BATTLE BOND

DEATH BEFORE DRAGONS
BOOK TWO

LINDSAY BUROKER

Battle Bond: Death Before Dragons Book 2
Copyright © 2020 Lindsay Buroker. All rights reserved.

www.lindsayburoker.com

Edited by Shelley Holloway
Cover and interior design by Gene Mollica Studio, LLC.

ISBN: 978-1-951367-04-6

BATTLE
BOND

CHAPTER 1

"It's a trap."

The slender wire was barely visible under the mulch and fallen apple-blossom petals, but even if I hadn't seen it, my half-elven blood would have allowed me to sense the faint hint of magic.

I'd taken three laps around the sprawling orchard, rows of trees stretching across dozens of acres, and it was my only proof that someone magical was in the area. Or *had* been in the area. Whoever it was hadn't been considerate enough to leave footprints.

I stood up, flicked my long blonde braid over my shoulder, and contemplated my options. Then impulsively chose one that wasn't that wise. I stepped into the trap.

Wire tightened around my ankle, then pulled at my leg hard enough to yank me off my feet. A second later, I dangled upside down, hands stretched toward the ground, like a cartoon hunter outsmarted by a clever rabbit.

My car keys, inhaler, and the stupid lavender-scented nose spray my doctor had recommended to calm my nerves tumbled out of my pocket. I hadn't needed so many silly things along on missions before my previously excellent health had gone off the rails. I still wasn't entirely sure what inflammatory markers did, but I was supposed to be de-stressing my life to improve them. Hard to do while dangling upside down from a tree.

Fortunately, Fezzik, my custom-made magical submachine pistol, stayed secure in its thigh holster, and Chopper, my even more magical longsword, remained in the scabbard strapped across my back. The hilt did clunk me in the back of the head as it shifted, but I deserved that. My leather thong strung with magical charms remained around my neck, but I had to tuck my chin to keep it there.

Val? Sindari's voice spoke into my mind—Sindari's *amused* voice.

I'd thought he was on the other side of the orchard, but when I twisted, I saw the great silver tiger padding toward me, his large paws barely stirring the grass between the rows of trees.

"Yes?" I answered aloud instead of in my mind.

With four of the neighborhood children missing, and dozens of local pigs devoured in the last week, the owners weren't wandering the property right now, so I wasn't worried about being overheard talking to a magical tiger.

Do you need me to rescue you?

"No. Actually, I need you to scoot off over the hill so whoever set this trap won't sense you when they come to check on what they caught."

Sindari sat on his haunches and looked up at me. *You intentionally stepped into that situation?*

"Yes. Now, scoot." I made a shooing motion. "You can come back and rescue me if more than four enemies show up."

You should be able to handle four kobolds by yourself. They're only two or three feet tall.

"That's why I said I'd only need rescuing if there were *more* than four."

Sindari's gaze shifted toward the next row of trees. *One approaches now.*

Good. I switched to thinking my responses, trusting the telepathic tiger would hear them. *Shoo.*

I am Sindari Dargoth Chaser the Third, Son of the Chieftain Raul, Feared Stalker and Hunter of the Tangled Tundra Nation on Del'noth. I do not shoo. He did, fortunately, engage his ability to fade from sight—and from the magical senses of anyone except the person holding his figurine.

Since that was me, I still felt him there. A few seconds later, I sensed more magical beings out there. Six of them, and they were spreading out around us. I resisted the urge to draw my weapons, instead letting my arms dangle over my head. I was just a helpless visitor foolishly caught in their trap.

Something pelted me in the butt, and I jerked, gasping at the pain.

"What was that?" I clasped a hand over the smarting spot. It felt like someone had cracked a whip.

A faint twang sounded, and something stung my opposite shoulder.

Are they shooting *me?* I twisted, trying to pinpoint the location of my assailants.

With slingshots. Do you wish me to rescue you now? Sindari sounded more amused than concerned for my welfare.

If these were the beings responsible for kidnapping—and possibly killing—children, this wasn't a laughing matter.

Another projectile—a rock?—buzzed past my head, stirring my hair. The leaves rustled in a nearby tree.

Just capture one. We need to question someone.

As Sindari sprang away, I yanked Chopper from its scabbard, pulled myself up, and sliced through the wire above me. The blade cut through the enchanted wire without trouble, and I had just enough room to flip a somersault and land on my feet. I still had to cut away the binding around my ankles, and I grimaced at the lost time. The kobolds had scattered as soon as Sindari leaped after them.

But I heard the one that had been in the tree jumping down. As soon as I was free, I sprinted after him.

The white-haired, two-foot-tall, gray-skinned creature darted into the next row of trees, a slingshot clenched in his small fist. I ducked branches and darted around trunks to follow.

My father's blood gave me better-than-human agility, but thanks to my mom, I also carried the blood of ancient Norse warriors in my veins, and they'd conspired to make me six feet tall. Branches clawed at my hair and smacked me in the face as I raced after the kobold. I lost sight of him, but my senses kept me on his trail.

As I surged out of the trees at the edge of the orchard, he came into sight again, sprinting for the native evergreens on the property's border. And the non-native, invasive blackberry brambles growing between those trees.

My long legs let me gain ground, and I urged them to even faster speeds as I saw his destination. A rabbit-sized hole in the dense wall of thorny vines.

I unstrapped Fezzik from my holster but hesitated to shoot him in the back. I wasn't yet sure these kobolds were responsible for the trouble, and my mother's words rang in my mind, that maybe the magical community would hate me less—would stop sending representatives to try to *kill* me—if they didn't fear me, if I helped them.

A split second before I would have caught up to him, the kobold dove through the hole. It looked too small even for him, but he slithered into it like a greased snake. It was all I could do to halt in time to keep from face-planting in the thorns.

Vines and leaves rattled, marking the kobold's passage as he found a route deeper and deeper into the brambles. Even my height wasn't enough to allow me to see over them and guess how far back into the trees the patch extended. Probably all the way to Puget Sound. There was a reason the Himalayan blackberry topped the lists of the most noxious invasive weeds in the Pacific Northwest.

As I was eyeing Chopper, debating how effective my treasured blade would be at clearing a path through the thorny tangle, I spotted the property owners heading my way.

I groaned. Had they seen me failing to capture a single toddler-sized kobold? They better have not seen me getting pelted in the butt by him.

Embarrassment heated my cheeks as I imagined snarky comments about how they thought they'd brought in the legendary Ruin Bringer, not some self-proclaimed bounty hunter hired off the internet.

Sindari? I asked silently as the middle-aged man and woman approached. *Any chance you've captured the rest of them and tied them up with a bow for me?*

Surprisingly, Sindari didn't answer. The cat-shaped charm on my necklace that could call him into this world warmed through the fabric of my shirt. Then it went ice cold, sending a chill through me that had nothing to do with physical sensation.

Sindari? I touched the charm.

Nothing.

CHAPTER 2

"It got away?" the man asked as he and his wife stopped, glancing at the blackberry brambles.

Worried about Sindari, I struggled to focus on him. "Yeah. Sorry."

The middle-aged couple didn't look much like my mental image of farmers—or orchard owners. He wore a Microsoft T-shirt and glasses, and she was in yoga pants and a hoodie displaying a stick figure doing the splits under instructions to *Stay flexible*.

Ayush and Laura were their names, I reminded myself. Colonel Willard had given me information on them and their lavender farm/apple orchard/cider house/winery when she'd given me the job.

"I told you we should have cleared all this." The woman pointed to the brambles and frowned at her husband.

"And I told you we'd need a hundred goats and a skidsteer with a brush-saw attachment to make any headway. It's been an epic battle just to keep them from encroaching on the orchard."

"I didn't object to the idea of goats," she murmured.

"Just the forty-thousand-dollar machine?"

"Yes. That's not in the budget."

"But goats are?"

"Goats are cute."

I was barely listening, my gaze scanning the orchard for signs of Sindari, even though I suspected he'd been dismissed from this world.

9

Usually, that was something only the holder of the figurine could do. But I'd once seen a powerful dark-elf mage force him away.

"Is this how they've been getting in and out?" Ayush pointed at the hole. The brambles had stopped rattling, and the kobold was far away now. "What *are* they?"

"Kobolds. I was trying to capture one to question. It wouldn't surprise me if they were the ones that stole and ate your pigs. I'm not sure about the children. They *are* known for playing pranks—" I resisted the urge to rub the incipient bruise on my left butt cheek, "—but they're usually smart enough not to pick fights with humans."

"Kobolds," the woman mouthed, looking at her husband.

From her face, it was clear she hadn't encountered magical beings before and wasn't sure she believed in them. Lucky her.

Her husband's expression was more grim and accepting. "You can find them, right? And find the children?"

I hesitated, aware that the missing children could be as eaten as the pigs, but I didn't want to steal their hope. "I can find the kobolds, and I'll question them about what's been going on."

I just had to figure out a way around the thorny brambles. I could sense more kobolds in that direction, but they were at least a half mile back. Unless Zav—the dragon who was determined to use me as bait to find the criminals he'd been sent to Earth to collect—showed up and breathed fire all over the place, I wasn't going that way. Besides, I hadn't seen Zav in two weeks. It was possible he'd completed his mission and left Earth forever. Dare I hope?

"I'll find a way around." I waved at the blackberry brambles and started to turn away, but Ayush lifted his hand.

"I know the government pays you, but if you can find the children, we'll give you some of our cider and wine and lavender chocolates. As much as you want."

Lavender chocolate? What strange thing was that? I wouldn't say no to hard cider, but I wasn't here for goodies.

"You don't have to give me anything." I waved and jogged off to collect my belongings from under the trap and to look for a break in the brush—and Sindari.

As soon as I was out of their sight, I would try summoning him again. And hope that whatever had driven him out of this world wasn't permanent.

Before I could reach for the charm, my phone buzzed in my pocket. "Yeah?"

"Ms. Thorvald," came Colonel Willard's dry Southern accent. "Did you not learn proper phone etiquette when you were in the army?"

"No. I was a pilot, not a secretary, and then they made me an assassin."

"Assassins don't answer phones?" Her connection was spotty, with voices in the background making it worse.

"Not politely. You're supposed to be fierce and vague in case an enemy is calling. Do you have something new for me? I'm hunting kobolds." Since the property owners were out of sight, I wrapped my fingers around the cat figurine and mouthed, "Sindari," to summon him back. I hoped.

"I do have new intel. I've lost touch with the forest ranger who was trying to find the kobolds' den, but the snitch in Port Townsend who first told me about the trouble has updated me. She says they may be taking orders from a leader and not necessarily acting of their own free will."

"Yeah, I guessed that."

The silver mist that always formed and coalesced into Sindari was slow to appear, as if it were fighting against some invisible force determined to quash the magic.

"You've encountered him or her?" Willard asked.

"Not yet, but someone knocked Sindari back to his realm."

"Try to find that person instead. Have you killed any kobolds yet?"

"No." This time, I *did* rub my butt cheek. "I just spotted them for the first time."

The mist thickened, and I exhaled in relief as Sindari's familiar features formed. It was taking longer than usual, but he was coming.

"Avoid killing them unless you can confirm that they're responsible. We're trying to create less animosity among the magical community for both our sakes." There was a grimace in her voice.

"I know. I will."

Willard's reply of, "Good," was almost drowned out by metal clanking in the background.

"Colonel, are you at the gym or are you recycling aluminum cans?"

"I don't drink anything that comes in a can."

11

"That's what I thought." I frowned my disapproval at the phone. "Shouldn't you be resting?"

"I'm doing some walking and light stretching."

"In the weight room?"

"I've been cleared for exercise, Thorvald." She'd called me Val when she'd been in the hospital dying, but it seemed we were back to formalities now. "It's fine. I want to get my health back."

"You had cancer two weeks ago. The best way to get your health back is to rest."

Finally, Sindari fully formed, once again a solid silver tiger at my side. I'd ask for details as soon as I got off the call but leaned against him and wrapped an arm over his back.

"It was a magically induced unnatural cancer," Willard said.

"So that means doing squats and bench presses right after is fine? You better not have signed up for a new triathlon."

"I'm *not* doing squats. Just light leg presses. And you do know that you're my lowly civilian contractor, not my boss, right?"

"Lowly? I tower over you."

"Two inches isn't towering. If I grew my hair out, I'd be taller than you."

"I'm positive that you with a six-inch afro isn't regulation," I said, though I suspected Willard could wear her hair and her clothes however she wanted at the office in Seattle. The soldiers stationed there were supposed to blend in to more easily monitor and control criminal activity from magical beings hiding out and traveling through the city.

"The regs just say it has to be off your neck and fit in your hat," Willard said.

"If I had more money, I'd bribe you to grow it out just so I could see that."

"You'll get your usual combat bonus if you bring in whoever is leading the kobolds. There's a school less than a mile from there. We can't let them keep kidnapping children."

"I know. I'm on it." I hung up.

I'd resumed walking as I spoke and reached a stream that flowed through the corner of the property. The blackberry brambles lay thick on one side but hadn't yet taken over the other.

"Looks like we can get through here, Sindari. What happened to…" I trailed off, realizing he wasn't at my side.

I whirled, afraid he'd been kicked out of our world again. But I spotted him rolling like a dog on his back under some apple trees.

"Sindari?" I called. "What are you doing?"

He stopped rolling, his legs splayed, his forepaws in the air, but he kept rubbing his head on the grass under the tree. *Rolling,* he replied.

"I see you're not overly traumatized by whatever punted you away from Earth. That *was* someone else's doing, wasn't it? You didn't simply get tired and want to take a nap?"

Of course not, Val. My stamina is amazing. And I've only spent an hour in your world today. Sindari kept rubbing his head in the grass.

"Well, if you wouldn't mind, we still need to find a kobold to question. And can you close your legs? I can see your junk."

My what?

"Never mind. I'm going this way. Please join me at your earliest convenience."

My boots squished in mud as I walked along a well-used trail on the clear side of the stream. It grew dim quickly under the forest of firs and hemlocks, the trunks rising a hundred feet and more. Dew dripped from the branches, occasionally landing on my head.

Every few steps, I knelt down to study fresh prints in the mud. They were smaller than mine but not as small as kobold prints. Maybe the local children used this path to cut through from property to property. That was another reason to find whoever was threatening them.

You're going the right direction, Sindari told me as he caught up. *Forgive my distraction. I could not resist.*

"Resist what? Did someone sprinkle catnip under those trees?"

Fertilizer, I believe.

"Isn't that stuff poisonous to animals?"

This was bone meal and fish meal fertilizer. Quite aromatic and delightful.

Maybe I would get some catnip later and see if my mighty silver tiger would roll around like that on my living room floor.

"Where did you go when you disappeared? Did you catch the kobold?"

No. I was close and then… ah, I found a trap of my own.

"You didn't step in a snare and fly up in a tree, did you?"

No, I'm not so foolish.

"Ha ha."

Follow me. Sindari sprang across the creek and onto another path. Here, the brambles had been burned back, as if by someone with a flamethrower. It was hard to imagine that being effective, since the forest was still very damp this early in the season. *The trap was expertly laid and camouflaged. I didn't sense the magic until it sprang, knocking me back into my realm with a blast of pain.*

I'm sorry you were hurt. Do kobolds have mages powerful enough to create such things? I eyed the burned-back vines, wondering if magic had been used rather than a flamethrower.

It wasn't created by a kobold.

Do you know what did *create it?*

Sindari didn't answer right away, instead leading me around bends in the trail, then on toward an opening in the trees ahead. Maybe he didn't know who had created it.

A faint tingle poked at my senses, like electricity under a high-voltage line. Magic.

Eventually, the trail led us into a large meadow of waist-high grass leading to an old windmill beside a creek. Sindari sat on his haunches and faced it. It was the source of the magic.

That *is who created it,* Sindari told me.

The windmill? I drew even with him, my instincts itching. The windmill represented a threat, but I also had the feeling that someone was watching us.

No, the being using it for its lair. He isn't there now, but I can smell dragon.

I gave him a sharp look. *Zav?*

I didn't sense his aura, and it was powerful enough that I usually did from a mile away. All I sensed, other than the windmill itself was…

Oh, damn. There were the kobolds again. I'd almost missed their auras since the windmill radiated magic. They were out in the tall grass. All six of them. Had they spotted us yet?

No. I recognize the scent of Lord Zavryd. This is another dragon.

"*Another* dragon?" I blurted out loud before I caught myself and switched to silent speech. *How can we have gone from no dragons on Earth for a thousand years to two in the same month?*

I don't know, but brace yourself. We're about to be—

All six kobolds rushed toward us, the grasses wavering madly with their passage. As I drew Chopper, the first one came into view. He'd traded his slingshot for a gun.

CHAPTER 3

I dove to the side, rolling into the grass, a split second before the kobold fired at me.

Sindari pounced as the bullet whizzed past my head. He tackled the kobold with the gun, but the five others burst out of the grass, armed with guns, daggers, and bows and arrows. The weapons were small enough to fit in their diminutive hands—but dangerous enough to be deadly.

I leaped up from my roll in time to greet two rushing kobolds, one male and one female, with Chopper.

The male had a dagger and the female a pistol. Faster than she could take aim, I whipped the blade across to strike the weapon. I'd only intended to knock it from her grip, but Chopper's magical blade cut through it like butter, leaving a glowing blue streak in the air.

Even though I could have finished her off, Willard's words came to mind. I spun on my heel and launched a low side kick. My boot slammed into her small chest, and she flew backward into the grass.

Her companion lunged at me with his dagger. His black eyes were glazed, and he didn't react to his comrade being kicked away. As I skittered back to avoid the sharp blade, he stabbed at me with a combination of robotic movements.

Like many magical beings, he was faster than the typical human, but my elven blood also gave me extra speed, and I was accustomed to quick and agile opponents. When he committed himself to a lunge, stabbing straight ahead with the dagger, I glided to the side and toward him, close enough to bend down and catch his wrist. I twisted it, but to my surprise he didn't yelp in pain or drop the weapon. He didn't make a noise at all as he tried to pull his arm away.

I hefted him into the air, knocked his hand against a nearby tree trunk, and finally his dagger fell to the dirt.

A roar came from the grass, and a disarmed and bleeding kobold sailed over my head and into the woods.

"Don't kill them," I yelled as I struggled to keep my prisoner subdued, so we could question him later.

They are not yielding to my superior power, Sindari told me, sounding exasperated. Another kobold flew into the woods. *It is impossible to stop them without harming them greatly.*

The one I held struggled and managed to get a fist past my guard. It clipped me in the chin enough to hurt, and I had to resist the urge to fling him away—or bash him in the head with Chopper.

Even as he battled me, his expression never changed and his eyes remained glazed. Someone was definitely controlling these guys.

I twisted the kobold so that his back was to me and pinned his arms, pulling him against my hip so he couldn't move.

To my left, the tall grasses parted to reveal the tip of an arrow pointing at me. The bowman hesitated, maybe afraid to hit his buddy, but he was too far away for me to reach with my sword. I plunged Chopper into the ground and yanked out Fezzik and fired.

My shot cracked through the top of the bowstave as I jumped back in case the kobold got the shot off. But I'd been fast enough. The arrow fell limply to the ground.

Sindari plowed into my would-be sniper from behind and batted him into a bramble patch with a swipe of his paw. The kobold's bow fell from his grip as he tumbled into the thorny vines. Like the male I'd captured, he did not cry out. Robotically, he tried to extricate himself.

They're going to keep coming if we don't do something to stop them, Sindari pointed out.

The two he'd first sent sailing had regained their feet and were stalking back toward us, even though they'd lost their weapons. The one I held kept squirming and trying to escape.

"Chopper," I blurted, a realization smacking me.

You wish to behead them? Sindari paused to knock another of the returning kobolds back into the woods. They only weighed about forty pounds, which meant his blows could send them far.

I winced as that one clipped a trunk with bone-crunching force. But it still had a dagger, and we couldn't let them continue to attack us without defending ourselves.

"No." I shifted my burden around and tried to put my sword's hilt in the kobold's hand without losing control of the blade. "Chopper's magic has protected me many times from mental attacks. Maybe it could break whatever hold is on him."

The kobold's small fingers wrapped around the hilt, and he tried to lift it, to use it to brain me. I was stronger than he was, but he made a valiant effort, and I started to think I had made a mistake.

Until he blinked in surprise and stopped struggling. He gaped at me, glanced around, and screamed.

It was right in my ear, and I almost dropped him just to get him away from me—or make it stop—but I needed to question someone.

"Stop," I said. "I'm not going to hurt you, and if you answer some questions, I'll let you go."

I hoped he understood English. Most of the magical refugees that had been on Earth and in America for years knew enough to get by, with some being experts at blending in, but newer arrivals often didn't know the language.

He screamed again. I couldn't tell if he didn't understand me or he didn't believe me.

Sindari sprang close and roared at the kobold.

"*That's* not going to help anything," I said.

But the kobold, eyes widening even further, stopped screaming… and wet himself.

I groaned and held him out at arm's length. "Gross, Sindari."

My apologies. I didn't anticipate that result.

"What *usually* happens when you roar at people?"

Stupefied acquiescence.

"This probably qualifies. He got my hip."

Perhaps you can roll in the fertilizer on the way out.

I don't see how that would help.

It would mask the odor.

17

So I'd smell like blood and fish instead?

Yes. Those are far more appealing scents.

If you say so. I pulled my sword out of the kobold's grip before realizing that might allow the mind-control to reassert itself.

But the glaze didn't return to the kobold's eyes. He struggled weakly—nothing like he had before—and stared at Sindari.

Two more kobolds, still under the mind-control influence, rushed at us. Once again, Sindari knocked them back into the brush. Though bruised and bleeding, they rose and came at us again.

I will keep that one from escaping, Sindari said. *You're going to have to let them all hold your sword to break the spell.*

I didn't hesitate to thrust my unwelcome and damp burden at him. As I trotted forward to catch the closest returning attacker, Sindari flattened our prisoner to the ground with a paw. He was kind enough to retract his claws.

It took several long moments to go through the process with the other five kobolds, and I grimaced at one holding a broken arm and limping, but Chopper successfully shattered the mind-control compulsion on all of them. As soon as they realized where they were and who they faced—one of them whispered my most common moniker, Ruin Bringer—they fled.

Since we had a prisoner already, I didn't try to detain them. I had rope back in the Jeep, but I assumed the kobolds would cease to be a problem once we took care of whoever was controlling them. Or *whatever*. I glanced at the windmill, an ominous, dilapidated gray structure that looked to be a hundred years old, worried about Sindari's warning about a dragon.

"I hope we kept one who understands English." I walked up to Sindari, the prisoner still pinned on his back under a paw, after the others disappeared into the trees. I hadn't missed that they had all run *away* from the windmill rather than toward it.

"I understand," the kobold whispered, staring up at me. He had a split lip that was bleeding. "You are the Ruin Bringer. We didn't do it."

"You didn't kill the pigs?"

He hesitated. "We didn't take the children. I mean, we didn't *want* to take the children."

"But you took the pigs of your own free will?"

Another hesitation. "No. We were forced."

"Why do I think you're lying?"

He probed his bloody, puffy lip with his tongue. "Pigs are delicious?"

He's not wrong, Sindari said. *On Del'noth, we have wild boars that are succulent.*

"Your kind would have an easier time hiding out in this world if you went vegan," I said.

You don't think the locals would also object to carrots being stolen from their gardens? Sindari asked.

"They might blame rabbits."

The kobold looked confused.

"Kobold—uh, what's your name?" Again, I thought of my mother's advice to make friends with the magical, with those who weren't criminals. I supposed I could at least be more polite. Maybe if fewer people loathed me, that would help with the issues I was reluctantly working on with the therapist.

"Bob."

I raised my eyebrows, suspecting another lie, but this one didn't matter. "Where are the children, Bob? Are they still alive?"

His eyes rolled toward the windmill. He couldn't have seen it through the tall grass, but he was looking in precisely the right direction. As a full-blooded magical being, he would sense its magic even more easily than I.

"We took them there," he said. "I do not know if they still live. He may have eaten them."

"He who? Who's been controlling you?" I should have asked that question first, but I dreaded the answer.

"The dragon," Bob whispered. "If you go there, he'll control you too. Or he'll kill you like the other human who went there."

Uh oh, was that the forest-ranger contact Willard had mentioned?

"Was it a black dragon?" I asked.

It didn't make sense that Zav would be killing people, when he'd pointed out more than once that he wasn't a criminal and that he was only here to take criminals back to his own realm for punishment and rehabilitation. But I would prefer to deal with the dragon I knew rather than some mysterious new dragon.

The kobold shook his head. "He's silver and as big as that windmill." Bob lowered his voice. "And meaner than a *tragothor.*"

Is that as mean as it sounds, Sindari?

Yes.

"He'll kill you." Bob grabbed Sindari's leg. "Please let me go. He'll kill *me* if he finds out I talked."

I waved a hand for Sindari to release him. Unfortunately, I didn't think the kobold was lying anymore.

I wished I had a way to contact Zav, not that he would deign to give me information about his fellow dragons. Or about anything. But he had given me a sample of his blood after I'd recovered his artifact for him. We hadn't parted on antagonistic grounds, never mind that he wanted to cart me around the world as his slave-bait to lure magical criminals to him.

What's the plan? Sindari asked as the kobold scurried away.

We check the windmill and hope the dragon doesn't come home before we're done.

And if he does? Neither of us is strong enough to kill a dragon.

I know. We're going to optimistically hope for the best. I marched resolutely through the grass.

Sindari glided past me to take the lead. *An interesting stance from someone with pee on her hip.*

I'm not sure I believe that you didn't anticipate that result.

His look back was not convincingly innocent.

CHAPTER 4

As we reached the entrance of the windmill, its original door long rusted off, I looked one last time at the cloudy sky overhead. I didn't sense a dragon, but that didn't mean he couldn't be on his way.

There is an enchantment on the doorway. Sindari twitched his tail as he gazed into the dim interior, where rotten rails and planks from a decaying staircase littered the stone floor. *Will your charm work on it?*

I stepped close and gripped what I thought of as my lock-picking charm, but it had actually been designed to nullify enchantments just like this. No, not just like this. Enchantments placed by dwarves and elves and magical beings of their caliber. It might not be able to handle something made by a dragon.

Not certain where to place my other hand, since the door was missing, I rested it on the nearby frame. An uneasy tingle ran up my arm and down my spine. The urge to flee back the way I'd come rushed through me. I gritted my teeth and kept my hand in place, willing the key-shaped charm to nullify the enchantment.

It heated in my hand, almost burning my palm.

I flashed back to the dark-elf lair where I'd been a prisoner, held by magical bonds, and had managed to break them with the charm's help. I hadn't expected it to be strong enough for the task, but somehow, it had worked. It had almost seemed to draw power from *me*, but I wasn't sure I remembered that correctly.

Just because my mom had boinked an elf back in the day didn't mean I had magical power. Sure, I had a few attributes that weren't quite human, but it wasn't as if I could cast spells. My charms and my magical weapons were the reason I could slay bad guys, not any secret power coursing through my veins.

The enchantment is still there, Sindari noted.

Annoyed that I'd let myself be distracted, I focused harder, willing whatever invisible protection was there to disappear.

Wood snapped and stone cracked, and I jumped back.

The doorframe I'd had my hand against split in a dozen places and crumbled inward. Several layers of the mortared stone of the surrounding wall collapsed atop it. Rock dust flew up, clouding the air.

Now it's gone, Sindari remarked blandly.

"Uh, good." I decided to pretend I'd meant to do that. It's important to be suave in front of a magical tiger.

I have not seen your charm perform so earnestly before.

Earnest, right. "I'm exploring its full powers."

Sindari padded slowly into the interior, ears alert and nostrils twitching as he sniffed the air. Since he was more likely to detect a magical trap, I let him go first, though I hated hiding behind anyone else.

As I stood on the threshold, a distant crying reached my ears. The kidnapped children? Dare I hope they were still alive? Or was it a trick? One designed to lure me into another trap?

The noise came from under the floorboards somewhere. Ancient floorboards that creaked as I walked into the windmill. Sindari weighed more than I did, but somehow, his paws didn't elicit the same response.

I searched slowly around the voluminous ground floor of the windmill, looking for a trapdoor or steps to a lower level. There were upper levels, too, but it would take some climbing to reach them. The wooden stairs that had once spiraled up the circular wall had collapsed, and the floor above was thirty feet up.

As I explored, I passed ancient wheelbarrows with wooden wheels, a rooster-shaped windmill weight, and millstones resting flat on the floor or leaning against the walls. One of the larger stones had fallen through the floor at some point, leaving a jagged opening to a dark basement.

"What kind of windmill has a basement?" I muttered, pulling out my phone and tapping on the flashlight app. I also had a night-vision charm, but there was too much daylight filtering in through the doorway and holes in the walls for me to use it here.

Val? Over here. Sindari's tone was grim.

He was on the other side of the cavernous room, behind a pile of rusty farm tools that looked like they'd been ordered back when the first Sears catalog had been mailed out. I shined the light down into the basement, spotting nothing but more millstones and a stack of wood boards, then headed toward him.

As I rounded the pile of farm tools, I almost tripped on a boot. A boot attached to a leg attached to a body. A body without a head.

I'd seen plenty of grisly sights over the years and didn't react to this one, other than to sigh. The man was wearing a blood-drenched green-and-khaki Jefferson County ranger uniform, and I knew right away this was Willard's missing contact. I wished the guy had waited for me instead of trying to find the children on his own.

"Where's the head?"

Sindari sat beside the body—this was what he'd brought me over to see. *It's not here.*

Judging by the stump of the neck, it had been bitten off. With one powerful chomp. There weren't many animals I knew that could have done that. I remembered how large Zav had been in his dragon form while standing on the rooftop of my apartment building. A dragon's maw was definitely big enough for the job.

"Do dragons eat humans?" I shuddered at the idea.

Not typically. They prefer fat herbivores of substantial size. But they're certainly capable of eating just about anything—and anyone. The dragon could have done this to make a point. Or as an efficient way to kill the man for snooping in his windmill.

"Is it really *his* windmill?" I looked toward the exit—the only way in or out, unless there was a big hole somewhere on a higher level. "How would a dragon fit in here?"

The only hole in the wall was the one *I'd* made.

They have long necks.

I thought he was joking, but Zav's neck *had* been long. Elegant but long. Could his big head have fit through the doorway to kill this man with a bite?

They can also shape-shift into smaller creatures, as you've seen.

"True."

I shook my head. I would let Willard know what had happened to this guy, but the children were why I'd been sent.

"Sindari?" I returned to the hole in the floor and pointed him toward it. "Can you tell if anyone is down there?"

He sniffed the air over the hole. That distant crying came again. No, not distant. *Muffled.* Maybe there was a door and another room down there.

"It may be another trap," I admitted.

If he didn't smell anyone, I would assume it was, that the dragon wanted to lure me down so it could later bite my head off.

I do detect other humans down there. Several of them. Stay here. I will look.

He disappeared into the darkness, dropping twenty feet and landing among the millstones without trouble. I dropped to my stomach and shined my light around below, hoping to spot a way to climb down—or climb back *up,* if I jumped down. Next time, I wouldn't hop out of the Jeep without a rope.

The circular stone wall of the windmill extended all the way to the flagstone floor of the basement. The area down there wasn't simply some pit that had been dug out after the initial construction. It actually looked like the original ground level of the mill and that the earth outside had been built up to cover it. Or maybe the windmill had been magically sunken *into* the ground. If so, to what end?

I pointed my flashlight beam toward the nearest basement wall. The mortar between the stones was crumbling or missing completely, leaving what I could turn into handholds for climbing. But the hole in the floor was more than ten feet from the nearest wall. There wouldn't be a way to get over to it without suction cups.

"Or making a new hole," I muttered.

A gouging noise floated up from below.

"I hope that's you, Sindari."

A loud thud followed.

"I *definitely* hope that's you. Please let me know if ogres live down there."

I am attempting to break down a solid oak door with an enchantment locking it. I may need you and your charm.

"I don't suppose I can toss it down and you can use it without me?" I eyed the exit, worried about the dragon returning while I was down in the basement.

I do not believe I can use your charms. Also, when you used it on the doorway above, you did something beyond the intrinsic power of that charm. I sensed it.

"Any idea what it was?"

You did it. Do you not know?

"I know less than you'd think." I located Sindari with the flashlight beam and saw the door. The muffled crying came again, and it came from that direction. That made up my mind. "I'm coming down."

But not without creating a way out. I trotted to the wall, pocketed my phone, and, apologizing to Chopper for using it as a crowbar, slid the blade between the board and the stone. A mundane sword would have snapped off at the hilt. Fortunately, Chopper was no mundane sword. I'd won the blade in a battle years ago and didn't know its history—Zav had hinted that it had powers I didn't know about—but I did know it was far stronger than a slender piece of metal should have been.

It glowed a faint blue when it was out of its scabbard, but today, its glow was fainter than usual. Maybe it was indignant to be put to this use instead of going into battle.

"Next time," I promised the blade.

A board shifted, nails wrenching free from their beds, and I flicked it away. As old as the windmill was, the floorboards were thick and solid, and I couldn't pull up the rest with my hands. I had to keep using the sword as a crowbar. Aware of the seconds passing, I forced myself to be careful and methodical—and not cut my leg off.

Another thud came from below. Sindari trying to knock down the door.

"Don't hurt yourself. I'll be down as soon as this hole is wide enough."

There isn't much time. He sounded certain.

"What does that mean?" I snapped another board free. A bead of sweat ran down the side of my face.

I sense the dragon approaching.

I swore. "How far away?"

The dragon wasn't within range of my senses yet, but Sindari's range was greater than mine.

Three miles, maybe four. He's flying this way.

I swore again and pried another board free. It clattered loudly as it landed. How well could dragons hear?

25

"Is someone out there?" For the first time, words reached my ears, as muffled as the crying had been and barely audible.

Sindari threw himself at the door again.

The hole was wide enough. I sheathed Chopper and scrambled down, willing my night-vision charm to activate, then wincing because there was still too much light filtering down from above, and it created a weird flare effect—and an instant headache.

Squinting, I clambered across the millstones to the opposite side of the basement. It grew darker as I moved away from the holes in the floor.

Directly under the ground-level entrance above, there was a short tunnel littered with pieces of stone that had fallen over the years. Sindari shifted aside, and I rushed forward, placing a hand on the oak door. The hinges were rusty but thick, and the wood was as solid as he'd promised. The zing of magic against my palm warned me of the enchantment sealing it.

"I'm here," I called. "We're getting you out."

"Please, please, help us," came the return call, a girl's voice.

I prayed the kids truly were alive in there and that some magic wasn't talking to me while beheaded children lay scattered among the upper levels of the windmill.

Two miles away, Sindari warned.

I closed my eyes and concentrated, willing the charm to unlock the door.

The enchantment broke, and the magical zing of electricity winked out. There wasn't a latch or knob, so all I could do was stick my finger in an empty knot and tug, hoping that was enough. The door glided soundlessly outward.

Four dirty, gaunt faces peered at me, and the scent of urine and feces wafted out. The children—two boys and two girls—must have been locked in there for days. Their lips were cracked—hadn't they even been given water?

"We have to hurry." I waved them out. "And you have to climb."

There's not going to be time. Sindari had moved to the hole and peered upward. *Unless you want me to distract another dragon. There's no cliff to leap off this time.*

He could turn this whole place into a bonfire while we're in the basement. I helped the children out, wincing at how slowly they moved, their bodies stiff after being locked up for so long. The youngest girl paused to wrap her arms around my waist. It was touching, but all I could think about was that we didn't have time. *Later*, there could be hugs.

My senses lit up as the dragon flew into my range.

A mile? I asked Sindari.

Yes. He'll be here in seconds. Sindari bunched his powerful leg muscles and sprang the twenty feet out of the hole, landing lightly on the floor-boards above. Dust trickled down between them. *I'll run into the woods and try to buy you time.*

Thank you. Make sure to dismiss yourself before he can hurt you.

I will. You make sure to irritate him enough that he doesn't follow me back to my realm. His tone was dry, but also concerned. Unlike most magical beings, dragons could instantly make temporary portals to the other realms.

I'm stealing his prisoners. I'm sure he'll be pissed.

I hope so. If he's taking prisoners, he's not going to be as easy to deal with as the other dragon.

I almost scoffed at the idea of Zav and his cocky arrogance being easy to deal with, but Sindari was right. However arrogant he was, Zav believed he was one of the good guys. He hadn't razed the city of Seattle to get to his dark-elf targets when he had the power to do so.

I half-pulled, half-carried the children to the wall. "We have to climb. Up that."

They stared at the vertical wall with wide eyes.

"It's easy," I promised them. "Lots of handholds."

They turned their wide eyes on me as if I were nuts. Maybe they would have been less daunted if they hadn't been weak from days without food and only whatever rainwater might have leaked through to them.

"Never mind. Here, climb on my back. One at a time."

They liked that idea better. I was halfway up the wall with one of the boys hanging from my shoulders when the roar of the dragon reached my ears.

Thieves! Intruders!

The children gasped, which meant the telepathic words were broadcast rather than drilled into only my mind.

"He's going to hurt us."

"He's going to kill us, like that man!"

"No, he's not," I promised, hoping I wasn't lying. "My friend is leading him away. Did you see the tiger? He's amazing."

Since Sindari didn't comment on the last—usually, he would agree—I assumed he'd already run out of earshot. Even now, the dragon might be diving down on him, like an eagle plummeting to snatch a fish out of a lake.

I climbed faster, reached the opening, and shoved the boy off my shoulders and onto the floorboards. Without hesitating, I jumped back down, rolling to keep the fall from breaking my ankles. I sprang back to my feet and swept one of the girls onto my back to repeat the climb.

Another roar sounded outside. The dragon was farther away now. Had Sindari made it to the woods? The tall, densely packed trees would make it harder for an aerial foe to swoop down on him.

I deposited the second child on the floorboards and jumped down again. Halfway there…

Val? Sindari's voice sounded distant in my mind. He had to be close to the end of our range—he could only travel a mile from the charm before the link would break, sending him back to his world.

Yes? I climbed up with my third hitchhiker.

I made it to the woods, and he followed me partway, but now he's leaving. I think he's going back to the windmill.

Ugh. He must have realized what you were doing.

I'm running back to you, but he's faster than I am. He'll get there first.

The second boy joined the other two children.

"You three, start running," I ordered as I jumped down again. "Run back to the orchard. Do you know the way?"

"Yes," the older boy said. "Is it safe out there?"

No.

"It will be for a bit, but you have to hurry." As I swept up the last girl, I again hoped I wasn't lying.

The idea of making it all the way here and finding the children only to lose them was heart-wrenching. Would the dragon capture them again, or would he incinerate them as they fled across the meadow? Why had he kidnapped them in the first place?

When I reached the top, I climbed out, not bothering to pull the girl off my shoulders. Panting from my exertions, I sprinted for the exit.

The first three children were running across the meadow toward the woods and the trail, but the high grass impeded them. The dragon flew into view over the treetops, heading straight toward the windmill. He was as large as Zav, but with silver scales instead of black, with a fist-sized, black onyx stone embedded in his chest. Instead of violet, his eyes were silver-blue, and I could see their angry glow from hundreds of meters away. They were boring right into me.

I ran after the children. If I could get them to the woods, I could come back out in the open and buy time for them to escape. Whether I would *survive* buying that time, I didn't know, but it was the only plan that came to mind.

With my longer legs, I caught up with the three children. They were only halfway to the tentative safety of the woods. The dragon was heading straight toward us and would be on us in seconds.

I shook my head in despair; there wasn't enough time.

"Follow them," I ordered, pulling the girl off my back and pointing to the others.

She could barely see over the grass that was waist-high to me and shoulder-high to her, but she scrambled after the others. I backed toward the windmill, drawing Chopper and waving the sword menacingly at the dragon.

He arrowed down toward the children, not toward me. His great fanged maw opened wide, and my heart sank. He was going to breathe fire at them, incinerate them while I helplessly watched.

"No, you don't, you bastard." I yanked Fezzik from its holster, flicked the selector to automatic, and sprayed magical bullets at the dragon's silver-scaled hide.

With a target that big, it was impossible to miss. But I'd seen Zav incinerate bullets, and I expected this dragon to do the same.

His jaws snapped shut, and his head jerked sideways. Again, those silver-blue eyes burned into me. He shifted his path away from the children—and toward me.

He hadn't incinerated my bullets, but they also didn't appear to have hurt him. That left me standing out in the open without a means of defending myself.

Arms pumping, I sprinted back toward the windmill, Chopper in one hand and Fezzik in the other. I tried not to think about the beheaded ranger and the fact that I wouldn't be safe even if I made it inside.

As I ran, I fired over my shoulder. The dragon dove down, talons outstretched. I wasn't going to make it as far as the ranger had.

I aimed for his eyes, the best I could as I was sprinting in the opposite direction. Maybe they would be a vulnerable spot.

One of my bullets bounced right off his eyelid. He didn't flinch. Hell.

The talons swept in. I flung myself to the ground, rolling onto my back and slashing upward with Chopper. The blade struck one of the toes on his scaly foot as the talons missed taking my head off by scant inches. Surprisingly, my sword gouged into its target.

The dragon didn't shriek in pain as his momentum carried him past, but he did grunt, jerking his foot up toward his scaled belly. I leaped up, thinking of taking another stab, but he passed out of my range too quickly. Already, he was flying upward and banking, so he could dive again.

I sprinted into the windmill, running to the far side and ducking under the overhang of the half-destroyed staircase. Sindari rushed inside as the dragon roared. Not with frustration at losing his prey—he knew he hadn't lost anything—but in preparation.

The sky outside exploded with brilliant orange light as the dragon breathed fire onto the windmill.

CHAPTER 5

I crouched beside Sindari at the back of the windmill, fingers wrapped around my fire-protection charm as flames obscured the exit.

The wood frame that I'd broken earlier charred and incinerated in two seconds. Much of the exterior was made from stone, but the heat was so intense that those stones were exploding or crumbling to ash. After twenty seconds under the dragon's fiery assault, the windmill already felt like an oven inside. My charm protected me from direct flame, but I doubted it would keep me from roasting alive.

Think it'll be cooler in the basement or worse? I silently asked, trusting Sindari to read my thoughts.

Possibly worse.

At what temperature do magical tigers burst into flame?

The same as half-elves, I suspect.

You better go back to your realm. I tapped the cat figurine. It was so hot to the touch that I jerked my finger away.

If Sindari burned to death here on Earth, would any part of him survive to return home? Or would he die as surely as I would?

I'm not leaving you here alone. Sindari pointed his nose toward the exit, the flames still roiling down at it from the dragon's maw. *I'll run out. Maybe he'll chase me again and you can get away.*

I don't think he's going to fall for that twice.

Smoke filled the interior of the windmill and made me cough. My airways tightened predictably, and I wondered if there was any point to

31

digging out my inhaler. Did it matter if I died of suffocation before being burned to a crisp?

The flames in front of the exit disappeared. I sensed the dragon standing right outside, so I knew we weren't safe. He was probably inhaling for another round.

"Hey, Dragon!" I called, mopping my brow. "Let's talk. Why are you kidnapping children? What do you want?"

I expected this attempt at dealing would work about as well as it had with Zav, but maybe I would be wrong. Maybe this was a chatty dragon who was misunderstood and longed for someone to listen to his plight.

A scaled snout came into view, one of those silver-blue eyes just visible at the top of the doorway hole. It gazed at me.

I did my best not to look toward the dead ranger and imagine the dragon chomping my head off. Chopper was in my hand and ready if he tried. I was slightly bolstered that the blade had managed to cut into him when Fezzik's magical rounds had not, but I hadn't even given him the equivalent of a hangnail.

The eye squinted.

You, the dragon spoke telepathically, his voice as powerful and resonant as Zav's as it rang in my skull, *smell of Zavryd'nokquetal.*

My mouth dropped. I didn't know what I'd expected, but it hadn't been that.

"That can't be. I've showered and scrubbed myself dozens of times since I saw him last."

The eye continued to squint at me. *I hoped to lure him here with my antics, but it's been days, and I grow weary of this game.*

"Antics? Wait, you've been commanding the kobolds to kidnap children, hoping to attract *Zav's* attention?"

Zav? Surely, he does not permit a mongrel to call him by that diminutive name.

"I can't pronounce his un-diminutive name."

That's pathetic.

"Sorry, I'm half-human."

Yes. I can tell. Even through telepathy, dragons could manage to be supercilious. *I am Dobsaurin the Most Magnificent.*

Great, he's even more pompous than Zav. I meant the words for Sindari, but the dragon's visible eye opened wide.

I can hear you when you think words to your stolen dragon slave!

"He's not a slave," I said as Sindari put in his own objection, an indignant roar that filled my ears.

The Zhinevarii are promised to dragons. You have no right to that charm.

"Uh huh. Why did you say you wanted to lure Zav here?" I asked, hoping to distract him from his new interest in Sindari—the last thing I wanted was for him to take the figurine away. "And why were you kidnapping children to do it? He thinks humans are vermin and is only here to get criminals that fled from your worlds."

He is insufferably righteous and resents those who prey on the small and weak, as if the small and weak are worth paying attention to. Dragons are gods in comparison to all the lesser species. Gods should not concern themselves with those who are so clearly inferior to us. But I knew Zavryd'nokquetal would come to challenge me if he found out I was meddling with the peoples of this world. I am disappointed by how long it's taking him to respond. I know he is here on this overpopulated, scum-infested planet.

"It's a big planet. He could be anywhere."

I suppose. But he has seen you recently enough to leave his mark on you. Will he come to see you again?

I didn't mean to hesitate, but I had to consider the answer. Reluctantly, I admitted that Zav had found me useful several times now, so he probably *would* hunt me down again.

Belatedly, I said, "No."

A lie. Your human half makes you weak and easy to read.

"Thanks for the analysis, but I already have a therapist that I pay for that. No need for dragons to butt in."

Have we not discussed the foolishness of irking dragons, Val? Sindari asked.

Yes, but you can hardly talk. You roared at him.

He called me a slave. That is worse than being called a pet.

Perhaps you will do. The dragon—Dob-whatever—studied me with new contemplation.

I'd liked it better when he'd been breathing fire at me.

Deliver a message to him. Tell him that my family does not appreciate his sanctimonious meddling, and that I have been sent to put an end to it. Permanently.

"Deliver a message? I'm not a Post-it note." I couldn't imagine anything more dreadful than being pulled into what sounded like dragon politics.

Other than dying. I supposed this was a step up from that. And, with luck, the children had made it safely back to their homes by now.

Tell him, or I'll flambé this structure with you and your tiger in it.

"I'll let him know."

Excellent.

The dragon backed away, sprang into the air, and flew off to the east. I wish he'd gone west. West was the Olympic Mountains and the Pacific Ocean. East was Seattle, my apartment, and millions of people.

As I stumbled outside, relieved to suck in a breath of fresh air, my phone buzzed. Expecting Willard again, I answered without looking at the number.

"Ms. Thorvald," Mary Watanabe, my therapist, said. "I'm glad you answered."

I wished I'd let it go to voice mail.

"Oh?" I couldn't help it that I sounded wary. She didn't call for social reasons.

"Have you been working on the 4-7-8 breathing technique we discussed? Are you finding it helpful for lowering stress in difficult situations?"

I coughed and dug out my inhaler. Right now, my lungs were too full of smoke for breathing exercises. They were busy working on just breathing.

"I didn't have time during today's difficult situation, but I've tried it a bit."

"Excellent. You mentioned being willing to try yoga too. Have you gone to a class yet?"

"I've been busy." I eyed the smoking windmill. The roof was burning heartily.

"Well, make room in your schedule. I was at a class this morning, and I learned of an opening at the Lotus Leaf Studio in Ballard. It's a membership-only facility, and the instructors are very good. They really care about their students. They don't just arrange your body in the right positions while in class but work on changing your mindset and teaching you to bring the tenets of yoga into your life as a whole. Of course we'll continue to work on the personal issues you've acknowledged, but I think it'll really help you if you can learn to take that philosophy into your daily life."

What would really help me was if dragons would stop trying to set me on fire.

CHAPTER 6

A salty breeze tugged at the strands of hair dangling free from my braid as I leaned on the railing of the ferry taking me back to Edmonds. My Jeep was down in the car compartment with boxes of hard cider, wine, and chocolate in the back, gifts from the grateful orchard owners.

The children had made it back safely, though I didn't think their parents had believed their story of being locked in a windmill by a dragon. Ayush, who must have had more encounters with magical beings in his life, had listened with wide terrified eyes. He'd been concerned that kobolds were still in the area and had spoken of listing the property and going back to being a software engineer in Seattle. I hadn't had the heart to tell him that far worse things than kobolds lurked in and around the big city.

Seagulls squawked as they flew overhead, and I couldn't help but look up to make sure they weren't fleeing a dragon. The sky had cleared and the sun had come out, so it would have been easy to spot the new one and even easier to see Zav's black form. Neither dragon was in sight.

How was I going to contact Zav? It wasn't as if he'd given me his cell phone number before disappearing.

Normally, I wouldn't care about delivering a message to him, but if there was a new, meaner, and more vindictive dragon in the world, he was the only one who could deal with it.

Fezzik's bullets hadn't done anything on that magical hide, and even

Chopper had barely cut it. I imagined fighter jets launching nukes at a dragon and wondered if even that would do the job. Dragons could probably make a shield that bombs would bounce off before they got close.

My phone buzzed, and I groaned. Who, now? I'd given Colonel Willard a verbal report of the incident—as usual, she wanted a typed report sent in by morning—and told Mary I'd go to a yoga class and see her later in the week for a session. I didn't want any more obligations, or to talk to any more people.

But when I saw Nin Chattrakulrak's name on my phone, I answered right away. Nin, owner of the Crying Tiger food truck and creator of magical weapons, never called me.

"What's up?" I asked.

"Val? I need to hire you."

It was after eight, but the June sun still hadn't set when I reached Occidental Square, the spot where Nin's food truck was parked today—and most days. The dinner rush had subsided, but kids wandering over from the busy outdoor Ping-Pong tables stood in line, paddles and ten-dollar bills clenched in their hands.

Nin's assistant was handing out paper-wrapped packages of the truck's signature beef and rice dish while Nin worked outside with a brush and bucket of soapy water. She was scrubbing graffiti off the side of the truck. Most of the message had already been cleaned off, but I could still read the word DEATH next to a noose around a clumsily painted skull. Despite the poor art, the message was an ominous one.

"Val!" Nin dropped her scrub brush in the water and rushed forward to grip my arms.

The kids in line looked curiously at us, or maybe at the polar opposites we represented. Five-foot-one Nin with her brown skin, tiny frame, and black hair currently dyed fuchsia versus pale, blonde, six-foot me looking like someone out of a comic book on the Valkyries my mom had named me after. I'd never been able to see much of my elven heritage in my face, but I also had never met my father and could only go by a painted portrait my mom had over her fireplace. My features were a little finer than hers, but I'd been in my twenties before I'd believed her origin story for me.

"What's going on?" I patted Nin on the arm.

She smiled and waved at the onlookers, then drew me around to the side of the truck. The *special* side. I ducked as we entered the little room sectioned off from the kitchen and smelling strongly of leather, metal, and gun oil.

Here, Nin had built Fezzik and continued to craft magical ammunition for it. That ammo might not have been effective on the dragon, but it could kill *most* magical beings.

A new order was in progress, a kris dagger with wavy edges that oozed menace. Guns hung on pegs on the walls, and parts rested in boxes under the counters on either side. All manner of tools were scattered around the compact area.

"You know that I have competitors in the magical-weapons business, right?" Nin spoke in her usual precise, calm English, but worry burned in her dark eyes.

"Sure. Before you showed up, I had a pistol made by Grifford down in Tacoma. I think he's still in business."

"He is. He specializes in small arms. And have you heard of the Pardus brothers?"

"They're up north, aren't they?"

"They work out of Bothell, but they sell magical guns all over the city. They were the major dealers of enhanced weapons here before I got into the business. In the beginning, they did not bother me or seem to care about me, but lately…" Nin extended a hand toward the wall with the graffiti outside.

"They did that?"

"I do not have proof. I did not see it happen. Tida and I were inside setting up this morning, and it was raining, so we had the window closed. When we opened for lunch, a customer pointed it out. It said my name and death is coming, and you saw the painting."

"Painting is an optimistic label for that skull. Let's call it graffiti. Why do you think the Pardus brothers are responsible, rather than some teenager acting on a dare?"

"They have threatened me before. Two weeks ago, Otto and Kurt came here to order food and tell me I had better get out of the weapons business or they would ship me back to Bangkok in a crate. In pieces."

"Oh? In front of witnesses?"

"They spoke softly so others would not hear."

"What did you do?"

"I told them," Nin said in her typical sweet but determined voice, "that if they tried to hurt me or my assistant, I would use my pliers to rip off their balls, dip them in batter, and fry them in hot oil."

"Good."

"They were not convinced. They said I had better close my *other* business or they would return. They are angry because, lately, some of their clients have left them and are purchasing weapons from me. You know my grandfather was a gnome tinkerer who learned his trade from a dwarf master smith, right? I am very well trained. I make high-quality weapons."

"I do know that."

"My weapons are superior. Their clients know this. That is why they are coming to me. What good is a weapon that a troll can snap in half?" Nin shook her head, her straight pink hair flopping about. "I do not want to give in to bullies, but it is scary and frustrating. They are full-blooded magical beings and much stronger than I am. I believe they are shifters. I wish my grandfather were here now to advise me."

"He passed away before you left home, right?"

"I am not sure if he died. He disappeared many years ago. And my father was already gone. He was a deadbeat and an alcoholic. My mother was not sad when he left, but that was when we had to go into the city to live. We struggled to make ends meet. That is why I want to earn enough here as a businesswoman to bring my mother and all my sisters to America and buy them a house."

That part of the story I'd heard before, and I nodded and patted her shoulder. "You will. You *are* good. I'm sure *many* of your clients would be happy to help you convince those guys to leave you alone."

"I would like *you* to help me, Val. You are the best, and you are my friend."

The words touched me more than I would admit, but they worried me too. As I'd told my therapist, I made it a point to avoid developing friendships, lest people be hurt or used against me by my enemies. It was a lonely life, but it was safest for those around me.

"Thank you." I patted her on the shoulder.

"How much would you charge to make the Pardus brothers leave me alone? I do not want them assassinated. I have no wish to do anything illegal or hurt them, even though they have threatened me, but I worry that their threats will escalate to more. I will compete fairly in business against them, but they do not wish to use fair tactics."

"I understand, but are you sure someone else wouldn't be better? It sounds like you need a negotiator, not an assassin." How was I supposed to get these guys to leave her alone when my main tactic was brute force?

"You have recent experience with a dragon."

All *too* recent. "I don't think Zav will go set fire to their workshop, if that's what you're asking."

"No, but they are now telling everyone that they can make dragon-slaying weapons. I do not believe this is possible for anyone but full-blooded dwarf and gnome masters in their native worlds. I do not believe it can be done at all with materials found on Earth."

"Why are they telling people they can make them?"

"Demand is very high right now. Many people saw your dragon flying over the city a few weeks ago. Also, there is footage out there of the kraken in Lake Union, and the houseboat residents are afraid more sea monsters will come. The police will do nothing. They do not admit that magical creatures exist."

I rubbed my face. "Zav isn't *my* dragon."

Nin shrugged. "You have spoken to him. Regardless, people are afraid. There is a huge demand for weapons that can protect humans from dragons. And the Pardus brothers claim to have them. They are selling their inferior weapons to scared people who believe they will work on a dragon. Val, people will be *killed* if they try to shoot a dragon."

Especially if they shot at the *new* dragon.

If I couldn't deliver a message to Zav, what might Dob do next to gain his attention? Something a lot more dramatic and showy—and deadly—than kidnapping a few rural children?

"I know you are experienced at dealing with the magical and also sensing magical artifacts and weapons," Nin said. "If you go there and see their offerings, you will know that they can't slay dragons. You could tell people, so *they* know."

I wasn't exactly a spokesman to the magical community—or the human community either—but if Nin wanted my help, I would do my best.

"I'll go visit them and learn what I can. Maybe paint threatening graffiti on their walls."

Nin smiled. "Good. Thank you. How much will you charge? I must negotiate with you, as I have learned from the entrepreneurship—" she pronounced that word with extra care, and I almost mentioned that I could barely say it either, "—lectures I take online. Even though you are a friend, this is business."

"I won't charge anything. You're my supplier of my weapons."

I wondered if the Pardus brothers somehow *did* have guns capable of piercing scaly dragon hides. If they did, I hoped Nin wouldn't be offended if I bought one. I would still threaten them on her behalf, but if dragons were going to keep showing up in the world, I needed a way to defend myself and others from them.

Her smile turned into a disapproving frown. "Val, this is a business deal. We must agree on a fair price, and you must be paid for your time. Also, it is possible you will be injured in your encounter with them. Have you met them? They are strong and dangerous. I know you are also very capable, but you must be paid for the risk you will take."

"What risk? I'm just going up to see if they have any good weapons for sale." I winked.

"There will be risk in dealing with them. You could be injured."

"I could be injured tomorrow at the yoga class I've been talked into going to—have you seen the pretzel shapes those people turn themselves into?—but it's all part of the job."

"I will pay you a fair amount when you return." Nin nodded firmly, then held up a finger. "Wait here. I will bring you dinner."

My stomach growled, reminding me that I hadn't stopped to eat on the way back. I would refuse to take Nin's money for doing a favor, but I'd happily take dinner.

When she returned, she carried *six* dinners wrapped in paper. She stacked them in my hands. "These will fill you up during your long journey."

"It's only a half hour up to Bothell at this time of night," I said dryly.

"That is only the beginning of your journey."

"Hm, probably true."

"It's also possible that you'll be mugged by a dragon on the way. They seem to flock to you."

I sighed. Had she heard about the new one?

A knock came at the side door.

Nin frowned. "Nobody has an appointment to come by now."

I sensed someone with a touch of magical blood out there, familiar magical blood. "It's my mom's roommate, Dimitri."

"He is your mother's roommate? He did not explain where he was from last time."

"Actually, he lives in the van in her driveway. I think he would love some of your business advice."

"I am still learning. I am not capable of being a mentor."

"Just show him some of your brochures." I opened the door and surprised Dimitri, who'd been about to knock again.

The six-and-a-half-foot-tall, pock-marked, refrigerator of a young man was standing outside and holding a pot with a fake cactus in it.

"Hello, Val," he rumbled in his deep voice. "I didn't expect to find you here."

"Am I in the way? Did you come to court Nin?"

Dimitri's eyebrows flew up, and he almost dropped his pot. "No, nothing like that. I… already met someone in town here. At the club." Looking flustered, he glanced at me, then at Nin, then back at me. "I just wanted to thank her." He looked back at Nin. "To thank *you.*"

"For what?" Nin looked puzzled.

"I've been watching your videos online for your food truck and figuring out some things I can do to help sell my yard art. I'm going to start recording videos for the internet, but I could use some help. My landscaping boss laughed when I asked him—he thinks my yard art is goofy. And Val, your mom only got footage of her nostril hairs when I tried to get her to use my phone to record me showing off one of my sentinels. This one, as a matter of fact." He hefted the pot.

"She's not that experienced with technological gizmos."

I eyed the blue metal faux cactus. Since I'd seen his work before, I had a feeling those barbed thorns could shoot out and fill someone with holes.

"It was just my phone," Dimitri said.

"Have you seen *her* phone?"

"The one where you pick up the receiver and make circles with your fingers to dial numbers by hand? Yeah."

"It's called a rotary phone. I promise you can't record nostril hairs or anything else with it."

"I know. I figured I might be more able to find help up here." He lowered his voice and glanced around the square. "I've also been talking to Zoltan."

I started to ask why but remembered the vampire alchemist supposedly had a huge internet presence, won by sharing videos of himself making potions.

"I drove up here because I got a booth at the farmers market in Woodinville. I'm going to sell my yard art and also some of his wares. In exchange, he said he'd show me how to get started building a platform online."

"Did you bring your cervical collar for protection?" I was joking—that wasn't going to stop the fangs of a determined vampire—but Dimitri nodded gravely.

I needed to make a trip to see Zoltan at some point too. I still had the notebook I'd taken from the dark-elf alchemist's lab, and I was curious if there was anything useful in it. Maybe I could convince Dimitri to take it to him for me.

"Anyway, this is for you, Nin." He thrust the pot at her. "If you press that button on the top of the cactus, it arms itself, and then you have five seconds before it starts spewing needles. Or you can automate it here." He flipped up a panel. "Sort of like setting a security system. If someone intrudes and doesn't know to turn it off, it'll fire. I wasn't sure if you needed something like this, but this neighborhood gets kind of rough at night, doesn't it? And I saw some graffiti on your truck."

"Yes." Nin nodded firmly, took the pot, and set it down on a counter. "Thank you for the gift."

"You're welcome. I'm hoping to find someone up here—" Dimitri waved vaguely toward the city, "—who programs apps, so the owners could also use their phones to set off my security devices remotely."

"Is all of your art hostile?" Maybe I ought to get a piece for my apartment.

The numerous deadbolts weren't doing enough to deter assassins, magical muggers, and snooping government agents.

"Some pieces are. Some just warn the homeowner if someone is trespassing. And some don't have anything to do with security at all. I have an automatic back scratcher made from old ski poles in my van if you want to see it. Oh, and a patio table and chairs made from a ski lift chair I found in a rummage sale." He pointed his thumb toward the street, though he must have parked somewhere out of sight. "I hope the van is all right. It's getting dark, and it doesn't have a security system."

"I don't think thieves break into vans for back scratchers."

"It's a luxury good, Val. You sure you don't want to see? Nin? I have a whole bunch of cool stuff I'm going to sell this weekend. Do you have any tips on negotiating?"

"Start higher than the price you want," Nin said, "and first show a very expensive item, so that the more modest item seems like a deal."

"Oh, that's good." Dimitri nodded. "Ski-chair patio furniture first and *then* back scratcher."

"I better get going. I'll go up to Bothell early tomorrow, Nin." I was tempted to drive up there now, but if I went during the Pardus brothers' business hours, I could pretend I was a customer. Maybe then, I could make an attempt at negotiating before falling back on my strength: beating people up.

I also wanted to talk to Willard first to see if she had any intelligence on them. Maybe I would get lucky and find out the government wanted them dead for heinous crimes.

"You're going to Bothell tomorrow?" Dimitri asked. "You should stop by the farmers market while you're in the area and pretend to be interested in my wares."

"Pretend?"

"So other potential customers will think there's a lot of demand. It's social proof. I've been studying."

"Why are you selling your stuff in Woodinville? Remember the houses we saw there? And the homeowners' association? They probably forbid yard art."

"Not *all* the houses there were like that. There were plenty of old farm houses and normal houses with big yards full of stuff. Besides, my art is fabulous. No HOA would object to it."

"If you say so." I eyed the blue cactus.

"Anyway, I have to pick up Zoltan's lotions and tinctures to sell."

"Lotions and tinctures?" I asked. "That doesn't really go with your steampunk upcycled bike parts style."

"My style is eclectic. And Zoltan said he'd give me a cut of whatever I sold."

"According to him, the dragon blood I gave him was worth a half a million dollars. What does he need to sell tinctures for?" And what was a *tincture* anyway?

"I think he's using that blood himself, not selling it. I better go find a place I can park my van for the night."

"You can stay at my place if you want." I didn't want a houseguest, but I felt obligated to offer.

"No offense, Val, but your place was ransacked when I was there and then invaded by a dragon."

"It's cleaned up now, and you slept through the dragon coming in. What's the problem?"

"I was creeped out later when I learned he'd been there making threats while I was sleeping. What if he saw me drooling? Or scratching my balls?"

"I promise he wouldn't care. He thinks humans are vermin and beneath his notice."

"I'll find a spot." Dimitri waved at us. "Don't forget to come by the farmers market tomorrow."

"I'm not sure whether to be offended or pleased that the possibility of visiting dragons has made my home unappealing to houseguests," I said.

Nin shook her head. "I do not know, but if I could pay a dragon to perch on my food truck, I would. I am concerned there will be more graffiti and perhaps worse."

"There won't be. I'll take care of those guys tomorrow, one way or another. And then go to the farmers market to buy vampire tinctures."

I was joking about that, but Nin looked wistful as she said, "Please buy me hand lotion if there is an appealing scent. I never have time to shop. Maybe someday…"

As her wistful gaze shifted toward the darkening sky, I vowed to find a way to handle the brothers for her. Nin had worked her ass off to build her business—both of them. She didn't deserve to be picked on by bullies.

CHAPTER 7

I sat in my Jeep in a gravel parking lot next to the Sammamish River Trail with the door open as I ate a breakfast burrito and ran searches on my phone. It hadn't occurred to me that the Pardus brothers wouldn't have a showroom or workshop address listed online, though I supposed Nin didn't technically have an address either. Maybe in the magical-weapons business, it wasn't a good idea to let anyone but trusted clients know how to find you. There were a lot of magical beings who would prefer that guns designed specifically to hurt them didn't exist.

When Colonel Willard's name lit up my phone, I answered it promptly. I'd left a message earlier, hoping she could get me the brothers' address. Nin had never been out here herself, so she hadn't known it.

"It's Saturday, Thorvald," Willard said, a little breathless. What workout had she been engaged in, while she should be resting, this time? Spin class?

"Crime doesn't stop on the weekend."

"What crime? Your message said you need the address of a gun dealer."

"A magical-gun dealer—two of them. The Pardus brothers have been picking on Nin. And by picking on, I mean threatening to destroy her business if she doesn't shut it down." I didn't think Willard had ever met Nin, but I'd mentioned her before and shown her Fezzik. Willard had politely oohed and aahed over the gun. "They're also selling what they claim are dragon-slaying weapons."

45

"Do you want to beat them up or buy one?"

"Both if they actually have them. But Nin doesn't think anyone on Earth can make such things. Any chance you have their address? There's a phone number listed, but when I tried calling it, I got a menu as convoluted as a bank's and eventually a prompt to put in a code. I do not have a code."

"Hold on. I have info on all the dealers in the area."

A pair of geese left the grass to waddle up to my open door. They eyed the second half of my burrito. One poked at the gravel, as if I would have littered crumbs all over.

"You're not getting my food, you winged mooch."

The geese were very well fed. On the trail, a biker had to brake to avoid ducks crossing from the brush to the river. They were also well fed.

"I assume that comment is not for me," Willard said. "Has your dragon returned?"

"To steal my breakfast burrito? No."

"You should eat higher-quality food. It might help with your health issues."

"I don't have health issues. Just an obnoxious case of intermittent lung inflammation that pops up at inopportune times, such as when evil alchemists hurl noxious potions at me and when dragons try to light me on fire."

"What do you think a health issue is?"

"Something serious that people die from. Like dysentery."

"I see you played *Oregon Trail* as a kid."

"I didn't need to play it. Mom and I lived it in our school-bus house on wheels. Do you have the address? I'm about to get mauled by geese."

One kept trying to pluck at my wrapper. I stuck it on the dash, then, worried the goose would jump onto my lap to get it, shut the door. They squawked in disappointed protest. Feeling guilty, I tore off some of the burrito and threw the pieces out the window.

"Yes, I'll text it. It's in Bothell."

"I know that. I'm already here. I'm popping in to deliver threats on my way to purchase vampire-made lotions at the farmers market."

"Zoltan has a stand? How does that work? Doesn't his skin turn to ash if he sees sunlight?"

"Dimitri has a stand and is selling Zoltan's products for him."

"Tell him to watch his veins."

"He'll be fine. He has a cervical collar and decorative metal cactuses that launch darts."

"Silver-tipped darts?"

"You're thinking of werewolves. The cactus would have to hurl wooden stakes to hurt Zoltan."

Willard paused before saying, "When you were going through Basic Training, did you have any idea your life would end up this weird?"

"I don't know what you're talking about, Colonel. You have Smurf coffee mugs. This is nothing."

"Ha ha."

The address popped up, and I thanked Willard and hung up. It was only a few blocks away in a neighborhood right on the river. That was surprising. Maybe their magical-weapons business did a lot better than Nin's. If so, it was doubly obnoxious of them to harass her.

After looking up the directions and how much traffic was clogging the streets this sunny Saturday morning, I decided to walk. The river trail would take me most of the way there.

The geese had multiplied by the time I got out of the Jeep, fastening Fezzik in my thigh holster, and making sure Chopper was secure in my back scabbard. A hint of magic made it so normal humans—mundanes—wouldn't notice the weapons, though I got a few odd looks from bicyclers and walkers as I strode down the trail in combat boots, my brown leather duster, and a utility belt out of a military supply store. Regular belts weren't sufficient for carrying ammo pouches. I'd experimented before.

Unfortunately for my antisocial tendencies, the trail was as busy as the streets. As a skater zipped past closer than I preferred, I thought about bringing out Sindari. His presence usually created questions I wasn't interested in answering, but I knew nobody would dare brush me on their way by. Further, people might entertain me by skating off the trail and into the slow-moving shallow river.

I chose maturity over whimsy, turned off the trail before it crossed the river, and trekked down a couple of streets. The noise of the nearby freeway grew audible, and I laughed as the posh riverfront neighborhood I'd imagined came into view. It was a mobile-home park.

As I wandered in, following the map on my phone toward a manufactured house near the river, I wondered how this place had avoided being razed and sold to a builder of overpriced luxury homes. The traffic noise was noticeable, but waterfront property was waterfront property.

Judging by the tenants wandering past, older ladies walking small barky dogs, it was a mobile-home park for seniors. The Pardus brothers were either older than I'd expected or had a granny tied up in a back room, who they pulled out whenever they needed to prove their eligibility to live here.

My senses picked up magic as I neared a drab gray-and-green house with the siding falling off and moss growing on the roof. It looked to be one of the original homes placed in the neighborhood, though nothing here screamed new and modern.

Tall evergreens and shrubs partially hid the house from the street, and there weren't any signs to suggest it was a business. A couple of beat-up trucks occupied a driveway with wide cracks spurting clumps of grass and weeds.

As I approached the front door, I was able to refine my overall sense of magic to pick out numerous artifacts—weapons, likely—and two magical beings inside. No, three. Two were on the ground level and one felt like he or she was on a lower level. But a manufactured house couldn't have a basement, could it? Maybe the lot sloped down behind the house and there was a shop back there.

The doorbell was broken with wires dangling out. I opened the rusty screen door and knocked. As one of the magical beings on the ground floor came to the door, I studied his aura with my senses. The brothers were shifters, Nin had said, but she hadn't specified what kind. There was a feline aspect to this one. Maybe a lion or tiger shifter?

I'd encountered numerous types of shifters over the years, all hailing from, according to Willard and her intelligence gatherers, a single world in the Cosmic Realms. They were always predators, and some shifters even said that many of our big predators here on Earth were descended from early visitors from their world. There was, as far as I knew, no science to back that up.

The strong-jawed, olive-skinned man who opened the door didn't look old enough to live in this park. His lips curved into a smile. If he was surprised to see me, he didn't show it, but a full-blooded magical being would have sensed my aura before I sensed his. He'd probably felt me coming as soon as I turned into the neighborhood.

"Well, well," he said, looking me up and down, his smile turning lewd as his yellow-brown eyes fixated on my chest. "What brings the Mythic Murderer to our humble abode?"

"A coupon. I hear you're selling dragon-slaying weapons."

"We might be, but I assure you, there aren't any coupons out there. We sell premium products and only to those who can afford them." His gaze dropped to my combat boots and utility belt. "I wouldn't think your assassination services came cheap, but to be frank, you're a bit shabby. Our last customer came in wearing a Versace dress and driving a Range Rover."

"Only in Seattle would those things go together." I plucked at a peeling piece of paint on the siding. "Are you sure she wasn't lost?"

"Not at all."

"Let's assume I can afford *premium* weapons. Why don't you show me what you've got?"

"Why don't you show me what *you've* got?" He eyed my chest again.

I drew Fezzik from its holster, pulled out the retractable buttstock and folding front grip that transitioned from a pistol to a rifle. "I've got a custom monster hunter here—it's taken a few shifters down in its day—and then there's Chopper." I pointed the barrel downward as I indicated my sword.

Since the shifter was magical, he would have no trouble seeing my weapons.

His gaze shifted from my breasts to the gun, and his smirk disappeared, his face growing hard and unfriendly. "That's one of that Thai girl's dinky little guns. I'm surprised you would carry something so inferior." He squinted into my eyes. "Maybe you're not as dangerous as I'd heard."

There was a challenge in his gaze, and it reminded me of the werewolves that had attacked me outside of Bend, just because they'd wanted to be able to brag to others that they'd taken me down.

I slid the stock back in and held Fezzik up with one hand. If he attacked me, I would be within my rights to defend myself. And if he died in the process, that would be unfortunate, but these things happened in this line of work.

"You're welcome to find out," I said.

His lewd smile returned. "I could kill you, but I could think of more fun things to do with you than fighting. I do love blondes, you know. And so does my brother. Why don't you come into our lair and meet him?"

"I'm more interested in meeting your dragon-slayer weapons, ah, what did you say your name is?"

"Kurt. My brother is Otto. And if you like guns, we have 'em. It sounds like you've got a fetish. We don't mind that. We don't judge." Kurt looked back as he headed inside, flashing white teeth that were more pointed than normal for a human. "Otto," he called. "We have a visitor."

"A visitor or a customer?" a gruff male voice said from a back room.

The living room, complete with wood paneling and old green-fabric couches, was covered in gun magazines, metal and rock posters, and racks and racks of weapons. Most of them weren't magical, but a few were on par with Fezzik.

In a far corner stood what looked like a liquor cabinet, but one door was cracked open to reveal boxes of ammunition. They gave off a faint magical signature. Interestingly, they were sealed, as if they had been shipped here rather than made in-house. Did the brothers get their weapons and ammo from someone else and then resell them?

"That's what we'll find out," Kurt called back. "If you can tear yourself away from your work."

As I followed him deep into the house, I peeked into a kitchen and dining room that had been converted into an office overflowing with boxes and papers. He led me down the single hallway, past two bedrooms that were messier than my apartment had been after the ransacking, and to a room with a couch and a TV.

Inside was another magical being, one that looked enough like Kurt to be his twin. He was playing video games from the couch, his shirt off and corn chips dusting the cushions next to him. Only slovenly magical shifters could eat like that and have the hard muscled bodies of fitness-magazine models.

In addition to the corn chips, there were boxes of cartridges and empty magazines. He was probably supposed to be loading them when he wasn't too busy playing his game. So far, it looked like more cartridges had fallen onto the floor than made it into magazines. They oozed magic similar to what had been in the cabinet out front. The magic seemed no more powerful than what Nin made for Fezzik, and I doubted the bullets could puncture a dragon hide.

"I could tear myself away for her any time." The brother—Otto, presumably—paused his game and gave me a long leer as his brother stepped aside.

I still had Fezzik in hand and planned to keep the gun there.

Ignoring their leers, I tried to identify and locate the third magical being I sensed. The aura was muted, and I struggled to guess what species it belonged to.

Before, I had thought the person might be out back, but it felt like he or she was under us. Maybe there *was* a basement. Or at least some pit that had been dug out after the mobile home had been installed. But how did one get down there? I hadn't seen stairs on my way in.

"She's interested in our guns." Kurt smirked again.

"Oh yeah? Mine's always loaded." Otto rubbed his cock through his jeans.

Negotiating was going to be futile. I could tell. I was starting to wish I'd driven by, tossed a Molotov cocktail on the roof, and gone to buy lotions and potpourri at the farmers market.

"Where's the showroom?" I pointed at the faded gray rug. "Basement?"

"The showroom is right here," Otto purred, shifting to his feet, his hand still on his junk.

"There's nothing in this room that can slay dragons."

"Don't be too sure about that." Kurt smirked and reached for me, his hand moving more quickly than a normal human's would.

But I was used to dealing with that kind of speed. I caught his wrist before he could touch me, and glared into his eyes. "Oh, I'm sure."

Not surprisingly, he wasn't daunted. He smirked wider, as if pleased with the development.

"The Ruin Bringer doesn't want to have some fun before making a purchase?" Otto asked. "That's disappointing. Maybe we could give her a discount if she spends the day with us."

"You ever do two guys at once, pretty girl?" Kurt asked. "Or maybe a man and a panther?"

He shifted, his wrist melting out of my grip as he transformed into a large black panther. My feline guess had been right.

As he shifted, I took the opportunity to touch my cat figurine and summon Sindari. I would fight two on one if I had to, but if these guys were as strong as their auras suggested, I wouldn't walk away unscathed. Evening the odds made sense, and Sindari always enjoyed a fight.

"I can't say that I have," I said as Sindari materialized in the hallway behind me. "Do you actually have urges and find humans attractive in that form? I've heard that shifters are only attracted to what they've shifted into."

"Not necessarily true." Otto strolled closer, coming up to rest a hand on Kurt's feline back. "We've hosted some killer parties here and experimented a lot."

Kurt's long black tail swished in the air and then demonstrated some possibilities for those who drifted toward bestiality. Otto laughed uproariously.

What were the odds that I could get any decent information out of them? Or think of a way to convince them to leave Nin alone?

"Put away your tail, furball." I took a last stab. "I want to see one of these dragon-slaying guns. I've had run-ins with a dragon lately. I'm a serious buyer."

"Later," Otto purred, loosening his belt and stepping forward.

"If you sell something good to me, maybe I'll put the word out to others. Then you won't need to threaten other people in your industry."

Kurt's tail stopped swishing, and he stared at me, speaking telepathically. *Other people in the industry can either join us and work under us, or they can get the hell out of the city. Did she send you here?*

"Stay away from her." The protective part of me regretted bringing up Nin, but I *had* come to convince them to leave her alone. With as much ice in my tone as I could manage, I added, "Or you'll deal with me."

"We'll deal with you *now*. Pleasure before business." Otto's gaze flicked past my arm toward the hallway. They must have sensed and smelled Sindari's appearance right away, but neither seemed concerned. "Your cat can play too. I don't suppose that's a female?"

Kurt's tail went back to swishing suggestively.

We're going to have a fight, Sindari.

I assumed so from the lewd tail gestures.

Do you want to handle the panther while I tangle with the human?

52

That seems right. Excuse me while I inform them that I am not female and that even if I were, I would rather hump a tree than some second-rate feline.

That must have been a brief conversation, because both brothers snarled, their voices surprisingly similar given their different vocal cord construction at the moment.

"Pin her down," Otto snarled. "I'll take care of the pussycat."

The panther sprang for me.

CHAPTER 8

The panther was so close that I wouldn't normally have had time to react, but since Otto's big mouth had issued a warning, I was ready. When Kurt's paws left the ground, I dropped into a crouch and dove under him and into the room, rolling and yanking out Chopper as he sailed above me.

Sindari roared and leaped, meeting Kurt in the doorway. As I jumped to my feet, Otto threw a punch at my face.

I blocked with my free arm, angling it to deflect a blow that came in like a battering ram. At the same time, I lunged in with Chopper, slashing at the shifter's bare chest.

Otto leaped back with the speed of a cat, and my blade sliced through air. It gave me time to back farther into the room, put a wall at my back, and give myself more room to swing. Otto shifted form, turning into a huge black panther, muscles rippling under his sleek flesh.

As snarls and growls filled the hallway, Sindari and Kurt biting and clawing at each other, we faced off. Otto sprang, a paw slashing for my eyes.

Aware of the couch to one side, I glided to the other. I feinted, as if I meant to cut off his paw, then shifted the blade mid-swing and changed targets. As he was busy jerking his paw out of the way, Chopper sliced upward toward his belly and vulnerable internal organs. Otto tried to twist in the air as he landed, raking his back claws at me.

My sword gave me the reach to avoid them while cutting into fur and flesh. It wasn't a deep wound, and Otto didn't cry out. As soon as he landed, he whirled to face me again. But shifters were always fast. I wasn't fazed. It would be a battle of attrition; it often was.

This time, Otto ran straight toward me instead of springing into the air. White fangs dripped saliva, and his intent was clear: he meant to ram me against the TV stand and sink his teeth into my neck.

I didn't dodge. With speed and strength I thanked the father I'd never met for, I slammed a straight kick into his chest as I thrust with Chopper, aiming the point into the panther's open maw.

The ball of my foot struck with the blade, driving Otto backward as I gouged the side of his face—he whipped his head aside before the blade could sink into his throat. Bleeding, he jerked away and backed up. Fury glowed in his yellow eyes, and he sank low, looking like he would spring again.

But as he met my gaze, he threw a mental attack at me, one I hadn't expected from a shifter. They were known more for brute force and magical regenerative powers than psionic finesse.

Power raked at my mind, evoking pain as if he were using physical claws on my brain. An image forced itself into my thoughts, one of me dropping to my hands and knees and letting the brothers have their way with me.

Though startling, it was a clumsy attack. I walled off my mind, pushing the pain and the crude images away. Even without Chopper and its assistance with repelling mental threats, I could have fought this idiot off.

He leaped for me again, coming straight in. Did he expect me to be so stunned by his mental attack that I wouldn't be ready?

I had plenty of time to spring to the side and swing Chopper at his neck.

More coming, Val, Sindari warned from the hallway.

The announcement startled me, and my blade sliced into Otto's shoulder instead of his neck. It struck bone and glanced off.

Otto crashed into the TV. I would have laughed when it hit the wall, then fell forward, glass shattering all over him, but I abruptly grew aware of more magical auras in the area. Four. No, six. Allies to the brothers?

A couple of them were coming from the direction of the river, but others were running down the street from the entrance of the neighborhood. And they were coming fast. Even as I finished counting to six, more magical beings surged into range of my senses. Ten? They were all similar to Otto and Kurt, shifters of one kind or another.

I sensed this one calling them, but I could not stop him in time, Sindari added, pausing to snap his jaws as Kurt, bleeding from a dozen wounds, charged at him to continue their fight. *They're converging on the front yard. You better go out the back. I'll keep these two distracted so you can get away.*

Sindari was fighting as he communicated with me, so I didn't respond. I didn't want to distract him.

Besides, there was nothing to argue about. We could have taken down the brothers but not the brothers plus ten *more* shifters.

Glass tinkled as Otto pushed himself up, the TV frame falling to one side. I snatched a few cartridges from the box on the sofa and jammed them in my pocket, then faced him as he looked at me. I took a step, tempted to finish him off while he was still dazed, so he couldn't hurt or threaten Nin again, but two of the incoming shifters had already reached the lawn. One sprang toward the window of our room even as the front door slammed open, another charging inside.

I raced into the hallway and jumped over Sindari and Kurt, the massive felines clawing and thrashing on the floor, their blood spattering the rug. Sindari had the advantage with his powerful fangs embedded in Kurt's thickly muscled neck. It wasn't smart, but I paused long enough to jab Chopper down into Kurt's haunch. Or at least, that was my intent. He twisted as he tried to tear away from Sindari, and all I got was the tail. My blade sliced through it at the halfway point.

"You won't be using that for your perverted sex shit again," I growled, then ran into a bedroom facing the back yard as another massive cat, a female jaguar this time, rounded the corner and entered the hallway. She sprang through the doorway after me.

By then, I had Fezzik out, and I fired at her. Bullets tore into her chest, and she jerked back out into the hallway and out of sight.

Don't linger, Sindari ordered as I rushed through the bedroom and slashed all the glass out of the window with four precise strikes from Chopper. It clinked outward, and I leaped after it, landing in mud and weeds outside.

My senses told me more shifters were pouring into the front of the house. I hated to leave without any real answers, but there was no choice.

I ran parallel to the river, leaped a hedge, and rushed through yards and common areas as I ran back toward the trail.

Sindari? I glanced back. *You're getting out of there, right?*

He could dismiss himself from this world any time, but he was doing his best to buy me time. As much as I appreciated that, I didn't want him to get himself killed fighting ten powerful cat shifters at once. It *was* possible for him to die if he took too much damage before he traveled the magical pathway back to his own world.

Sindari?

Have you made it back to your vehicle yet? he asked.

Yes, I lied.

Running through muddy yards and leaping fences and hedges wasn't the fastest way to travel. But the bridge and the busy trail were in sight up ahead. I doubted the shifters would chase me through such a public area during the day.

I ran across the wide lawn of an apartment building, ducks quacking and paddling away from the bank as my passage disturbed them. The quacks grew uproarious, and several ducks took flight. That was when I realized that it was more than me bothering them.

A bloody silver tiger was running after me. Fortunately, nothing was running after him.

You have not *made it back to your vehicle,* Sindari told me sternly.

Before I could reply, an unfamiliar voice spoke into my mind. *Help me.*

The brothers' house was no longer in sight, but I was positive the telepathic words came from that direction. Had it been one of the brothers? I couldn't imagine them asking me for something. More likely, it was a trap designed to lure me back.

"Did you hear that?" I asked.

Sindari had caught up with me and ran by my side. *No, what?*

A telepathic voice spoke to me. It came from back there.

There was another magical being—not a shifter—under the house.

I know. Do you think that's who's reaching out to me? I had the telepathic abilities of a rock, but I tried to open my mind and project back toward the house. *Who are you? What kind of help do you need?*

A brown panther and a lion leaped over hedges and into the yard of the apartment complex as we ran out onto a street on the other side.

Flee, Ruin Bringer, one of them taunted me. It was not the same voice that had asked for help. *Flee with your pussycat.*

Yes, a female voice purred into my mind. *Run away from the power of the Northern Pride. Let it be known that the supposed Scourge of the Magical wets herself at the first sign of real might.*

There's only two following us, right? I asked Sindari.

Yes. The rest remain in the house.

I stopped in the street and turned to face the panther and the lion— they were loping lazily across the lawn. The fact that they weren't truly trying to catch us told me plenty. They'd seen Kurt and Otto with the snot—and blood—beaten out of them and weren't eager to fight us, not just the two of them.

I fired at them, not caring if any mundanes wandering past heard the noise. As the weapon opened up, bullets slamming into enemy flesh, the two big cats screeched and wheeled to run away.

The lion ran across the lawn and jumped, trying to clear the river in one leap. He didn't quite make it. Three-quarters of the way over, he splashed down and swam like a furry Olympic medalist to the far side, where he scrambled up the bank and disappeared.

The panther launched herself onto the two-story roof of the apartment building, a man holding barbecue tongs gaping at her as she sailed past and out of sight. A raw steak ready to go on the grill dangled from those tongs as he turned his gape on me. I smiled and waved, then holstered Fezzik. After digging out a cleaning cloth, I wiped down Chopper and put the sword away too.

My telepathy is weak, I told Sindari as we walked toward the trail. *Please deliver appropriate parting remarks regarding their power and might.*

Already done. I also pointed out to the lion that he is the only one wet around here.

Perfect, Sindari. Thank you. I paused to hug him, careful not to touch any of the open gashes in his hide.

Then I headed glumly to the trail. Even if we'd been ridiculously outnumbered, I couldn't help but feel that I had lost. I hadn't confirmed whether the Pardus brothers did or did not have weapons capable of hurting dragons, and I definitely hadn't done anything that would keep them away from Nin. I might have made things worse. Maybe I would get lucky, and they would turn any thoughts of revenge on me and leave her alone, but I couldn't count on that.

A part of me wished I'd killed them before I ran out. Maybe there wouldn't have been time—shifters were resilient as hell—but if I'd been determined, I bet I could have done it. They were assholes, and the world would be better if they were gone.

But, as I'd promised Zav more than once, I wasn't a criminal. I worked for the government and only executed those who'd committed heinous crimes. It was possible the panther brothers fell into that category, but I didn't have proof of that.

"It's a pain in the ass being a good guy." I sighed dramatically as we turned back onto the trail.

If it helps, I prefer working with righteous handlers. Having that charm in the hands of a vampire was dreadful.

I grimaced, thinking back to how Sindari and I had met. "I understand. I'll try my best to stay righteous. While plotting ways to put those guys out of business and drive them out of the country. There's nothing morally questionable about that, is there?"

I don't think so.

"Good. I need to come back again, ideally when they aren't home, to find out who's in their basement, but there's no point as long as their pride is hanging out in the house." I had no idea what I would do if the pride didn't leave. "Do panther shifters go out on Saturday nights?"

Tigers prefer to hunt at dawn and dusk.

"I'm not sure how much hunting those two do. They'll probably be licking their wounds for a while. Unfortunately. I'll have to mull over our options while I'm shopping for lotions at Dimitri's stand."

I halted, the memory of the boxes in that living room cabinet coming to mind. I had swiped some of their cartridges. Maybe I could find out who was supplying them to the Pardus brothers.

"I wonder if Zoltan knows anything about Kurt and Otto and this Northern Pride. These guys aren't operating that far from his home."

Zoltan might also be able to use his alchemy to tell who'd crafted the ammunition.

He did seem well informed, considering his limited ability to travel.

"Maybe the haunted house gives him tips." I glanced at the clock on my phone. It wasn't even lunchtime yet. "I suppose I can't visit a vampire at high noon."

Not if you expect him to be awake.

"He may think I'm going to rob him if I sneak in and knock on his coffin."

Perhaps if you arrived with Dimitri, you would be more welcome, since they now have a working relationship.

"Zoltan and I have a working relationship too. I got a bunch of blood for him. He should be oozing fond feelings for me."

Never mind that I'd killed his giant guard tarantula. Maybe going to visit with Dimitri *would* be a good idea. Especially if he already had to return to Zoltan's lair later, with whatever the vampire's cut of the day's earnings was.

Wrapped up in my conversation, I'd forgotten to dismiss Sindari when we got back on the trail. Someone zipping across the bridge on inline skates saw him, let out a startled yelp, and made the turn down the ramp harder than necessary. He hit the grass, flailed and almost caught his balance, but then ran into a rock. He flew off the bank and into the river.

"I think it's time for you to go, Sindari," I said as bicyclers came into sight. "You need to heal, and you're scaring people."

Me? You were the one talking about blood deliveries and oozing.

That's not nearly as alarming as a giant silver tiger. I smiled as I made a shooing motion, then hurried to add, *Thank you for your help this morning,* before Sindari faded into mist.

Always a pleasure to pummel lesser great cats, came his parting words.

CHAPTER 9

I passed people selling early-season vegetables, fresh-cut flowers, and local honey, and found my way to Dimitri, who stood like a brooding giant under a white awning stretched over his table of yard-art specimens. More of the metal statues crowded the ground around the table. A few people gave him curious looks as they passed, but nobody came close to admire his goods. Which was probably why he was brooding.

"How's business?" I asked, walking up.

"Deplorable." His shoulders slumped. "Nobody even comes up to ask questions about them. They only glance from the walkway and hurry past. I don't know what the problem is. I've had some luck selling them from my website."

"I hate to break it to you, Dimitri, but…" I reached up to put a hand on his shoulder. "You've got a face for internet sales."

"What does that mean?"

"You're big and scary looking. If you smiled more, that would help, but when you're standing there being broody, you look like someone's mafia bruiser." I wasn't sure smiling would make that much of a difference, but it couldn't hurt.

"Oh. You're not telling me anything I don't know, but why would it matter for selling art?"

"Do you see anyone else manning these tables who looks like a security guard?" I waved to the predominantly female vendors, including two women at a soap table who had a box of puppies. I wasn't sure if they were for sale or only there to bring people in. A lot of exclamations of, "Oh my God—they're so cute!" came from that shop, and the hand-made goat-milk soaps were flying off the table.

"You think you could do better?" Dimitri squinted.

"Me?" I gestured to my assassin-on-the-job couture, including a few tears where flying shards of the broken television had sliced through the fabric of my shirt. Given how the morning had gone, I was lucky I didn't have black eyes and broken ribs. "I'm not dressed for sales."

"That place across the way has all women's clothes. I bet that floral midi dress would fit you."

"Floral what?"

"Midi dress. You know, the hem at mid-calf."

"I don't know. How do *you* know?" Now I squinted at him.

"I'm an artist, Val. Not a mafia bruiser. Even if my father would have been more approving of that as a line of work." He shooed me toward the clothing stall. "I'll buy it for you if it's less than twenty dollars."

"Wow, you're a regular sugar daddy."

"Also, you have to stay for an hour and see if you can sell things better than I can."

I was about to tell him that I wasn't a sales clerk or here to work for him, but then I remembered my reason for coming. "I'll try to sell some stuff for you if you do a favor for me. I need to talk to Zoltan tonight. Are you going to take him his money when this is over?"

"His money or, with the way things are going, his inventory back, yes."

"Good, you can take me with you."

"I agree to this scheme, but why can't you go without me?"

"The last time I walked into his place, he sicced a giant woman-eating tarantula on me. I proceeded to kill it. I think we parted on decent terms, despite my ravaging his security system, but I'm not positive I would be welcome to return. If I walk in at the side of his new business partner…"

"We're not business partners. I'm more like his gopher. Or maybe his apprentice." Dimitri's eyes lit at this more prestigious title. "He's already given me some tips for growing a following online. I bet he'd approve of me using a pretty girl to sell my stuff."

I snorted. "You'd be better off with a twenty-year-old ingénue."

"I don't have one of those. I have you. And that dress." Dimitri pointed. "Go get it before someone else does."

"You'll throw yourself in front of me if there's a new tarantula?"

"Deal."

He had to point me past three dresses to the one he'd had his eye on. The floral wasn't as bad as I'd feared when he'd said the word. There were roses on the ivory fabric, but they were sage green, a color I didn't usually look ridiculous in. I was less enamored with the buttons up the front. They seemed too much of an invitation for some thuggish panther shifter to unbutton, but the Northern Pride didn't likely do business at the farmers market. Judging by the women pushing strollers, this wasn't a gun-buying clientele.

"Are you interested in that dress?" The vendor strolled up. "It's vintage from the nineties. It'll look fabulous on you. What great height you have."

Hearing that something from the nineties was vintage now made me feel old, and I was pretty sure *vintage* also meant it was used, but I guessed it would do for selling yard tchotchkes. Besides, it was getting warm, and being in something sleeveless might feel good.

The price was right—Dimitri had made a good guess—though the vendor was disappointed that I wouldn't try on any of her sandals. The table would hide my combat boots. They wouldn't matter.

A few minutes later, changed and with my weapons stashed under the table, I listened to Dimitri tell me what his gizmos were and what recycled bits and pieces they'd been made from, and attempted to look personable to anyone who wandered past. That wasn't my strength. He should have held out for an ingénue.

Still, as soon as he faded into the shadows at the back of the stall, interested people started coming up.

"How much for that big fish made out of wrenches?" asked a bearded man in green plaid who was clearly practicing the lumbersexual look. He wasn't as flagrant about checking out my chest as the panther brothers had been, but his gaze skimmed past on the way to the metal fish statue.

Dimitri hadn't given me prices, since he was standing nearby. After taking in the latest iPhone sticking out of the guy's pocket, an Apple watch on his wrist, and a BMW logo on the car keys he dangled, I said, "Three hundred."

Dimitri sputtered. Because the price was too low or too high? I hoped he hadn't brought thousand-dollar pieces of art to hawk from a tent.

Green-plaid Guy lifted his eyebrows. "How much for your number?"

I grabbed one of Dimitri's business cards. It had the name of his business, Sculpted Rain, rather than his name, along with a website and phone number. Perfect. I held up the card. "It comes with the purchase."

"I'll give you two hundred."

"The price is three hundred, my friend, but I'll throw in the Scorpion Stinger lotion. It's got a nice zing."

"All right." He pulled out a wallet thick with twenties and hundreds and counted out the money. "Don't forget the number." He paused, noticing Dimitri in the shadows for the first time. "Er, is that your partner?"

"Nope. He's the hired help. This stuff is heavy. Dimitri, wrap up the fish statue and take it to the man's car for him, will you?"

Dimitri squinted suspiciously at me but glanced at the money and silently went along with my suggestion.

I stuck the bills in his cash box and soon sold an owl with eyes framed by horseshoes to an older man who said his wife "loves this crap." He wasn't clad in overpriced techno-gadgets, so I only charged him sixty for his piece.

When Dimitri returned, he said, "You know that man is going to call me later, looking for you."

"He'll be disappointed that this was my last day at work and I sold the business to my porter."

"This isn't quite how I expected this to go."

"You're selling products and making money. No complaining."

"Fine," he said as another man approached the stall and started admiring wind chimes made from bicycle chains. "But for future reference, the Scorpion Stinger isn't a lotion. It's a tincture you can brush around your doors and cracks in the foundation of your house to keep rodents and insects out."

"Handy. I hope you let Mr. Plaid know. We'd hate for him to break out in hives."

"I told him. He seemed more interested in it then. He even gave me a tip." Dimitri held up a five.

"You've got a future in carrying people's merchandise."

"Whatever gets me my own property to park my van on."

"I thought you were saving for a house."

"Houses are expensive to build. That can come later."

"Maybe you can build your own from recycled bicycle chains."

"It crossed my mind. I might throw in some wood too."

"Rebellious." During a lull in passersby, I lowered my voice to ask, "Are any of the things for sale here magic?"

I'd wondered if I should be toting extra features or not.

"Not in any significant way. I think I'm going to have to be like Nin and sell those items through word-of-mouth. The times I've tried to explain to non-believers about the magical elements, it hasn't gone well."

"If it's any consolation, I doubt there will be non-believers for much longer." Not with dragons sprouting like dandelion seeds. The government might have been able to somewhat hide the existence of kobolds and werewolves that mostly kept to themselves, but dragons soaring over the cityscape were another story.

"I'm not that consoled." Judging by his grimace, Dimitri was also thinking of the proliferation of deadly magical beings in the world.

When I handed him another hundred from a sale, he perked up. If only money could solve my problems.

As the hour I'd promised Dimitri limped past, I wore out my lip muscles by smiling and my self-respect muscles by letting men ogle me. And I sold five more pieces for him.

"You're actually pretty good at this," Dimitri offered, stuffing his cash box. "You could get a job in sales."

"This may shock you, but I'd rather lop off the heads of murderers than smile pleasantly at people for money."

"I'm not shocked. I've known you for a couple of weeks now."

"Got the lay of the land, eh?"

"More or less. Thanks for helping."

As my hour of service—or was that servitude?—was ending, a powerful aura lit up my senses. I groaned.

Soon, gasps came from a couple of the shoppers wandering down the aisles, and they shouted and pointed toward the sky. Everyone else looked up, but they only shook their heads in confusion. I realized the people pointing all had the faint auras of those with a quarter or an eighth magical blood.

I stepped out into the open aisle in time to see the silver dragon flying high overhead, soaring toward the river. I'd been afraid he would show up on this side of Puget Sound.

Where was Zav? He needed to confront this guy and tell him to go back to his world.

My phone buzzed.

"It's still Saturday, Colonel," I said as soon as I answered it.

"No kidding." Willard sounded irked. "What were you doing out in Bothell this morning, Thorvald?"

"I told you. Looking for dragon-slaying weapons that probably do not exist." I wouldn't make that proclamation for sure until I'd seen what—and *who*—was in that basement. "I also got in a fight because I didn't want to have sex with strange panther shifters."

Dimitri's eyebrows rose.

"Would that be the Pardus brothers?" Willard asked.

"Yes."

"Respected officers in the Northern Pride?"

"Respected? Are you sure?"

"I ask," she said without answering my questions, "because the Pride's lawyer called our office to lodge a verbal complaint. He said you broke into their house, threatened them, and busted their television when they refused to back down."

"That's not how it went. They threatened *me*. When Sindari and I defended ourselves, the TV was an innocent bystander."

"The brothers say they have video footage of everything."

"Highly edited, I'm sure."

"If you don't stay away from them and their house, the lawyer is going to call the police and press charges."

"The lawyer? What kind of panther shifter brutes hire lawyers?"

"The ones with a lucrative business. Look, I believe you, Val, but don't go back to their house. If Nin needs protection, tell her to hire a bodyguard. Stay out of trouble this weekend. I'm collecting some intel, and I should have a new assignment for you next week. The dark elves have disappeared, at least out of the sections of the tunnels that were revealed by the sinkhole, but I'm hearing that they've been bribing members of the magical community. They may still represent trouble."

Of that, I had no doubt. The alchemist had said she'd wanted me—and Willard's office—out of the picture because of some plan her people had. She was dead now, but the two dark elves Zav had been hunting weren't, and there could have been hundreds more living in those tunnels. At least.

"Fine, but here's an intel tip you might not have yet: there's another dragon in town. And he's flying around looking for trouble."

Willard digested that for a long silent moment. "Maybe you should try to find a *real* dragon-slaying weapon. If the dragon starts attacking people... we're going to be called on to deal with it."

"By we, you mean me?"

"Very likely."

"Wonderful."

CHAPTER 10

The headlights of the van brightened the For Sale sign at the driveway of the upscale residence in front of Zoltan's haunted, dilapidated carriage house. It had been amended since our last visit, and a blue rectangle on the bottom now promised the sale was pending.

"Maybe Zoltan sold the dragon blood after all," I mused as we drove up in Dimitri's van. I'd left my Jeep at a park in town, trusting that we wouldn't need to go off-roading tonight.

Dimitri shook his head, his neck already armored in his white cervical collar. "He didn't."

"The real-estate agent must have finally found a sucker. And cleaned up the blood in the driveway and the slightly exploded playhouse in the back. Maybe the owners dropped the price. A lot."

"It's not a bad house." Dimitri looked wistfully at it as he parked on the opposite side of the street, even though it didn't look like his style. "I mean, it's a hideous amalgam of architectural styles, and those nubs on the roof don't make any kind of structural sense, but I'd take it anyway. It's peaceful out here but not that far to Seattle. You could build a huge workshop in the back."

Dimitri grabbed a toolbox and a canvas grocery bag with the remainder of Zoltan's merchandise from the back of the van. His bed and belongings were covered in unsold yard art, but I'd helped him move quite a few pieces. He'd been flummoxed by my method of pricing objects based on what I guessed people could pay, but it had evened out by the end of the day, and I hadn't shorted him.

Dusk was settling as we strolled past the house—fortunately, neither the real-estate agent nor any HOA patrollers were around to stop us—and to the vampire's dominion. I eyed the broken door warily, but Dimitri went around to the back, where there was a secret entrance to what had once been a root cellar. He nudged a root in the grass to open it, then clomped down wide earthen stairs, ducking low to keep from hitting his head.

"Any security systems on this side we need to worry about?" I considered summoning Sindari as I followed Dimitri down. I didn't sense any dark elves this time, or any other magical beings lurking around the property, so the only trouble might come from Zoltan himself. His aura placed him in the laboratory I'd visited before.

"He said they wouldn't bother me."

"Will they bother *me*? I'm unexpected."

"In all senses of the word." Dimitri smirked back at me.

"Ha ha. I'm debating if I should summon Sindari. Cats like spiders."

It had been more than twelve hours since our battle that morning, so he should have had time to magically heal the majority of his wounds.

"Including giant tarantulas?"

"He's always up for a challenge."

Dimitri used his phone's flashlight app as he walked past dusty shelves filled with jars of what I at first thought were tomatoes and pickles from some long past harvest. But they were fetuses, organs, and who knew what other disgusting things a vampire alchemist collected. Did he do biology experiments too? I didn't want to know. I walked past quickly, also not wanting to know if they were human.

"Great place to bring a date on Halloween," I muttered. "If the girl you met at the club likes being scared, I highly recommend it."

He gave me a weird look over his shoulder.

"What? *Is* there a girl? Or did you make that up because you're not interested in Nin? I think you could just tell her. She's got a lot going for her. It's not like she'd be crushed if you're not interested."

"I never said it was a girl."

"What do you mean?" Sometimes, I was exceedingly swift.

"I mean Sindari would be closer to my type."

"Animals?"

"*Guys.*" This time, he gave me an are-you-dense look over his shoulder.

"Oh." I followed him through a secret door and into a dark tunnel. "In that case, you shouldn't have been upset about the BMW-lumberjack calling you later."

"He wanted to call *you.*"

"You're the one he gave five dollars. Maybe he swings both ways."

I couldn't even interpret the third look. I touched my charm and summoned Sindari, more because I needed a rescue from my bumbling half of the conversation than because I expected another tarantula.

Dimitri had reached the door to Zoltan's abode, but he waited while the tiger formed.

Is it time for another battle? Sindari asked as soon as he solidified.

I hope not, but be prepared. We're visiting Zoltan.

I see Dimitri is better armed this time. Sindari wandered up and sniffed the canvas grocery bag with avocados, bananas, and strawberries on the side. *This smells like lilacs and rattlesnake venom.*

That's what you get when you carry stuff for an alchemist.

"Sorry I don't have any cat food." Dimitri knocked on the door.

Cat food! Sindari glared at me. *Does he believe I would eat mush made for small domestic felines?*

"Sindari doesn't need to eat while he's in our realm," I informed Dimitri. "But if he were to eat, it would be a steak, not a can of cat food."

A steak? I would prefer the steaming bloody liver from a fresh kill. A zebra or a syrentitops, perhaps. Yes.

You and Zoltan should get along well. He's into steaming blood too.

The door opened before Sindari could respond, and the red glow of the laboratory's infrared lights flowed out into the tunnel.

"Ah, my robber and my business partner." Zoltan was dressed in a sharp gray suit with a white button-down shirt and red bowtie. "Excellent timing. I'm working on a project you can help me with, Dimitri." His dark eyes narrowed as he regarded me. "And perhaps you can help me test it when it's complete."

"Lucky me."

Dimitri walked in after him but only took a few steps before staring at a pile of circuit boards and metal parts on the floor. "Is that it?"

"It will be." Zoltan strolled to a counter that had been full of chemistry equipment the last time I'd been here. Now it held welding tools and a giant metal...

"Is that a spider head?" I asked.

"A fused head and thorax, yes." Zoltan beamed. "I am replacing my biological tarantula with a robot version that I will infuse with alchemical power. It will be a superior defender of my humble abode. It also will not smell of spiders, and it will make less of a mess if it's destroyed." His pleased expression transformed into one of utter distaste. "You do not know how long it took me to get rid of the smell and the *stains*. And the carcass itself." He flattened a palm to his chest and shook his head. "I had to drag the body way out to that trail back there. I couldn't leave it to decompose near my home, or there would have been all manner of rodentia swarming the area."

"So it's decomposing on one of the most popular riding trails in town?" I asked.

"I believe some park rangers came one morning and discreetly disposed of it. Thankfully. That whole incident was dreadful. I should have you slain on principle for leaving such a vile mess."

I rested a hand on Sindari's back. "I knew I was wise to come with allies."

Zoltan looked to where Dimitri had fallen to his knees in front of the parts and was already sorting them like someone prepared to build a LEGO structure. "I believe that is *my* ally."

"Oh no. I put on a dress and sold metal doohickeys for him all afternoon. He's definitely my ally."

"Doohickeys?" Dimitri threw me an aggrieved expression. "Art, Val. Functional, magical, and aesthetically pleasing art."

"Zoltan," I said, "I was wondering if you could look at a few things for me."

"Is our deal not complete? Pardon my rudeness, Ms. Thorvald, but you are not welcome among the magical community, and as you can tell, I haven't quite forgiven you for removing my loyal guardian from me."

It sounded like it was more the mess that had aggrieved him than some fondness for the giant tarantula.

"Today, I sold four tins of your Scorpion Stinger, two of the Fount of Youth skin rejuvenator, and nine bars of your no-more-ingrown-hairs ox-horn shaving soap."

"Please, come tell me what you need." He flashed his fangs at me and patted the counter beside him.

Keeping a wary eye on those fangs, I pulled out my purloined cartridges from the Pardus house. "First off, have you heard of the Pardus brothers?"

"Certainly. They sell magical weapons and are high-ranking officers in the Northern Pride."

It seemed everyone knew about that association but me. I should have come here first.

"I'm hoping you can tell me whose work this is. I believe someone is selling magical cartridges—maybe even the weapons themselves—to the Pardus brothers and that they're reselling them to clients." It had occurred to me that I might have an easier time turning the screws on their supplier than on the brothers themselves, and that might give me a bargaining chip when it came to negotiations. If their supplier stopped making things for them, there would be nothing for them to sell. "Also, I have a notebook I got from the dark-elf alchemist when I was in their lair, and I'd like you to translate it for me."

"You want so much of my valuable time, so much valuable information. How many bars of the ox-horn soap did you say you sold?"

"Nine. All in all, I made two hundred dollars for you."

"By yourself?" Zoltan looked over his shoulder. "Is this true, Dimitri?"

"Yes. Apparently, I have a face for internet sales."

Zoltan's smooth pale brow wrinkled.

"I also got you that vial of dragon blood," I reminded him. "You mentioned it was worth slightly more than two hundred dollars."

"Indeed, indeed. So it is. I was delighted to show my interweb protégés how to make lyngurium with it, a stone capable of healing everything from gallbladder stones to jaundice. There's much misinformation about lyngurium on the interwebs—many sources say it's solidified lynx urine, can you believe?—but dragon blood is the true key ingredient. My instructional video has already been watched over a million times."

"There are that many people with jaundice?"

"Gallbladder stones, my dear robber. Unfortunately, none of my young acolytes have access to dragon blood. Yet. I am considering starting a mail-order ingredients business. For the right price, I could part with a few drops of that liquid gold." Zoltan pressed his fingers to his lips and kissed them flamboyantly, then tapped the cartridges. "I recognize the signature of the enchantment melted into the metal of these projectiles, yes. There's a local enchanter who works for a fence company here in Woodinville. They install *enhanced* wrought-iron and chain-link barriers designed to keep out werewolves, zombies, and other savages. Given how easy it is for assassins to intrude upon my domicile, I may have to consider purchasing one of their fences."

"Don't you think the new homeowners will believe it odd if their carriage house is behind bars?" I asked.

"Oh, I'm sure they won't be here for long. They never are. Strange, isn't it? I'm a charming neighbor. And a deterrent to riffraff. Most riffraff." Zoltan gave me a pointed look. "Only the Mythic Murderer would wander willingly into a vampire's abode."

"Not *only*." I pointed to Dimitri, who was now using pliers and a wrench to make a spider leg.

"He's an invited guest, not riffraff."

"You found someone who isn't intimidated by your stature, Dimitri." I pulled out my phone to look up the fencing businesses. "Is this it?"

I pointed to the only one in the list that mentioned *enhanced* offerings.

"It is, yes," Zoltan said distractedly. He'd pulled over the notebook to study.

Assuming it took a while to translate a language, I made myself wait patiently for an entire minute. "Anything interesting?"

"Perhaps, but I'll have to dig out my academic tomes on languages to find out. Unlike that sigil you brought me, these pages aren't in the dark-elf alchemical language."

"One of the other three?" I remembered him explaining that the dark elves had four.

"Yes. The one reserved for religious ceremonies, I believe. It will not be a simple matter to translate it." Zoltan straightened and looked at me, his gaze drifting to my neck.

"How many bars of shaving soap do I have to sell to make it worth your while? You're not getting my blood."

"No? That's unfortunate. I can tell you've been in the presence of dragons again." His dead eyes gleamed like wet marbles. "More than one.

Amazing. It's like you're a magnet to them."

"The only thing amazing is how inadequate my loofah is. I can't believe I spent twelve dollars on an extra-fibrous one and it doesn't get dragon aura off me."

"Believe it or not, I wasn't going to ask for remuneration. You can simply owe me a favor."

I shook my head. "I refuse to owe people favors. Or anything else."

"Yet you ask for them."

"I'm not asking for a favor. I'll pay you for your time. Why don't you translate the pages, find out what the information is, and then give me a fair price? I'll decide if I'm willing to pay it. If I'm not, maybe someone else will be so you won't have wasted your time." I wondered if Willard's department had funds dog-eared for information on the dark elves.

"Has it occurred to you that the dark elves might want their notebook back, and that I could be in danger while translating it?"

Actually, it hadn't. The alchemist was dead and their lair was in disarray. Who would even know the notebook was missing?

"I am assuming that you stole it from them," Zoltan continued. "They wouldn't give this to their closest ally, much less an enemy. You *are* a robber, aren't you?"

"I am not." Memories of Zav calling me a criminal came to mind. I *had* stolen the notebook, but my mind refused to accept that it had been an ignoble act. "The alchemist was trying to kill me. I only grabbed that because I was seeking the ingredients to make a concoction to fix my lungs. You were the one to tell me the ingredients for that, by the way. Thank you."

"You are most welcome, but I am positive I didn't list dark-elf diary pages among the ingredients."

"Is that what you think those are? I assumed they were from an alchemy recipe book."

Zoltan smiled enigmatically. "We shall see."

CHAPTER 11

Sunday morning found me with my bare feet and hands planted on a mat in a downward-dog position. The fence manufacturer in Woodinville, my only lead, wasn't open on the weekends, and Willard had told me to stay away from the Pardus house, so my investigation was at a stand-still.

What better use of my time than to contort myself into strange positions that caused my T-shirt to dangle about my head? Now I understood the need for a yoga-specific wardrobe. We'd been holding the position for five breaths, supposedly, but I was positive it had been five minutes. I was thinking about my daughter instead of listening to the instructor guide me through an unpronounceable form of breathing that involved channeling Darth Vader and the back of my throat.

While waiting for the class to start, I'd seen a social-media post from Amber, not the usual swim-meet information, but something about a book she was struggling with for her last school essay of the year. I'd read it, even though it had been long ago, and had the urge to call her and ask if she wanted to talk through her ideas for her paper. But it had been ages since we'd spoken, and she would probably hang up or be horrified if I called.

Mary, the therapist I'd seen a few times now, wanted me to reestablish a relationship with my daughter, even though I kept assuring her that was a bad idea. I made new enemies every month—every time I walked into someone's moss-covered, sagging mobile home. It was better that none of them knew I had a family.

Knowing that didn't keep me from feeling regretful and wishing things were different. I'd also caught a post from my ex-husband that morning mentioning that he and Amber were planning a trip to a lake in Northern Idaho this summer. I couldn't help but imagine hanging out with them on some dock, having a normal familial relationship…

"I can't hear you, Val," the instructor said in a sweet sing-song voice.

She was walking between the staggered yoga mats, saying a few words to people about their downward dogs—thankfully we were done *flipping* the dog now—and paused beside me.

"Uh?"

"Breathing. We're working on our Ujjayi breathing. You need to inhale through your nose, fill your lower belly with air to activate your first and second chakras, then move the air up to exhale through your nose. You move your glottis as the air passes in and out of your throat to make the ocean sound."

I rolled my eyes at the talk of chakras, made a note to later look up glottis, and wondered what it said about me that I would rather be fighting with the panther brothers than doing this. "Right. Ocean breathing. I'll work on it."

"Excellent. I want to hear you." The instructor wandered off to harass someone else.

A clank, followed by glass breaking came from a window at the front of the room. I jumped to my feet, reacting before the projectile—a grenade, damn it—hit the bamboo floor. Startled shouts came from the other people in the class. I sprinted up, grabbed the grenade, and threw it back out through the hole it had made in the window.

An explosion roared out in the street, fiery orange light flashing, and the windows shook under the force. The already-broken window shattered inward, glass tinkling across the hard floor. Women screamed and ran for the changing rooms. I ran and jumped out the window, grimacing as glass cut my bare feet.

Not only did I not have shoes, but my weapons were all in the Jeep. Fortunately, I wore my charm necklace and could call Sindari if needed.

The explosion faded as I landed on the sidewalk, crouching behind a mailbox for cover and looking for who had thrown the grenade. Tires squealed at a nearby intersection, and I glimpsed a truck peeling out of sight around the corner. That truck looked a lot like the white one that had been in the Pardus brothers' driveway.

I was tempted to run after it—horns honked, promising plenty of traffic that would slow down their getaway—but I saw someone walking toward me wearing slippers and a black robe that wouldn't fit in anywhere except maybe a fantasy gaming convention.

The power of Zav's aura buffeted me like a strong wind, and I couldn't believe I hadn't sensed him sooner. Maybe he'd been flying nearby, spotted the explosion and landed immediately, turning into his human form so he wouldn't attract attention.

"What are you doing here?" I blurted as soon as he was close enough to speak with over the honks of horns and shouts of people on the opposite side of the street. Already, a siren wailed, the police and maybe the fire department heading this way. Nothing was burning—thankfully, the grenade had exploded in the air over the street. "I know you didn't come to get your chakras aligned."

"That is not the proper way to greet a dragon." Zav looked me up and down, his gaze lingering on my bloody feet. "Nor is this appropriate attire for battling criminals."

"I'm not battling criminals. I'm exercising and contorting my throat to do ocean breathing."

His forehead creased. "You must always be prepared to battle criminals. They are attracted to you. That is why I keep telling you that I will use you as bait."

"No kidding." A police car turned onto the street, and some of the yoga students were peering out the broken window and the front door. "Look, I've got a message for you. Let's go over there." I pointed to an alley.

I hurried to it. Zav considered his surroundings before clasping his hands behind his back and strolling after me.

"You leave blood on the ground as you walk." He pointed to a spot. "This will make it easy for enemies to track you. Do you wish me to heal your injuries?"

"No, I don't want anything from you." Owing Zav a favor would be even worse than owing Zoltan a favor. I waved for him to keep following me, so I could go to the parking lot in the back where I'd left the Jeep. "But there's a dragon who does. You know a Dob-something-or-other? Big silver dragon, likes to kidnap children?"

Zav's face grew frosty. "I know Dobsaurin and am aware that he is in this world."

"Did you know that he's been trying to get your attention?"

"I do not know his reason for coming, but I have sensed him here. I have been far to the east and south, capturing rogue djinn in a hot desert region."

"What brings you back? You missed me?"

He regarded me blandly again. "You do make it easier to locate criminals. They are drawn to you like a *vylorni* to a flame."

"I've noticed." I waved in the direction of the soot-stained sidewalk and broken window. My first yoga class, and I'd endangered all the students there. How had those idiot brothers guessed I would be there? They couldn't have tracked me by scent in a city so large, could they have? "But you attract irate dragons who don't like your current criminal-capturing gig."

"Dobsaurin's family does not like anything that my family does. We are rivals."

"Yeah, I guessed." I walked across the parking lot to my Jeep. Nobody else from the class had come out the back yet. Maybe they were waiting for the police to question them. I would need to go get my shoes and bag eventually, but I hadn't locked my door, so at least I could grab a towel out of the back and wipe my feet.

A warm heat washed across my soles, followed by the itching of new skin forming, and I glared suspiciously at Zav. He stood a few feet away, his aura tingling all over me and probably making it even easier for magical beings to find me. His hands were still clasped behind his back.

"You're healing me? Listen, I appreciate that you'd rather do that than incinerate me, but I *really* don't want to owe you any favors."

He cocked his head. "Why not?"

"Because you'll try to redeem them. And tell me I need to travel with you and be your bait."

"I do believe your reputation might have stretched even to the distant deserts. You may have attracted the djinn, thus making it easier for me to locate and capture them. Lesser magical beings tend to hide when dragons come near."

"Shocking."

"Your tone is not properly respectful. Do not forget that you are addressing a superior being."

I only partially managed to muffle my scoff as I rubbed the towel across my feet. The blood had dried, and the wounds had completely disappeared. It wasn't just that they'd turned to scars; it was as if the injuries had never occurred.

"Thank you," I made myself say, however grudgingly. Now that I'd met a dragon that liked to kidnap children for fun, it made me realize I should be a little nicer to the one who was a law enforcer. Even if laws put forth by the Dragon Justice Court had little in common with Earth laws, Zav seemed vaguely reasonable to deal with. "Why are you here? I don't suppose the Pardus panther-shifter brothers have committed crimes and you've come to capture them for rehabilitation."

Dare I hope? If he was after them, it would make sense that he'd shown up.

"No. I do not know who they are. I brought you the gift you requested, even though your tone reminds me that you are not deserving of gifts from a dragon."

"Uh, what?" I was positive I hadn't requested anything from him except that vial of blood, and he'd already given me that.

"A poster of myself that you can throw hatchets at."

"You're joking, right?"

"I am not." Zav drew, seemingly out of an invisible poster carrier attached to his back, a rolled-up tube.

Had he actually found a print shop and had one made? I couldn't believe it. I squinted at him as I accepted it, still expecting a joke.

"I suppose dragons aren't known for their senses of humor," I said when I didn't find any sign of amusement on his face. It was a handsome face, with a strong, angular jaw and high cheekbones, everything enhanced by a perfectly trimmed beard and mustache, but it was a haughty one. It had to be hard to laugh when one's haughtiness mask was affixed so tightly.

"Who told you this lie? Dragons have riotous senses of humor, but we only tell jokes among our own kind. Inferior species would not have the necessary mental acuity to grasp them."

So much haughtiness.

"Oh, I bet."

As I opened the tube and tipped the poster out, I noticed a twelve- or thirteen-year-old boy with a skateboard under his arm eyeing us from across the parking lot. He was watching but pretending not to be watching. Maybe he liked Zav's robe and wanted to know what Etsy shop he could order it from.

"I also came because Dobsaurin told me he left a message with you." Zav's violet eyes narrowed. "He was exceedingly coy when he spoke to me, and it was from a great distance. I know he is here in this geographical region, but I cannot pin him down." He gazed at the walls of the buildings around us, as if he could see through them to the snow-capped Cascades to the east and the Olympics to the west. "I believe some magical artifact is assisting him in evading my senses. He taunted me with his words, as if he had some knowledge that I did not."

"Uh, the only knowledge I have is that he wants to kill you for sanctimonious meddling, and he's a dick."

"I already know this." Zav paused. "What is a… dick?"

"The thing hanging between your legs." I unrolled the poster but almost lost my grip when Zav bent to look down. Did he think I meant his robe? "The sex organ that's there if you gave yourself all the human parts when you shape-shifted. I guess I don't know if you did. And," I hurried to add, "I don't want to know."

Zav straightened. "I would not shape-shift into an ill-considered amorphous blob. When I am in human form, I am anatomically correct."

"I'm so glad for you."

I held out both sides of the poster. It wasn't the big black dragon I'd expected. It was a blown-up photograph of Zav, with his familiar haughty and handsome face and wearing the same black robe with silver trim. He was posing with one leg propped on a chair and his chin on his fist, his elbow on his knee. I assumed it had been the photographer's idea. It wasn't a bad one. The photo was attractive. If he wanted to retire from enforcing dragon laws, he could easily get modeling gigs here. Or, if he was as anatomically correct as promised, a career working in the sex industry.

"I have to admit, I was imagining throwing hatchets at the *dragon* form of you."

"The dragon form of me couldn't fit in the booth, and the photographer was unsettled. He would not consider going outside with me. I decided not to magically compel him. People don't do their best work under such conditions."

"Imagine that." I turned the poster, wondering at the plausibility of setting up a hatchet-throwing arena in my small apartment. And if I could truly bring myself to hurl blades at his face. "Mangling someone who looks human seems sadistic."

"You would not consider it sadistic to mangle a dragon?"

"Nah. It would be like operating a crane with a wrecking ball and swinging it into a building marked for demolition. Satisfying."

Zav gazed at me. Something about it made me feel guilty, like I was morally wrong to find the idea of mutilating a dragon appealing. It wasn't my fault he was so pompous and annoying. His arrogance invited fantasies of mutilation.

Across the parking lot, the boy was still not-watching us.

"Do you have any idea what that kid wants?" I asked to change the subject—and because I was curious.

Zav shouldn't have been able to see the boy from where he stood, but it didn't surprise me that he knew what I meant. "He wishes to deliver a message to you, but he's not certain if I am your mate and will drive him off in a fit of jealous rage." Zav's forehead crinkled. "His thoughts are alien to me. It's possible I misinterpreted them."

"Yeah, I think so. Don't sweat it. Teenage-boy thoughts are alien to other humans too." I looked over at the kid, caught his gaze before he could pretend not to be looking, and waved for him to come over.

"I truly need the message that Dobsaurin delivered to you," Zav said earnestly. "If he is here to openly challenge me, this is unprecedented, and something must have changed between our families. I must warn my kin." His gaze drifted from my eyes upward to my forehead. Well, that was better than all the guys whose gazes went down to my boobs. "You are not wearing your magical sword. It is interesting that I have difficulty reading your thoughts."

"You're probably distracted by my great beauty."

His gaze drifted downward, more considering than interested, and I wasn't positive he'd even been aware that I was female. Not that the baggy T-shirt I'd chosen for this class was form-flattering.

"Never mind," I said. "Look, he kidnapped some children, and he said it was because he wanted to get your goat. He didn't say why, just implied that he would kill you. That's really all he gave me. He spent most of our time together trying to flambé me."

"My goat?"

"Your attention."

"If he wishes my attention, he has it. If he wishes to challenge me, I am not afraid to battle him. Why would he use you to deliver this challenge and then hide?"

"How would I know? I didn't even know he existed until the other day."

Zav frowned at me. "It is true you are ignorant of politics in the Cosmic Realms."

"Yes, I am. I'd like to stay that way. And also not to be incinerated by dragons trying to get your attention."

The boy had skated over and was close enough to hear that last sentence, but he didn't react to it.

"I think you're the one," he said.

"I'm sure that's true." I eyed him again, hoping the kid wasn't here to take revenge for a parent I'd killed. That had happened before. But there wasn't a drop of magical blood in his veins—this close, I would have sensed it—so he couldn't be descended from any of the magical beings I'd assassinated. "One for what?"

"A guy paid me five dollars to deliver a message to the big blonde chick that he said would run out of the yoga studio after an explosion. He said she'd probably be on fire."

"I'm tall, not big. Don't call women big. They don't like that." I held out my hand, already imagining the idiocy this message would contain if it had come from the panther brothers.

"If you are big, people will fantasize about hurling wrecked balls at you," Zav informed the kid.

"*Wrecking* balls." I gave him a weird look—the kid gave him an even weirder one.

I wasn't sure if Zav was trying to be personable, but he'd been less alarming when he'd simply been calling humans vermin and telling me how deplorable this planet was.

"Let's have it," I told the kid.

He'd taken out a wrinkled envelope, but he hadn't given it to me. "The guy said you'd also give me five dollars."

"He said I'd do that while I'm on fire?"

His face screwed up as he considered the logic. "Yes."

I snatched the letter from him faster than he could jerk it away, then shooed him back across the parking lot. "Thanks. Go spend your big earnings at the arcade."

He looked like he wanted to object, but Zav frowned at him, made his eyes glow violet, and the kid jumped and ran away.

"Nicely creepy," I said. "I think the villains in *Stargate SG-1* did that."

"It is sometimes a warning among my kind, sometimes an indication that power is being used." Zav returned his scrutiny to me.

I had a feeling he thought I knew more about his dragon nemesis than I did. I had no idea how to convince him otherwise.

"Are you stronger than Dob is?" I tore open the envelope.

"The law and the righteousness of my beliefs will aid me against him."

"Oh man, you're really screwed, aren't you?"

What would happen if Zav lost and Dob won? Would Dob be satisfied and go back to his own world, or would he stay here and terrorize more people?

"I am not. But he occasionally uses methods that are unacceptable to the Dragon Justice Court and myself. If we were to do battle, it would be important that bystanders were not nearby."

I imagined people bursting into flames as dragons battled overhead, spewing gouts of fire everywhere. "Yeah, if you're going to fight, please lure him away from the city."

"That will be my goal. But I must locate him first. That is why I am questioning you."

"I knew you didn't just come to give me the poster." I sighed as I read the short note.

Stay out of our affairs, or you and your weapons-making friend will be forcefully deported.

It wasn't signed, but it wasn't a big mystery who'd sent it—and tried to bomb the yoga studio.

"Are you *sure* you don't have a couple of panther-shifter brothers named Pardus on your list of people to send through a portal back to your court?" I asked.

"I do not."

"I don't suppose you'd like to punt them through a portal anyway?"

"Not if they have not committed a crime against the tenets of dragonkind."

"They're advertising that they can make weapons to slay dragons."

"I assume that is untrue."

"From what I've been told, probably. But don't you think such claims might offend your court?"

Zav tilted his head. "Why do you not slay them yourself? This is what you are known for, is it not? Assassinating the magical." Judgment oozed from his tone.

"Only if they've committed crimes—specifically murder. I don't get sent out against magical beings unless they've been killing humans." There was also the matter of the ten shapeshifter allies the brothers claimed. At least ten. Who knew how many were in that Northern Pride? Maybe I could get Willard to send me what the office had on them.

"If you cannot give me further information on Dobsaurin's whereabouts and intentions, I must go." Zav looked to the sky.

"You have another dragonkind-irking deadbeat on your list?"

"I must find Dobsaurin." His gaze returned to me, speculative. "I do wonder…"

He was thinking about dangling me out in the woods to attract the dragon. I could tell. But Dob wasn't from Earth, and he shouldn't have had time to build up a grudge against me, so I doubted that would work, even if I were willing.

"He's after you, not me," I said. "Don't even think of putting a compulsion on me or whatever you did last time. I'm my own free person, not somebody's puppet."

"I must consider the needs of the court over the needs of one mongrel."

"Must you call me that? My name is Val. I'm a capable warrior."

"Of mongrel heritage. Be pleased that your mixed blood gives you an advantage over the typical vermin that inhabit this foul, infested place."

"You're a dick too, FYI. But I'm still going to give you something." I opened the car door and pulled out the wine that I had no interest in drinking. The cider and chocolate I could find a use for—even if it was weird huckleberry cider and lavender chocolate—but wine was only slightly more palatable to me than coffee. "Try this." I shoved the case of twelve bottles into his arms. "Probably in human form. Maybe you'll like it. Wait, here." On a whim, I grabbed one of the boxes of chocolate and put it on top. I'd been given enough to share. "That too. I bet if you sample the offerings of this vermin-infested planet, you might agree that we come up with some good stuff."

"Doubtful." Zav wrinkled his nose as he surveyed his gifts.

"Humans love chocolate. Good chocolate is a delicacy."

"Is it made from meat?"

"Uh, no. Do dragons only eat meat?"

"Meat and occasionally fish."

"Nothing with any fiber? How do you stay regular?"

He gave me a blank look. It was just as well. I couldn't believe I'd brought up toilet habits with a dragon.

"Never mind. Just try it. And if they're awful, you can pelt Dobsaurin with them."

"I will pelt him with fire and brimstone."

"Also acceptable. I'm going to find my shoes." I waved and headed for the door.

"Wait." Zav spoke in a normal tone, but power laced the word.

I froze, my body unwilling to disobey him. As I knew from past experience, it wouldn't have mattered if I'd had Chopper with me.

As he strolled up with the boxes, walking around my unmoving form to face me again, I gritted my teeth. I wanted to curse at him and his presumptuousness, but my lips and tongue weren't working either.

"You know how to research the locations of magical beings in this world. Can you locate Dobsaurin for me?" Zav flicked a finger and muscle control returned to me.

"Maybe," I said slowly, realizing someone from another world and without a phone and a cell plan would have a hard time using the internet on the fly, "but—"

"This would be more efficient than if I flew all over the mountains, hoping to unmask the camouflage he has placed on himself. Yes, this is a good plan. You will do this for me."

"Pardon you, but I'm on my own quest right now." I glowered at him.

If he said I owed him because he'd healed me, I would aim a kick right at his groin and find out if he was as anatomically correct as he promised.

"I understand this. Once we have found Dobsaurin and dealt with him, I will assist you in negotiating with these panther shifters who are an obstacle to you."

"I don't want to negotiate with them; I want to blow up their house and drown them in the river."

He gave me that judgy look again. "I am impassive in regard to them. This will make me a superior negotiator."

I wanted to argue, mostly because he was trying to make all the decisions, but I'd already admitted I couldn't rightfully kill the Pardus brothers unless they did something worse than attacking me and painting graffiti on a food truck. If they had killed people with that grenade, it would have been different, but I couldn't feel anything but relief that they'd failed.

"The fact that you can breathe fire and melt people probably helps with negotiations too."

"People do not melt. They char and incinerate."

"Good to know." I rubbed my face and tried to set my ego aside to agree to his deal. Negotiating on Nin's behalf was what I'd had in mind, and it would be a lot easier to cow the brothers—convince them to comply—with a dragon standing at my side. "All right, I agree to your proposal, but if we're going to work together for even a moment, we have to establish some rules."

"I agree. I am bound by the laws and regulations of the Dragon Justice Court. You will swear an oath to uphold the same laws."

"That's definitely not what I had in mind. I'm talking rules—boundaries—between me and you." I imagined Mary talking about the distance I created between myself and others and almost laughed. "You promise to stay out of my head. None of that magical compulsion bullshit. No freezing me in place while you stalk around me and touch my stuff. No using me for *bait* to get this silver dragon to come calling. And finally, no making me want to obey and *please* you." I still wasn't positive the compulsion he'd put on me weeks earlier had faded. Maybe I was only here talking to him because he'd made me want to be nice to him.

Zav gazed at me. I couldn't tell if it was a thoughtful and considering gaze or if he was ignoring my speech while making a mental to-do list. Whatever that looked like. Clean the cave, pick up fresh sheep to eat for dinner, compel innocent maidens to service him.

"I find you a surly mongrel," he said, "and do not care for this manipulation."

"Tough. You want me to research your silver nemesis, you agree to my stipulations, or forget it."

His eyes narrowed. They were glowing a soft violet, and I remembered what he'd told the kid. It occurred to me that he might be able to magically compel me to go do that research for him, while massaging his feet and pumicing his corns. Especially since Chopper was in the Jeep instead of in my hand.

"Listen." I lifted my hands in a placating gesture that probably worked better on humans than dragons. "I'm my own person, and I'll do my best work if I'm a willing participant. If you were in my shoes, you wouldn't want someone with superior power manipulating you, would you?"

"It is the way of the Realms that those with superior power use it to maintain their dominant positions."

"Yeah, yeah, survival of the fittest. But you wouldn't like it if someone more fit than you manipulated you, right?"

"It happens. That is the way."

"It's happened to you?"

Zav lifted his chin without answering. Great, did that mean that some other more powerful dragon could come along and compel *him* to do things? Like Dobsaurin?

"I will agree to your terms for the duration of this time that we are working together," Zav said, "but you may wish to rescind your rules if we encounter Dobsaurin. If you are under a compulsion from me and under my control, it will be more difficult for him to put a compulsion on you."

"I'll risk it. Besides, I'm researching where he is, not going with you."

"You will come with me to make certain we can find his lair and deal with him."

"No, I won't."

Zav tilted his head. "You already agreed to this."

I reviewed the moments of our conversation, wishing I'd thought to record it. Already, it looked like he was treating this as a binding agreement. As I thought about it, I realized that, yes, he'd said he would help me with the Pardus brothers after *we* found Dob and dealt with him. Damn it.

"Why do you want me along? Won't I just be in your way?"

His eyes went from a faint violet glow to full-on beaming. "You will be in *his* way."

CHAPTER 12

When I walked up to Nin's food truck, the graffiti had been removed—or painted over—and she was outside on a ladder installing security cameras while men in the lunch line offered suggestions. There weren't as many customers as on a weekday, but they all had opinions about installing cameras. Nin thanked them politely, smiled, nodded her head, and ignored them in favor of carefully following the instructions.

"Hello, Nin." I wished I had better news for her. "I visited your competition, found them unpleasant, handsy, and with unexpected allies. I'm in the process of researching and regrouping and coming up with a Plan B. I can't openly go back to their house, since they had their lawyer complain to my boss, the whiny gits."

I didn't mention the new dragon duties I had to fulfill before I could finish Nin's assignment. Since Zav's departure, I'd started researching the social-media sites for news on the silver dragon, and I'd found a few videos of him that had been posted the day before, when he'd been spotted flying around the Woodinville and Redmond areas. Unfortunately, a dragon could fly hundreds of miles a day, so there was no telling where he was now.

Nin climbed down from the ladder and regarded me solemnly. "I am sorry that your yoga studio was attacked."

"Oh, you heard about that?"

"There are many rumors going around—my customers share them

with me. A new dragon threat has arrived, pedestrians are being plucked off the Burke Gilman Trail, and a yoga studio with the Ruin Bringer in it was assaulted."

"Pedestrians are disappearing?" I grimaced. I hadn't stumbled across that yet, but I'd been searching specifically for news of the dragon. Any number of people, magical and mundane, could be responsible for missing persons. Still, I'd seen the silver dragon soaring toward the Sammamish River Trail, a trail that turned into the Burke Gilman Trail once it hit Lake Washington. Coincidence?

"Three that I have heard of so far. The demand for dragon-slaying weapons is increasing. I have fielded many inquiries but have been forced to admit I cannot make anything that powerful. I worry that people will believe the Parduses' claims and go to them."

"I'm afraid of that too."

Nin hesitated. "Do you think they are the ones who attacked your yoga studio?"

I also hesitated, since I didn't want her to feel bad about getting me involved with this. "It's not my yoga studio. That was my first class there. We were only halfway through, and I hadn't even figured out what ocean breathing was yet."

"Val…"

"Yes." I sighed. "It was probably them. Like the manly men they are, they had a boy deliver a message for them." I fished it out of my pocket and showed it to her.

She shook her head as she read it, her pink pigtails flopping sadly forward.

"Don't worry about it." I rested a hand on her forearm. "I get threatened all the time. It's part of the job. And nobody was hurt." I shuddered to think what might have happened if I hadn't reacted quickly enough to throw that grenade back out. "I'll just avoid being barefoot and without my weapons in enclosed spaces full of people until I get this resolved. And I plan to. Zoltan pointed me toward the person who's supplying their magical bullets, and I'm going to visit tomorrow and find out what I can. Maybe see if I can convince the person to take a nice vacation for a while. I'm also thinking about going back to the brothers' house tonight and sneaking around—not going in, mind you, since I have orders not to do that—to see if I can figure out who they've got working in the basement. I don't think either of those two lumps of coal has enchanting skills of their own."

"I wish you would let me pay you, Val. This is dangerous work."

"I'll take some ammo. A lot. I have a feeling I may need it."

"To fight the Pardus brothers?"

"Maybe." I decided not to mention how Zav thought I should go with him to vanquish his dragon nemesis. "Why don't you take a break? Let's get some lunch."

"I can make you some—"

"Nope." I lifted a hand. "I enjoy your food very much, but let's get something else for a change, eh? Something you don't have to cook."

"I should not leave my truck."

"You have an assistant."

Nin looked from the line of customers to her kitchen helper manning the window and up to her security camera—or maybe the spot where the graffiti had been. Her fingers twitched, as if she would grab the corner of the truck if I tried to pull her away.

"You're not *sleeping* here, are you?" I asked.

"No. I cannot park the truck here overnight. It is stored at a secure commissary and truck yard." She waved vaguely to the south. "They do not allow you to sleep there."

"You know this because you've tried?"

She hesitated. "Maybe. I am concerned right now that I will lose the truck—and my business. I have set magical traps in case someone tries to go inside, but…"

"I understand. I'm not trying to drag you away for a week. Just for lunch. I'm buying. You could use a break. I can tell."

Nin appeared more reluctant than grateful about my offer, but she did tell her assistant to call someone else in if she got busy, and she walked resolutely out of the square with me. She let me drive us up the hill to Capitol Cider, where I sat facing the windows so I could see any trouble coming. I ordered the fish and chips and fire-roasted pepper cider. I could pass on wine or beer, but I was a Washington girl, and apples were my favorite fruit. Juice was too sweet for my taste buds, but hard cider was perfect and not a stiff enough drink to impair my reflexes or judgment.

Once Nin had ordered a suspiciously healthy-sounding mushroom-

and-kale grilled cheese sandwich, I leaned in to ask, "You seem to get a lot of gossip from your clientele. Have you heard anything more specific about the silver dragon?"

I'd left a message on Willard's voice mail that morning, asking for everything she had on the Northern Pride, but I didn't know if she would get back to me before Monday. And now I had a new problem.

"I have heard of one being sighted but not much more. What are you trying to learn?"

"Where he's hiding. And ideally *why* he's hiding. This is the ugly brute that almost toasted me over on the peninsula. He gave me a message to give to Zav, which I've done now, but apparently, he's playing coy and not letting Zav find him."

"I know very little about dragons. Until last month, I would not have believed they ever came to Earth."

"If a dragon would kidnap children to attract attention, would he also kidnap joggers?"

"I do not know. I would expect a dragon to kill people outright."

"Dead people can't be used as bait."

As I sipped my drink, the spicy dry cider leaving a smoky note on my taste buds, I poked around on my phone, looking for news stories mentioning the missing pedestrians that Nin had brought up. The news sites were worthless—for years, the mainstream media had been looking the other way, presumably under government or corporate influence, and not admitting to the existence of magic or magical beings. The socials were more reliable, but even they only mentioned that a couple of joggers had gone missing that morning, one from Log Boom Park near Lake Forest Park and another from a secluded stretch of the Sammamish River Trail between Woodinville and Bothell. There were trees in both of those areas, I decided, closing my eyes to picture the different sections. A dragon swooping in early enough could have grabbed joggers without being noticed, especially if he had means to camouflage himself. If Dob could hide from Zav, he could definitely hide from humans.

"Here's another missing person. A walker disappeared from Cold Creek Natural Area in Woodinville." I dropped pins, zoomed out, and gripped my chin as I studied the map. "The three spots are almost in a straight east-to-west line. Too bad the times when the people were kidnapped, if that's what happened, are imprecise. With that information, we could tell where he started and which way he was going when he picked up the last one." I tapped the map. "The farmers market in town is roughly on that line too. I saw him yesterday, not this morning, but that could indicate his lair—that was what Zav called it—is nearby."

"What does a dragon lair look like?"

"My Dungeons and Dragons experience tells me it's a cave full of mounds of treasure. Dragons are the Scrooge McDucks of the mythical kingdom."

Nin's forehead furrowed in confusion.

"I'm going to be disappointed if neither Dungeons and Dragons or Scrooge McDuck exist in Thailand."

"I do not know. I was not familiar with them. But I have heard young men at my food truck speak of the dungeons. It is a game, yes?"

"Yes. There are books too."

The food arrived, and my mouth watered at the aroma of the batter-fried cod sitting atop a mound of fries with a lemon wedge and tartar sauce on the side. I hadn't eaten before going to the yoga class, so this was my first food of the day, and I stuffed fries in, determined to set my phone down and appreciate them. But I couldn't keep my gaze from straying back to the map.

To the west of the first missing-person location, Log Boom Park, was the populous suburb of Shoreline and eventually, Puget Sound. Unless I was way off on what dragons liked for lairs, it was hard to imagine a promising spot existing among the houses and apartment buildings of the area. Or out in the Sound with the krakens and dolphins. I supposed the dragon could be shape-shifting and staying in a hotel, but if he was kidnapping people and not eating them, storing them at a Motel 6 would be tricky.

I scrolled to the east, my finger drawing an imaginary line. "Somewhere around Duvall, maybe? There's a lot of farmland out there, but also a lot of forest, and eventually, you get up into the foothills of the mountains. There are some hiking trails, old logging roads, and an access road to the Tolt River reservoir and the water-treatment facility out there but not much more. Some topography to the area." I typed in a search to see if information on any caves popped up.

"Has your colonel assigned you to find this dragon?" Nin was nibbling at her sandwich.

"Not yet. She promised I'd have an assignment coming, but I think it was related to those dark elves, not dragons. That was before people went missing." I set down the phone, realizing Nin might be wondering why I was obsessing about this rather than researching her problem. "I ran into Zav this morning. Or maybe I should say he stalked me down. We made a deal. I'm helping him find the silver dragon, and he's going to help me negotiate with the panther brothers." Assuming I succeeded in assisting Zav in dealing with his foe first, and the silver dragon didn't kill us both.

"Negotiate? Are dragons good at that?"

"He mentioned hurling fire and brimstone as a tactic."

"Hm. I wish the Pardus brothers would simply leave me alone. I have no wish to see anyone burned or otherwise harmed."

Remembering the brothers' willingness to force me to have sex with them, I had no such objections. "We'll figure something out. Promise."

"Good. I like it here, and I am making progress at saving up the money I need. I do not take any days off, because I am working toward a goal."

"Nin, you should take days off. People who don't know how to relax develop health issues and end up being prescribed a bunch of drugs and being tortured by breathing loudly through their glottis because their therapist insisted."

She gazed blandly at me. "I do not know what a glottis is."

"I don't either. I think it's in here somewhere." I waved at the front of my neck. "Take it from me, you need to enjoy a day off now and then."

Nin pushed her plate to the side, her sandwich only half-eaten, and linked her fingers on the table. "I want my family to come to America. I am appreciative that technology lets me see and speak with my mother and sisters, but their lives are not good. They are cramped in their apartment, because work that pays well is so hard to find there. And I am... missing something. In here." She touched a hand to her chest. "Because I am not with them. I grew up with all my siblings and my mother and grandmother. It is difficult not to be with them." She blinked moist eyes. "You must have a family. Do you understand?"

"Our situations are a little different..." A pang of self-doubt and regret filled me as I thought of Amber again, of her working on a book report this weekend while I was tramping around the city, dealing with hostile shapeshifters and arrogant dragons. "But I understand."

"This is why I must work a lot, and this is why I cannot let the Pardus brothers drive me out of the city. After many years, I am established here. To start over would be very difficult. It would delay everything."

"I know. I get it. They're not going to drive you out of the city."

"Thank you."

The waiter brought boxes for our food—I hadn't finished my mountain of fries—and I paid the bill, then reached for my phone to look at the map again. My fingers paused mid-air.

Did I really need to spend my day researching for Zav when I knew exactly where the people who were threatening Nin were? Yes, Zav would make a good ally were I intending to *negotiate* with them, but I'd handled dens of shifters on my own before. With some high-powered grenades from Nin and the element of surprise, I could take out the Pardus brothers and their house and weapons supply. It wasn't as if I hadn't killed magical beings before. I just didn't make a habit of doing it if they hadn't been condemned as criminals and someone wasn't paying me, usually the government. Freelance stuff was iffier, but I'd always been careful to stick to criminals where footage or other strong evidence showed their evil-doing. I'd never counted crimes against myself as a justifiable reason to kill someone, since they all hated me. But was there truly any doubt about the Pardus brothers? They'd threatened Nin, not just me.

"The glottis," Nin read from her phone, saying the unfamiliar word carefully, "is the part of the larynx consisting of the vocal cords and the opening between them."

I shook away my musing and smiled. "Yes, that sounds right. Thank you."

"Perhaps I will recommend it to my word-of-the-day apps."

"Is that how you learned English?"

"I took night-school classes. I thought I knew English when I came to America, but nobody could understand me. It was strange."

"I'm sure." My phone buzzed. "Hey, Willard."

"Some people address me as *Colonel* Willard."

"I could do some research, learn your first name, and call you by that."

"Willard is fine."

"I thought so. Did you get my message?"

"Yes, and even though it's Sunday and I'm relaxing and recuperating, I went to the office to do some research for you."

"You were at the gym again, weren't you?"

"I was doing a leisurely bike ride along the Burke Gilman Trail."

"If it's more than twenty miles, you can't count it as leisurely."

"You're a nag, Thorvald."

"I know. Watch out for dragons while you're on that trail." I eyed the phone. "You weren't looking for the new one, were you?"

"No. I only found out about the missing joggers when I came in. You think this silver dragon took them?"

"He's into kidnapping. I'm trying to pinpoint the location of his lair, especially if those joggers may still be alive in it."

"Good. Your next assignment may get preempted if there's a hostile dragon to deal with."

I grimaced. "I don't have a weapon capable of *dealing* with a hostile dragon."

"Point the other one at it, open the chute door, and slap him on the ass."

"The chute? Zav isn't a bull. Also, your countriness is creeping me out."

"I can't help it. I was stationed in Texas for six years. Just be ready. If we have to find a way to deal with him, you're going to be our best bet. Especially if he's lurking around the city. We can't send bombers to drop nukes in the suburbs."

"I'll try to get him out of the woods. Did you get my request on the Northern Pride?"

"Yes. I'm putting together a file for you with everything I have on them, and I'll email it over. But tread carefully around them, all right? Or avoid them altogether. There are a lot of those cat shifters in the North End. They're well financed, and it's going to be a legal hassle if we irk them."

Nin had been reading on her phone, not trying to listen, but she must have heard enough, for she looked up and frowned.

"In other words," I said, "don't get caught if I blow up the Pardus house?"

Willard sighed. "You can't blow up a house in the middle of a mobile-home park."

"I can if there are ten crabby shifters inside."

"Don't do anything unwise, Val. I appreciate that you helped me out, and you do good work, but there are only so many times I can get your ass out of legal trouble."

"I know, I know." The file came through. "Maybe I'll point Zav at their house and try that open-the-chute thing."

"Don't forget the ass slapping."

"I'm sure that'll excite him."

"I'll expect the wedding invitations by next spring."

"Ha ha. Later." I pocketed my phone, grabbed my little box of fries, and waved to the door. "I've got some files to study. Let me give you a ride back down the hill."

Nin nodded and headed for the door. Out of habit, I trotted past her so I could go out first.

A dirty white van squealed around the corner at Broadway and Pike, almost mowed over two pedestrians in the crosswalk, and sped toward us. The side door flew open, and two masked figures with guns leaned out.

CHAPTER 13

"Get down!" I yelled, aware of people dining at sidewalk tables to either side of the door.

As I shoved Nin back into the restaurant and dove behind a parallel-parked car, the two gunmen hanging out of the van fired. Those gunmen had the auras of magical beings.

Glass shattered and wood splintered as bullets hammered into the building and parked cars. But from the way the masked men twisted and leaned out the door to track me, I knew I was the target.

I reached for Fezzik as the van sped past, but there was no way I could open fire on the busy street. Instead, I sprang out from behind the car and yanked out Chopper as I sprinted after the van. They would have to switch from the side door to the back door to target me—which could happen. But I planned to catch up with them first.

The van did its best to peel away at breakneck speed, but traffic didn't move fast on Pike at the best of times. They made it to the next block and roared up on the sidewalk to go around a car and make a right turn. They knocked one of their mirrors off on a stout wooden lamp-post peppered with flyers, and their wheels wobbled as they dropped back down into the street.

I cut the corner closer and caught up with the van. The men leaned out the side door to fire again, but I sprinted and leaped onto the back fender before they could target me. As the van picked up speed on the straightaway, I pulled myself onto the roof.

When the driver zigzagged in his lane, trying to hurl me off, I plunged Chopper through the metal roof to create a handhold. Someone inside shouted.

Realizing I was vulnerable if they fired through the roof, I started to crawl to the right so I could swing down through the open side door. But the driver veered again, taking us up on another sidewalk and knocking over a trash bin. The roof tipped as the wheels on the right side ran along the curb. The van shuddered as it crunched into a newspaper vending machine. Metal squealed, and if not for my grip on Chopper, I would have flown off the roof.

Before I could pull the blade out and swing down into the van, a low-hanging tree branch almost took my head off. Swearing, I flattened myself in time to avoid being clubbed. My enemies chose that second to open fire at the roof.

Hot fiery pain blasted my side as a bullet sank in. I swore, pulled out Chopper, and rolled sideways, flipping down and through the open door. My boots entered first, and I adjusted my swing to ram each of the sturdy gunmen in the chest. My momentum knocked them backward against the far side of the van—the seats had been removed so we had an open arena.

Good. My side hurt like the fiery circles of hell, and I wanted to take it out on someone.

Using the pain to fuel me, I plowed into the gunmen. There wasn't room to swing Chopper, but I punched and kicked and bashed skulls with the weapon's hilt. And my enemies had *thick* skulls. No matter how hard I hit, the masked beings didn't cry out in pain, only grunted and snarled. Orcs, I guessed, though the driver was masked, too, and I couldn't tell for sure.

When I stunned one of them with an uppercut, Chopper's hilt cracking his teeth, I almost threw my back out hurling my foe out of the van. Three hundred pounds of solid muscle.

The other one leaped toward the back of the van, trying to give himself room to aim his rifle at my chest. But I didn't cooperate. I found the room to slash Chopper into the weapon before the gunman could fire. The blade cut through the barrel as easily as it had the roof, and it almost shaved his knuckles off with it.

The orc cried out and threw the destroyed rifle at me as I lunged in, the point of my sword leading. I dodged, and the weapon sailed past, cracking against the back of the front seat. The driver grunted and veered down an alley, the van going up on two wheels as it turned too fast.

My opponent was hurled against the side. I sank low, keeping my balance, and used the opportunity to grab him and throw him out the door as we veered onto another street.

He swore, twisting in the air and catching the edge of the door. I launched a side kick at his fingers. He let go and bounced three times before landing in a heap on the sidewalk.

I was alone with the driver. He kept glancing back, kept swerving as if doing it hard enough would also hurl me out of the van. It didn't. I lunged up to his seat and pressed Chopper into the side of his neck.

"Park it."

Cursing, he tried to jerk away from the cold kiss of my blade and managed to run the van up on the sidewalk again. It clipped a telephone pole before slamming into a tree. I grabbed the seat with my free hand, sinking low for balance. The van pitched sideways and landed on its side in the street. Keeping my feet under me was like staying up on a surfboard in a tsunami. We had been heading down a hill, so the momentum carried the van half a block, metal squealing and smoke pouring from the hood, before it slowed to a stop.

I sliced the driver's seatbelt strap, grabbed him, and tried to haul him out of the van, but even with the strength of my father's blood, three hundred pounds was too much for me to lift from a dead stop. I pressed Chopper's blade against his neck again.

"Get out. We're going to have a chat." I glanced through the broken windows, expecting the other orcs would come running up.

"Got nothing to say to the Ruin Bringer," the orc growled.

I yanked off his ski mask, revealing blue-tinted skin and a short snout full of pointed teeth, including two tusks that hung over his lips, giving him a lisp when he spoke English.

"You attack me just for fun or were you after something else?" I could question him here as well as anywhere, but the wail of sirens in the distance promised it wouldn't be long before the police showed up. I kept my ears and my senses open so I would know when the other two orcs came close.

"Not for fun. To *kill* you."

"I take out some relative of yours?" I'd killed two orc rapists the winter before—they'd sworn a biological imperative forced them to take women to breed and repopulate their species here on Earth—but none since then.

"You hunt the magical, you tray— traitor— traitorous bitch."

"You shouldn't use vocabulary words too big to get out around your tusks. And I'm not a traitor. Earth is my home, and these are my people. I'm protecting them." I thought of the people dropping below their tables and wondered how many had been hurt in the shooting, hurt because these jackasses had been after me. I pushed my blade deep enough to draw blood. "What prompted you to shoot me today?"

"The Pride's got an extra good bounty out on your head. Freshly issued. You better stay out of town, bitch."

"Thanks for the tip. Very magnanimous considering you were trying to shoot me thirty seconds ago." I started to lean back—I could sense the other two orcs coming, only two blocks away and running toward us—but I paused. "You know where that silver dragon is living?"

"Screw you."

I dug Chopper in deeper, not enough to sever an artery, but I bet I was tickling his glottis. He hissed with pain.

"I have no qualms about killing someone who opened fire on a restaurant and probably put people in the hospital—if not the graveyard. But if you give me a lead on the dragon, I'll let you live."

"How should I know? Dragon lairs are in caves, not in cities. You want a lead, go for a hike." He jerked his head away, banging it against the window hard enough to knock out the already-shattered glass.

But there was nowhere for the orc to go—that side of the van was flat against the street. He roared, yanked out a knife, and twisted in his seat, lunging toward me. I had little choice but to defend myself, and with Chopper already near his neck, I sank it in, cutting his throat. His body stiffened, and the knife fell from his fingers as his life's blood spurted from his neck.

Frustrated with the situation, I climbed out of the van and leaped to the sidewalk. Pain erupted from where the bullet was lodged in my hip. I swore and barely kept from screaming and pitching to the ground.

Why couldn't I protect humanity without being at war with every magical being on Earth? The irritatingly familiar tightness came to my chest, but I couldn't stop to dig out my inhaler yet.

My senses warned me seconds before the other two orcs ran around a corner and into view. I was waiting with Fezzik out and pointed at their chests and Chopper in my other hand, blood darkening the blade. It glowed a soft blue, always pleased when it had the opportunity to do battle.

I kept my injured hip turned away from the orcs, hoping they wouldn't notice it, though I knew they would smell the blood. They should smell their dead comrade too. Maybe that would make them pause.

The orcs saw me and stopped altogether. I had no idea what expression was on my face, but it must have promised their impending death. They lunged back around the corner and ran back the way they had come.

As the sirens drew closer, I walked toward the nearest alley. My grimace deepened as I sensed another magical aura, this one sailing in from above. By the time I was halfway through the alley, Zav had landed somewhere close and shifted into his human form.

When he stepped into the end of the alley, he was impeccable, as always, not a short curly black hair out of place, not a smudge on his dark robe. I had orc blood on my disheveled clothes, and my own blood was making my shirt stick to my side.

"What?" I demanded, barely remembering not to point any weapons at him. We were allies now, at least for as long as we both had a use for each other.

"The proper address is, Lord Zavryd, you honor me with your presence—how may I be of service to you and dragonkind?"

"I'll keep that in mind should the day ever come that I want to kiss your ass. What do you want?"

He squinted at me and then looked over his shoulder. At his ass?

I would have laughed if I hadn't been gritting my teeth in pain. The bullet had done more than graze me. I could feel it inside, grinding against my hip bone. I'd have to go to the hospital to have it removed, and I'd have to do it soon. As I'd learned in the past, my fast healing became an impediment if it healed *around* a bullet lodged inside me. A military surgeon had cut me open again the last time that had happened.

"I came to see how you are progressing with your research. Dobsaurin had a message delivered to me." Judging from his tight jaw, it hadn't been a party invitation with the address to his cave on it. Zav's gaze shifted to my hip.

I wasn't favoring it or holding a hand to it, and my black tank and duster hopefully hid it, but his sense of smell had to be at least as good as an orc's.

"You are injured again," he stated.

"Yes. You're as perceptive as you are magnificent."

"You are mocking me?" His dark brows rose.

I couldn't tell if it was surprise or indignation or both. Ally, I reminded myself. Ally.

I forced myself to lift an apologetic hand. "Yes, but I mock everybody who gets in my way. It's a bad habit. I'm sorry. I'm in pain and that makes me cranky. I'm also worried about all the people who might have just been hurt—or worse—because some idiot orcs got an itch to take me out and make some money."

No, that wasn't even it. It was because I'd gone to the Pardus brothers' house and turned them into enemies. Looking back, I wasn't sure how I could have avoided that, but someone with more smarts and more charisma surely could have managed it. I'd only made things worse for myself and for anyone standing next to me.

A wave of dizziness washed over me—how much blood had I lost?—and I stumbled over and pressed a hand against the cool brick wall for support. I closed my eyes, struggling for equilibrium and calm, but thoughts raced through my head. I had to check on Nin and the people at the restaurant, and if I didn't want to deal with talking to the police, I needed to hobble out of the area. And back to my Jeep and to the hospital. I didn't even know where we were. Miles from where I'd parked by now, I was sure.

It was only because I sensed Zav coming closer that I opened my eyes. And almost pitched over because he was less than a foot away. Only the wall kept me upright.

I planted my hand against his chest, remembering the times I'd been close to him before. It had been so he could touch my head and put his stupid compulsions in my mind. That tingle of power that always emanated from him stirred goosebumps on my skin, and I grew aware of the hard muscle of his chest through the fabric of his robe. He was another shifter who opted for the bodybuilder persona when in human form.

"Whatcha doing?" I asked as casually as I could manage, though having him so close unnerved me.

He looked down at my hand, a faint glow to his violet eyes. He was probably appalled that I was touching him. *Presuming* to touch him. "There is a metal projectile lodged in your hip."

"No kidding. I hadn't noticed."

"I must remove it to heal you."

I wanted to push him away and say something flippant about how nobody had asked him to heal me, but a wave of hope washed through me at the notion of having the pain taken away now, instead of hours later in the hospital, after a surgery that I would have to pay for, since my self-employed freelancer insurance was lousy. But was it worth it to owe him another favor?

While I was waffling with indecision, he pushed my duster open and rested his hand on my hip, right on the hole in my tank top—and my flesh. I expected the touch to bring another blast of pain, but some cool magic flowed from his palm, curling gently into my wound and numbing the hot snarl of agony. It was like one of those cough-drop commercials promising soothing relief, and I could almost hear the angelic choir in the background.

A quick burst of heat punctured the relief, and I bit my tongue to keep from gasping in pain. I wasn't gasping in front of some dragon, damn it. "What was that?"

"I withdrew the projectile." He held up the flat bloody bullet, then flicked it onto the ground. It burst into flame and disappeared. Incinerated. "Now I will heal the wound."

"Is it hard to heal humans when you're used to dragons? I imagine we're rather anatomically different." I glanced at his face, meeting his eyes briefly, then looked over his shoulder. Looking him in the eye from this close seemed too intimate.

Besides, I needed to pay attention. We were standing in a public alley. Those orcs might wander down it at any moment. Though that was unlikely. They would sense the aura of a dragon from even farther away than I had. But the police could show up. We weren't that far from the wreck.

Oddly, nobody entered the alley. Nobody even walked past. Was he oozing some magic to deter people?

"You are half-elf. I have spent time with elves."

"They're not as loathsome to you as humans?"

"They are among the most powerful of the lesser magical beings."

Lesser. I snorted. "So you rank people and decide who's worth spending time with by their power."

"By their power, by what they do with their power, and by how obnoxious they are to be around."

I could feel his gaze upon me and knew exactly what he was implying. As if *he* wasn't more obnoxious than I was. In his arrogance, he didn't even see it.

Warmth replaced the cool, and my flesh tingled with intensity. I sensed the muscles knitting together, the chipped bone being regenerated, and the skin regrowing over the wound. Even though the power came from him, my legs grew weak, as if some of it was also drawn from my own body. When he removed his hand and stepped back, I slumped against the wall. I wanted to slump all the way to the ground, but my pride—and the old pieces of gum stuck to the cement at my feet—kept me upright.

"Thanks." For someone who hated being beholden to others, I was thanking him a lot. I didn't like that. "Maybe next time, I'll greet you with some ass-kissing."

His eyebrows flew up, and he took another step back. "I do not wish to be intimate with you."

"That's not what I meant, but thanks for clearing that up. When you talk about kissing someone's ass, it's an expression. It means you're sucking up, currying favor." There we go. The way to define an idiom is by using a bunch more idioms, right? "I just meant that maybe I'll call you Lord Zavryd the next time you plop down in front of me."

I rubbed my face, more embarrassed than I should have been at explaining that I *wasn't* interested in his ass. Why couldn't I keep my sarcastic tongue clamped down?

And why did it bother me that horror had flashed in his eyes when he'd made his announcement? It wasn't as if he hadn't been perfectly clear that he thought humans were vermin. And it wasn't as if I wanted to sleep with him. My mind hurt at even imagining how that would go. It was more the implied insult, that humans—that *I* wasn't good enough for someone as lofty as a dragon.

"That would be a wise policy to adopt. Not all dragons are as lenient as I am." He'd recovered from his surprise and reaffixed the haughty expression. "Tell me what information you have learned about the location of Dobsaurin."

"It's only been three hours."

He gazed at me expectantly.

"Look, I have some ideas based on where he's been seen flying and where people have disappeared, but I'm going to need more time."

Zav clasped his hands behind his back. "I should have gone to see the lava golem. But Dobsaurin is in this territory, not her territory. I thought you might be a more logical researcher."

"Sorry to disappoint. If you give me more than three hours, I can dig more up. I didn't know I was on such a tyrannical deadline."

He looked thoughtfully at the sky. "We *will* go to see her."

"Greemaw?" The only lava golem I'd met had been on the trip to Oregon to see my mother. "And what do you mean *we*?"

"Greemaw. Yes. You will come with me to speak with her and give her the information you have gathered. Together, you may more effectively pinpoint Dobsaurin's location." He squinted at me. "Assuming you *have* gathered information. Have you?"

I glared at him. "I told you I had. I've got the points on a map where three joggers were kidnapped, and I have some ideas about where his lair might be." Granted, it was all supposition. I didn't even know for sure that Dobsaurin had been the one to kidnap the joggers.

His face smoothed. "Yes. Yes, I remember. You do not lie. Good."

Not strictly true, but I knew what he was talking about. The conversation I'd had with Greemaw while he'd been hiding behind a wall and listening in like some police interrogator.

"How about you fly down there and ask her about it yourself? That's a long drive for a human. No wings." I was pleasantly surprised when my hip didn't hurt when I stepped away from the wall to make flapping motions with my arms.

"Your ground conveyances are slow."

"Sorry, I haven't renewed my pilot's license in a long time. Mostly because I can't afford a plane."

"You will fly with me. Come."

"Uh." I raised a finger to protest—was he saying what I thought he was saying?—but he'd already leaped up to the rooftop of the building, as if he were some comic-book superhero.

I sensed the ripple of power as he shifted into his dragon form.

Come, he spoke into my mind.

I looked up at the three-story building and rolled my eyes. "Sure, I'll be right up."

Even though I had reservations, I found a drainpipe I could climb and shimmied up it like a burglar. My hip didn't hurt at all. Man, I wished I could bottle his power and keep a stash in my kit for emergencies. *Dragon essence: pour directly on injury for instant healing.*

Maybe that was what the dragon blood did in alchemical potions. If so, no wonder Zoltan had been so delighted to get some.

Zav waited on the roof, his great black body taking up the entire top of the building. Scales gleamed in the sun, as sleek as fur over the powerful muscles of his legs and arms. He hadn't spread his leathery black wings yet—if he did, they would stretch out over the street and the alley.

"How is it that people aren't noticing you left and right?" I glanced toward an apartment building across the street, one that rose six stories and had rows of windows overlooking us.

Only those with magical blood can see a dragon, unless he wishes to be seen.

"You think so? I've seen video footage of you on the internet." I walked to his side, wondering how I was supposed to get on, and if that was truly what he wanted. Maybe he intended to hold me in his talons and fly hundreds of miles with me dangling helplessly.

Video footage taken by people with magical blood.

"I think anyone can see you once they're uploaded."

His big reptilian head canted like a dog listening to a strange sound. He didn't have ears, not that I could see from down below, but I assumed he could hear. *It is possible the technology thwarts the natural magical camouflage. I have spent little time in this world, and I am uncertain how such things work.*

Which was likely the reason he'd asked me to do his research. It was better to have use, I supposed, than be useless, though if I was of no value to him, maybe he would leave me alone.

But who would have healed my wound then?

Get on my back.

Before I could ask if I was supposed to climb, my feet grew light and I dangled in the air. Levitation. I'd never seen a magical being capable of doing that, but my mother said the legends about elves proclaimed that some of them could.

My skin started tingling again as I came closer, settling onto his back. His power was even more noticeable now. When he was in human form, it was electrical against my skin, raising gooseflesh and even feeling appealing. Like I had the urge to step closer and bask in it. In his dragon form, it was too much. It made my head ache. Hopefully, he would fly quickly.

"No saddle?" I'd envisioned this being like riding bareback on a horse, but his back was too broad for that. If I had a picnic blanket, I could have laid out a basket, champagne glasses, and a charcuterie tray.

A what? his voice thundered in my head.

Such indignation meant he knew the word... He just didn't find the word appropriate.

"Is it less offensive if we call it a harness?"

The next sound echoing in my mind was either a grunt of disgust or a dragon hawking a loogie.

"A seatbelt? Except that there's not exactly a seat." I patted the smooth scales, positive I would pitch off as soon as he jumped into the air. Why had I agreed to this?

Why did I suggest this? he asked.

"I have no idea. Sindari has never offered to let me ride him."

The Del'noth tigers are not unwise.

"I'll let him know you praised him so profusely."

My magic will keep you in place.

"What if you're distracted?" I envisioned the silver dragon zipping out of the mountains and attacking us.

A second before I could change my mind, slide off his back, and tell him to visit Greemaw on his own, Zav sprang into the air. I flattened myself against him, arms spread wide, positive I'd made a huge mistake.

But as he flapped his large powerful wings, quickly gaining altitude, the air barely stirred around me. Right away, he took off to the south, flying over the buildings of Capitol Hill. I expected the breeze to tug at my hair and clothing, but it either streamed past, his head blocking it, or some bubble of power kept it from disturbing me. He did seem to radiate even more power as he flew, its presence surrounding me and filling my senses. I felt overwhelmed, like the time I'd gone to a laser music show as a teen, colored lights flashing all over the domed ceiling while *Dark Side of the Moon* boomed from the speakers and the floor vibrated underneath me.

I closed my eyes. This was going to be a long flight.

CHAPTER 14

I t wasn't as long a trip as I'd expected. After an hour, we soared over Bend and toward the forest near Paulina Lake that held Greemaw's hidden valley sanctuary.

I'd taken a few peeks down as we flew southward following the mountains, but Zav's wings blocked the view, and I hadn't felt adventurous enough to crawl up to his long sinewy neck for a better look. Heights didn't usually bother me, but the lack of a seatbelt kept me from risking rocking the dragon boat. Also, I'd been busy watching the sky behind us, worried about what would happen if the other dragon showed up and we had to fight.

A part of me had been tempted to summon Sindari, if only so he could see the world from up here, but I'd envisioned my leather thong of charms somehow slipping off my head if I fiddled with them, and I hadn't dared. I'd flown countless hours in numerous models of planes and helicopters when I'd been undergoing my army training, and somehow, this was nothing like any of it. Maybe because I had no control and didn't trust the being who did.

"Do you really fly three hundred miles an hour?" I asked, guessing the distance from Seattle to Bend in my head. Admittedly, if he'd taken me as the crow flies—as the dragon flies—it would have been shorter.

I am not familiar with your units of measure, Zav responded telepathically as he pulled his wings in, his head dipping toward the ponderosa pine forest below.

I could see the lake over his head and did my best to grip his scales, but it wasn't as if there were gaps between them. They were smooth and tight, leaving nothing to hold.

For my sanity, I closed my eyes as he arrowed down, only spreading his wings at the point where collision seemed a certainty. We slowed until he landed in an easy crouch. Not outside of Greemaw's valley, as I'd imagined, but right in it, on the main road that wound through what seemed as much refugee camp as village. There were permanent structures, yes, but most of the people—everyone from orcs to kobolds to dwarves and goblins to shifters in wolf form—seemed temporary. Transient.

The orcs eyed me hostilely, several resting their hands on the hilts of bladed weapons or maces. Could they have already heard about the orc I'd killed in Seattle? Or had word of the Northern Pride's bounty made its way down here? If so, I would have to watch my back even more than usual. I refused to hide behind Zav's robe.

Before I could slide off his back—a dwarf with a rifle changed his grip on the weapon, making me pause—Zav shifted into his human form. I let out a startled squawk as I dropped more than a dozen feet and landed, my hands now gripping his shoulders.

"A warning would have been nice," I grumbled, letting go and backing up.

"It is a great honor for a lesser being to fly with a dragon. It is typical for them to be grateful and effusive afterward."

I caught myself before I could make another comment about ass-kissing—he would probably think I was obsessed with his butt—and limited myself to saying, "I'm atypical."

"Yes."

Grumbling further, I straightened my duster, checked to make sure Fezzik was still secured in my thigh holster, and touched Chopper's hilt to reassure myself of the weapon's presence on my back. The orcs were trading whispers. So were the dwarves. A dragon had landed in their midst, and everyone was glaring at *me*. How was this fair?

Zav strode off without acknowledging anybody, heading toward the alcove at the back of the valley where I'd spoken to Greemaw before. Not trusting a dragon's presence to keep me safe, I gripped the cat figurine and summoned Sindari.

Only after he materialized did I walk in the direction Zav had gone, my hand resting on Fezzik's grip. I didn't want to pick a fight here, but I would defend myself.

We've returned to the sanctuary valley, Sindari observed, striding at my side. *To do battle?*

I hope not. I replied silently since there were so many ears and eyes pointed this way.

Lord Zavryd is here.

Yeah, we came together. We made a deal this morning. I'm helping him with his problem, and afterward, he's agreed to help me with mine.

Sindari gazed up at me with his green eyes, as if he wasn't quite sure I was his regular handler. Maybe he thought a lookalike had replaced me. *How long has it been since you last summoned me?*

We fought the panther shifters and visited Zoltan yesterday. It seemed like it had been much longer ago than that. This weekend had been eventful. *If I'd had the opportunity, I would have summoned you to help me with some angry orcs a couple of hours ago, but there wasn't time.*

How long does it take you to touch my charm and call my name?

More time than I had. Keep an eye on those orcs, will you? And everyone with a weapon who's glaring at me.

So everyone except for those three small children over there. Sindari's gaze shifted toward a trio of green-skinned goblins with white hair.

One of them has a slingshot.

Ah, yes. So only the toddlers fighting over that orange foam tube are safe.

It's a pool noodle, and yes. The last time I'd been here, I'd seen a few pool toys and an inner tube in a pond in the tunnel leading in. They weren't the only things here that looked to have been salvaged after floating away from their owners on the Deschutes River.

Imagine my embarrassment at not knowing the correct terminology.

Do tigers actually get embarrassed?

I do if I fail to perform adequately or fall and don't land on my feet.

We followed a bend in the only real road through the valley, leaving the last of the dwellings and market stalls lining it, and Greemaw's alcove came into view. The moss-haired, gray-skinned lava golem sat on her conference-table-sized bench and towered over Zav, who stood in front of her, already speaking. He seemed almost puny next to her mass, but I sensed their auras, the potential for power that each carried, and it was easy to tell that Zav was far stronger than anyone here.

That was why these detours were worth it; he could probably walk into the Pardus brothers' house, tell them to knock it off, and they would. Whereas I'd have trouble achieving that without starting a war. That made me bitter, but if Zav was willing to help, I would bury my resentment. Whatever it took to keep Nin safe was what I would do.

An elf approaches, Sindari informed me.

I turned, hand tightening on Fezzik's grip as I followed his gaze. Sindari's tone hadn't warned me if he was only making an observation or if the elf represented trouble.

The tall, lean, and powerful elf glided across the packed earth toward me, a bow and quiver on his back and a short sword belted at his waist. If he were human, he would have been roughly forty, but purebred elves reputedly lived centuries, so maybe he'd been alive during the Crusades. A torc of gilded woven twigs wreathed his neck and emanated power, but the rest of his brown and beige clothing was ripped and stained, as if he'd been on the road for a long time. I remembered seeing an elf when I'd been here with my mother weeks earlier, but I hadn't gotten a good look at his face and wasn't sure if this was the same person.

He lifted a hand to stop me.

I glanced at Zav and Greemaw to make sure they weren't looking back expectantly and waiting for me. Neither of them was looking in my direction at all.

"Glad I made the trip," I muttered.

The elf stopped a few feet away and bowed to me.

I had zero bowing experience so I lifted a hand and said, "What's up, Legolas?"

He straightened and regarded me curiously.

"I guess you haven't been on Earth long enough to get signed up for Netflix," I said.

"I have recently arrived on this world. I chose to help some refugees escape the wrath of the Silverclaw Clan, and now, I am waiting and hoping to chance across someone who can create a portal so that I may return." His gaze shifted toward Zav, then back to me. He touched his chest. "I am Syran Moonleaf."

"That sounds about right." I held back a quip about the probability that an internet fantasy-name generator would spit that out within the first five tries. He wasn't holding any weapons or glaring at me like he wanted to drive a sword through my gut. I could be polite. "I'm Val Thorvald."

"Thorvald... That is your mother's name?"

"Good guess." With the certainty of a fist connecting with my nose, I realized this guy knew who my father was. He hadn't *said* that, and I couldn't imagine how he would know—especially if he'd just come to Earth and hadn't heard anything about my reputation—but that question... What else could it mean?

Moonleaf was studying me with more than his eyes, I sensed, as a hint of magic brushed my awareness.

All the curiosity I thought I'd long ago given up bubbled to the surface, and I wanted to know everything he knew about my father. "It's Norse. It means Thor's ruler. My first name is even better. Valmeyjar. It means Battle Maiden or Corpse Maiden. My mom named me that and then was surprised when I became an assassin for the army. Weird, huh? Did you know my father?"

Moonleaf blinked. The color of his silver-green eyes reminded me of the lavender leaves on the plants potted at the front doors of my apartment building.

"I traveled with him once long ago when we were diplomats and explorers, serving the three kings." Moonleaf smiled wistfully. "That was before our fates veered onto different paths."

"Is he still alive? What's his name?" I knew the name my mother had given me and figured it would mean something if this elf gave me the same one. If not, Moonleaf could have mistaken me for someone else. How could he tell from looking at me who my father was?

"Oh, he is most certainly still alive. I would tell you to visit him, but I fear there are few here who know how to make portals to the Cosmic Realms. I was warned about that ahead of time, but I didn't quite realize how barren of magic this world would be."

And here I'd been thinking about how many more magical beings were in it lately.

"I am debating what I could offer a dragon to send me home." Moonleaf looked at Zav again. "But one does not presume to ask favors of dragons."

"No. I assume you're probably in trouble if you owe a dragon a favor too."

"It depends on the dragon. The Stormforge family has always been fair." Moonleaf waved at Zav, his fingers long and elegant, exactly what one would expect from an elf. "It is unfortunate that their hold over the Dragon Justice Court is not what it once was and that so many crueler and more insular dragons are working against them to steal their positions. That is why so many refugees have been forced to flee to this world. It is—it was—a place that nobody believed dragons would come."

"Not anymore."

"So I've heard," Moonleaf said grimly.

"Val," Zav called, power in his voice as he looked over—as he summoned me.

It was the first time I remembered him using my name, and I had the urge to trot over obediently. Which I refused to do. I planted my feet in stubborn rebellion, held a finger up to him, and finished my conversation with Moonleaf. "Would a half-human be welcome in… the place where my father lives, if she were to show up?"

Not that I had plans to leave Earth any time soon, even if it somehow became a possibility. It wasn't as if I could hunt down a portal charm. At least, I assumed not. But I was curious and wanted to know.

"Few humans have ever been taken from this—pardon me, but this is how the rest of the sentient species feel about it—savage world and into the Cosmic Realms, so I could not say for certain." Moonleaf glanced at Zav, lifting a hand in a fingers-down gesture that seemed like an apology. He was speaking quickly. "But humans as a whole have not traditionally treated the other races well when they've visited this world."

"So there may be grudges."

"Yes."

"And such a trip would be dangerous."

"Probably so, but if you ever get the chance…" His blond brows rose as some new thought occurred to him. "Does he know you exist? Your father?"

"I don't know." My mother had told me that he and his kind had left before she'd known she was pregnant with me. She'd never allowed me to voice anything negative about him—using the phrase *deadbeat dad* when I'd been about ten had gotten me slapped, the only time I could remember her hitting me. She had never agreed with me that it had been an asshole thing to choose to leave Earth with his people instead of staying with the woman he had supposedly loved. "Probably not," I added.

"Ah. That is interesting." Moonleaf sent Zav another nervous glance—Zav had his arms folded over his chest, that haughty expression tinged with impatience. "I must not keep you from your meeting. I'm pleased to have made your acquaintance."

He bowed again and turned toward the other end of the valley, toward the exit tunnel I'd originally come in through.

"Wait," I blurted. "If I ever get a chance to go looking for him, where would I start? There are a lot of worlds in the Cosmic Realms, right? Like seventeen?"

"Yes. You need only to ask to be taken to the Sylvan Court of the Elves. There are many portals that lead there, from all the worlds where elves have colonies."

I thanked him and started toward Zav and Greemaw but noticed that two of the kids who'd been watching had scooted closer. Their dirty faces were lean, and they looked hungry. I reached into one of my inner duster pockets and pulled out the box of fries I'd stuffed in there as I'd left the restaurant. It was smashed after the battle with the orcs, but the fries ought to still be edible. When I tossed it to them, they snatched it out of the air together and raced off behind a tent.

Are you delaying on purpose? Sindari asked. *Your dragon looks cranky.*

He's not my dragon, and he always looks like that.

True.

Trusting I'd made my point—that I would not be summoned like a slave—I joined Zav and Greemaw. I did feel a little bad for making her wait, especially since we were intruding on her time, but she oozed the calm serenity of one who had lived a thousand years and more and was never in a hurry. I wondered if Zav was young for a dragon.

Fortunately, he didn't snipe at me when I arrived. He returned to their conversation.

"The mongrel said she has a map with points that may be useful," he told Greemaw.

"The *mongrel?*" I stared at him and pointed back to where I'd been talking. "You *just* used my name. Did you forget it that quickly?"

As soon as the words came out, I realized he might have only used it because names had power and he'd known I would be more likely to come to it than *mongrel*.

Greemaw stirred on her bench as Zav turned his violet gaze on me. His eyes weren't glowing at the moment, but her stony face looked worried. Did she think he would flatten me for my presumptuousness?

Even Sindari stirred, bumping my side. *Have you not yet learned to avoid being contrary with dragons?*

I didn't know asking to be called by name was contrary.

To him, you are a lesser being.

A lesser being with a name.

"It's Val," I told Zav. "Or Ms. Thorvald if you prefer formality in our relationship." That ship might have sailed sometime after I discussed ass-kissing with him.

"I am aware of your name, battle maiden." One of his eyebrows twitched. Had he been eavesdropping on my conversation from over here? How rude. "I did not know if Greemaw would be."

"Greemaw, I'm Val." I lifted a hand. "You've met me before. And my mother."

"Yes," Greemaw rumbled. "Is she well?"

"I think so." I hadn't spoken to her since I'd gone back to her house to pick up Willard's cat. It did feel strange to be here outside of her town without calling, but... with more people than ever gunning for me, I didn't want anyone to know about her. Especially if others here had ears as effective as Zav's at eavesdropping.

"Good. Please show me the map."

"Right." I dug out my phone, chose the satellite map view, and adjusted the screen to show the three points where joggers had gone missing. As soon as I lifted it to show Greemaw, someone who could have held six phones in her palm, I felt silly. How were the eyes of a thousand-year-old golem? Did they work like human eyes? Could she see the screen decently? There was no way she would be able to manipulate it with those giant stone fingers.

Greemaw looked at Zav, as if waiting for him to explain it.

"You can't make it larger?" Zav asked.

"I can zoom in, but then we wouldn't be able to see all the points. Sorry, I didn't have time to get a physical map."

"I meant the device it is displaying on."

"Uh, no. I can't will my phone to double in size." That would have been handy. Or a way to project the screen holographically. I looked at Greemaw apologetically. "This was an impromptu trip."

Zav took the phone from my fingers without asking—I resisted the urge to yank it back, though I feared he would hurl it into a rock wall out of some frustration for the stupidity of human technology. Or vermin technology as he could call it. But I hadn't seen him truly angry since we first met, when he flung my Jeep into the treetops.

He studied the screen, then handed it back to me and crouched, resting his palm in the dirt.

Back up, Sindari warned me.

I glanced around, making sure nobody had a gun aimed at me.

Because of dragon magic, not assassins, he added, his telepathic tone dry. *There's a difference?*

Innocent bystanders can be taken out by both.

I scooted off to the side of Greemaw's alcove and stood beside Sindari. Zav hadn't moved, but I could sense him doing something.

The packed earth rippled and shifted, as if it were water instead of dirt. Parts rose up to form tiny mountains while others sank to show valleys and gullies with rivers flowing through them. Flat sections represented farmlands, and tiny dots the buildings in the towns of Bothell, Woodinville, and Duvall. About six feet by six feet, the map was impressively detailed and much larger than what displayed on my phone screen.

"Show me again the locations the humans disappeared," Zav said, rising, the fine dirt on his hands trickling away and leaving them clean, even though he didn't dust them off.

This guy does not know how to say please, I thought to Sindari. "Right away, Lord Dragon."

Zav's eyes narrowed and glowed violet.

Val... Sindari warned. *Why do you not simply accept that he is extremely powerful and should be respected, if only because he can squash us like insects?*

Because power *isn't what makes someone deserving of respect.* I pointed to Zav. "See, isn't it better to be called by name? You call me Val, and I'll call you Zav."

"My name is Lord Zavryd'nokquetal."

"My tongue would fall out if I tried to say that."

"How unfortunate that would be."

I grinned at him before I could catch myself. Maybe it was petty, but having Lord Zav-butt getting snarky with me felt good. Like I was rubbing off on him. Or he was becoming more human. A thought which would surely make him projectile vomit.

The grin must not have been the response he expected, because for a split second, a flustered expression crossed his face. It disappeared so quickly I might have imagined it.

He walked over, took the phone from my hand again, and pressed the button to turn the screen on—I was impressed he knew that much, since I assumed this was his first cell phone. Judging from his exasperated look, he didn't know what to do with the lock code prompt that came up.

"Don't watch." I leaned over, covered my hand with my other hand, and tapped in the code. "I don't want you getting lonely in the middle of the night and ordering naughty videos with my banking information."

He didn't comment, only looked at the map and thrust the phone back at me.

Are you flirting with him? Sindari asked as Zav crouched to touch the earth again.

I fumbled the phone, almost dropping it on the dirt map. *What? No.*

I have observed humans and some of the other species like elves and dwarves using humor in an attempt to win mates.

That's not what I'm doing.

That is good. Because I don't believe he finds you humorous.

Yeah, that's my read on him too.

Dragons are impressed by power and raw physical strength, not humor.

I'll be sure to hit the gym later and work on my bench press. You know I want him to find me sexy.

Sometimes, I don't know when you're joking.

I'm joking. But thanks for the advice. Maybe if I ever meet a non-arrogant dragon who likes mongrels, I can put it to use.

You are welcome. I believe if you call him Lord Zavryd and refrain from sarcasm, he will treat you—us—fairly.

I'll keep it in mind.

As I watched Zav pluck up little hills of earth to show the spots where the people had disappeared, I silently admitted that Sindari was probably right. I might be able to have a cordial, business-like relationship with Zav if I stopped giving him grief.

The problem was my aversion to having anyone boss me around. I'd struggled with it in the military, and it was even harder now that I was older and used to calling the shots. I worked for people, but I didn't bow and scrape. They either hired me as I was, or they could find someone else to fix their problems.

When Zav was done, I stepped forward and pointed to the forested hills east of Duvall. "This is where I'm guessing his lair is. He could have picked up someone here, here, and here and then continued east to a cave. I think that land is either owned by the state or by the big logging companies. There's a lot of wilderness out there, plenty of places for caves. He could be farther up in the mountains, too, but I assume there's a limit to how far a dragon would want to tote people."

Zav looked at me, and I almost expected a comment about how he'd toted me three-hundred miles, but he was apparently done being sarcastic. "If he picked up all three of his kidnap victims in the same trip, yes. There is a limit to how much weight even a dragon can comfortably carry, especially on this world."

"What's different about this world?"

"It is one of the planets with higher gravity on which sapient life evolved. My kind evolved on a world with less gravity."

It was strange hearing him talking in scientific terms instead of magical. I supposed it made sense that these Cosmic Realms were actually planets in different star systems, but I hadn't considered it before.

"Long ago, before the cities of men existed, I walked in those foothills." Greemaw was studying the map, not paying attention to us. "It was too long ago and for too short a time for me to remember all the caves, but I may be able to speak to the earth up there through the earth here and learn a few things. All is connected."

"We will wait," Zav said without the impatient vibe he'd had for me earlier. Maybe golems were up there with elves as lesser beings that dragons considered more pleasing to spend time with than others.

Greemaw shifted off her bench and leaned against the stone wall of her alcove, closing her eyes. How *long* would we wait, I wondered. Could I wander off and call Nin to check on her? For that matter, I should call Dimitri and make sure he hadn't had his blood sucked by Zoltan the night before.

As minutes passed, neither Greemaw nor Zav stirring, I stepped away. There wasn't enough reception for phone calls, so I texted them both.

Dimitri replied right away, saying he was still at Zoltan's place, eating pizza and finishing up the giant robot sentry tarantula. Imagining a delivery driver tramping into the back yard and leaving a pizza on the stoop of the haunted carriage house amused me. Dimitri also said Zoltan was working on translating the notebook. That was promising. I wondered how much he would charge me.

"Val," Zav said, calling me back. By my name. Huh.

Greemaw stepped away from the rock wall and faced me. "There are not as many caves in that area as there are higher in the mountains, but there are a couple dozen. Many will not be easily accessible by a human vehicle, but a dragon could reach them."

"The advantage of flight—and of not needing a runway." I looked at Zav, wondering if he planned to tote me all over the foothills on his back.

But he'd stepped away and wore an abstracted expression, like someone listening to a podcast and not paying any attention to his surroundings.

"I will show you the locations." Greemaw gestured for me to approach her.

She radiated magic similarly to, if to a lesser degree than, Zav, but I didn't feel wary around her. Something about her ancient eyes made me trust her, so I didn't flinch away when she lifted a massive hand and rested it on top of my head. When Zav had intruded on my thoughts, he'd left desires to do his bidding. Greemaw gently placed locations in my mind. Her point of view was strange, often looking up from the earth instead of down from above, and I knew I would struggle to translate the locations to spots on my map, but I did my best to remember each of the areas.

While Zav stood, his gaze toward the canopy of branches hiding the valley from the outside world, I put dots on the dirt map. After each one, I looked up for confirmation. Greemaw hesitated a few times, but I got a lot of nods. Once we'd marked all of the spots, I took a picture of the dirt map with my phone.

"I must go for a time," Zav said.

"Go?" I asked.

"Back to my home." He looked at Greemaw. "Family matters."

I thought of Moonleaf's words of how Zav's family was struggling to maintain control.

"Does Dob's presence here have something to do with it?" I asked, even though he was looking at Greemaw, not me, and probably didn't want me to butt in.

Zav looked sharply at me. "It is possible he was sent to distract me. Or to vanquish me here where there would be no witnesses."

Ugh, I thought to Sindari. *I knew I wasn't crazy to worry about what would happen if I was riding on his back when that other dragon showed up.*

I am surprised that you did not insist on coming here in your automobile.

It was faster this way.

Zav looked at the map, then faced me. "I will take you back to your city. When I return, we will find Dobsaurin with this information Greemaw has provided us."

Even though he was far more polite with Greemaw than with me, he didn't thank her. Maybe *please* and *thank you* weren't in the dragon vocabulary. You'd think a race with a language that favored words twenty characters long would have room to squeeze in pleasantries.

"How long will you be gone?" I asked.

"I don't know."

If he was gone as long as he'd disappeared last time—weeks—I doubted I would have the patience to wait for his help with the panther brothers. And if I had to deal with them by myself, this detour and research for him would have been a waste of time.

No, I corrected. That wasn't true. If the silver dragon was kidnapping people, I needed to know everything about him, because as Willard had pointed out, it would fall to me to deal with him. Which I might also have to do on my own if Zav didn't return in time. A bleak thought.

CHAPTER 15

Someone had broken into my apartment again.

I stood in the hallway, staring at the door slightly ajar, all four of the deadbolts I'd coerced the landlord into letting me install unlocked. A three-year-old with a couple of hairpins could have thwarted the cheap doorknob lock but not the deadbolts. They weren't even visible from the outside.

Sighing, I summoned Sindari. Whoever had done this had probably long since gone, but there was a chance he or she was still inside. Or *they*.

I didn't sense anyone magical, but mundane humans could ransack my apartment as effectively as an irritated panther shifter.

There is nobody inside, Sindari informed me after he materialized. *Do you wish me to go in first in case the thief left booby traps?*

I don't know. Are you more in the mood to be dangled upside down from the ceiling than I am?

With my speed and agility, I am unlikely to be dangled at all.

In that case, you should definitely go in first. I pulled out Chopper.

Sindari pushed the door open further and padded inside.

A click sounded from across the living room. Still in the hallway, I dodged to the left, whipping my sword across defensively. Something *tinked* off the edge of the blade and clattered against the floorboard before hitting the thin gray carpet. A tiny silver dart.

Warily, I picked it up. A gunky blue residue smeared the tip. Poison?

"Clearly, I need a taller tiger," I said.

My height is perfect for seeing over the tall grass on the Tangled Tundra on Del'noth.

"Helpful."

Very much so in hunting there, yes. Sindari padded farther into the room, avoiding the lamps, books, and clothes strewn across the floor. I'd just gotten everything cleaned up from the *last* break-in.

"It may be time to move again."

Perhaps you should not use your real name when you lease an apartment.

"You have to. They do credit checks before renting you a place. Gone are the good old days when you could lie about everything and pay in cash."

Living in the human world requires an unsettling lack of privacy.

"Tell me about it." I itched to go inside and try to figure out if the intruders had only come to ransack the place or if they'd taken anything. My giant wine jug of change was still sitting on the bookcase beside the door. Nobody ever stole that. Either it was too heavy for the average intruder to lift, or nobody wanted to deal with rolling coins to get the bank to take them.

I see the slender tripwire leading from the door across the ceiling and to this shelving unit. Sindari looked up at the ceiling, then put his paw next to my signed hardback of *Elric of Melniboné*. By some miracle, the Moorcock books were still on the shelf. *Harry Potter* and *Lord of the Rings* hadn't fared as well. A heavy vase I'd picked up at a thrift store was the bookend on that shelf and the object of Sindari's attention.

Something akin to a miniature crossbow has been affixed in here. It looks like that was the only dart.

I held it up and sniffed the tip, but my olfactory senses weren't good enough to identify poisonous substances more exotic than arsenic and cyanide. "I may need to visit Zoltan again."

Sindari checked the kitchen, small dining area, and bedroom and bathroom. I eyed the deadbolts. They hadn't been forced open, at least not with a clumsy tool that would have damaged them. When I squinted across the apartment, I saw that the sliding glass door to the balcony was still closed and the recently added wood board that kept it from being forced open was in place.

When Sindari's perusal resulted in no other ominous clicks, I walked inside and picked up a box of sandwich baggies on the floor. Almost everything from the kitchen drawers was on the floor. All of the cabinets had been rummaged through and most of the plates and cups knocked off the shelves. Because this had happened before, I kept plasticware instead of glassware now. Nothing classy and breakable for assassins with enemies.

Whoever did this appears to have been looking for something specific, Sindari said. *Everything was searched, but little seems to be missing.*

"You've inventoried my whole apartment already? You *are* impressive." Despite the joke, I was inclined to agree with him. The television I never used was on the stand, and my laptop was still plugged in and sitting on the little desk in the living room.

I have been here numerous times, and I have the keenly observant eye of an apex predator.

After slipping the dart into a plastic baggie, wrapping it up, and using masking tape to bundle it so the needle wouldn't poke out, I walked toward the shelf with the crossbow. As I passed my laptop, I noticed the poster Zav had given me was rolled in a different way than I'd left it when I tossed it on the desk. Before, it had been rolled in a tight tube. Now, both ends furled toward each other, with a small bone dagger thrust through the paper and into the wood.

I gripped my chin and stared at the dagger for a moment, then nudged the furls open enough to see where the blade had gone into the poster. Zav's stern, haughty face.

"Even though that's roughly what I had planned for this poster, I feel affronted that someone sneaked in here and defiled it."

I tugged out the dagger. Whoever had thrust it in there hadn't been weak. The design was smooth and simple, and there weren't any markings. For some reason, I thought of the dark elves and the big statue on the pedestal that had been made of bones and fossils.

Val? Your bathroom door has a dagger in it.

"Another one? Was there a two-for-one sale at the local hunting-supply store?"

Sindari, whom I'd never taken shopping, did not respond to that.

"Is it made from bone?" I headed to the compact bathroom, where he stood halfway inside, his neck craned to peer around the back of the door.

It appears so, yes.

"It's not stabbing a picture of a shape-shifted dragon, is it?"

Do you keep such a thing in your bathroom?

"Oh, sure. They're all the rage now."

This one is stabbing your underwear, and there's a note. Sindari scooted out, so I could step inside.

"My underwear? That's more disturbing than a poster."

Indeed. I wouldn't have suspected you to wear anything black and lacy.

"Every now and then, a girl likes to dress to impress." I grimaced at the bone dagger that impaled a black bra that hadn't seen action for a while. The intruder would have had to dig it out from deep in my underwear drawer. "It goes through the left cup. Is that supposed to be where my heart would be? It's a little low."

Dark elf hearts are on the left side, lower than human hearts.

"Ah. So this is exactly as creepy as I think it is."

I pulled out the dagger and grabbed the note. It was written on a single piece of paper—army stationery from a pad I'd kept after Willard had thrown it at me for saying something snarky.

"Huh. It's in English."

You were expecting Dwarven?

"Dark elf, actually." I perused the handful of dark brown lines of text—I'd wager the ink was blood—then read them aloud for Sindari. "Do not believe you have defeated us or that we did not notice that you stole something of value. Return it, or we will slay everyone dear to you."

Did you steal something from the dark elves?

"Just the artifact they supposedly stole from Zav's people. You wouldn't think they'd be so uptight about something that wasn't theirs to start with." I gazed toward the living room and the poster of Zav. The message had to be for me, but they must not have forgiven him for his part in ruining their ceremony and destroying part of their tunnel system. "Oh, and that notebook. The one I gave to Zoltan for translation. You think that's what this was about?"

A dark elf would have been able to sense if the magical dragon artifact had been here before even entering the building. If the notebook is only pages and a binding without an element of magic, he or she would have had to search manually for it.

"While leaving a few bone daggers stabbed into things along the way?"

Perhaps the dark elf was frustrated by the search. You left the notebook with Zoltan, did you not?

Yeah.

And Zoltan had even warned me someone might come looking for it. Ugh. I would have to warn him.

"I'll let Willard know in the morning that the dark elves are still active. They might try to search her office too." I scowled. "It would be nice if they could have waited a few weeks. This week is already reserved for dragons and shifters. I don't have room in my daily planner for dark elves."

Perhaps if you left a note and a calendar pinned to your door outside, your enemies could schedule their assaults and break-ins for more convenient times.

"I think my sense of humor is rubbing off on you."

My phone buzzed from my nightstand, waking me up. It was pitch dark in my apartment, and I felt like I'd just fallen asleep. After fumbling for the phone and checking the time, I realized I *had* just fallen asleep.

"What is it, Nin?" I answered without turning on the light.

"Val! I got a call from the commissary yard where I park my truck. Somebody I do not know said it is on fire."

"Shit." I was going to *kill* those shifters, whether I had evidence that they'd committed these crimes or not.

"Will you meet me there?"

"Yeah. Send me the address." I threw the covers aside, climbed out of bed, and grabbed my clothes. "And don't go in without me. Whoever started it could still be there."

"If they are there," Nin said, her voice as hard and determined as I'd heard it, "I will shoot them."

"Good, but wait until I'm there to do it. If you kill someone and get arrested, you'll spend the rest of your life in jail, and your family will never get over here."

She hesitated. "What if *you* kill someone and get arrested?"

"It won't be the first time." The address of the storage yard popped up on my phone. "I'll be there in twenty minutes. Don't go in without me," I repeated.

"Thank you, Val. I will be there." Nin hung up.

She hadn't confirmed that she wouldn't go in without me.

Cursing, I dressed as fast as I could, shoving my feet into my boots and grabbing my weapons. My gaze snagged on the military flak vest hanging in my closet, the supposedly bulletproof Kevlar still riddled with holes from magical projectiles and claws. I'd worn it consistently for a while, but as I'd found out during three encounters in a row, the sturdy material didn't do much against magic.

Still, getting shot earlier in the day almost made me grab it anyway. No, I'd ask Nin to make me something magical if we both got through this. She'd mentioned something about branching out into armor, and with the way my month was going, I had a feeling I'd need some. Badly.

CHAPTER 16

The address Nin gave me was on the southern end of town, near the Old Rainier Brewery. That meant it was a lot closer to her apartment than mine. Even with little traffic, it took me more than twenty minutes to get there from Ballard, and I worried that was enough time for Nin to have gotten in trouble.

Who had called her, anyway? Someone she didn't know, she'd said. The police? The fire department? Someone laying a trap for her?

Plumes of smoke floated from behind the obscured security fencing of the compound, hazing the city lights as they rose to mingle with the cloud cover. Surprisingly, there weren't any police or fire trucks at the front gate when I pulled up. How could this not have been reported? It wasn't a residential area, and everything was closed for the night, but still. The smoke had to be visible from I-5.

As I parked my Jeep outside the gate and hopped out, the tingle of magic washed over my awareness. I couldn't tell if whatever artifact or charm I sensed was keeping the outside world from knowing about the fire, but it was a possibility. I also sensed the aura of a magical being—several of them.

Nin's pale blue Volkswagen Beetle was also parked out front, but she wasn't inside. Damn it. She hadn't waited.

Where are you? I texted her as I approached the front gate. It was ajar, not enough for a vehicle to drive in, but enough for a person. The lock had been melted off.

Val? a text message came in, but it wasn't Nin. It was Dimitri.

Unless you're in trouble, I can't talk now. Nin's food truck is on fire.

With Fezzik in hand and my ears and magical senses alert, I stepped inside. The crackling of fire came from beyond a large building, a commercial kitchen and bakery, the lit sign over the door promised. Twenty food trucks were parked in parallel spaces across from it and a few more were in the back where the smoke was coming from.

I opted for following the fence instead of going straight down the wide center aisle. One of the magical beings I sensed was close to the fire, maybe crouching atop the fence and looking down. The others—I picked out two more beings—were on the far side of the compound. Nin would have gone straight to her beleaguered truck.

When I stepped into the shadows between the commissary and the fence, I paused to summon Sindari.

Can you take me to Nin? I asked as soon as he materialized.

With only one-quarter gnomish blood, her magical aura was very faint. I wouldn't be able to pick her up until I was standing next to her, but Sindari could smell her.

Yes. Are we going into battle?

My grip tightened on Fezzik. *I hope so.*

Excellent. Sindari continued along the fence, padding silently through the shadows. *Is Nin in danger?*

She may be. She didn't wait for me outside like I told her to.

And she hadn't answered my text. What if that shifter or whoever was looking down on the facility had captured her?

Oddly, Dimitri hadn't responded to my text either. I didn't want to have a conversation while we were sneaking up on an enemy, but the lack of a prompt reply was puzzling. Maybe that magic I felt *was* a spell that isolated this fenced compound from the rest of the world. I'd messaged him from outside and then stepped inside.

As I trailed Sindari, the crackling of fire was the only thing I heard. Before entering the gate, I'd been able to hear the freeway traffic a few blocks away and a horn from a train passing through the city. In here, we had quiet isolation.

You sense the magic around this place, right? I asked silently.

Yes. An insulating bubble covering the same area as the fence.

An insulating bubble that would keep anyone from seeing or hearing what's going on in here? And keep calls from getting through?

That is a possibility. I smell kerosene.

The light of fire bathed the fence ahead and reflected orange on Sindari's silver-furred head. We were almost to the burning truck.

A gun fired from that direction. From atop the fence, someone returned fire.

Sindari sprang up to the fence and ran along the top. I rushed forward, using the building as cover until I saw Nin's food truck.

The roof and back side were burning despite the material not looking like it should be flammable. What had been white with cheerful signage was now charred. The back door was open, and someone crouched there with a gun in one hand and a hose in the other. Nin.

Charred boxes had been thrown out onto the pavement, bullets spilled all around them. Because they were ignitable?

A squawk came from atop the fence, the figure obscured by the smoke, followed by a feline roar. Sindari had reached whoever had been firing at Nin.

As I rushed forward, I called her name so she would hear me coming and wouldn't turn her gun on me.

"Val. Here, take this." Nin handed me the gun and claimed the hose in both hands, going back to what she must have been doing before her attacker had fired.

Flames burned inside the kitchen, and she sprayed them down, even as she lifted her hand against the heat roiling out of the truck.

"Let me trade you." I thrust the gun back at her and took the hose. "I've got protection from fire. But be careful out here. Sindari is after the shooter, but there are two more people on the other side of the compound."

"I know. There were three here when I got here. Dimitri's cactus thorns drove two of them away. I punched that one." She pointed at an unconscious man slumped against a dumpster. One of those cactus thorns protruded from the fence above him, but he didn't appear to be perforated himself.

I hadn't seen him or sensed him as I'd come up. "You *punched* him? With what, a tire iron? He's out cold."

He wasn't magical, so he wasn't one of the three I'd been counting.

"I also hit him with a cast-iron frying pan. After he laughed at my punch."

"That would do it."

"Then I grabbed one of my newest rifles—the bear grinder—and threatened him with it. He ran backward so fast he tumbled into the dumpster and cracked his head on it."

"You are a fearsome woman."

"I am a mad woman. Val, my truck."

"We'll get it put out. You've got insurance, right?"

I jumped into the middle of the kitchen fire, spraying water on anything that looked like it could be put out that way. Two empty fire extinguishers already lay spent on the floor. The remnants of grease in the bottom of the drained fryer station were burning brightly, but I vaguely remembered that water would only make a grease fire worse. I grabbed towels and aprons to wet down and tried to smother the flames.

"I tried to call nine-one-one, but I have no reception." Nin crouched outside the truck, watching the wall and shadows in all directions. "I am in the middle of the city. There *should* be reception."

"I know."

I sensed Sindari had knocked the man off the fence and into the street outside and was chasing him down. The two other magical beings were still on the far side of the compound. I couldn't tell what they were doing, but one of them had to be responsible for the spell blocking our phones. They felt like full-bloods. A shifter, maybe a member of the Northern Pride, and someone else I couldn't identify from a distance. As soon as the fire was out, I would visit them and find out what.

"Or maybe not," I muttered as my senses told me they were on the move. And heading this way.

"Here, Nin." I waved for her to take over with the hose. "We've got more trouble coming."

She took the hose, but she also leaned around the corner of her truck, facing in the direction I pointed, a big double-barreled shotgun at the ready. I ran to the truck next to hers, not wanting to draw fire her way. After activating my cloaking charm, I crept closer to the aisle, keeping the truck at my back.

The two people heading our direction paused. I must have dropped off their senses.

They didn't pause for long. The light of the fire made it hard to see people in the shadows, but my senses told me they were looking at Nin from between two trucks across the way. Finally, I picked out the cloaked figures against the black siding of a burger truck.

They were whispering to each other. I crept closer. The bigger person's voice carried.

I ducked around a truck, activated the screen on my phone where they couldn't see it, started a recording, and returned to the other side. As I snuck closer, I caught something about the Pardus brothers and having already been paid.

He drew a handgun and said, "Nobody cares if she gets hurt or killed, and if I killed the Ruin Bringer..."

Whoever his partner was didn't answer, or answered too quietly for me to pick it up. He strode closer to the aisle—and Nin.

He pointed the gun in her direction. Nin was behind cover but kept leaning out to look for approaching enemies. He might get lucky.

"Not on my shift." I shot him in the shoulder.

He flew backward, hit the ground crying in pain and rolling, then jumped up. He shifted into an ocelot and sprinted at me.

I fired twice, the bullets slamming into his chest, then switched to Chopper as he reached me, springing for my face. I darted out of the way fast enough to avoid the claws slashing for my eyes, then drove my blade into his side. He screeched and crashed into the truck I'd been standing in front of. As he landed, I lunged in and pressed the tip of my sword to his throat. At the same time, I grabbed Fezzik with my left hand and aimed it toward his buddy, who was watching but hadn't moved or drawn a weapon yet. The shifter transformed back into human form and tried to roll away, but I stepped on him and kept the blade to his throat.

"How much are the Pardus brothers paying you?" My phone was still recording in my pocket. I wasn't sure he'd been speaking loudly enough before to pick up his words, so a confession would be nice.

"Not enough to deal with you," he spat between pained panting breaths.

"They just want Nin out of the picture?"

"Oh, they want you dead too."

His buddy finally moved, facing me and lifting bare hands, the palms strikingly pale, fingers long and lean. A woman's? At first, I thought she was showing me that she was unarmed. Then a mental attack poured into my mind like a thousand fire ants burrowing through my ear canals and into my skull.

The shifter rolled away as I gasped, distracted by the pain. He turned into an ocelot again and sprinted down the aisle and out the front gate.

Snarling, I tried to fire Fezzik at the woman, but my finger didn't want to obey. The mental attack grew stronger, more intense, and it felt like a cable was pulling my arm down as I struggled to keep the weapon aimed at the person. At the *dark elf*. The magic was familiar and I belatedly recognized those albino hands.

I fired, even though I was aiming at my assailant's foot. I couldn't force my arm up to shoot at her chest. She sprang more than ten feet in the air, avoiding the bullet that gouged a hole in the pavement, and landed lightly atop the burger truck.

The attack on my mind lessened, but she wasn't done. She drew her hand back, as if to skip a rock.

Not a rock. I leaped sideways as a disc glinting orange with reflected firelight sped toward me. I whipped Chopper across but didn't connect with the projectile. It slammed into the truck next to me and sank in deep.

Do not meddle in our affairs, a female voice spoke into my mind.

Your affairs? What are you doing partnering with some scruffy cat shifters?

The time of humans infesting and destroying this world is coming to the end. All who do not stand with us shall perish along with them.

Are you offering me a chance to switch sides? I wouldn't, of course, but I was curious.

You chose your side long ago, mongrel.

"Yes, I did." The weight pulling my arm down had faded when she shifted from a mental attack to a physical one, so I aimed Fezzik and squeezed the trigger.

But she waved her hand, and the bullets slowed as if they were flying through molasses instead of air. Before they reached her, she dropped off the other side of the truck. I sensed her run to the far fence and leap up and over.

She didn't go the same way the shifter I'd shot had gone—nor did she head toward the one that Sindari had chased off—so maybe that meant they weren't truly working together. Just that, for some reason, she'd lent her magic to them tonight. In exchange for a favor?

Sindari hopped over the fence as if it were three feet high instead of twelve and rejoined me. *I chased the other one until he went into what I believe is called a night club. It was very noisy and filled with people. I assumed you would not want me to follow him inside.*

Were service animals not allowed?

Sindari placed a heavy paw on my foot. *If you're partial to this, you'll remember that I am not some servile animal.*

If you tear off my foot, I'll have a hard time battling dark elves.

He squinted at me. *I thought I sensed an elf or dark elf. What was he doing here?*

She was delivering threats.

How novel.

I thought so.

Someone honked out front. Maybe the police or fire department had finally figured out what was going on.

"You all right, Nin?" I checked on her, found her finishing hosing down the last of the flames, and got a thumbs-up.

"Hello!" came a familiar call from the entrance gate.

"Back here, Dimitri." Fairly confident we'd dealt with all the trouble—Sindari would alert me if more showed up—I stepped out into the main aisle. "Are you alone?"

"Who else would be with me?" He pushed the gate farther aside and stepped in.

"Your hot date."

"Jeremy from the club? I haven't had time to get together with him yet."

"Zoltan," I said dryly.

"He doesn't leave the premises except to hunt, and he said he stays local for that." Dimitri strode toward me, frowning darkly when the charred and smoking food truck came into view. "Fresh, local food. That's his preference." His mouth twisted. He wasn't wearing his cervical collar, but I wagered it was still in the van.

"How fortunate for the people of Woodinville."

"Is Nin all right?"

"Yes. Physically. Mentally, she's probably already stressing out about disappointing her regulars when she can't show up for the lunch hour tomorrow."

"Maybe she can use the kitchen there, then set up a table with some warming trays." Dimitri waved at the building, then rested a hand on the soot-covered hood of the truck.

"Do you think there's any chance of fixing it?"

"I don't know much about cars, so if the engine was damaged, don't ask me. The rest..." He shrugged. "I'll have to take a look. Do we know who did this?"

"Shifters and a dark elf. One of them confessed that the Pardus brothers paid them and didn't care if anyone was hurt or killed. I recorded it—" I pulled my phone out, "—but I've been told that confessions that I extract at sword point aren't admissible in court."

"They're not?"

"Some legal mumbo jumbo about duress and threats." I shrugged indifferently.

"Have you actually been to court?"

"To testify? A few times. Colonel Willard has learned to pull strings to keep me from being subpoenaed."

"Are you an unreliable witness?"

"I'm a sarcastic witness. I've been held in contempt of court three times."

"How many times have you been in court?"

"Three."

"I can't believe you said *I'm* the surly one who shouldn't be hand-selling my wares."

"I'm pretty sure I just implied you weren't quite as cute as the box of puppies next door."

"Who is?"

"Nobody."

Sindari came to sit by my side, his shoulder reaching as high as my shoulder. *Please tell Dimitri good evening. And let him know he may pet me if he wishes.*

He may? Like it's an honor for him?

It is certainly an honor. We have discussed my status and importance among my people, and that I am essentially an ambassador here.

Ambassadors get assigned by other people, not summoned through charms.

You'll find that, as you travel to different worlds and learn different languages, the definitions of words are nebulous and imprecise.

Are you sure? I think the definition of bullshit is universal.

That's because you are unworldly and untraveled.

"Is he talking to you?" Dimitri looked from me to Sindari and back.

"Yeah. He says he wants you to scratch behind his ears."

Sindari narrowed his eyes at me.

"Also that you should feel honored when you do it."

"I always do. He's soft." Dimitri stepped to Sindari's side and rubbed his ears.

Soft? Assure him that I am made from fang and sinew and akin to the hardest metal alloy your people have discovered.

"He likes belly rubs too," I said.

I am thinking of chewing your arm off.

I need my arms to wield my weapons. Chew off something less vital, please.

A kneecap?

I'm partial to those too.

You are a difficult handler.

I know.

Sindari pretended aloof indifference to Dimitri's behind-the-ear rub, but I caught him leaning in for better access. While this was going on, Nin came out, her face smeared with soot, her shirt torn. Her eyes were moist with tear tracks streaking her dirty cheeks. Her forlorn expression made me want to beat the crap out of the brothers' minions again.

"Thank you for coming, Dimitri, and Val." Nin hugged me and then hugged Dimitri. She paused and looked at Sindari. "Does your tiger like to be hugged?"

Sindari lifted his chin. *She may embrace me.*

"He says it's okay."

Nin hugged Sindari, who was looking quite pleased by all this attention.

"I'm sorry I didn't get here in time to do anything," Dimitri said. "I was way up in Woodinville."

"Is the farmers market not over for the week?" Nin asked.

"Yeah, but I'm forging a new business relationship with Zoltan."

"You will become an alchemist?"

"No. I'm assembling something for him, and he's teaching me about building a following on social media."

"*I* could teach you about these things. Your cactus shot one of my enemies in the scrotum."

143

I blinked. "We usually just say balls, Nin."

"That is imprecise. Also, it was the word yesterday on one of my word-of-the-day apps. Once I use it five times, it will be mine forever." She nodded with the determination of one seeking to master the entire English language, including the anatomy part of it.

"What kind of word-of-the-day app pops up scrotum?" Dimitri asked.

"It is medical-themed." Nin pulled out her phone. "Do you want the sample sentence and definition?"

"No," Dimitri and I said together.

Outside the compound, police lights flashed, and I glimpsed a fire truck pulling up. With the spell cocooning this place lifted, the authorities must have finally learned about the incident.

"I'll take a look at your truck while you talk to them, Nin," Dimitri said. "I'm sure you have insurance, but I've done some bodywork. Maybe we can get things up and running again quickly."

"That would be wonderful." Nin touched her hand to her chest and smiled warmly at him. "Thank you."

"I'm sorry I haven't been able to find a way to keep the brothers from attacking you yet, Nin," I apologized softly. "This is unacceptable. I'm going to do something tomorrow."

"Thank you, Val. Please let me know if there is anything I can do to help you. Like paying you." She raised her eyebrows.

I held out a hand. "No payment, but I could use some magical armor if you have time to work on it. There are officially more days in the week now where I'm being shot at than when I'm not."

"Oh yes. I would be pleased to make you something. Lightweight, yes? That is important."

"Very much so."

"I have some prototypes, but I will design something new for you."

"Thank you." I would still insist on paying her for her time and the materials, but I didn't mention it now, since she looked relieved to have something to trade.

Another vehicle rolled up outside the gate, and a car door slammed shut.

I patted Sindari. *You better disappear before the police see you.*

Your people need to learn to accept that there are many beings that exist beyond those native to your world.

Yes, they do. But not tonight.

As he faded into nothingness, I braced myself for the inevitable questions. I was tempted to disappear as well, but I wanted to make sure they didn't give Nin a hard time about anything. She had a permit for the food truck, but my understanding was that one couldn't get permitted for selling magical weapons since the government didn't admit that magic existed. Everything in the back compartment of her truck was hush-hush.

I endured the police questioning with a minimal amount of sarcasm. It wasn't their fault they had shown up late. The sorcerous dark elf had been the problem, and it worried me more than a little that she'd been working with the Pardus brothers' thugs.

Tomorrow, I vowed, I would figure out how to deal with them. One way or another.

CHAPTER 17

As soon as I left Wilmot Gateway Park in Woodinville, jogging along the trail toward the section looking across the river to the Pardus brothers' mobile-home park, I activated my cloaking charm. A bicyclist heading in my direction swerved, face screwing up in confusion as I seemed to disappear to his eyes, but shrugged and continued past. I ran to the side of the paved trail so I wouldn't be in anybody's way.

Freeway traffic zipped by to my right, but my attention was focused to the left, across the water. I hadn't wanted to risk driving through the neighborhood—the charm would only camouflage me, not my Jeep—and this would make it more difficult for the shifters to give chase if they somehow detected me. They would have to come after me on foot and go for a swim first.

As the house came into view, half hidden behind brush and trees in the little lot's back yard, I sensed the auras of the brothers and... eight more magical beings. My shoulders slumped. What were they doing? Running an Airbnb for shifters?

After last night, I ached to take those two jerks down, but I couldn't fight that many shifters, and definitely not on their own turf. By now, the brothers had to expect me, and they'd likely added magical fortifications.

I could still sense the aura of a magical being in the mysterious basement that shouldn't have existed, but it seemed weaker now. The memory of the plaintive call for help came to mind, and I longed to go over there and rescue whoever was down there. If I'd spotted a window or entrance to the basement, I might have tried sneaking in, but there wasn't anything visible to indicate there even *was* a basement. The entrance had to be in the house.

A spotted leopard wandered out the back door and onto the un-kempt lawn. I didn't know if he'd been assigned patrol duty or was going out to take a leak, but the shifter's presence deterred me from thoughts of rescues. At least for the moment. I had to figure out a way to even the odds first.

The spotted feline, easily three times the size of a normal leopard, wandered to the river's edge and sniffed the air. I wasn't moving, but I stood even stiller. The charm should mask my scent and hide me from view, as well as camouflage my aura, but it was always possible someone would see through it someday. I was encouraged that it had worked on Zav that day we'd first met in the wyvern cave, but there were all sorts of magical tools and trinkets scattered across the realms. I might one day run into someone carrying one that nullified stealth magic.

The leopard scanned the trail, eyeing a couple ambling along and pushing a stroller. They were oblivious to the potential threat across the river.

I dropped a hand to Fezzik, ready to attack if the shifter decided it would be worth getting wet to prey on a couple of humans. I wished he would. Then I would be justified in attacking him, in whittling away the brothers' houseguests one by one, until I only had to face them.

The leopard crept closer to the bank, eyes focused on his potential prey.

Do it, I thought, as if I could telepathically send the message. I pulled Fezzik from its holster.

The leopard's tail swished and he crouched, preparing to spring. He was in the shadow of a tree. The couple didn't see him. But I did. I lev-eled my gun at his eyes.

Someone called from inside the house—it sounded like Kurt's voice. The leopard's tail stopped swishing and he glanced back. He looked torn, his gaze turning back to the couple.

My sights were focused on his head. It would be easy to shoot, to take him out before he could return to the house. If I were to tell the authorities that he'd been in the middle of attacking the couple, who would know the difference? A clean shot could end his ability to tell anyone otherwise.

The leopard, no doubt communicating telepathically with Kurt, rose from his crouch and walked across the lawn toward the house.

Reluctantly, I lowered my gun. Even though I wanted to take out the brothers' allies, I couldn't kill someone who hadn't committed a clear-cut crime. Maybe the leopard had killed humans numerous times, but maybe he hadn't.

The spotted feline disappeared back inside. Nobody else came out.

I walked back to my car, planning to check the fence company next. Maybe the person who'd been making bullets for the shifters would have some good intelligence. And maybe it would give me ideas for how to lure away members of the Pride—or even lure the Pardus brothers out by themselves—so I wouldn't have to deal with so many enemies at once.

The Sepes Fencing Company was located near the river in Woodinville, on the industrial side opposite the trail. I entered through a door in the front of the corrugated metal building after checking out the fenced side yard full of vinyl posts and rolls of chain link. Everything inside registered as completely normal to my senses. I could, however, detect something magical inside the building. Maybe that was where the *enhanced* fence bits were kept. So long as the worker who made them was also kept back there.

A petite, bronze-skinned woman with a knitting needle stuck through her loose gray bun was manning the front desk. The door didn't ring or buzz, and I walked up and leaned over the high counter before she noticed me. Two more knitting needles were fast at work in her hands, crafting a scarf that proclaimed her, or some future gift recipient, a *Ravenclaw*.

"Can I help you?" She looked up without pausing her knitting. "Are you interested in a fence?"

"Home security is a concern for me," I said without lying. "I've had a few break-ins, and a friend of mine just had an arsonist take out her most prized possession." Never mind that a fence would be useless to either of us.

"That's awful. Where do you live?"

"Ballard."

"I hadn't realized any parts of Ballard were still that rough."

Mostly just my apartment. "I live in a transitional neighborhood. I'm particularly interested in your *enhanced* fences. Is the person who makes them available for a consultation?"

"That's not quite how it works. We come out to your house or business, take some measurements, talk about what you hope to achieve, and then give a quote."

"I'd like to see if your fences are truly enhanced before going through all that hassle. And talk to the person who does it."

Her eyes narrowed, and she set aside the knitting. "The people who do our in-house builds aren't the ones who interact with customers. You'll be working with the installers and a supervisor. I can see if Timothy can come out and talk to you, but I'd rather get your information and set up a time for a consult at your house. Ballard is a little out of our usual service area, but we can probably accommodate you."

"How about a tour of the facility first?" I waved to the closed door behind her. The grinding of metal being cut emanated from the back.

"We don't give tours."

"Can you make an exception?" I pulled out a fifty and laid it on the counter. I would prefer to bribe the woman before resorting to threats, especially since she was my mom's age, or breaking into the facility and risking being caught by a security camera.

"It's not typical."

I laid another fifty on top of the first. "Are you sure? I hear good yarn is expensive."

She slid the bills off the desk and stuffed them into her bra. The blue dress she wore must not have had pockets. "I suppose it wouldn't hurt to show you around. No recording allowed though. We create some custom fencing materials that our competitors would love to know about. We can't have the videos getting up on the internet."

"I understand completely."

The three people who would watch a video about fences could ruin the company.

"This way. What's your name?"

"Val."

"I'm Martina." She glanced at me—up at me—as I rounded the desk to join her. "You've got great height. Are you in the market for a scarf? I know it's only June, but this is the time to order."

"Not really."

"I can customize it. I have an Etsy shop." She handed me a card. "Please look at my reviews. People are very satisfied."

Everyone was an entrepreneur these days.

"Do you know what house you're in?" she asked.

"Pardon?"

"You know, for *Harry Potter*. Those are my most popular scarves."

"Oh. Gryffindor." I didn't know if it was weirder that I had taken the online test and could answer this or that she nodded sagely, as if she now knew *everything* about me. "I stand up for injustice."

By shooting people who caused it. Had the original books mentioned assassins? I couldn't remember.

"I would have guessed Slytherin, but I don't judge. I just knit scarves. In your preferred colors. You would look fabulous in a vibrant red."

"Good to know."

Slytherin. That was what I got for bribing her.

The grinding noise was much louder inside. Martina headed toward the man making it—he was cutting wrought iron rods to uniform length—but my gaze went to a tall, stout woman in the back who looked like the female version of Dimitri.

There was a hint of the magical about her, and I guessed her a half- or quarter-blood. But of what species? Dwarf? Like Dimitri? Her short white-blonde hair had a frizzy kink to it that looked untamable, and with those shoulders, she could have defended a hockey goal without need of pads or a stick. She reminded me more of a troll.

All around her, stacks of stakes and artistically bent pieces of iron rose, most of them oozing a faint magic. Nothing was as strong as my weapons, but for passive protection, they could work to convince thieves to wander off and try another target.

Martina tried to introduce me to the metalsmith, who looked at my ass and gave her a thumbs-up—maybe this meant I was an acceptable client—but after a hurried hello, I went straight to the big lady.

"Hi, I'm Val." I stuck out a hand.

The woman had been hunched over a worktable, her hand resting on an ornamental disk that looked like it would be welded to a gate. She looked at me and straightened, towering six inches taller than my six feet. Definitely troll blood. That was interesting because they weren't known for being natural enchanters or craftsmen, though their shamans put together some legendary potions that Zoltan would know all about.

"Inga." Her deep voice matched her barrel chest. She started to lift a hand to shake mine but paused and dropped it. "I know who you are."

That sounded ominous.

Martina had caught up to me. "Inga, this is Val. She's a Gryffindor."

Inga's blonde eyebrows twitched. "Is that right." It wasn't a question.

"So the internet test told me." I lowered my hand.

Inga eyed Fezzik and Chopper, clearly having no trouble seeing the weapons that were invisible to most.

"Do you have a couple of minutes?" I asked. "I'd love to talk to you about your work."

"I can't believe the Mythic Murderer is in the market for a fence."

Usually, only full-blooded members of the magical community knew my nicknames—and held a grudge against me. Inga must have had ties to her kin.

"I'm in the market for information, and I'm willing to pay."

Martina's forehead furrowed as she looked back and forth between us.

I put a hand on her shoulder. "If I buy a scarf, will you leave us alone for ten minutes?"

"I will for another fifty dollars."

And Willard wondered why I insisted on being paid in cash and could only afford a one-bedroom apartment with a view of a brick wall.

"Easier money than knitting, huh?" I pulled out another bill and gave it to her.

"It doesn't require me buying yarn or paying the Etsy fees." Martina winked and slid it into her bra with the others.

Inga looked disgusted.

"Be careful," Martina whispered to her before leaving. "I think she's really a Slytherin."

"No doubt," Inga grumbled.

Bribing her might not be effective. I would have to figure out what I could offer her that she wanted. Information rarely came free, especially from someone who knew my reputation and didn't like it.

"I believe I've seen your work in the ammo boxes of a couple of werepanthers," I said, getting straight to the point. "They're trying to run my friend, Nin, out of the magical-weapons-crafting business, and I object to that. Any chance you'd like to give up your side gig working for them if I can help find you something more profitable?"

"I wouldn't take a gig from you even if it paid three times what I get working here."

"What about if it paid better than you get working for the Northern Pride?"

"I don't work for them anymore. Any ammo you saw was old."

"Oh?" I hoped that didn't mean I was wasting my time.

Inga bent over the disc again, crimping a pattern into it with a tool as palpable magic flowed from her fingers and into the iron. She seemed to be saying the conversation was over.

"Were they not agreeable to work for?" Maybe if she had left in disgruntlement, she might be tempted to rant. Rant and share valuable information.

"They're assholes."

"I agree, but they must have paid you decently, or you wouldn't have started working for them, right?"

"It was a side job. It didn't matter that it didn't pay that well. I just wanted enough for a house. Not even a house. A little condo here, something with decent ceiling height, so you can take a shower without bending in half."

"That is annoying."

"You're short. You wouldn't know."

"Even at six feet, I've cracked my skull on some showerheads."

"Showerheads, doorways, car roofs…" Inga thunked her tool down and gave me an exasperated look. "They didn't even pay me for the last batch. They just ended our deal, said they'd found someone else who would make ammo for them and modify their guns cheaper. As if any sane person would work for less than what they paid me. It sucks to be a woman in a man's business. The bastards are always trying to lowball you, treat you like some commodity rather than the skilled craftsperson you are." She turned a scathing expression on the man manipulating the grinder, but he'd gone back to work and wasn't paying attention.

"If I get a chance to pummel them mercilessly in the near future, I'll let you know."

"If you do, take pictures and send them to me, so I can blow them up and throw axes at them."

I laughed. Who would have thought I'd find someone who shared my interest in hurling weapons at posters of obnoxious magical enemies?

"I will definitely do that. I should have done it the last time I visited. Otto looks good wearing a broken TV on his head."

"That the one that can never put a shirt on?"

"He did seem to have that proclivity. Do you know *who* is working for them now, by chance?"

I still thought that if I could convince their bullet-maker—and it sounded like Inga had also enchanted their guns—to sever her relationship with the brothers, then that would help convince them to take their business elsewhere. If they suddenly couldn't supply their customers with their promised goods, competing with Nin would be the last of their worries.

"No idea. Like I said, it has to be someone slaving away for nearly free, because my work was good and way underpriced. Maybe they've got someone tied up in their garage and they're forcing him to work."

I rocked back. "It's the basement."

"What?"

"I sensed a magical being in the basement when I was there. A full-blood, I'm sure."

Her thick brows rose. "I was joking. Besides, even shifters couldn't keep a full-blood enchanter imprisoned. It would be easy for him or her to use magic to escape."

She laid her hand next to an iron bar on the table, and I sensed magic flowing again. The metal turned liquid and flowed over her wrist, re-forming into a shackle and locking itself. A second later, it unformed and returned to its original shape on the table.

"So whoever is in the basement is an ally and being paid?" I asked skeptically. I remembered that telepathic request for help.

"That's my guess, even if it's hard to imagine those two with allies. Still, they've got all those other cat shifters that visit their place. They must have some mysterious allure that's unfathomable to me."

"Maybe it's their sex parties." I grimaced, remembering the brothers' suggestions.

"I can't talk to that. I don't get invited to a lot of those." She sounded more wistful than happy about that.

"I don't think those are parties that any sane woman would want to be invited to. All right, Inga. Thanks for the information." I wasn't sure how she would react, but I laid a hundred and fifty dollars on the table. It didn't seem right that the receptionist should make more than the person I'd come to talk to.

"I don't want your money, Mythic Murderer."

"It's the government's money." Technically, it wasn't anymore, since this was part of my combat bonus from the wyvern job, but I had a feeling Inga would be more likely to accept it if she didn't think it came out of my purse.

She snorted and stuffed it in a pocket. "You're definitely Slytherin."

I shook my head and walked out. I needed to work on my reputation.

CHAPTER 18

Tuesday morning found me in a grumpy mood as I sat in Mary's waiting room with the magazine-tidier I'd met before and another patient who was wearing running shoes, a hoodie, and spandex shorts that left little to the imagination. His leg hair would have put Chewbacca to shame.

Google had promised me that normal people went to therapy, but I hadn't seen evidence of it yet. What did that say about me?

But I'd long ago given up any notion that I was normal. Normal women didn't spend their nights battling pyromaniacs in food-truck parking lots or having nightmares about all the people they'd killed coming back to life and mauling their family members.

I rubbed my gritty eyes, wondering what it was like to sleep well and through the night. My joints ached, and my lungs were tight. I hadn't had to use the "rescue" inhaler—how I loathed that term for it—much since starting on a new steroid one, but my body was telling me I hadn't managed to do anything to address those elevated inflammatory markers my doctor kept talking about. How was I supposed to de-stress my life and lower inflammation when my attempts to do so ended up in yoga studios being bombed?

Ironically, the place on my hip where I'd been shot didn't ache. Dragon healing magic had to be the best in the galaxy. I wondered if it could work on chronic conditions. Even if it could, there was no way I'd admit to Zav that my lungs were anything but sublime. Nor would I ask him for help.

My phone buzzed, and Mom's name came up. Worry flashed through me. There wasn't any reason she should be in danger, but I couldn't help but imagine the worst.

"Hi, Mom," I answered. "What's up? Everything okay?"

"Yes." She sounded puzzled that I'd asked. Her dog barked in the background, and she added, "Rocket misses Maggie."

"I think you misread that bark. Nobody except Willard could possibly miss that cat."

"He keeps looking up at the loft, expecting her to throw something down to him."

"*To* him or *at* him?"

"He may not know the difference. He can catch anything. Are you going to Idaho?"

The abrupt topic switch surprised me. "Idaho? No, what for?"

Then I remembered Thad's Facebook message announcing the vacation he and Amber would take next month.

"Thad and Amber are going to get a cabin on Lake Coeur d'Alene in July. They invited me."

"Oh." I should have said something more articulate, but I felt a numb disappointment that was completely illogical. They hadn't invited me, but *of course* they hadn't invited me. I hadn't spoken to either of them in years. They probably didn't even know I lived and worked in the state—or that I'd gone to several of Amber's swim meets and her sixth- and eighth-grade graduations, always standing too far back to be noticed.

I rested my forehead on my knees, regrets and sadness settling on my back like a hundred-pound barbell. Maybe, if I could somehow finish dealing with Nin's shifters and get all the dragons out of my life, it would be safe to take a trip to Northern Idaho. I'd only had a few assignments over there, so I shouldn't have *too* many enemies in that state. Maybe if I visited for a few days, no bounty-hunting orcs would show up to pester me. Maybe it would be safe to walk up to Amber and Thad and say hello. And say… I was sorry I hadn't been around.

Thad knew the reason why—I'd told him before I left—but I doubted Amber remembered. She'd been so young at the time. And I had no idea what Thad had told her in the interim. Had he made me out to be a deadbeat and a villain? Or just explained that my work was dangerous so I couldn't stick around? Either way, I couldn't imagine a scenario in which Amber would understand and forgive me. It was almost better not to get in touch and never to know for sure how she felt about me. That would be less painful than walking up to the face of anger and rejection.

"Val?"

I sat up. "Yes. Sorry. You should go."

"I will." Mom paused. "*You* should go."

"I'll think about it." My phone alerted me to another incoming call. "My boss is on the other line. I need to go."

"Tell my roommate his rent is due soon if you see him."

"I think he's in Woodinville working on... a project for someone. His van is there too. Can you charge someone rent if he's never there?"

"Of course, you can. He has a lease."

"Right." I said goodbye and switched over in time to catch Willard's call.

"It's about time," she said.

"I like to keep people waiting so they're extra eager to talk to me when I pick up."

"You weren't sleeping, were you?"

"No, I was talking to my mom. Her dog misses your cat."

"Really. Nobody's ever said they missed Maggie before." A screech sounded in the background—it was either Maggie complaining about something or Willard had adopted a cranky baby in the last week.

"Rocket is a golden retriever. They like everyone—and everything. It's in the genes."

"I have bad news for you."

"You're sending me after the dragon, aren't you?"

"How'd you guess?"

"My fate seems inextricably intertwined with dragons these days."

Mr. Hairy Legs was listening to my conversation and raised his eyebrows at this. I resisted the urge to threaten him with a weapon and instead walked over to the window and spoke more quietly.

"Inextricably intertwined?" Willard asked. "Nice vocabulary words. If I didn't know better, I'd think you went to college."

"I read books now and then."

"From what I've been able to dig up, the silver's full name is Dobsaurin of the Silverclaw Clan."

"He introduced himself to me as Dobsaurin the Most Magnificent."

"I'm sure. According to my informant, his family is reputed to rule over the second most powerful clan among the dragons. None of my snitches have any idea why he's here on Earth. Do you? And do you know for sure if he kidnapped those joggers?"

"I don't know that for sure, but he seems to be here to harass Zav. Maybe even kill Zav."

"So why kidnap kids and joggers?"

"To irk him. Or lure him into a trap, maybe. I have a map of some possible locations of caves where Dob might be staying. I can go out today to look for them."

I'd been hoping Zav would return so we could do that together. It wasn't as if I could take down Dob alone. But who knew when he would be back? Maybe I could find the lair, sneak in and rescue the kidnapped people, and then point Zav to Dob when he returned. Then they could fight it out in a dragonly way, *mano a mano.*

"Good. Do that. This Dobsaurin was caught on a video yesterday evening. I'll send you the footage. He swooped down and killed four horses and riders near Kathryn Taylor Equestrian Park in Redmond. Right on the Tolt Pipeline Trail." She hesitated. "It's grisly."

"I'm used to grisly."

"I know. The dragon isn't in the video—this was taken by the police in the aftermath—but two witnesses saw him and confirmed the scales were silver. They ran into the woods to the side of the trail when the dragon showed up. Others who were interviewed said they couldn't see him, just people being torn to shreds, seemingly by nothing."

"Zav said that only those with magical blood can see dragons unless the dragons *want* to be seen." I pulled up Kathryn Taylor Equestrian Park on my map, and a weird knowing feeling twisted my gut. "It's not straight east from the spots where the joggers were picked up, but it's very close. Just a little jag to the southeast. I've been theorizing that he's got a cave out in the woods east of Duvall. For some reason, all of his kidnapped joggers were on an east-west line from there. Maybe he likes to take a morning dip in Lake Washington."

That was a joke, since there were plenty of rivers and lakes closer to where I thought he was staying, but Willard said, "Maybe, or maybe he fishes there in the mornings. There's a big variety in there, I've heard. Do dragons like fish?"

"Zav said they eat fish and meat. He was skeptical about the lavender chocolates I gave him."

"You're giving him chocolates? Val, it works the other way around. The man gives the *woman* chocolate."

"I'm trying to get him to believe humans don't suck and that there are some good things on Earth."

"By wooing him with chocolate?"

"I'm not *wooing* him." I must have spoken too loudly, because the eavesdropper was looking my way again. Either that, or my half of this conversation was the most interesting thing going on this morning. I scrutinized him briefly, making sure he didn't have any magical blood. The last thing I needed was some spy from the Northern Pride giving the brothers another location to bomb. "I didn't even buy it. The people I helped on the peninsula gave it to me, along with a case of wine."

"Did you give that to him too?"

"Well, yes, but only because I don't drink it."

"Did *he* drink it?" Willard sounded fascinated by this development. Maybe some secret girlie part of her heart wanted to attend a dragon–half-elf wedding.

"How should I know?" I grimaced as the video she'd promised popped up on my phone. I was used to death and gore and violence, but that didn't mean I enjoyed watching footage of it. "Are you officially putting me on assignment to get this dragon?"

"Yeah. The military is prepared to send in jets to attack it from the air, but we need someone who can see it to pin it with a locator device."

"Oh, that'll be easy. I'll just tag him like he's a bear."

"I was told without much subtlety that this is the least preferred method of dealing with him. They would prefer you simply get rid of him."

"Even easier."

"When your dragon sobers up, maybe you can try that chute-opening-ass-swatting suggestion I made."

"If only. Zav went back to his world. I'm not sure when he'll be back."

Willard swore. That spoke volumes about her belief that I could handle this without Zav. Maybe she'd assumed from the beginning that he would be there to help—though I wasn't sure why she would. Unless she knew more than I did, which was usually the case.

She took a deep breath. "We need to convince Dobsaurin to leave, one way or another. I've been authorized to double your combat bonus if you can kill him. Regular combat bonus if you can pin him with a transmitter that he can't remove."

I rubbed my head. How was I supposed to do *that*? A dragon wasn't a wolf. I couldn't staple something to his ear that he wouldn't be able to remove—or incinerate. Dragons didn't even *have* external ears.

"I'm having something prepared now. Something very durable. You can pick it up at the office this afternoon. If you're successful, there's a team at McChord ready to take off after him."

I lowered my head, staring bleakly out at the gray sky and the darker gray water of Lake Union. Dealing with the dark elves seemed like a simple affair compared to this new assignment. I'd *have* to kill Dob. Or somehow convince him to leave. There was no way a dragon wouldn't be able to remove a transmitter tag, even if I had a weapon that could pierce his hide to pin him with it. Chopper was the only thing I knew of that could make a dent. A tiny dent.

"You have the option to say no," Willard added quietly.

I hadn't spoken for a long minute.

"You're not sworn to follow orders anymore," she added.

"Yeah, but if I don't do it, who will?"

"Nobody as good as you."

"That's what I was afraid of. I'll be there soon."

As I hung up, Mary leaned out of her office. "Val? I'm sorry my last appointment ran a little late. Will you come in?"

"I have to go." I waved my phone before pocketing it. "Work."

"You can't take a few minutes to talk?" She raised her eyebrows. "You look tired."

"Because I slept for two hours last night. I *am* tired."

"I won't nag you. I'm certain you already know that the best thing you can do for your health is get at least eight hours of sleep in a dark, quiet environment."

"Trust me. I would love to do that."

"Do you turn your phone off at night or at least keep it in another room?"

"No. When a friend calls and says her food truck is on fire, I want to be there for her."

"It is difficult when your job requires you to be available around the clock. I know. I work with firemen and police officers. Will you make time to come in next week?"

"Yes. I figure everything will either be resolved by then or I'll be dead."

Mary smiled, but it faltered. Maybe my expression told her I wasn't joking. I wished I were. The conversation I'd had with my mother returned to my mind, and even though I hadn't decided anything yet, the idea of dying before I'd had a chance to speak with my daughter bothered me. A lot.

"Mary? My mom told me that my ex-husband and my daughter will be going on a family trip to Idaho in a few weeks. They invited her to join them, and she suggested I come along. I haven't spoken to Thad or Amber in years, and they didn't invite me, but... would it be weird if I showed up there? Just to say hi?"

"After years of silence? Yes."

"Oh."

"That doesn't mean you shouldn't do it, but maybe you could call them first, instead of unexpectedly showing up."

"Yeah." But Thad never called me, and it was hard for me to imagine calling him first out of the blue. Of course, I'd told him *not* to call me unless it was an emergency, but I'd expected... I didn't know. I'd thought he might reach out occasionally over the years. He hadn't.

Why was it easier to face killer dark elves, vampires, and werewolves than to call my own family?

Because I didn't care how those other guys reacted to me, I answered my own question. More than that, I *expected* them to be hostile. I could deal with hostility from strangers. Hostility, or even indifference, from people I should have had a relationship with... That was different.

"Or email," Mary offered. "Couldn't you email them without people realizing you have a connection?"

"So long as none of the magical people who want me dead are hackers or get ahold of my computer or phone, yes."

"Is that likely?"

"It's not an impossibility. My apartment gets broken into often. Someday, I'm going to hunt down a trinket that can keep everyone out of there." I sighed with longing, having heard that artifacts like that weren't uncommon in other worlds. Dimitri's cactus home-security doo-dad wasn't quite in the same league. Maybe with a little encouragement, he could learn to create something more useful.

"Get in touch with your family." Mary put a hand on my shoulder. "Whatever reception you fear is probably the worst possible iteration of what will really happen. Even if they reject you, at least you'll know. That would be easier than living with the uncertainty."

I wasn't sure about that. As long as things were nebulous, there was still hope. Hope of them forgiving me for the long silence, for walking out all those years ago.

"I'll think about it. Thanks."

As I headed for the door, Mary repeated, "Don't randomly show up on their vacation like a stalker, please."

She must have decided her previous, more circumspect wording of that hadn't been sufficient.

"I won't. I'm not a dragon."

Her brow furrowed in confusion. I *definitely* wasn't a normal patient.

CHAPTER 19

When I pulled into the Moss Lake Trailhead parking lot, a place that could get me back into the forest where Greemaw had marked the caves, there weren't any other cars there. I didn't know whether to take that as a good sign—there wouldn't be anyone to see me illegally let myself through the locked gate—or an ominous one. The hiking spot was out of the way and not that well known, but there were usually a few other people here.

I left the Jeep running and walked up to the gate, reaching for the magical charm that unlocked secure doors and gates. But I paused, my hand dangling. Someone had shot off the padlock securing the metal gate that kept people from driving back onto the old logging-road-turned-trail. Fresh tire marks had disturbed the grass and mud. The bar creaked as I pushed it up.

I trotted up to the bend and peered around it to make sure there wasn't a bevy of park-ranger trucks waiting. The wide trail stretched back into the trees, straight and empty for as far as I could see, but the fresh tire marks were visible all along the way.

"Maybe someone else is hunting dragons," I muttered and thought about calling Sindari.

But I needed to save him. If I ran into Dob back here... Well, I hoped I wouldn't. Not yet. I wasn't ready to run into him. I had Willard's transmitters—there were three of them, and they'd been built into custom cartridges I could fire with Fezzik—but I was skeptical those rounds would pierce dragon hide. The memory of Zav incinerating bullets before they touched him came to mind.

All I wanted today was to find Dob's lair. If I could slip in and out and leave one of the transmitters tucked behind a rock, maybe Willard's pilot buddies could bomb the cave one night while he was snoozing.

Rain drizzled from the gray sky as I drove onto an old dirt road that had been allowed to narrow to something more suitable to hikers than automobiles. High grasses, trees, ferns, and other dense foliage I couldn't name made it claustrophobic. Long beards of green moss dangled from the evergreen branches and carpeted their trunks.

Some of those branches reached out over the trail, clawing at the roof of the Jeep and reminding me of when Zav tore off the soft top on my *last* Jeep. The black one the army was lending me had a hard top, though I doubted it would deter dragon talons. Even though I couldn't sense anyone magical nearby, I kept leaning my head out and trying to see the sky.

I caught a glimpse of Moss Lake off to the left but soon passed it, along with narrow trails branching off into the woods. I stayed on the wider path—given the density of the trees, there wasn't any other option—until I came to a grass-choked crossroad, then turned right and gained access to a larger system of old roads. The rain picked up as I weaved along routes long forgotten by all but determined hikers and the wildlife that lived here.

When I got as close to the first cave as possible, I parked, put on a wide-brimmed rain hat, and went on foot. I cut my way through wet foliage, forging a path toward one of the creeks that ran through the area. Rain pattered off my hat, and the going was slow. My thought of checking all the caves Greemaw had marked by the end of the day turned into a plan to check them all this *week*.

The first one had been claimed by a skunk, and it drove me out of the area more effectively than a dragon would have. A bear had made a den in the second cave but was fortunately not home. The third was high on the bank of the Tolt River and too small for a dragon, unless he shape-shifted to get in. Since that was a possibility, I climbed up to it and shined my phone's flashlight inside. Nothing.

"Three caves down, twenty-eight more to go..."

I'd searched all the ones in this area and would have to return to where I'd parked and head into the brush on the other side of that road. I was halfway back when gunshots fired.

Reflexively, I tore Fezzik from its holster and sprang behind a tree for cover. But my brain caught up to my instincts and informed me those shots weren't near me. It was hard to tell how far away they were with the forest muffling sound, but at least a mile.

More shots fired as I continued warily back toward the Jeep. Hunters? If so, they weren't very good hunters. Who needed that many shots to fell a deer? It wasn't even hunting season. If anyone was back here, they were illegally poaching. Not that I particularly cared, so long as they didn't shoot up my rig.

The gunfire continued, and the roar of vehicles grew audible. It sounded like I was heading right for it. I broke into a run, imagining drunk idiots smashing into my Jeep.

I leaped ferns, mushroom-studded logs, and great roots jutting out of the earth. I couldn't wreck another vehicle in the same month, damn it.

Their trucks came into view before my Jeep did. A white Nissan and a black Ford, mud spattering the sides as they navigated down the old logging road. Men leaned out the windows and knelt in the beds, aiming rifles into the brush on the other side of the trail.

Just as I was thinking that any deer would have long ago fled at the noise, I sensed magical beings in the woods in the direction they were shooting. A half dozen of them at least. I couldn't identify their species by the auras, but they seemed smaller than humans. More kobolds? Goblins?

Two shots fired, and a female scream came from the woods. That was no deer.

"Got one!" a man yelled.

I ran to the edge of the woods and leaned out enough to see the trucks. They'd stopped. The men—they were young and definitely human—sprayed fire into the trees.

A whispered argument in a language I didn't understand came from the trail opposite me, and I spotted two green-skinned goblins with shaggy white hair also hiding behind trees. One was male, one female, neither more than four feet tall.

They pointed at the men, then pointed back into the woods in the direction the scream had come from. Neither of them appeared to have weapons. Clad in ripped and oversized jeans and flannel shirts, they reminded me of the refugees in Greemaw's village. Their faces were lean, cheekbones prominent, and I doubted they'd had a good meal in a long time.

Even though I'd never met a goblin that hadn't made trouble for me—the ones I'd run into were notorious for stealing things—I'd also never met one that was a killer and deserved a death sentence. In short, *I'd* never been sent out after one.

I tapped my translation charm and willed it to activate.

"They got Teenah. We have to help."

"*How?*"

"Go pick her up and get her out of here."

"They're shooting all *over* the place over there."

More gunshots erupted from the truck beds.

"Get 'em, get 'em!" one of the drivers urged, yelling through the open slider window to his gun-happy buddies.

Two of the men leaped out and ran into the woods. What were they going to do? Cut off the goblin's head and mount it above a fireplace?

I pulled out Fezzik, visions of stalking down the road and opening fire on them filling my head. More sane visions of staying in the trees and shooting out their tires from behind cover replaced them.

I ran parallel to the road, leaping brush and logs, landing as lightly as I could, not that they'd hear me over their yammering and shooting. Once I was close enough, I found a stout red cedar to hide behind and leaned out. Though I was tempted to randomly rain fire on their trucks—and maybe sink a few bullets into their asses—I calmly and methodically aimed for their tires.

Still firing their own weapons, it took them a minute to even realize they were being shot at.

"Shit," one of the drivers called out the back. "One of you jackasses hit my tire."

"That's impossible."

"I'm losing tire pressure." The driver pointed to some warning indicator on the console.

"You probably ran over some glass."

"My tires are losing pressure too," the driver in the second truck hollered.

Man, these guys were geniuses.

"It's the goblins," one of the men in the bed said. "They must be shooting back at us."

"You said they wouldn't have guns!" All of the men in the truck beds dropped to their bellies, only their heads and rifles visible over the sides as they fired into the woods again.

My senses told me that the goblins had managed to get their comrade and were carrying her out of the area, but the idea that these guys had come out here to hunt prey that couldn't fight back—intelligent prey, not animals for the dinner table—pissed me off.

I fired again, this time aiming for their rifles. My shots knocked two guns out of their hands before the rest of the men spun in my direction.

"Over there!"

They finally returned fire in the right direction. I ducked behind the tree and touched my charm to call Sindari. Their bullets flew all over the place. None of them had seen me or knew exactly where I was.

You're supposed to summon me before *you enter into a firefight,* Sindari said as he finished forming, the silver mist fading.

Is that how it works? I do struggle with order-of-operations problems.

You must have been a pox to your mathematics instructors. Shall I go rip off the legs of the men firing vaguely in our direction?

As tempting as that is, I doubt the police would appreciate it if we mutilated poachers in the woods. Especially goblin poachers. As far as I knew, it wasn't a crime to shoot magical beings, since the government didn't acknowledge they existed or give them rights. I thought of my mother pointing out that this kind of thing wasn't uncommon down in Oregon. Maybe it wasn't here, either. I just hadn't known because I lived in the city. *But do me a favor and scare them, will you?*

Gladly.

Bonus points if they wet themselves.

I'll give them my special roar.

I knew you knew your roar could elicit that response.

Sindari grinned back at me, inasmuch as tigers could grin, as he bounded toward the road.

His innate stealth kept the gunmen from seeing him until he sprang into the bed of one of the trucks, knocking men and their rifles over the side. He must have kept his claws retracted, because nobody screamed when he struck them with his powerful limbs, but the men did shriek and yell at the drivers to get them the hell out of there.

I trotted out as the trucks rumbled down the road, the poachers who'd been knocked out running after them. Sindari sprang from the roof of one truck to the bed of the next, knocking over more people. They couldn't shoot at him without risking hitting each other, though that didn't keep a few from trying. They weren't even close to fast enough to graze Sindari with a bullet.

I could have shot out more of their tires—the ones I'd hit were deflating with impressive speed—but there wasn't much point. Sindari had them on the run. So, being the mature person I was, I took out my phone and recorded their flight as Sindari leaped back and forth, evading the men stupid enough to still be in the truck beds attempting to shoot him. I was fairly certain my stoic, regal tiger was deliberately taunting them—and having fun doing it. By now, most of them had lost their weapons.

Once the wobbling, lopsided vehicles turned onto the road that led to the parking lot, I stopped recording.

"Maybe it's time to start a YouTube channel," I said. Nin and Zoltan would call it marketing. Who wouldn't want to hire me after they saw how delightfully effective Sindari was?

As I turned, trusting he would be back, and strode up the trail toward the Jeep, I sensed the goblins scattering deeper into the brush. Soon, their auras faded from my awareness.

If they felt any gratitude or cared that I'd stepped in, I would probably never know it. That was fine, though there was a wistful part of me that wanted them to know. It would be nice if some members of the magical community believed I was a good person and only hunted the legitimate criminals among them.

As I got closer to the Jeep, I noticed something on the ground next to it. Ugh, had those idiot poachers done something to it? The tires weren't flat, and I didn't see any bullet holes… Was that a paint bucket? And… brushes?

When I stepped around to the driver's side, I found myself staring at stick figures painted in red on the door. My first thought was that it was mindless graffiti, but there was a definite message being conveyed. A stick dragon with a round belly was knocking a stick person—someone with a braid of long hair—into a ravine. At the bottom of the ravine, the stick person was duplicated, this time lying dead among jagged rocks.

Sindari caught up to me as I considered two words written next to the stick figures in an unfamiliar language.

"How's your Goblin?" I was positive the truckers hadn't done this.

I understand many languages. That's your name.

"Val?"

Mythic Murderer.

"Wonderful. And that's also my fate, I suppose."

I wouldn't worry about it. Goblins are known more for being mischievous than prophetic.

"I don't feel comforted."

CHAPTER 20

Your new colleague is coming, Sindari informed me.

I'd pulled a towel out of the Jeep and was doing my best to wipe off the paint that hadn't yet dried completely. It wasn't working well.

He's not a colleague. I sensed the approaching dragon aura and looked up in time to spot violet eyes sailing into view over the trees.

I thought you were trying to get him to see you as an equal. A dragon would typically think of your relationship as something closer to master-slave.

In that case, I guess he can be my colleague.

I thought you might see it that way.

Zav landed on the road in front of us, radiating power like a sun. Too bad he hadn't appeared earlier. His fanged maw, muscled body, glowing eyes, and sheer size might have convinced the hunters not only to flee but to never step foot in this forest again.

Even with his wings tucked in, the trees to either side of the road hemmed in his great dragon form. I wondered if the foliage on his world was courteous enough to grow farther apart.

Zav shifted into his human form, opting for his usual silver slippers and black, silver-trimmed robe. The rain, mud, and puddles all around might have suggested hiking boots and a poncho, but maybe shifters could only change their forms, not their clothing. If so, that was too bad. Zav wearing a vibrantly colored Mexican poncho would have amused me vastly.

As he walked toward me, wind blowing damp leaves off the trees and batting at his robe, I debated how to admit my lack of progress without sounding like I'd been slacking off these last two days. Or like I was incompetent. Willard had only given me this assignment this morning, but I'd been researching it longer. I'd hoped to be able to hand him the location of Dob's lair, but all I'd found were poachers tormenting goblins.

"You're early," I told him. "I'm only doing preliminary scouting."

Zav stopped in front of me. "You assisted magical beings against humans."

I shrugged, surprised he'd gotten here soon enough to see that. I tried not to feel a twinge of disappointment that *he* knew about it and the goblins didn't. It wasn't that I wanted a reward, but my mother's words had been in my mind, that maybe if I helped more magical beings, the innocent ones would stop fearing me as much as the guilty ones did. Then maybe there would be fewer break-ins of my apartment and drive-by shootings. But that would only happen if the magical community *knew* I was helping them.

"From what I've learned, this is not usual for you," he continued. "Typically, you side with the vermin—the *humans*—infesting this world instead of the magical, even though you are half magical."

"That's because I was born here, and *humans* are my people."

What did he want from me? His gaze was impossible to read when it latched onto me—and more than a little disconcerting. He was close enough that I could feel that now-familiar tingle of power emanating from him, like high-voltage electricity crawling over my skin. Except less unpleasant. I didn't have the urge to hurry away from it, like I would from power lines. No, I had the urge to step closer, to intensify that sensation, and that disturbed me. It was too much like the pull of a moth to a flame—or a bug zapper.

"That is no reason not to embrace the superior half of your heritage," Zav said. "Your father could teach you much."

"I'm sure he could, but it's not like I can look him up on LinkedIn."

A gust of wind swept down the road, blowing more soggy leaves off the trees and threatening to give me a glimpse of Zav's legs under his robe. I wondered if he was wearing socks with his slippers and smirked at the thought.

He frowned, no doubt thinking my twitching lips indicated some disrespect or another. "He has left this world?"

"All elves did. And dwarves. Forty-odd years ago. Nobody knows why, but there are lots of theories. Nobody left behind knew how to make portals, so it's not like I could get a ticket and go looking for him, even if I wanted to see him. And I don't."

"Why not?"

"He left my mother before I was even born." I pulled my collar up against another chilly gust. It was almost summer, but I was wet, and the rain was threatening to turn into a more serious storm. "She forgives him, or so she says, because he had to choose between leaving with his people and staying here with her and only her. He chose his people."

Why was I speaking about this to a dragon? What did he care?

"Look, never mind any of this. I've been searching this area using the points on the map that Greemaw gave me, but I haven't found anything yet. That's why I didn't call you. Also, I don't have your number."

"My what?"

"I don't know how to get in touch with you."

Zav touched his temple. "I do not have my mental shields up against telepathic intrusion, not in this world. There is little need. You can reach me telepathically."

"Uh, sure. If I could do that, I would." Actually, I wouldn't. The idea of trying to touch my mind to his seemed disturbingly intimate. Either that, or he'd give me a headache with the power of his responses. Thus far, that had been my experience with telepathic communication with dragons.

Zav lowered his hand. "You cannot?"

"Nope."

"What magical powers do you have? Besides your charms and your weapons. It would be useful for me to know before we confront Dobsaurin."

"I don't have any magical powers besides healing quicker than normal for a human."

"That cannot be possible."

"Oh, it is."

"You are half-elf."

"Yeah, and I tried to do magical things when I found out. Nothing ever happened. I don't have any powers." I remembered the magical bonds I'd broken in the dark-elf laboratory—and how I wasn't positive the lock-picking charm had been responsible for that. Or at least *wholly* responsible.

"You were trained by a practitioner and failed to show abilities?"

"No. I tried to teach myself. That's how it goes for most mixed-bloods here. There's nobody left to teach. You muddle through and figure things out on your own. Lots of people manage it."

"Magic must be taught. Muddling is unacceptable."

"That's how it works here. Let's drop it, okay? My charms and my weapons and my ambassador are plenty." I waved toward Sindari. He'd moved farther up the trail to sniff at something in the woods. The sky was growing darker, and his fur glowed a soft silver.

The wind gusted again, tugging at my braid and leaving a soggy leaf on Zav's broad shoulder. I snorted and stepped forward, reaching for it. He caught my wrist, his movement too swift for me to jerk away in time.

"What are you doing?" He squinted at me, eyes flaring with violet light. Had he thought I was reaching for his neck? If so, there was something amusing about him being as wary about me getting close as I was about him getting close. Though he was probably more worried about me kissing his ass than strangling him.

"Keeping you from a fashion faux pas." I looked pointedly at the leaf.

He eyed it, then eyed me, then released me. I brushed off the leaf and stepped back. He was still eyeing me. I couldn't imagine what was going on in his mind.

"I'm not going to make a pass at you, if that's what you're worried about."

"A what?"

"A pass. Romantic moves. You're not my type."

That was a lie. He was *exactly* my type, at least going on looks and that hard chest I remembered feeling, but I couldn't forget that he was an obnoxious, haughty dragon who thought nothing of mentally compelling people to do his bidding. Besides, he'd made it clear I wasn't *his* type from the day we met. Maybe he thought I would be so overcome by his virile masculinity that I wouldn't be able to keep my hands to myself.

"I see." Zav clasped his hands behind his back and nodded toward the woods. "Let us walk. One of the caves is near, but I believe the forest canopy would make it difficult to find from above; nor could your conveyance fit between the trees."

"I guess that means we're using Chopper as a machete." I didn't point out that a cave that was hard for *him* to see from above would have been equally hard for another dragon to find. I'd planned to check all of Greemaw's locations regardless.

Zav glanced at the hilt over my shoulder. "That is not a fitting use for that blade. I am capable of clearing brush if necessary."

"Can you breathe fire when you're in human form?"

"I can *make* fire in this form."

I imagined him crouching with flint and steel and dried pine needles. A snort escaped my lips. It was almost a giggle, but I am a mature woman and do not giggle.

I hadn't meant for it to sound sarcastic or dubious, but Zav's eyes narrowed, then glowed violet. I'd been walking at his side, but I paused warily, expecting something of mine to burst into flame. A long beard of moss dangling from a nearby branch caught fire and burned within a second. The rest of the tree was not damaged.

"No flint and steel required, eh?"

"No."

Zav veered off the muddy road, and I made a mental note of the Jeep's location and nearby landmarks in case he disappeared again. There wasn't any cell reception out here, so the GPS map was useless.

Zav took the lead. Along the way, not much burst into flames, but the ferns and bushes leaned away from him to make our passage easier. It was still slow-going. The roar of the river drifted to my ears, but I didn't know if we were five minutes from it or thirty.

"What made you help those goblins?" Zav asked without looking back.

Surprised he was bringing it up again, I shrugged. "I don't like big guys picking on little guys."

He kept walking, still not looking back, and I wondered if he thought I was insinuating that dragons did that.

"Given your reputation, I wouldn't have expected you to help the magical, size regardless." He sounded like he was trying to work through a puzzle.

"Reputation is what other people believe about you. It isn't always an accurate reflection of who you really are, but it's damn hard to alter the perceptions of others."

"That is true among all the races." Zav stopped, framed by two towering cedars, and faced me. "You will probably not believe that I also do not like big guys picking on little guys." His emphasis on *guys* was careful, as if the word wasn't familiar to him. It probably wasn't. What dragon freshly arrived from another world could have fully mastered English in a few weeks?

"Actually, I do believe that. Ever since you told me you were a cop."

"A what?"

"Police officer. Or your world's equivalent."

"Hm, that is not precisely my position, but I do help my clan uphold the law. I have not made it a secret that I find this assignment—" he waved to the forest, or maybe the vermin-infested planet in general, "—unappealing. It is beneath me."

"It must be hard being so magnificent."

"*You* and your trinkets could do what I am doing."

"Just when I think you aren't a complete asshole, you get all arrogant and superior on me."

I expected him to glare and maybe flare his eyes at me, but he only gave me a considering look. "Dragons are long-lived but not fecund as a species, so there are not many of us. We must serve where we can be of the most use—those of us who actually care about serving something other than megalomania. My abilities are needed back at home."

"So you're frustrated."

"*Yes.*" He looked at me as if this should have been evident from the start, as if I knew anything about dragon politics and his clan. "Yes," he said more quietly, more reserved.

Zav turned and resumed walking. I was tempted to ask him for more details, but I doubted he would give them to me. It sounded like he was low-man-on-the-totem-pole back home. Who would want to admit that to some scruffy mongrel? What ranking did Dob have, I wondered. Zav had been evasive when I'd asked if he was stronger than Dob, and it might be telling that he'd dragged me along. Maybe he wanted me to be a distraction if they fought. Or a sacrifice.

"Comforting thought."

Zav had drawn ahead, but he paused and looked back.

"Just wondering what the odds are of me surviving a battle if we actually find Dob."

"You need not risk yourself."

"You said you were taking me to get in his way."

Zav smiled faintly. "I was hoping there would be another windmill and you could convince him to burn down his own hideout again."

"I see you got the details from someone."

"One of the kobolds. It pleased me that you vexed Dobsaurin." He turned the smile on me, and my stomach did a weird little flipflop.

Oh, no, Val. You are not attracted to the dragon. Especially the dragon who calls you a mongrel and grabs your wrist if you presume to touch him.

"But it doesn't please you when I vex *you*," I noted casually, ignoring his smile—and my stomach's theatrics.

"I prefer it more when your biggest weapon is pointed at someone I detest."

My biggest weapon? I raised my eyebrows and touched Fezzik.

"Your mouth."

Ugh, I'd walked right into that one. Had I truly been pleased earlier that my humanness—my sarcastic humanness—was rubbing off on him?

"If my mission places you in danger," Zav added, "I will protect you."

That would have made me feel better if I wasn't certain that Dob could kick his ass.

Zav returned to the walk. "Come. We are close to the first cave."

I didn't point out that I'd already investigated three caves.

Zav paused, lifting his nose in the air like Sindari. "I cannot sense him, but I *smell* dragon."

CHAPTER 21

Zav, who kept sniffing the air for dragon scent, took me not to any of the caves I'd already checked but in a new direction. I dismissed Sindari, aware of the limited time he could spend on Earth, and trailed Zav on a meandering route around dense copses of trees, through depressions, and up hills. Now and then, we would pass some rusty saw blade or other century-old detritus of the logging past.

We came out on a bluff overlooking the churning water of a river, and Zav led the way down a steep slope thick with ferns, their fronds heavy with rainwater. In the rare spots devoid of vegetation, years' worth of fallen fir needles and cones lay decomposing in soggy clumps.

Though Zav obviously knew where he was going, we were almost on top of the cave entrance before I spotted it. Mossy boulders were mounded to either side.

Anticipation ran through my veins. This was the first cave that looked large enough for a dragon to fly into and, thanks to the waterway, the canopy overhead was open enough that one might reach it from the air.

I peered into the dark passage. It looked to go back quite a ways.

Even though I didn't sense another dragon, I let Zav go ahead. *Way* ahead.

After all, Zav was struggling to sense his nemesis too. Dob clearly had a way to hide his aura. And even if he wasn't here, he could have left behind booby traps.

That thought rang in my mind so strongly that I hurried to catch up to Zav so I could warn him.

"Watch out for traps," I blurted when his robed back came into sight, my flashlight beam illuminating it.

"I am. I suspect he has set many for me." Zav looked back and down at the beam. He squinted, even though I wasn't shining it in his eyes.

I angled it toward the lumpy dirt-and-rock floor of the cave.

"That is obnoxious," he said.

"My need to see?"

"I suppose you have no power over that, but I refer to the beam of light shooting out of your hand device."

"It lets me see in the dark. See? Light." I flashed it onto the wall next to us, then beyond him and into a wider section of the cave that appeared partially natural and partially hollowed out by human hand. Or dragon magic.

Zav raised his hand, and Chopper loosened in my back sheath.

"What are you doing?" I reached for the hilt, catching it before he could levitate it away.

His eyes narrowed, but he didn't try to force it out of my grip. He stepped forward and wrapped his hand around mine. The warmth of his touch—and the fact that he was touching me at all—startled me.

Before I could again ask what he was doing, he spoke a single word that meant nothing to me. "*Eravekt.*"

Chopper often glowed a faint blue, usually during a battle or in the presence of magic, but the blade flared to a much brighter blue than I'd ever seen. It pushed back the shadows of the cave, but the glow remained soft enough that it didn't make me squint and look away.

"*Eravekt?*" I said experimentally.

The glow faded.

"*Eravekt,*" I said firmly.

Chopper flared back to life.

Zav didn't exactly roll his eyes—did dragons know about that gesture?—but he did lift them heavenward and issue a long-suffering sigh. "Why do you even have this weapon if you don't know how to use it?"

"I know how to use it just fine. The pointy end goes in the dragon."

"*That* is unlikely to happen, especially given your command of its power. Perhaps later, a small rodent will skitter through, and you can skewer it."

"Perhaps later, I can poke you in the butt with it and see if you feel it. Dob has known its bite."

One of his elegant eyebrows arched. "Has he?"

"His front right toe was in extreme agony for at least seven seconds."

"It's good to know you've so weakened my foe."

"I'm here to help. Are you going to let go of my hand?"

He looked at my hand under his, as if surprised he had touched me. Or surprised by something. No doubt, how beautiful and feminine my hand was, despite the scars and sword calluses.

Oddly, I didn't mind that his fingers were still wrapped around mine—I usually would have kneed a guy in the nuts by now. I told myself it was only because he knew things about my sword that I didn't. Naturally, I wanted to be agreeable so he would share his information.

Still, I couldn't help but add, "Because among humans, this would definitely be considered making a pass."

He released me immediately.

"And here I thought you'd overcome your aversion to humans and wanted to woo me."

"No."

"I'm crestfallen. Meanwhile, what's the deal with that word? And do you know how to spell it?" I flipped my phone to the notepad app with my free hand.

"I'm sure a phonetic spelling will suffice. It's Dwarven."

"What's it mean?"

"Light."

"That's not as imaginative as I would have guessed."

"Dwarves are a prosaic people. It takes someone with power of their own to activate one of their enchanted blades, the word notwithstanding."

"Oh." I lowered Chopper in disappointment. "So it only worked because you were holding my hand?" No wonder he'd kept the grip so long.

His eyebrow drifted upward again. Just the right one. Like Mr. Spock. Maybe he'd stayed in a motel and caught some old *Star Trek* episodes when he'd been away hunting criminals.

"No." Zav extended his hand toward the sword.

An invitation to try it again? I was starting to feel self-conscious, and more than a little dumb for not knowing activation words for a sword I'd carried for ten years, but it wasn't as if I had any dwarf acquaintances who could have told me.

"*Eravekt,*" I said.

It worked. I grinned at Chopper's new feature. It was a big, goofy grin, but I couldn't help it.

I expected Zav to lift his gaze heavenward again, but the faintest hint of a smile curved his lips.

"Are there other things it can do?"

If we were going to fight a dragon that was stronger than he was, any extra advantage I could find would be great.

"Many things, likely. I'm not familiar with that blade specifically, but most dwarven weapons are enchanted with that command. You may be aware that dwarves usually dwell in tunnels. They can see in much dimmer illumination than humans, but, as with felines, their eyes do need a small amount of light to function. Even their simplest tools are enchanted with the power to create illumination. If there is time later, we can try other commands, but you should thoroughly research your sword."

"Oh, sure. I'll hit up the Seattle Public Library when we get back. The magical swords section."

"Good." Zav headed into the cave.

Thinking again of traps, I lingered in the entrance to the larger chamber and peered around using Chopper's pale blue light. I supposed it was wrong of me to wish that Zav would fall into some kind of nefariously clever pit trap with magical bindings and dragon-eating lions, and that I could heroically rescue him and prove I wasn't an imbecile.

Fortunately—or unfortunately—the ground didn't open up, nor did any obvious trap spring. Zav stopped in the back to stare at mounds of dried fir and cedar needles that might have been a very large bed. Not a very comfortable one. The mounds were low and didn't do much more than even out the lumpy floor.

"He slept here," Zav said. "At least one night."

"No sign of kidnap victims, eh?" I peered at the walls, remembering the niche under the floor of the windmill where Dob's young prisoners had been stashed.

"No." He lifted his nose in the air again.

I wondered if he still had superior olfactory senses when he was in

184

human form. Most shifters took on the characteristics and gained the attributes of whatever creature they turned into, and then largely lost them in their human form. But I didn't think dragons were the same as werewolves and werecats and the like. Dragons *were* their native forms, not the other way around.

"Can you smell if any other humans were here?" I asked.

"Only you."

"Do you know how long ago Dob was here?"

Zav turned and gazed at me.

"Sorry. I'm annoying you. I'll stop asking questions. Carry on." Since no traps had enveloped him, I wandered in and poked around.

There wasn't much to poke at. Other than the mounds of needles that could have been brought in by animals, there was no hint that this was the home of an intelligent being. Even if it was temporary, I had expected more from a dragon. Something to suggest the cave was lived in by someone more sophisticated than a bear or badger.

"Like what?" I mumbled to myself. "A wall unit and a throw rug?"

Zav, who had been considering the needle bed with his chin in his hand, looked at me again.

I started to apologize once more for interrupting his contemplation, but then I remembered: "It was *your* idea for me to come with you for this."

"I didn't realize you would be so verbose."

"You *didn't*? The first time we met, I burbled nonstop in the hope of chancing across an argument that would keep you from killing me."

"You did burble," he agreed, then pointed toward the exit. "Wait outside. I'm going to set a trap in case he comes back."

Normally, I would point out that he should have added a *please*, but if he was going to make something that would spew fire from the walls at anyone inside the cave, I didn't want to hang around for an etiquette discussion.

Outside, with the river rushing by below, I stood in the rain and worried that this whole trip would be a waste of time. Was there any point in checking more caves? Would Dob be stashing people in one, wrapping them up with some magical binding, and then sleeping in another? So they wouldn't get their human cooties on him while he dozed?

As I gazed at the water, I realized there was no guarantee he'd kept those joggers alive. I'd been assuming it was a possibility since he'd kidnapped the kids, but then he'd slaughtered those horses and riders on the trail. Was all of this to keep Zav distracted from the criminal-capturing mission he'd been on? Or distracted from things happening back in his world? What had he learned when he'd gone back home for a visit, and who had called him back?

I grew aware of more auras than Zav's and dropped my hand to Fezzik's grip. There were several magical beings in the trees higher up the slope behind me. Knowing that made my shoulder blades itch, so I turned to face them as I glided behind a sapling growing up between two boulders. It wasn't much cover.

A couple of the auras were familiar. My goblin graffiti artists were back. And they'd brought friends.

To pick a fight? It was hard to imagine. As full-blooded magical creatures, they had to sense Zav in the cave. Unlike Dob, he wasn't doing anything to hide his aura.

A few of the goblins shuffled down the slope, coming closer. Two females and two males came into view, stopped, and pointed at me and my tree. Then they pointed at one another. One of the females was pointed at more often, and she threw up her hands and walked closer. The elected speaker?

I activated my translation charm and hoped she understood English. If she didn't, I would be able to understand her, but unless they had similar devices, they wouldn't understand me.

"Mythic Murderer," the female goblin said in guttural English, stopping about ten paces from my tree.

I hadn't drawn Fezzik, but she glanced toward my thigh, so she knew about the weapon.

"You can call me Val."

Goblins higher up the slope and hidden by the foliage chattered to each other too softly for my charm to pick out their words.

"I am called Work Leader Golgitha. I was chosen by my slightly cowardly kin to tell you about the dragon."

My ears perked up. "The silver dragon?"

"Yes." Golgitha glanced toward the cave opening—Zav must have sensed the goblins out here, but he hadn't come out yet. "Do you seek him?"

"Yes." I saw no reason to make a secret of that.

"He sleeps sometimes in the woods out here, but he has also been seen frequently in the water factory."

"Water factory? Oh, the Tolt Water Treatment Facility?"

I'd biked out to it once years ago. It was at the end of the Tolt Pipeline Trail, which we weren't that far from now. I was positive the old logging roads winding through the area could take us to it. It had been locked up the time I'd reached it, and I assumed the public wasn't invited inside for tours. If memory served, the facility oversaw a big reservoir farther back in the foothills that supplied a lot of the water for the city.

An uneasy feeling wound through my gut as her words sank in. The water-treatment facility would be the kind of place a terrorist wanting to wreak havoc on Seattle might target. But would a dragon from another world think to mess with the city's water supply? Maybe.

"It is a large building with many tanks and pipes of water rushing through," Golgitha said. "I have been inside a couple of times at night on acquisitions quests."

I gathered that meant stealing tools and materials that might be useful for goblin projects.

"But not recently. Several days ago, one of our acquisitions teams did not come back. We believe the dragon killed or captured them." Golgitha shook her head, her full lips, yellow eyes, and bulbous nose forming a grimmer expression than I was used to seeing from goblins. "Most likely, he killed them. Their kind believe goblins have no worth."

"I think dragons feel that way about everybody who's not a dragon."

"Not everybody." Golgitha squinted at me. "You are part elf?"

"Yes, but half human too. Zav tells me humans are vermin."

She mouthed "Zav" as if she couldn't believe I'd called him by such an ignoble moniker, but she didn't otherwise comment on it. "Yes, then perhaps you understand. The silver dragon hides his aura, but we have seen him flying in and out of that place. Once, he was carrying a human in his talons."

"How long ago?"

"Three days, perhaps."

That was when the joggers had disappeared.

"Do you have any idea what he's doing inside?" I asked. "Just storing captives or something else? And how has nobody from the city noticed him? There's a staff that works there, right? I'm sure it's not completely automated."

Actually, I wasn't sure of that. I remembered seeing a utilities truck parked there the time I'd ridden close, but it was possible everything was automated these days and someone only came out if there was a problem. It wasn't as if we were that far from the city.

Golgitha shook her head. "We do not know. We have discussed putting together a team to look for our missing comrades when the dragon is not there, but we worry about traps. Dragons are not as clever as goblins—" she said that with a straight face, and I imagined an eavesdropping Zav rearing up in indignation, "—but they have so much power. They do not have to be clever to create effective traps."

"I'll check it out. Thanks for the information."

"Good." She drew the outline of a wrench in the air with her finger, a typical goblin gesture used for greeting and parting, then touched her forehead. "If you see our people alive in there and help them escape, we will be grateful. This is the only place we have found that is not claimed by others—humans or magical beings—and we would like to make it our place."

I imagined that Weyerhauser or whoever owned all the logging land out here would object, but I wouldn't tell them. "I'll keep an eye out."

Golgitha made the wrench-gesture again, then scurried back up the slope, disappearing with her comrades into the woods.

Zav walked out of the cave and joined me beside the sapling.

"We had a visitor. You missed it."

"I missed nothing."

"I thought you might be eavesdropping."

He eyed me. "That word implies improper behavior."

"Are dragons never improper?"

"I am not. I waited inside so that my presence would not inhibit them."

"You *are* an inhibiting presence." I was a little impressed they'd even had the gumption to come talk to me, their Mythic Murderer.

"Not to you." He sounded more irritated than pleased by it.

"I'm not easily inhibited. Shall we go check out the water-treatment facility?"

Zav gazed into the woods, not after the goblins but toward the north.

I had a feeling he was looking toward the facility, perhaps already close enough to investigate it with his senses.

"Yes."

"Can you sense anyone there? Dob?"

"No, but I have not sensed him at all since I started looking for him. It is surprising, since even dragons must sleep, and there is a limit to how much manipulation of magic you can do while you slumber."

I was surprised they could do *any* manipulation then. All I managed to do in my sleep was have nightmares.

"It is possible he has some artifact or tool that is assisting him. Something like your trinket." He pointed to the collection dangling around my neck from my leather thong.

"Oh," I blurted, remembering my encounter with Dob at the windmill. "I'd forgotten—or hadn't thought anything of it at the time—but he wore an oval-shaped black onyx stone in a gold setting that was either embedded in his scales—" I touched the spot just below my collarbones, "—or magically adhered. I didn't see a collar or necklace."

"You did not think to mention this earlier?"

"No. Like I said, I didn't think anything of it. My experience with dragons is limited. I figured he was accessorizing."

"*Accessorizing.*" Zav gave me an exasperated look.

"Yes, you should try it. Maybe a nice amethyst or sapphire gem to go with your eyes. Though neither of those is quite the right color. What's the crystal the New Age woo-woo people like?" I snapped my fingers. "Sugilite. You should get a sugilite collar."

"A collar. Like one of your *hounds*?" It was hard to tell if he was truly disgusted or only feigning offense. Probably truly disgusted. I hadn't yet seen much of the sense of humor he'd promised that dragons possessed. "Do you think dragons are similar to dogs?" he added.

"No. Dogs are friendly, fun, and eager to please. You are... not those things."

"Neither are you."

"I cannot deny that."

He shook his head in disgust. "Come. We will search this facility."

I smiled at his back. It was immature, and I knew it, but somewhere along the way, it had become fun to goad him. The Mythic Murderer clearly had a death wish.

CHAPTER 22

We took the Jeep to the water-treatment facility, though Zav grumbled at the delay, saying he could have flown there in minutes. I'd pointed out that if we found a bunch of injured people, it would be easier to get them out and back to town in a vehicle. As broad as his back was, I assumed there was a limit to how much weight a dragon could carry. And then there was the awkwardness of explaining the method of transportation to everyone who rode along.

As I wound down muddy, weed-choked roads, jostling my refined dragon passenger, who looked very out of place sitting in the passenger seat of a Jeep in his robe and slippers, I did start to wonder if I should have driven back out and around via paved roads. The thought had seemed silly, since we were only a couple of miles from the facility, but this was anything but direct.

I glanced at the dyspeptic expression on Zav's face, not sure if it was for the bumpy ride, the delay, the company, or the overall indignity of sitting in a human vehicle. "You can go ahead on your own if you want. I won't be offended if you're not here at my side, regaling me with your sublime company."

Zav gave me a considering look, then focused on the route ahead again. "No. If he is there and sees you by yourself, he may attempt to circumvent me and come get you. Since he has this ability to hide his aura from me, it's a real possibility."

"Why would he want me?"

"To irritate me. Everything he has done here has been to vex me."

I would call Zav full of himself, except it had seemed true when I spoke with Dob at the windmill. The only reason he hadn't killed me then had been because he sensed Zav's aura on me. That pesky aura that I never seemed to be able to scrub off.

"Why though? Why would he follow you through a portal to Earth?"

"Because this place is lawless. *I* am the only representative of the Dragon Justice Court. If he kills me here, there would be no witnesses who could go back and tell my family, so there would be no repercussions for him."

"Why does he want to kill you?" I gunned the engine to climb up a hill that couldn't possibly be an acceptable grade for a logging truck. I wondered if there was a map anywhere that covered the snarl of old roads and trails back here.

"Because I support my mother."

"And she's important on your Justice Court?"

"Yes." Zav didn't sound like he wanted to speak of this further, not with some nosy half-elf, but there was definitely more to the story than he was telling me.

Maybe he and Dob had personal history that went way back. Didn't dragons live hundreds or even thousands of years? That was a long time during which to accumulate enemies. I knew. I'd accumulated plenty in the twenty years I'd been doing my job.

The road flattened out, and we plowed into a surprise pond-sized puddle at the top. Mud sucked at the tires, and the water lapped at the side rails under the doors. The Jeep sturdily maneuvered through without much trouble, and I was glad Willard had arranged a loaner almost identical to my old rig.

"Just in case you're curious to know," I said, "I owe eighteen thousand dollars on the Jeep that you threw up in the trees and that was too wrecked to repair. The insurance company refused to pay it off because dragons aren't considered an act of God."

"Why do you tell me this?" Zav didn't look at me. He was peering at a hint of black asphalt ahead.

We were coming to the road that led into the water-treatment facility, and nervous flutters started up in my stomach.

"In case you feel guilty now that we're allies, and you want to pay off the loan for me." And because I would rather talk than think about the dead goblins we might find on the floor of this place. Even though I'd just met the pack of goblins living out here, I felt protective of them after witnessing those poachers trying to kill them.

"I do not have money."

"No money? No piles of gold in a cave somewhere? Our stories talk about how dragons hoard treasure. All kinds of knights went on quests to try to slay dragons and take their hoards."

"That is ridiculous. Money is of no value to us. We value strength and power and take what we need from nature."

"I guess that means you're not going to chip in for gas money then."

This time he looked at me, but the look suggested he didn't know what I was talking about.

"I'm afraid, good Zav, that you'll never star in a romance novel. In those, the women are always falling for the hunky billionaire who somehow manages to develop six-pack abs while working eighty hours a week to build his software company."

I drove us out of the mud and onto the nicely paved road, looking left and right. To the far left, I could make out the bend I remembered that would lead down to a gate and the main road. To the right, the water-treatment plant wasn't in view yet, but I knew it was that way and turned in that direction.

"Human women desire males with money," Zav parsed this.

"Not always, but it's definitely a trend in romance novels."

"Is this what you desire?"

"No. I would have stayed with Thad if that were what mattered. He does well for himself."

"You have been mated before?"

"If by mated, you mean married, yes. I don't need a man with money, but a man who pays for something he destroys would be nice."

He returned to studying the route ahead. "I am not a man."

"But you say you gave yourself all the anatomical parts." I arched my eyebrows. I wasn't sure what I was angling for. I didn't truly expect him to pay off the loan, especially if dragons didn't have money, but an apology would have been nice.

It was interesting that he hadn't objected when I called us allies. I'd assumed that, no matter what he'd agreed to when we'd finalized our

Lindsay Buroker

deal, he still considered me nothing more than bait to be used to lure in his enemies. Like a wriggling worm on a fish hook.

"You have acquired another conveyance," Zav said, rather than commenting on his anatomy.

"It's a loan from my boss. I need to pay off the wrecked one before I can afford to take out another auto loan."

He gripped the dash and leaned forward as a locked gate came into view with the large treatment facility beyond that. Two city utility trucks were parked in the small lot. Everything looked normal from here. Maybe the goblins had been playing a trick on me.

"I can open that with my charm." I nodded to the locked gate as I slowed, intending to get out.

Zav looked at it, and the lock fell away. The chain-link gate rolled open.

"Never mind." I parked next to the trucks and got out, eyeing the concrete walls, metal roof, and large timber supports at the front of the building. It was more architecturally interesting than I would have expected.

As we walked to the front, where glass walls and two glass doors showed off a large, empty foyer, Zav waved at my weapons. "I should be able to handle Dobsaurin—the main reason he is a challenge for me is that he will use battle methods that kill innocent beings and destroy cities, whereas it is my duty to protect these things. Out here, I do not think that will be an issue. But stay close to me, and if you see an opportunity to even what he would doubtless try to make uneven odds, do so. Your gun will be useless on him, but the sword may injure him."

"You're certain he's in there?" I glanced at the foyer visible through the glass doors. "I thought everything looked normal."

"I sense people in pain inside."

"Maybe they don't like their jobs."

"No."

I waved for him to go in, the flutters intensifying in my stomach. I was always nervous before a battle and tried to tell myself this wouldn't be any different from usual. It didn't work.

The front doors weren't locked. As soon as we entered, I joined Zav in believing something wasn't right. The only light came through the glass doors. The wall sconces weren't on, and when I found a switch and flipped it, nothing happened.

194

Without hesitating, Zav strode toward a metal door that led deeper into the facility. I hurried to keep up, and we entered a vast chamber full of tanks and pipes, with catwalks barely visible in the shadows overhead. In here, there were no exterior windows, and the lights were also out, though the walls of computers and machinery were working, their colored LEDs glowing in the darkness.

I drew Chopper and thought about using my new Dwarven word to brighten its dim glow, but drawing upon power might alert Dob that we had entered. Instead, I activated my cloaking charm and my night-vision charm. There had been too much daylight to use that one in that forest cave, the trinket designed to work in complete darkness, but the red and yellow computer LEDs weren't bright enough to interfere.

Zav paused and looked back, and I almost bumped into him. I took that to mean I'd disappeared from his senses.

That one is effective, he murmured directly into my mind.

Because he worried Dob was out there to overhear us?

Good, I replied silently.

If Zav couldn't sense me, Dob shouldn't be able to either. That would make it easier for me to jump out and make a sneak attack.

Should I get Sindari too? If I'd been walking in alone, I wouldn't have hesitated.

Your choice, but even when he's using his magic to camouflage himself, I can sense him when he's within about twenty feet of me.

You didn't sense him in the wyvern cave, did you?

Not at first, but I felt him coming before he sprang at me.

That was good to know before we faced off against another dragon. *I'll wait until I see if there's a battle.*

Zav nodded and continued on. He'd surprised me by speaking gently into my mind, not the booming headache-inducing demonstration of power I'd gotten from previous mental communications with dragons.

After a few steps, he paused, lifting his nose in the air. He turned down a walkway between two big tanks. The sound of rushing water reached my ears, and we walked over grating in the floor with a channel of water running through ten feet below. To me, the air smelled faintly of chlorine, but Zav must have detected something else.

He turned down another walkway, following it to the end where the only choice was to climb a ladder up the side of a tank or go back. He crouched and scraped at something on the textured flooring. My night vision wasn't good enough to see what it was.

Straightening again, he looked up, not at the tank but at something hanging from the high ceiling.

I swallowed and followed his gaze. Four bodies dangled down from ropes tied to beams.

CHAPTER 23

"They're the missing goblins," Zav said.

I nodded numbly as I stared upward. At first, I'd thought they were children—my night-vision charm couldn't distinguish skin color well—but the ragged clothing was similar to what the other goblins had worn. Only it was more torn and dark with bloodstains. The victims' faces were mutilated, gouged by talons, and their throats had been slit open.

I managed not to react with horror—I'd seen enough death to be somewhat inured to it—but I did spin a slow circle, searching the shadows above as I thumbed Chopper's worn grip. All those towering tanks would make excellent perches for a predator—and what was a dragon but a massive predator?—to spring down from.

Zav turned, brushed past me, and headed back to the main walkway. *I will attempt to lead us to the people who are still living but in pain.*

Good.

Be wary. I suspect they were only kept alive because Dobsaurin was laying a trap.

As he had been doing with the children in the windmill. Had Zav been in the area a week ago, he might have walked into Dob's trap then.

I'm always wary, trust me. I followed him past more computer equipment as we paralleled the water streaming through the canal under the floor. *Any chance he left a trap but isn't here himself?*

Possibly, but I hope he is here. Better to face him here than in the middle of a populated area.

I wasn't sure I agreed, but I kept scanning the shadows and eyed the top of every tank we passed.

Zav hopped over the railing and off the walkway. He strode toward the grate above the canal, but it wasn't until he crouched down that I saw anything unusual.

Pieces of rope were looped through the grate from below, attached to something out of sight. I came up beside Zav and tried to pick out what was in the dark shadows down there, mostly obscured by the grate. Something hung above the water. No, I realized as one of the shadows stirred. *Someone.*

Three humans dangled from the ropes, which were tied around their wrists to hang them from the grate, their feet dragging in the current. Their heads were bent forward, and I couldn't tell if their faces had been mutilated by dragon talons. If not for the movement one had made, I would have been certain they were dead. Were these the missing joggers?

Zav touched the grate but jerked his hand back. *He put a protective ward on it, no doubt to delay me. Keep an eye out.*

I will.

I stepped back a few feet so I could see up and down the walkway, and I alternated checking that and peering at the tanks all around and the catwalks high above. Even though I couldn't sense the other dragon, my instincts told me there was a threat here. Instincts that even humans had, the ancient genes that warned when something inimical was watching you.

While I waited, I pulled out a fresh magazine for Fezzik. I fished out the three cartridges that Willard had given me, the ones laden with transmitters, and replaced three of the magical ones with them. Then I loaded my gun with the new magazine. I still didn't think it would work, that those cartridges or Nin's magical ones would pierce Dob's hide, but I owed it to Willard to try.

Once I'd re-holstered Fezzik, I caught myself gazing toward an alcove between two banks of computers. It was dark, and I could barely pick out an open door there. Had that door been open when we'd first walked by it?

The urge to investigate it came to me with startling intensity. I would find something in there. I was sure of it.

I started to tell Zav that I would be right back, but he was busy trying to disarm that ward. I shouldn't disturb him.

I frowned because that thought seemed to come from somewhere else. It wasn't like me—I had no problem disturbing Zav with my big mouth. But I found myself climbing back onto the walkway without warning him, my feet turning down that side path and toward the alcove and the door.

My heart thudded in my chest, far faster than made sense given my minimal exertion. It was afraid. And I was too. But for some reason, my feet kept walking, leading me to that open door and the dark chamber beyond. I tried to stop myself—the hand gripping Chopper shook from my effort—but I couldn't.

This was similar to the time that Zav's compulsion had almost driven me to fling myself into that chamber of dark elves in order to get his artifact. Dob was here, and he was using his magic on me. That was the only thing that made sense.

Even knowing that, I couldn't break the hold. It was too strong. *He* was too strong. Chopper's protection wasn't enough. Dob was either more powerful than Zav—I'd feared that all along—or Zav had intentionally made his compulsion less strong. Maybe Zav hadn't been truly trying to get me killed. This guy was another story.

I entered the lightless chamber. Soundlessly, the door shut behind me. And locked.

As my treasonous legs took me deep into the dark chamber, farther and farther from Zav, I envisioned myself ending up gouged and disemboweled and strung up next to the goblins. I tightened my grip on Chopper, hoping I could overcome the compulsion for a few seconds when I needed to and attack the bastard.

Laughter rang in my mind. My hand lifted against my wishes and sheathed Chopper in the back scabbard.

A yellow light started glowing nearby, gleaming off whitewashed walls. I squinted, pain lancing through my head because the night-vision charm amplified the existing light so much. Thankfully, the charm detected the illumination level and turned itself off. As I blinked at blurry spots in my vision, Dob came into view.

This time, he wasn't a dragon. A male elf with flowing silver hair, wearing a green V-neck tunic and loose gray trousers, strolled toward me, a smug smile on his handsome face. Despite the guise, there was no doubt this was Dob. He had the same silver-blue eyes he'd had as a dragon, and that black onyx stone gleamed from the flesh below his collarbones. As my memory had suggested, it didn't hang on a necklace but appeared embedded. Too bad. Maybe I could have found a way to knock off a necklace.

Not that I could move a finger. I was rooted to the cement floor, Chopper put away and Fezzik in its holster. My fingers were a scant inch from the gun's grip, but they might as well have been a mile away.

Dob stopped in front of me and smirked as he looked me up and down. "He doesn't know you're gone."

My mouth wouldn't move to answer him, so I thought my words, figuring he was as telepathic as Zav. *How'd you detect me through my charm?*

I have useful trinkets of my own. He touched his throat, then slid his fingers down to the black onyx. This close to him, I sensed a hint of his aura, but I couldn't sense the stone at all. It had to be what was cloaking him. *And unlike some dragons, I'm not too proud to use external assistance to defeat my enemies.*

Dob prowled around me, his gaze probing.

The first time I'd been in Greemaw's valley, Zav had done something similar, but Zav's gaze had been professionally assessing. Dob touched me a few times, and his eyes held sexual interest. He lifted the hem of my duster, checking out my ass, brushing his fingers against me, cupping me. I didn't let myself shiver in horror or flinch away, not that my body could have moved anyway.

Apparently, *some* dragons weren't so superior that they weren't interested in having sex with humans. Though I would have much preferred it if Dob didn't have that interest, especially when I couldn't do anything to defend myself.

Frustration boiled up in me, but I couldn't even grind my teeth. I wasn't used to feeling helpless. Being hit on, sure, that happened, but I'd always been strong enough and fast enough to handle myself. This gave me a lot of sympathy for all those people who weren't. And it filled me with rage.

Dob stopped in front of me again. "Zavryd'nokquetal has claimed you as a mate, yes?"

No, I thought.

"No?" He twitched a finger.

I found I could move my mouth and tongue enough to speak but little more. "He's made it clear humans are vermin and he's not interested in me."

"No?" Dob's eyes crinkled with laughter. "I find this difficult to believe. He likes elves just fine, or he did once. I suppose that didn't end well for him, though he's still alive, so what is there to complain about? He screwed one of their princesses for a while. Of course, he was cavorting around in elven form then. These days, he's rounded his ears and put on some more muscle to blend in with the locals. He should have the same urges as any human male while he's in that form."

Why was Dob acting like he had all the time in the world to discuss this with me? Even if my cloaking charm was working against me—if I hadn't activated it, Zav would have sensed me being pulled away—Zav would eventually glance back, find me missing, and come looking for me. Any second now, he would charge in here.

Dob leaned in, brushing his knuckles down the side of my face. "I think even an elf would find you worth mounting."

I spat at him. Before I could be pleased that my muscles worked well enough to manage the act, my spittle struck some invisible barrier and never hit his face. Damn it.

"So feisty too. Truly, I do not believe he has not claimed you. I am certain he wants to." Dob's fingers drifted down to stroke my breast.

Such rage filled me that it blurred my vision. First, the panther shifters and now this. What was it, bag a half-elf month?

"I bet you're wrong about a lot of things, asshole."

His eyes flared with silvery light. Oh, how I wanted to whip out Chopper and slam the blade between them. I willed my arm to move, to let me reach up and grab the hilt. Zav had implied I had power. Why couldn't I use it for something useful, like braining this murderer?

Smirking again, Dob lifted his hand and pressed it against my left temple. A new fear charged into my mind. Zav had done that when he'd compelled me to want to get that artifact for him. What would Dob try to make me do?

"Provide a distraction for me, will you, sexy elfling? I do not know why he brought you here, but since I'm positive he feels something for you, I will use that to my advantage. This will be even better than leaving wounded people in his way for his annoying noble self to heal."

Images popped into my mind, images that were not of my own making. I saw myself striding out there and seducing Zav, having sex with him on the walkway while Dob did… Dob did not show me what he planned to do. Bite Zav's head off while he was in the throes of passion?

I couldn't believe this idiot thought that would work. He would have been better off putting me in danger, not that I was going to speak and give him that idea.

"I will be curious to see if you are telling the truth—it's interesting that I can't read any of your thoughts except those you vocalize in your mind to me—or if it's clear that you and he have rutted like animals before." Dob tilted his head. "After he's dead, you'll come with me. I believe you'll find this encounter too brief to be satisfying, but I'll make sure you don't go away longing."

He gripped my shoulder and turned me toward the door. "Ah, but that won't quite do."

He unbuckled Chopper's harness. Fresh horror filled me. I'd have an even harder time breaking his compulsion without the magical protection the blade lent me. Not that it was helping right now anyway… Asking it to stave off a dragon was too much.

After Dob pulled off the harness, he tugged off my duster. My limbs moved enough to let him do so, but they still wouldn't respond to orders from my own brain. I felt like a doll being manhandled. He dropped the duster on the floor, then surprised me by putting the sword harness back on me.

"He would be suspicious if you returned without your weapons."

Right, because me walking up and kissing him wouldn't be at all suspicious.

Dob prowled around to my front again, eyed my chest, and lifted a finger. A long claw—or was that a dragon's talon?—sprouted from it like a macabre press-on nail for Halloween. He sliced it down the front of my shirt. Not the whole way, but enough to show my bra and the tops of my breasts.

"I do not get paid enough for this bullshit," I growled, refusing to show any fear.

"Ah, that's enough talking." He patted my cheek, the claw clipping my ear and drawing blood. "I don't want you doing anything but kissing that righteous bastard."

A warm drop of blood ran down the side of my face. He smiled, leaned in, and licked it off. My stomach roiled. What would happen if it tried to vomit while none of my muscles were working?

"No clues to let him know you're anything but the eager concubine he's been working with all day."

At least it was clear Dob hadn't been spying on us all day. Eager concubines didn't promise to shove swords in their masters' butts.

He circled behind me again, swatted me on the ass, and whispered, "Go to him," in my ear.

Where will you be? I wanted to ask it out loud, but as he'd promised, I couldn't move my lips again.

Poised to take advantage of his distraction. He chuckled into my mind.

My legs started moving, taking me toward the locked door. As it unlocked and swung open, I saw bodies wedged behind an equipment console. They hadn't been visible to me when I'd been walking in. My heart sank even further. They wore the uniforms of the staff. Dob had killed everybody here, aside from the few he'd left alive to distract Zav.

And I was going out to distract him further. I shouted obscenities in my mind. Zav had warned me this could happen if I didn't let him put a mental compulsion of his own on me. I'd been too proud to even consider it. Now that choice might get us both killed.

CHAPTER 24

The door opened, and I walked back into the main room. The cool air stirred gooseflesh on my bare arms and made me wish I'd chosen a sweater to wear under my duster, not a tank top. I couldn't sense Dob behind me, but then I'd barely sensed his aura when he'd been standing in front of me, shredding my shirt.

On the other side of the walkway, Zav knelt, a hand on the shoulder of one of two people lying on the floor beneath him. They wore grimy, damp exercise clothes. A puddle and a trail of water showed a spot where the third person might have been hauled up before walking—or running—out. I chose to believe that rather than that the third person had been lost to the current.

The grate was open—no, Zav had torn it off and tossed it across the water channel—so I could tell nobody was left in the canal. I sensed him using his magic, healing the two men. Had Zav noticed I was gone? He must have.

He glanced back at me as I approached and frowned. "Where did you go? You shouldn't have wandered off in here."

Wandered off? He thought I'd decided to roam of my own accord?

One of my usual sarcastic responses rose to mind, but what came out was, "I thought I saw something. I checked on it. I don't think he's here anymore." My tongue felt thick in my mouth, but the words came out sounding normal to my own ears, and my shoulder twitched in a shrug.

Zav's first glance had been quick and dismissive, but he looked longer the second time. "What happened to your clothes?"

His gaze didn't linger on my chest the way Dob's had, but even the brief perusal sent a flush of hot desire through me. When his violet eyes met mine, that heat turned molten. My hips swayed as I drew closer.

As if I ever walked like that. Would my puppeteer move my limbs for me for all of this?

"I got hot," I said.

One of the people sat up, but I barely noticed anything except Zav. A strong carnal desire coursed through me, urging me to get closer, to wrap my body around his.

Zav? I thought, my mind the only thing I was in control of. *Can you hear me?*

He was scrutinizing me, but he didn't give any indication that he heard the words. Was Dob blocking my thoughts somehow?

"What's going on?" the man asked, rubbing his shoulder and staring at me in confusion.

The guy next to him groaned and rolled to his hands and knees, more out of it than his colleague.

"You should be healed enough to get out of here now," Zav told them without looking away from me. "Go the way the woman did and do not look back."

His voice rang with power, power that sent a shiver of desire through me, and the two men, though confused, hurried obediently away.

"Any chance *you're* hot?" I smiled and stepped close enough to Zav to rest a hand on his chest. "I've never seen you without that robe on, and I'm terribly curious what's under it."

That cheesy line made me want to gag. *Zav!* I shouted in my mind. *Listen to me. Can't you hear my thoughts? Dob is in the other room. Maybe he's in here by now, sneaking up behind you.*

"Are you?" He arched an eyebrow and let his gaze dip to my half-bared chest. He slid an arm around my back and pulled me closer, then gazed into my eyes.

Dob wasn't *right*, was he? That Zav was actually attracted to me? It was ridiculous.

Zav leaned closer, his forehead resting against mine. *I see his compulsion on you,* he spoke into my mind.

Thank his scaly ancestors! My hand caressed his chest through his robe. I sure hoped he could tell Dob was making me do that and that I didn't *want* this. It was irritating as hell that his gaze and his hand on the small of my back were turning me on. I was going to blame Dob for that, too, not the long, *long* time I'd gone without male companionship.

I can break it, Zav added, *but as soon as I do, he'll know.*

Can you hear my thoughts?

From the way he was peering into my eyes, as if seeking an answer there, I assumed not. Great, how was I supposed to tell him he was in danger right now? I envisioned Dob sneaking around behind him with some giant dragon-slaying weapon. Or would he simply shift into his regular form and snap down with massive fangs and break Zav's human neck?

I assume he wants to catch me off guard and take advantage of my distraction. Zav rubbed my back through my thin shirt, fingers trailing up my spine.

Pretending to be into it, as Dob expected?

My body responded with embarrassing enthusiasm, and I leaned into him, aroused by the tingle of power washing over me, by his roaming hands, by his gaze locked onto mine.

I still can't sense him. Zav lifted his other hand to my face, fingers gentle and caressing where Dob's had been cold and cruel. *Play along for a minute, and we'll see if I can make him think I'm more distracted than I am.*

Play along? I wished it were a game, that I had control over my body and that I wasn't doing this, that I wasn't mashing my breasts to his chest and lifting my lips to his for a kiss achingly full of longing and desire. The raw power that raced over my skin lit my nerves on fire, and I struggled to remember what was going on, to think of the danger and not of his hand on my ass, his lips nibbling at mine. My ragged breaths echoed in my ears between our kisses.

I hoped Zav believed I was only responding this way because of Dob, that I wasn't this pathetically into him. That I wasn't groping him through his robe, wondering where the seam was so I could touch real flesh and lean, sculpted muscle. That I wasn't pressing against him, tempted to wrap both legs around—

My brain snapped like a rubber band, and Dob's influence vanished in an instant.

Zav whirled away from me, leaped across the canal, and crashed into

Dob. He was still in his elven form, and he'd been approaching with a glowing white sword I hadn't seen. I'd been too busy being horny.

Snarling, I yanked out Chopper and Fezzik as Zav flung up his hands and Dob was hurled twenty feet. He crashed into a tank hard enough to dent it and tear one of the bolts from the floor. The impact would have broken a man's back, but Dob bounced off, landed on his feet in a crouch, and pointed his sword at Zav.

Already chasing after him, Zav dove to the side as a beam of white energy poured forth from the sword. It shot past him, just missing his shoulder, and slammed into the catwalk near me like a missile. The catwalk blew, shrapnel pelting me in the back as I whirled away. Pieces dug through my thin tank top—and my flesh—but I gritted my teeth, refusing to cry out. I would *not* distract Zav.

As Zav flung a magical attack at Dob, I took aim with Fezzik. In his dragon form, those special bullets would never pierce his hide, but maybe he would be more vulnerable as an elf.

All three bullets slammed into his chest, but they bounced off as if they'd hit titanium.

Dob leered across the water at me. *Don't worry, little elfling. I'm not offended. I'm still going to screw you later.*

I fired again, aiming for his glowing silver-blue eyes. Maybe Nin's magical rounds would have better luck.

But an invisible shield protected Dob now. Even my magical bullets bounced off. One slammed into a tank full of liquid, and the stuff dribbled out onto the floor.

Zav and Dob hurled waves of pure energy at each other at the same time. I sensed the tremendous power even though the attacks were invisible to the eye.

Zav crouched low, bracing himself as if against a hurricane. The blast of power riffled through his hair and batted at his robe, but it didn't knock him over. When Zav's attack struck Dob, it hurled him all the way to the wall. He crashed against the cement, snaps sounding and cracks zigzagging up to the ceiling.

Dob snarled, shook his head like a dog, elven hair flying, and between one blink and the next changed into his dragon form. He sprang into the air and rushed at Zav, but Zav must have sensed him changing, for he did the same. The black dragon was ready for the silver's charge.

I stared as they clashed, knowing I should do something to help but not knowing what. They moved so fast, jaws snapping and talons raking, that I couldn't follow the battle. One of their tails bashed against a tank, and it toppled as if it weighed nothing and hadn't been secured by steel and cement. If I tried to get close, they would knock me over—or *kill* me—without even noticing.

"Sindari," I whispered, holding my charm.

Maybe he would have better luck helping.

But as Sindari formed at my side, I realized something. Zav was larger than Dob and just as fast and agile. He kept coming out on top in their skirmishes. Blood flowed from a dozen gashes in Dob's silver scales, whereas Zav only had one significant cut.

Zav maneuvered atop his foe and pinned him, sinking his teeth into Dob's shoulder. He snarled, shaking his head like a massive Rottweiler killing a rabbit. He snapped his jaws with lightning speed, changing his grip and biting into the onyx gem embedded in Dob's chest. Snarling savagely, he tore it out, along with a huge chunk of scale and flesh.

Dob screeched and flailed, growing more desperate. His wild, pained eyes glanced my way, and I saw the threat an instant too late.

I ran, diving behind the remains of the walkway. I expected him to hurl a fireball or a wave of pure energy, but he attacked my mind, his power lancing into it like a dagger to my brain.

A scream escaped my lips before I could bite down and stop it. I curled into a ball, almost dropping my weapons, but at the last second, I tightened my grip. Chopper had always helped me repel magical attacks before, and I needed its help now.

Agony stabbed behind my eyes, but I willed myself to push it away, to build an impenetrable wall around my mind.

A roar penetrated the haze of pain, Sindari running away from my side to attack Dob. Another roar came from the dragons. Was that Zav?

I sensed part of his power wrapping protectively around my mind. The mental attack disappeared, and the pain left so abruptly that the cessation almost made me pass out. I growled, pushing back the darkness encroaching at the edges of my eyes. Weapons in hand, I shoved myself to my feet.

I was in time to see Zav go flying backward into two tanks. Dob pushed off, wings flapping madly. He hurled another attack, not at Zav but at the back wall of the building. It blew outward as if he'd ignited explosives.

He was escaping.

"No, you don't." I raced toward the new exit, hoping to cut him off. I jammed Fezzik in my holster as I ran—the bullets had done no good—but I kept Chopper.

Dob banked right in front of me, struggling to navigate in a facility that was cavernous to humans but cramped to the great dragons. I leaped and slashed at his foot, lamenting that I couldn't reach a more vital target.

The blade glowed a fierce blue as it cut through one of the dragon's toes. Dob screeched and glared back as he flew. I dropped flat to my belly as angry power blasted toward me, crackling over my skin like wildfire. It didn't strike me full on, but the force was enough to send me skidding ten feet and rolling onto my back.

The next time we meet, Dob's words thundered in my mind, *you will die.*

"So much for him wanting to screw me," I muttered.

Black wings flapped past above me. Zav was giving chase.

"Get the bastard," I yelled after him and sat up.

Don't get in the way again, Sindari warned me, coming to my side. Or maybe to stand on me if I got up. *He was distracted when you screamed and the silver knocked him back.*

It wasn't my fault Dob attacked me.

You were shooting at him.

Yeah, ineffectively. *Zav asked me to help if I could. It's not like coming with him was my idea. He—*

I halted and gaped as green lightning streaked up from the pavement outside the exit hole Dob had blown. Dob had already escaped, flying out of my sight, but the lightning caught Zav, wrapping around him and crackling with power that held the sun's intensity. Even from a hundred feet away, I felt it, like a swarm of wasps attacking from all sides.

Zav crashed down, hitting the pavement like a wrecked airplane. The pain assailing me faded, and I pushed myself to my feet.

Outside, Zav lay crumpled on the ground. I swore. If it had felt like wasps from a hundred feet away, what had it been like to be right in the middle of it? And what if Dob came back to press his advantage now that his trap had sprung?

I ran for the exit, my body aching from my harsh ride across the hard floor. With Chopper in hand, I envisioned protecting Zav from an attack. As if cutting off the tip of Dob's toe had actually done anything.

When I reached Zav's side, my blade raised as I scanned the gray sky, a soft mist fell on my warm cheeks but nothing more. I didn't see the silver dragon. But I kept my sword up. Dob could be above the low cloud cover, preparing to swoop down.

He is fleeing to the south, Zav spoke wearily into my mind. *I can sense him now.*

He spat weakly and the black onyx oval—and a chunk of Dob's chest—tumbled out onto the pavement.

"Gross," I said, though I was relieved that he—and I—would be able to sense Dob's aura now. "Uhm, will you be all right?"

Concerned that Zav wasn't making an attempt to get up from the pavement, I stepped close enough to rest a hand on his cool side. Guilt crept into me. He was only injured because Dob had attacked me and Zav had paused his own attack to protect me.

I *hated* that I'd been used as a pawn in this, hated that I'd been someone's weakness to exploit. Not once but *twice* that bastard had used me.

It didn't matter that me coming along had been Zav's idea, not mine. He'd probably expected me to be able to take care of myself or at least do enough to be useful. I remembered him asking what powers I had beyond my charms and weapons and having to admit that I had nothing. Only a sword that was death to dragon toes. Maybe it could hurt more than a toe if I could ever reach anything higher. How did the knights that slew dragons in stories do it? Trampolines?

I knew there would be traps, Zav admitted, not answering my question. *He had days to work on them. But in the bloodlust of the hunt, I wasn't thinking. I should not have charged out recklessly.*

Self-reproach was going around. "*Are* you going to be all right? Is there anyone I can get to help?"

In this forsaken world?

"Maybe Zoltan the vampire alchemist has a nice potion."

Zav pushed himself into a sitting position, his wings drooping at his sides. *I am in pain, but I still have my power. I will create a portal and go see someone who can heal me more efficiently than I would naturally. I have no wish to crawl into a dank cave in these woods and spend weeks regenerating.*

I almost said that if he could regenerate in human form, he could stay in my apartment, but I couldn't think of anything more awkward after that weird compulsory kiss that had ended up far too real, at least for me, than I could have imagined. Besides, if he could go home and get healed by another dragon, that would be best.

"Do you think that's what Dob will do?" I didn't like the idea of him hanging out in the area when Zav was gone, especially now that he wanted to kill me instead of simply using me.

Possibly. I hope he returns to that cave where I set a trap. Zav clacked his jaws together in what sounded like appreciation—or delight. *Either way, he should not be strong enough to bother you for a few days. With luck, I will return by then. He killed goblins and humans cruelly and for no point other than to vex me.*

"Will you try to hunt him down and kill him for that?"

It is against our laws to kill dragons and dragon-kin. It will be my duty to capture him for punishment and rehabilitation.

"Will that be as difficult as it sounds?"

Yes. Not because I can't capture him but because his family has powerful allies on the Dragon Justice Court and in prominent positions throughout the Cosmic Realms. It is likely they will, through political maneuvering, be able to have him set free without punishment.

I didn't like the sound of that.

Zav turned his gaze toward me. *You will be able to make your way home safely?*

My cheeks flushed at the insinuation that I'd be helpless without my dragon bodyguard. But after my performance today, how could I expect him to think anything else?

"Yeah." I jerked a thumb toward the parking lot on the other side of the building where my Jeep waited. "No problem."

I didn't ask him if he would come back and help with my problem, not when we hadn't accomplished what I'd said I would help him with first. As I'd feared all along, I would have to figure out a way to deal with the shifter brothers on my own.

"Sorry I wasn't more help," I added. "And that you got hurt because of me."

Zav continued to gaze down at me. I was still standing there, holding Chopper. He probably thought it was silly that I'd run out, thinking I could actually do something to protect him.

I asked you to come. It was my mistake.

That made me feel worse instead of better. Pathetically useless.

He opened a portal, a great shimmering silver puddle of energy in the air. But he paused before stepping through it. He transformed into his human form, and it was a startling reflection of the injuries he'd received as a dragon.

His eyes held pain, his dark hair was tousled, and blood dripped from a gouge in his temple. Even his robe was shredded, hinting of wounds to his body.

But he still radiated power, and seeing him in human form again rekindled memories of that kiss. *More* than memories. Even bruised and battered, and with Dob's influence fading, I wanted to step closer to him, to bask in his power. In that stupid alluring aura of his that I couldn't wash off. It was definitely for the best that he was leaving for a while. As it was, I feared my dreams would be distressingly erotic for the next few nights.

Zav stepped close and lifted a hand to the side of my face. I froze, afraid he was going to leave me with some new compulsion. But all he did was send his healing power through me, stealing the aches and pains throughout my body, and mending the tiny cut Dob had left on my face.

Tears welled in my eyes. Why was he wasting his energy on me when he should use it for healing himself? Did he feel guilty because I'd been hurt trying to help him with his foe? Could a haughty, arrogant dragon even *feel* guilt?

He rubbed my cheek with his thumb and gazed into my eyes as the healing energy faded, but my awareness of him and his touch didn't fade. The urge to kiss him returned to me. But that would be a bad idea. He would snort and remind me that he wasn't attracted to me. There would be no reason for him to play along a second time.

He leaned his face toward mine, and for a startled moment, I thought he would kiss *me*, but he pressed his forehead against mine instead and murmured two words. "*Aryoshanti sharyo.*"

Was I supposed to say that back? Would it kill the moment to ask what it meant? More importantly, was he looking at my lips and thinking how sexy they were, or was that my imagination? Definitely my imagination. He was probably disgusted that he'd pretended to be into me back in there. Though he didn't *look* disgusted. He looked… contemplative.

Zav shook his head slightly, as if he'd reached some decision, then lowered his hand and stepped back. Without another word, he walked into the portal and disappeared.

I bit my lip, afraid my reaction—or non-reaction—had been the wrong one. I should have closed my eyes, leaned into him, and let myself appreciate his gesture. It had seemed meaningful. But my irreverent mind had been too busy yammering for me to realize it.

Now, with Zav gone and sweat drying on my skin in the damp air, I felt cold and alone. The moment seemed a representation of my life. Always alone. Never with someone to go home to, or go home with. I'd picked that life, but it didn't mean I didn't regret it. It didn't mean I didn't sometimes long for companionship.

I rubbed my face, trying to push aside the funk. It wasn't as if I was missing *Zav*. The epitome of infuriating arrogance. I'd have to be nuts to want that in my life.

"You're losing it, girl," I muttered and headed inside to fetch my duster.

I didn't need any more dragon distractions. I had a friend to help.

CHAPTER 25

Hammering noises came from the inside of Nin's no-longer-charred food truck. It was still parked in the same spot in the commissary compound, but I'd heard she'd successfully driven it around the block and nothing had fallen off. With *Crying Tiger* freshly painted in bright blue letters on the side, the truck was starting to look like it had before the fire.

I knocked on the door, and Nin came out with a paint-stained rag. She smiled warmly at me, then waved at a security camera mounted under the awning.

"Is that a new one or did it survive the fire?" I asked.

"It is the old one, and it *did* survive the fire. Once I was able to get the footage downloaded, I learned that it caught the face of the person who started the fire." She pulled out a folded piece of paper and showed me a color printout.

"That's the leopard shifter I pummeled. Too bad it wasn't one of the Pardus brothers themselves. I'd have an easier time getting backup if they were being blatant about their illegal activities."

"Do you need backup? You had mentioned that the dragon might assist you with negotiations."

"I know, but he got injured and is back in his world recuperating."

Nin's eyes widened. "What could injure a dragon?"

"Another dragon. Specifically, a magical trap set by one." I waved in dismissal, not wanting to think about Zav or Dob. It was time to focus and complete this mission. "I need to handle this without him. I shouldn't have been relying on some outsider anyway. I'm capable of dealing with shifters by myself... though I do acknowledge that I'll need a few distractions, things going on outside while I'm sneaking in. Why, you ask? Because when I drove by this morning, there were even *more* of those cat shifters loitering at the Pardus house. I'm honestly flummoxed. What could possibly be there that's so interesting?"

"Sex, drugs, and rock and roll?" Nin seemed earnest about the suggestion.

"Probably, but that can't be all of it." I shrugged. "I don't care what they're doing. I just want to solve your problem. So, as I said, I'll need distractions. That's why I called this meeting. Let's wait until Dimitri and his phone get here before I explain things."

"His phone?"

"Zoltan has agreed to be on a call with us." I glanced at the time. "In fourteen minutes. He was unwilling to wake up before his regular evening rising hour."

"I will assist you in any way I can," Nin said.

"Thank you. I've already made some arrangements, but you can definitely help by providing some weapons for—"

My phone buzzed with a text message, and I nodded.

"Good, one of my distractions has been confirmed. Someone from Willard's office is making arrangements for the police to visit the Northern Pride's headquarters tomorrow at nine p.m. They've got a warehouse near the freeway at the north end of Woodinville. It seems that people have been complaining about them operating a meth lab out of it, so a warrant is being issued for a search." I tapped the file Willard had sent about the Northern Pride. I'd finally had time to read everything about them and brainstorm ideas.

"I have not heard of a shifter-operated meth lab," Nin said.

"Me either—Willard's research says the shifters meet at their headquarters regularly to socialize and play with boxes and that's about it—but it's amazing how rumors can catch on and spread like wildfire. I'm hoping that a strategically timed visit from the police will prompt a number of shifters to be called back north and leave fewer for me to deal with at the brothers' house."

216

"Play with boxes?" Dimitri said, rounding the corner of the truck and joining us.

"I may have filled in that detail myself. The report only mentions pool tables. But workers in the neighboring buildings *have* reported suspicious activity at their headquarters at night before, so it wasn't hard to get a couple of them to snitch to the police."

Willard was also going to send a couple of subtle plainclothes agents to the mobile-home park tomorrow to clear out the houses around the Pardus house—an unfortunate gas leak would require the homeowners to stay in a hotel for the night. I *hoped* to take care of the brothers without causing collateral damage or hurting anyone nearby, but it was better to be safe than sorry.

It had taken me some time, and a reminder of past favors done, to convince Willard to do any of this, since this wasn't an assignment she'd given me or even wanted me on, but I'd promised I'd be back on the dragon problem sooner once I knew Nin was safe.

I pointed at Dimitri. "Is it late enough to get Zoltan on the line?"

"I'll check." Dimitri tapped his phone screen.

"Thanks. Nin, got anything we can use to sit on? Let's get this party started."

While she brought out coolers to serve as chairs, explaining that she would have to use them for food storage until she could get her refrigerator repaired, I answered a text regarding one of my other distractions and summoned Sindari. Since I would need his help, it made sense to include him in the planning.

I perched on the edge of a blue Coleman cooler while Nin and Dimitri sat opposite me on some knockoff brand called the Insulation Sensation.

"I am here," Zoltan's Hungarian accent came from the phone.

Dimitri held up the screen, the vampire's infrared lights glowing red behind him, so we could see each other.

"Zoltan, I'm going to infiltrate a compound of panther, lion, and tiger shifters up in Bothell. One-on-one, I can usually handle these guys, but there have been at least ten hanging out there every time I've gone by."

"A shifter compound? I am not aware of such a thing in the area."

"Technically, it's a manufactured house in a senior mobile-home park."

"How formidable."

"*They're* formidable, and I think they've got magical defenses on the house."

"I should hope so. You really can't call it a compound otherwise. Unless there are some turrets and a portcullis, I believe I'm going to have to downgrade it to a lesser structure."

I rubbed my face, remembering the first time I'd visited Zoltan and tried to extract information from him. He did have a tendency to wander off topic.

"Is there at least a moat?" Zoltan asked.

"There's a river behind the back yard."

He pursed his lips in disapproval. "I fear that is insufficient. How could a river contain half-starved alligators strategically placed to munch on invaders foolish enough to attempt crossing when the drawbridge is up?"

"Zoltan, can you make me some alchemical weapons by tomorrow? Ideally something especially effective on felines, though that's not a requirement. I can go in wearing a gas mask if I have to. I just need to get this out of the way soon. There's an injured dragon out there that wants me dead, and I'd like to make sure Nin is safe before he shows up to kill me."

Dimitri's brow wrinkled. "Zav?"

"No, Dob. Zav went home."

"I do not wish you to be killed, Val," Nin said gravely.

"Thank you. I'd prefer to avoid it too."

"You are one of my best customers. You go through ammunition like candy corn in a bowl at Halloween."

"So it's true love that has spurred your concern for me."

She grinned, then smiled shyly at Dimitri. She was probably appreciative that he'd been helping her fix her truck. I wondered if Dimitri had explained yet that he was into guys. And tigers. Though his interest in those was probably platonic—and shared by many. Sindari had strolled over to sit between them, his head level with their heads, and Dimitri was absently running a hand down his furry back while Nin rubbed his ears. Sindari's tongue lolled out slightly, a blissful expression on his face.

"What are you doing, Sindari?" I asked.

Sitting regally and politely allowing your human allies to touch me, as would be proper for an ambassador of Del'noth sent to foster peace among our peoples.

"Your tongue is hanging out."

Regally.

"Does he talk back to you?" Nin asked curiously.

"Yes, telepathically."

"Does he mind having his ears rubbed?"

Sindari leaned his head toward her.

"I highly doubt it. Just don't turn your back on him. Sometimes, his predator urges kick in and he has to pounce."

I assume I will be permitted to pounce on those obnoxious panthers tomorrow, Sindari told me.

Absolutely.

"I do not know of any formulas that would specifically target felines." Zoltan had opened an ancient tome and was flipping through it. "There are a number of human chemical substances, such as antifreeze and insect and rodent bait, that can cause seizures and death in cats if they lick it off their paws."

"I don't think I can get panther shifters to lick their paws for me. I was thinking more of an aerosol."

"Hm."

Time to move on to the next request. "Dimitri, if I give you some money, can you make some projectile yard art that spits poisoned darts?"

"Projectile yard art?" He arched his brows.

"Whatever I need to call it to put it in your wheelhouse and make you interested in working on it."

"I'm not sure how much I can get done by tomorrow, but I can see what I can come up with. You don't need to pay me. I'm here to help Nin. Er, wait. You probably need to give me enough money to get some good parts. The campground I'm staying at is expensive, so I've almost gone through what I made at the farmers market already."

"Why don't you stay in a hotel?" Nin asked.

"Hotels are *more* expensive."

"You can sleep on my couch if you want," I said.

"Didn't you say your apartment got broken into again?"

"And ransacked, yes, with bone knives left sticking into things. But the inoffensive couch was not targeted."

"I'll keep your offer in mind."

"And, yes, I'll pay for any parts you need."

"It must be nice being rich," Dimitri said wistfully.

Rich, right. I wasn't getting paid for this, and there was no way I'd be able to complete the dragon-slaying gig and earn the big money Willard had teased me with.

My phone alerted me to a new text. Confirmation of a job accepted.

"Nin, I mentioned that I could use some loaner weapons. I've just finalized another part of my distraction. Some toughs are going to park in front of the Pardus house and shoot any shifters that run out—and maybe put a few rounds in the front door for decoration. It would be nice if they had bullets that could bite into shifter hide."

"Yes, of course."

"What toughs will you hire?" Dimitri asked.

"Why, do you want to volunteer?"

"I'm an artist, Val."

"Too bad. That sliding door on your van would be great for drive-by shootings."

"Is it okay to find it strange that you've considered this?"

"I can't help it that I've been the target of frequent drive-by shootings. Gregor's Gang over in West Seattle is who I've hired to come up north for this. They're werewolves. They won't risk themselves or feel any loyalty to me—" when I'd contacted them, I'd done it anonymously and offered to pay in cash, "—but for enough money, they're happy to arrive en masse and shoot up an establishment."

"I see you also agree that it must be downgraded from a compound," Zoltan murmured, flipping the pages in his book.

"Don't werewolves hate you?" Dimitri asked.

"That's why I'm not telling them who's paying for the job."

"You don't think they'll figure it out when they arrive and see you there?"

"Nobody's going to see me." I tapped my cloaking charm. "Not until I'm ready to strike."

"Will you kill the Pardus brothers?" Nin asked softly, her eyes dark with concern. She'd asked me to find a way to get them to leave her alone, not to assassinate them.

"Ideally not, especially since Willard told me to stay away from them—something about the Northern Pride having a hotshot lawyer—but I have an idea."

"Cutting off their fingers so they can't bother *anyone*?" Dimitri asked.

"I don't think that would work. Shifters heal quite well. They might be able to regenerate digits." I wondered if Dob would regrow the toe I'd cut off his foot. Maybe he would be less bitter if I hadn't permanently scarred him. Probably wishful thinking. "I'm going to assume, since I spent the greater part of yesterday in close proximity to Zav, that his dragon aura is on me, noticeable for those full-bloods who can sense such things."

"Oh yes," Zoltan said in a distracted tone as he continued to read. "I can smell it all the way over here."

I started to ignore him but frowned as I debated if that was possible. It couldn't be. He couldn't smell me from more than ten miles away—not even a cat or wolf shifter could do that—and a magical aura didn't travel over cell waves.

"Are you joking?" I asked.

"Yes, but I trust I'm correct. Have you mated with him yet? It seems inevitable."

Dimitri fell off his cooler.

I rubbed my face and did not allow my mind to return to that kiss. "No, but that's actually what I'm thinking about."

"Mating with him?" Zoltan asked.

"*No*. But if you believe that and Dob believed that, then maybe the Pardus brothers will too. And instead of denying it, as I keep doing, what if I let them think it's true? I won't lie, just smile and let them believe what they will. Pissing off a dragon is generally regarded as a bad idea—"

Generally? Sindari asked. *It's regarded unanimously in all seventeen of the Cosmic Realms to be a horrific idea.*

Yes, thank you. "—so wouldn't they be more inclined to negotiate with me if they think Zav could show up at any time and stomp them like the furry little maggots they are?"

As much as I hated the idea of pretending I had a super powerful dragon backer, it was hard for me to imagine an alternative other than killing the brothers. I wouldn't cry if that happened, but I'd hate to make trouble for Willard and her office. I also didn't want to earn the ire—and the arrest warrant—of the local police, which could happen if the Pride's lawyer was good and the Pardus brothers didn't yet have a criminal record.

Besides, Zav kept wanting to use me. Wasn't it fair if I used him?

Dimitri maneuvered himself back onto the cooler. He still looked stunned and didn't resume petting Sindari until Sindari looked expectantly at him.

"Well," Dimitri finally said, "it would make *me* want to be in your good graces."

"And me as well." Zoltan closed his book and looked up.

Nin nodded in agreement.

"Since cats of all types have extremely good noses," Zoltan said, "and feline shifters retain that feature even in their human form, I believe a particularly potent gas could debilitate them. I happen to have here the odor of a weasel and the tears of a griffin—" he pointed to rows of bottles on shelves behind him, "—which can not only take out a basilisk but can be combined with a few other ingredients to make a sulfur-based chemical agent that causes severe burning of the eyes, skin, and respiratory tract. A cat's nose would be particularly susceptible."

"What about *my* respiratory tract?" The last thing I needed was to have an asthma attack in the middle of the enemy lair. *Again.*

"I suggest a gas mask that covers your eyes, nose, and mouth."

Memories of the gas chamber in Basic Training came to mind, of how hot and stuffy it had been under the chemical suits and masks we wore. I'd never had the delightful experience of being gassed in actual combat, but I could envision how fun it would be to fight in that getup. And then, if the shifters managed to tear off my mask, there was the possibility that my lungs would be more susceptible than a cat's nose to the horrific stuff.

I was about to ask Zoltan if he had anything else when he added, "Alternatively, I can make you a small charm that would protect you from inhaled threats."

That sounded much more appealing. I could always make room on my necklace for more charms.

"How much is all this going to cost me?"

"Oh, a great deal." Zoltan beamed a smile at me. "These ingredients do not come cheaply, nor is my exceedingly valuable time inexpensive."

"How much does odor of weasel go for?" Dimitri asked. "And how do you bottle it?"

"You bottle the whole weasel," Zoltan said, "and open the jar to let out the odor as needed."

"Ew."

"Did you think a horrific mustard gas could be made from something appealingly fragrant?" I asked him.

"I guess not."

"Send me the invoice, Zoltan," I said. "And keep in mind that I am a lowly servant of the government employed only on a part-time basis."

"Don't you also freelance?" Zoltan asked.

"I'm freelancing right now. Pro bono."

"Pro bono! That's horrific. What kind of entrepreneur are you?"

I squinted at the phone. "Are you Slytherin, Zoltan?"

"What?"

"Google it. Send me the invoice." I waved for Dimitri to close the line.

Nin stood up and hugged me. "You must let me pay you for this, Val. How much will all this cost you?"

"You're going to make me some snazzy magical armor, right? That'll make us even."

She twisted her lips dubiously, as if she didn't believe that would be sufficient to make us even. I disagreed.

"Val, I would like to pay you."

"Nope." I patted her on the shoulder. "Don't worry about it. If you want, you can throw in a few free lunches. And some nice magical grenades for my incursion."

"Grenades are free of charge for my best customers."

"Nin, you have to count some of this stuff toward what you think you need to pay me."

"I will. The lunches." She nodded firmly. "Free lunches for the rest of the year. At an average of ten dollars a meal, if you come every day, that would be just under two thousand dollars in lunches."

"That sounds good." I traveled far too frequently to take advantage of that many days, and the armor and grenades would be a lot more valuable to me, but if it would make her feel better... "Is it a deal?"

Nin stuck her hand out. "Deal."

"Val?" Dimitri sounded concerned.

"You're not going to ask me about mating with dragons, are you? Because I'm not doing that, I have no plans to do that, and I wouldn't know the first thing about it." I already wondered how I would keep from flushing in embarrassment every time Zav came around in his human form. Was it wrong to be relieved that he'd had to leave Earth instead of awkwardly riding back to town in the Jeep with me?

"No, I was wondering what you should do when you're ready to get up but there's a tiger sitting on your foot."

CHAPTER 26

The next night, as the last of the long June daylight faded from the western sky, I crouched in the reeds by the river, looking toward the back door of the Pardus brothers' manufactured home. By now, the police should have knocked at the door of the Northern Pride's warehouse a few miles to the northeast, but it hadn't drawn away any of the magical beings inside yet.

I sensed ten shifters and the same magical being with an unidentifiable aura that had been in the basement on my previous visits. Presumably the person Inga had said was making enchanted weapons and bullets for the brothers—for less than the awful pay they'd been giving her.

"I want to find that basement before I confront them," I murmured.

Sindari crouched at my side. We were both in stealth mode, mine delivered by my charm, and his a natural part of his magic. So far, the only being I'd encountered who could see through my charm was Dob. I was crossing my fingers that he was still wounded and holed up in a cave somewhere—maybe the one Zav had laid a trap in. Even if he wasn't, he shouldn't be able to detect me anymore now that Zav had ripped that onyx stone out of his chest.

Dimitri was in his van at the entrance to the mobile-home park, lined up on the side of the road with two white vans, each with four werewolf shifters inside, all armed with Nin's magical weapons. Dimitri was acting as my liaison. I would text him to send them in, and the werewolves would come raise a ruckus for an hour, and then receive the second half of their payment. The wolves didn't know I was the one footing the bill.

I will circumnavigate the premises and look for an outside entrance to the basement we suspect. Sindari trotted off, disappearing into the shadows.

That's a lofty word to describe walking around the house.

My people are articulate.

They do a lot of wordsmithing out on the tundra where you hunt?

We use poetry to woo female Zhinevarii.

I wouldn't have guessed. On what subjects? Philosophy? Feelings? The beauty of nature?

Often on the exultation of the hunt, of the excitement of stalking and chasing down one's prey, and of feasting on sumptuous fresh, hot, still-twitching meat.

I was sorry I'd asked. *And that works on females of your species?*

Naturally. Would it not work on you?

I guess I don't know. Nobody has ever penned me poetry about meat.

A shame. No wonder you are lonely.

Had I ever admitted that to him? I rarely even admitted it to myself. This conversation had gotten less fun.

I've never asked, Sindari. Do you have a mate?

I do not currently have a partner, but I have sired children. My people usually have several mates in their lives.

They're not into monogamy?

Only during mating season. Sindari padded back into view. *I have heard dragons mate for life, if that's of interest to you.*

I squinted at him. *Why would it be?*

He didn't truly think I'd been flirting with Zav the other day, did he? He hadn't been in our world when Dob had been diddling with my mind.

Since you're so often the object of dragon interest of late, it would behoove you to know more about them.

That was probably true, but... *Not their mating habits.*

Are you sure? I would allow you to use some of my poems to woo Lord Zavryd if that is your desire.

It is not. I pushed aside the horrifying image of me spouting lines about stalking prey and consuming still-twitching meat to Zav. *Did you find the basement?*

I could not detect an outside entrance, nor sense any magic in the ground that would hint of an enchanted secret door.

Too bad, but I wasn't surprised. I didn't see any vents or openings to suggest a lower level even existed. Only the magical aura of the being trapped down there.

A bedroom window is open in the back— Sindari pointed his nose toward the house, —*and I do not believe anyone is inside that room currently.*

Let's give it a try.

I wanted to find a way in and to check out the basement before all my local distractions started. I still had a vain hope that whoever was down there could be freed or turned against the brothers to force them out of business—or at least make them have to stop fulfilling orders until they found someone else to use.

Before trotting across the lawn after Sindari, I checked my ammo pouches and the small backpack I'd grabbed to hold the glass bulbs of mustard gas that Zoltan had made for me. They were insulated in a case, not where I could get to them easily, but the fragile glass hadn't made me inclined to keep them in a pocket. I also made sure the small charm Zoltan had given me was hanging on my leather thong with the others. It was shaped like a bulbous nose, and I wished I'd thought to make a design request before he'd made it.

The lights were on in the messy bedroom—it smelled like an animal den from ten feet away, even to my weak half-human nose—and the door was open, voices coming from the hallway, but Sindari was right. Nobody was inside. I started to draw Chopper, intending to cut through the screen, but Sindari eased past me.

Allow me.

He lifted a paw, one of his claws extended, and soundlessly sliced open the screen on all sides.

Handy. I pulled myself through, landing lightly on the clothing-strewn carpet inside. *Next time the electricity is out, I'm coming to you to open cans.*

The den smell was stronger inside. It seemed strange that all these cats were living together, even temporarily, when I associated most of the big feline predators with being solitary. Prides were a lion thing, and I assumed whoever had started the Northern Pride was a lion shifter, but these other members were all going along with it. Maybe there were perks. Like lawyers and assistance with beating the snot out of pesky government assassins.

Someone is coming. Sindari slid into the closet, knocking off the handful of garments hanging up instead of piled in a heap on the floor.

Light footsteps sounded in the hall, just audible over the voices of people in the living room. I hadn't moved from the window yet, so I crouched down behind the bed, Chopper in hand. There was nowhere to hide my six-foot frame even if there had been time. I was about to see how well my cloaking charm worked on these guys. The dark-elf apprentice alchemist had seen me when we'd been within a couple of feet of each other.

A male shifter in human form stumbled in, his jeans halfway off his hips. I wasn't sure if that represented a stylistic choice or if he was in the middle of undressing, especially when a giggling blonde slinked in after him. They embraced, tumbled to the bed, and started a noisy kiss-and-grope session a foot away from me. They reeked of alcohol. Maybe everyone here would be drunk and this would be easier than I thought.

Do you think he recited poetry for her first? Sindari asked.

No. Moving as soundlessly as I could, I headed for the door, stopping only to peer in the closet to see if there was a panel in the floor. There wasn't. I'd already been in the room with the TV—now replaced, judging by the video-game music drifting out of that corner of the house—and hadn't seen an access panel in there either.

Sindari and I checked the master bedroom next—it was also empty and even grimier than the first room. As we checked the closet, voices roared in laughter scant feet down the hall. Someone went barreling past and tried to get into the bathroom. It was locked, and the person rushed into the master bedroom. I barely had time to flatten myself to the wall and avoid getting hit as the man sprang into the small bathroom. But he—another shifter, this time a big man with shaggy blond hair who might have been a lion—paused with his hand on the jamb.

He sniffed a few times, and I held my breath. He was looking right at me, and it was hard to stay still, but his eyes weren't quite focused on the right spot.

He shook his head and disappeared into the bathroom, shutting the door.

There is an entrance here. Sindari backed up so I could check the closet.

There was a rectangle cut in the carpet. It looked like an access panel to a crawlspace under the house and nothing more. I almost backed out, thinking there had to be stairs and an actual doorway somewhere, but I had seen most of the house by now, and I hadn't noticed anything like that.

Chopper's soft light shined over dirt in the carpet. I touched it. It was fresh dirt. Someone had been down there recently.

The sound of the man peeing echoed through the wall, so I was careful not to make any noise as I pressed Chopper's tip into the crack and wedged the panel open. The smell of mold and mildew and dampness rose up, and I frowned. My sensitive lungs were going to love this.

There was no light below, so I crouched and lowered Chopper. I was tempted to use my new Dwarven command, but not until the man with the bladder the size of a canteen finished his work.

Val? Sindari had been next to the bed and watching both doors, but he looked gravely in my direction. *The dragon is coming.*

Please tell me you mean Zav.

I do not. The other one.

Why? I barely resisted the urge to thunk my head against the wall. *He shouldn't be able to sense me while I've got the charm activated.*

Or was that wishful thinking? He'd lost his ability to cloak himself when he lost that onyx stone, but I had no proof that he didn't have other magical tools or an innate sensitivity. Just because Zav hadn't seen through my cloaking charm didn't mean another dragon wouldn't.

It's possible he's not after you.

And just wants to visit the cat-shifter party in Bothell?

Maybe he's not coming here. This is along the route he was flying when he was kidnapping people.

True.

The bathroom door opened, and the lion shifter walked out, heading for the hallway. Once again, he paused, nostrils twitching as he tested the air. He stood right between me and Sindari.

A part of me was tempted to jump out of the closet, shut the bedroom door, and try to knock him out before the others heard anything, but a lion shifter wouldn't be easily subdued. He would fight back and make noise.

He turned toward Sindari. His innate stealth was different from what my charm granted me. As his handler, I could see him, but nobody else should have been able to. Maybe this guy was extra sensitive.

Sindari glided out the door into the hall. *He's catching a hint of my scent. I'll lead him away from you.*

I hated the idea of being separated from Sindari, but it was better than being discovered too soon. *Don't leave me for long. I pine without your companionship.*

I know this.

The shifter left the room. Trusting Sindari to evade him, I slid the closet door shut and lifted the panel the rest of the way. I leaned it against the wall then whispered, *"Eravekt,"* and Chopper's blue glow flared bright.

It illuminated a chamber dug into the dirt below the house with mud and puddles on the ground. Something that looked like cement had been sprayed on the lumpy walls, maybe in an attempt to keep water from seeping in. Droplets lined a few cracks in the hardened gray material. Fuzzy growths of mold dotted two of the walls, and my chest tightened.

While I debated whether to dig out my inhaler *before* I started wheezing, I lowered my head, twisting to see what was on the wall underneath me. A door. A huge metal vault door with a spinning handle that looked like something out of a submarine.

How had they gotten it down there? There was no way they could have fit it through the access panel in the closet.

The dragon that Sindari had already sensed came into my range. Dob. No mistake.

I pulled out my phone and texted Dimitri. *Stay ready, but don't send in the brute squad yet. Dob is around.*

Isn't that a reason to *bring them in, not the other way around?*

They're not going to fight a dragon.

Is he coming for you? Dimitri demanded.

I could sense him wanting to help—he'd made a few enchanted weapons to use on the shifters, but they would be laughable against a dragon.

I hope not.

That's not an answer.

Just hold tight.

I hopped to the muddy ground, wanting to see what was behind that door. I could still sense someone with a magical aura, but as before, it was nebulous and hard to identify. The door itself held some magic, and I wondered if it was what was making it hard to get a good read on who was inside.

Easing forward, I gripped my lock-picking charm and rested a hand on the cool steel. The metal tingled under my fingers, a testament to an enchantment on it. I tried to open the door, in case someone had left it unlocked, but the spinning wheel of a latch didn't budge.

That was fine. This was what my charm had been designed for. But when I closed my eyes and urged it to thwart the enchantment, nothing happened. Oh, I sensed the magic from the charm trying to obey, but like a true bank vault door, this had state-of-the-art security. Or state-of-the-art magic?

I could try to hack it open with Chopper, but if it was as thick as it looked, that would be asking a lot even from a magical sword. Besides, that would make a ton of noise. I couldn't forget that I was right under a house full of shifters with very good hearing.

One more try, I decided, resting my hand on the exact spot where I guessed the locking mechanism would be. Once again, I willed the charm to work, and I imagined funneling some of my own energy into it. Zav was positive I had some inherent magic, and I *had* seemed to draw upon something like that when I'd broken the dark-elf bonds.

You can do this, I told myself, ignoring the offensive moldy air curling down my trachea and the tightness of my chest.

A *thunk-clink* came from the door. I felt the reverberation in my hand. Was that it?

I tried the wheel again. This time, it turned.

With no idea what was on the other side, I only opened the door a crack and paused, listening and waiting. I didn't hear anything, but intense magic flowed out, startling me so much that I scurried back several steps and lifted Chopper in a defensive gesture.

Nothing rushed out besides the magic and a faint lavender light, but the magic called to me, inviting me.

I tried to sort through what I sensed. I hadn't encountered anything like it before. The being with the aura was still in there, close to the door, I thought, but there was something else that was the source of this power. It was what was trying to draw me in, almost like one of the compulsions the dragons had put on me. But it was easier to resist than a dragon's commands, at least from here and with Chopper in my hand, lending its protection to my mind. That might change if I got closer.

Footsteps sounded in the room above me. I wasn't sure if I was still under the bedroom or had moved under the hallway. It occurred to me that the shifters would feel this magic, too, that someone would know their vault had been opened. I needed to shut it—but not without seeing who was in there first.

A *ding-dong* echoed down from above, almost amusing in its mundaneness. The doorbell.

The footsteps stopped. A few muffled shouts echoed from above.

The dragon is here, Sindari informed me.

He rang the doorbell? Why did that seem ludicrous to me?

He did. I can sense him standing on the stoop in his elven form.

I couldn't tell where Sindari was. Still in the house, I thought.

Stay safe. Don't get closer than twenty feet from him—Zav said he felt you at that distance. I'm going to find out who we've been sensing in this weird basement.

Be careful. I just felt an immense powerful swell from somewhere under the house.

I know. I opened a door.

I think it's something menacing.

I had a feeling it wasn't a fairy handing out lemonade.

Be careful, Sindari repeated. *That's probably the only way in and out.*

I'm not sure about that. There's a two-ton vault door down here. It wasn't brought in through the crawlspace opening. I eased the door open a little wider, enough for me to slip through.

Maybe it was here before the house was built.

I had been about to step in but froze at the thought. The door looked new, far newer than the house above, but Sindari's suggestion was possible. If so, maybe it—or whatever was behind it—was the reason the shifters had picked this place. Maybe it had to do with why so many other cat shifters were willing to come hang out here for days. To protect a secret?

Only one way to find out. *I'm going in.*

CHAPTER 27

I stepped through the doorway, leading with Chopper, though I was tempted to switch to Fezzik. Images of enemies firing at me from behind crates popped into my mind.

A moan came from the left, behind the door, and I spun, almost attacking before my brain registered what I was seeing. A dwarf. A full-blooded, full-bearded, old male dwarf with wild white hair and olive-gray skin that reminded me of dirt and stone. His slate-colored eyes were sunken and vacant, and he didn't react as I stood gaping at him with my sword poised to strike.

He sat on the floor with his back to a stone wall—the walls in here were natural stone, not the lumpy cement of the other room. Unlike the muddy floor outside, this one was flat, rock, and bone dry. Boxes of ammunition rested to the dwarf's right and a crate full of loose rounds to his left. As I watched, he took a single bullet from a box, held it in his hand and murmured something too soft to hear, then placed it in the crate. A faint magical residue emanated from the bullet. Before he'd touched it, it had been plain.

The dwarf moaned again, the sound soft and full of pain. His left ankle was shackled with iron, a chain running from it across the floor of the small chamber and into a tunnel. The chain was the source of the lavender glow, but it wasn't the source of the magic calling to me. Whatever that was came from down that dark tunnel.

The door thudded shut, sealing with a hiss. I lunged for it a split sec-

233

ond too late to grab it and hold it open. My stomach sank. There wasn't a latch or wheel or anything but flat metal on this back side.

Trapped.

No, I'd opened it once. I could use magic to open it again. I hoped.

You will not believe this, Val. Sindari's voice sounded far, far away, as if he'd run to the end of the mile range he could get from his charm.

What? I lowered my sword and crouched in front of the dwarf.

When I waved my hand in front of his eyes, he didn't react, didn't seem to see me at all. Was he blind? His face was gaunt, his weathered hands so lean that I could see every tendon and vein along the backs as he worked.

Dob has heard that the brothers sell dragon-slaying weapons, and he wants to purchase one.

Is he the reason the shifters aren't checking out the magic that flowed from their vault? I reminded myself that it was a good thing that the door had shut, insulating that magic inside again. Maybe, distracted by Dob, they would forget they'd sensed it.

Yes, I think so. Two of them were on their way to check the orb—that's what they said—but everybody is in the front room now. They're very wary of Dob.

As they should be.

Orb? I eyed the tunnel. Was that what was back there, calling to me? Not with words but with pure magic that promised something good if I came to visit it. My curiosity almost pulled me away from the dwarf to investigate, but I remembered my mission, to get the shifters to leave Nin alone. If I took away their dwarf slave, they wouldn't be able to create magical weapons or ammo anymore.

Besides, this poor guy needed to be freed.

"I'm going to let you go, all right?" I patted his shoulder, but again, he didn't react.

An uneasy thought stirred, and I moved my hand to his throat. What if he wasn't alive any longer? What if he'd died here and his undead body was chained by magic to forever carry out the whims of the shifters?

But his skin was warm, and a slow steady pulse beat under my fingers.

"Good."

I reached for the glowing shackle on his ankle, thinking I could unlock it with my charm. I'd barely touched it when a surge of power slammed into me. It hurled me across the chamber like a cartoon character who'd stuck his finger in an outlet. I tried to twist in the air to make sure I didn't break anything landing, but I struck the wall first. *Hard.*

My breath whooshed out of my lungs as pain struck me like a lightning bolt. Groaning, I slumped to my hands and knees.

"You could have warned me," I growled between gasps for air.

The dwarf hadn't moved. He still wasn't reacting.

It was a long moment before I could climb to my feet and pick up Chopper, and the ache that remained after the initial burst of agony worried me. Since I didn't see a way I could escape the night without fighting, I worried about cracked ribs making everything even more difficult.

I shambled back over to the dwarf, careful not to bump the chain with my boot.

What's going on out there, Sindari?

Since the door had shut, I hadn't heard any noises from above. It was almost as if I'd been transported to some other dimension. I didn't get an answer, and that worried me, but he probably wasn't monitoring my thoughts because the shifters and the dragon were having an interesting conversation.

"Wait here," I told the dwarf, as if he was going anywhere. "I'm going to explore."

Maybe I could turn off the source of the magic powering the chain and keeping him in zombie mode.

I padded down the tunnel, rounding bend after bend, careful not to touch the chain that ran along the wall the whole way. The passageway sloped slightly downward, and I lost track of where I was in relation to the neighborhood above. Definitely not still under the shifters' house.

The lavender light grew brighter as the tug on my mind grew stronger. Whatever was trying to get me back there seemed... hungry. But it was full of promises too. Images started to pop into my mind of me and my daughter skipping rocks into a lake, of me sitting out on a sunny beach with no weapons in hand and nobody trying to kill me, of me dragging a handsome and laughing version of Zav into bed with me. All the things I wished I could have? I grunted skeptically at the last.

By the time I reached a chamber about twenty feet by twenty feet, the lavender light was so intense that I held up my hand to protect my eyes. An orb hung in the center of the chamber, not suspended from anything, simply floating in place. Dark purple veins were visible on its glass-like surface, overshadowed by the brilliant light it exuded. The orb throbbed, reminding me uncomfortably of a beating heart. I could even feel the faint pulses emanating from the walls and floor around me.

More images flooded my mind, these more intense than the first. They were carnal and erotic and promised great pleasure if I came forward and touched the orb.

"Given how it went the last time I touched something down here, I'm going to pass." I gripped Chopper's hilt with both hands and willed the blade to help protect me, to push the intrusion out of my mind.

It helped but only a little. Energy crackled in the air, something both similar to and different from what I felt in Zav's presence.

Shaking my head, I focused on the chain on the floor. I was here to free the dwarf and end the brothers' ability to do business.

The chain did not lead to the orb as I had expected. Instead, it ran under the orb and to the wall at the far side of the chamber, a dead-end wall. I hadn't found another exit, so the mystery of how the vault door— and the orb for that matter—had gotten down here would remain.

The chain ran up the wall and into something that looked so mundanely like a fuse box that I almost laughed. Had the shifters picked it up at Home Depot? But no, this fuse box oozed power. It was barely noticeable with the massive sun of an orb throwing off magical energy in front of it, but it had a slightly different feel. I was looking at two different magical artifacts.

Too bad I had to go around one to get to the other.

Warily, I skirted the orb, sticking as close to the wall as I could. By now, it was obvious that the closer I got, the stronger its pull became. Even with Chopper's help, it was hard to resist the call to creep over to it, to touch it, just for a moment…

"*No*," I growled and focused on the box.

When I reached it, I prodded it with Chopper's tip, afraid it would be as booby-trapped as the dwarf's shackle. A zing went up my arm, but I wasn't thrown across the chamber. I reached for it with one finger, tapping it lightly. A surge of power knocked my arm back behind my head.

It *was* booby-trapped in the same way. Maybe Chopper acted as an insulator.

"What happens if I thrash you with my sword?" I whispered to the box.

It didn't answer. Before committing to that, I tried to pry open the front panel with the blade. My arm tingled the whole time and started to go numb, but I managed to flip it aside. As soon as I pulled Chopper back, the numbing tingle faded, and I could see into the box.

The chain came up through a hole in the bottom and fused with a gray metal rectangle that looked like a slab of solid steel but radiated power. It had three other places—ports?—where chains could be attached. So it could keep up to four slaves working at a time? Or had this place originally been designed for something else?

Val, Sindari spoke into my mind, *we're coming down.*

Who's we?

The dragon, the Pardus brothers, and several other panther shifters. I'm following them at a distance. They haven't noticed me yet. Make sure your charm is activated and pray the dragon doesn't see through it.

It was only then that I realized Sindari's voice was loud and clear in my mind again. That meant he—and everyone he'd named—was already down here. Why did I have a feeling they hadn't just come to look at the dwarf?

CHAPTER 28

In a fit of desperation, I was tempted to bash at the magical fuse box with Chopper and hope it would set the dwarf free before Dob and all the shifters showed up, but that would be pointless. Grandpa Dwarf wasn't in any shape to fight battles or go anywhere quickly. And it would alert the shifters to my presence. It was still possible they would come and go and not see me.

Maybe.

Voices sounded in the tunnel, and I flattened my back against the wall by the fuse box. With luck, the orb and its intense magic would distract them from whatever they were doing. Not looking for an intruder, I hoped.

I'd pulled the closet access panel shut after me, and the vault door had closed, so there shouldn't be any sign down here of my presence. Unless the shifters caught my scent. But the charm *should* still be masking that...

"That dwarf is too comatose to even begin to make a dragon-slaying weapon," a familiar voice said. Dob.

"He promised he could make them." That sounded like Kurt Pardus. "Technically, the people who kidnapped him from his realm, brought him here, and sold him to us promised he could make them. But you're right that he's mostly only produced bullets with minor enchantments so far, but he *was* able to do some impressive mods on the military rifles we snagged. It's a lot better than what that ugly troll wench we were working with before could do, but it's still not ideal."

"Why then do you waste my time?" Dob's voice rang out in irritation.

"We thought you could take a look at the mechanism controlling him."

The shifters and Dob came into view in the tunnel, the lavender light brightening their faces.

"The Northern Pride has claimed control of this place, but we did not build it, and we're not sure who made the original artifact, just the orb. That's a recent upgrade to this hole."

"You got that right." That was Otto.

"If you can alter the dwarf's controller," Kurt said, "maybe he can make the kind of sword or bullets you want. Then we can make a fortune selling *real* dragon-slaying weapons."

"Are you not making a fortune selling fake ones to idiots who do not know better?" Dob's voice oozed disdain.

"We've made some, yes, but we could make so much more if we had legit goods. We'll cut you in."

"I care nothing for your grubby peddling of wares. I want only one thing."

It occurred to me for the first time that Dob had come here hoping to find an advantage he could use against Zav. He'd almost gotten his ass handed to him in the water-treatment facility, even with his tricks and trying to use me, so he knew he needed help to kill him.

My grip tightened around Chopper. I wanted to plow my blade into his vile heart.

"Well, there's the control box over there." Kurt pointed, almost right at me.

"We'll let you play with the orb while you're here." Otto was shirtless again, rubbing his chest as he gazed at the floating artifact.

As I scooted soundlessly away from the fuse box, Otto chuckled and trotted to the orb and flattened his chest to its pulsing purple side. He laid his cheek against it, his eyes pointing right toward my section of the wall, but he didn't see me. I doubted he would have seen me even if I hadn't had the charm. His mouth opened and his head fell back as orgasmic pleasure contorted his features.

"Idiot," Kurt muttered. "We're here for business, not a mind fuck."

I thought of the images the orb had promised me, the ones still dancing and teasing me, inviting me in, and I could imagine what was playing in the shifter's mind, especially when his hips started moving against the orb. What *was* this thing? Somebody's fancy sex toy? I remembered that it had promised me less lurid pleasures, as well, so maybe it wasn't just about sex. But about promising vivid wish fulfillment?

"I have no interest in fondling some dark-elf scientist's gewgaw," Dob said.

"You're the only one then," Kurt said. "The Pride's headquarters building has been empty since we let others know about our new toy."

So, dark elves had sold or given them this orb. But why would the dark elves want to do favors for these guys? Maybe the brothers had stolen it from them after their lair had been damaged. No, a dark elf had been helping one of their minions the night of Nin's fire. There was definitely some kind of alliance.

"It's amazing," Kurt continued, sending a wistful look toward the orb. Otto was still engaged with it, the lavender light glowing all around him, his body blocking enough of it to create a weird shadow on the wall. "Even dragons must like to have fun now and then."

"You are a fool," Dob said, "if you think any pleasure a dark elf gives you comes without a price."

"We paid for it already. She said it was a prototype with some quirks, so they wouldn't be able to use it."

"I'm sure." Dob stalked past it, not showing any interest in flattening himself to it like Otto.

Too bad. It might have been my chance to slice Chopper through his neck.

"Wait," Kurt blurted, watching Dob approach the box. "Why is it open? We didn't leave it open."

One little mistake…

Dob examined the interior of the box without responding. Kurt grabbed his brother and yanked him away from the orb.

"I wasn't done yet, you bastard."

"Did you leave the control box open?" Kurt pointed over Dob's shoulder.

"No."

"Then someone's been down here."

"Who?"

"I bet it's that Ruin Bringer bitch." Kurt spun toward the other shifters still in the tunnel—their gazes were all fastened on the orb. "Fan out. She could still be down here."

He waved them into the chamber, then sprinted back down the tunnel. Otto sucked in a shaky breath and followed him. Unfortunately, the four shifters in the hall entered the chamber, two going left around the orb, two going right. Their hands shifted, growing fur and changing from fingers with fingernails to paws with long, razor-sharp claws. They swiped at the air, as if they knew I was camouflaged somewhere in there. Maybe they did. One of the shifters was the lion from the bathroom.

Sindari, I'm in a bit of a bind. I scooted out of the way the best I could, but the chamber wasn't *that* large. Any second, these guys would be close enough to see through my charm.

I had to back out of the tunnel to avoid being seen. The Pardus brothers just rushed past. They're searching the chamber with the dwarf and also the room outside the door. Do you want me to charge in and attack?

Ugh, did I? With Dob less than ten feet away fiddling with that box?

The lion shifter was almost to me, swiping his claws in the air. Hoping I wasn't about to get myself in deeper trouble, I moved away from the wall and dropped low to crawl under the orb.

As I'd feared, its effect on me intensified. It floated only a couple of feet above my head, its pulsing power beating in sync with my heart. Not letting go of Chopper—I was positive that was the only reason I hadn't thrown myself at the orb yet—I worked my backpack off my shoulders.

"I heard something," someone said.

I froze. Sound was the one thing the charm didn't hide. It was hard to imagine hearing anything over the throbs of the orb, but the shifters had ears far better than mine.

"What happens if you touch it?" one of the shifters asked. A new visitor?

"Don't. We have to find that bitch."

Two sets of legs came closer to me. Careful not to make any noise, I removed and opened the case holding the small spheres of the gas compound that Zoltan had made. I also pulled out four magically enhanced grenades that Nin had given me. What were the odds that they would take out this whole chamber, including the orb and the control box enslaving the dwarf?

I laid out my goods on the floor and shifted into a crouch, hair almost brushing the bottom of the orb. I struggled to keep my thoughts my own, not to let in the images of pleasure it kept promising me. Nothing had ever been harder.

Dob was still facing the control box, but two of the shifters came right up to the orb, their feet pointing toward me. Any second, they would crouch down and swipe their paws at me.

I lifted one of Zoltan's spheres, on the verge of hurling it out and against the wall—maybe I would get lucky and even Dob would gag on the noxious gas—but neither of the shifters crouched down. They reached out and pressed their arms and their bodies to the orb. They were so close that I could have kissed their knees.

"You idiots," one of the shifters closer to the wall said. "Not *now*."

Groans of pleasure came from above.

A scream of pain echoed back down the tunnel. Had Sindari attacked?

Was that you? I asked silently.

No. You didn't give me the command to attack. The dwarf just cried out. Nobody's next to him.

Dob chuckled, his hand lowering from the control box.

The dwarf screamed again. Dob strode past and back into the tunnel. Maybe he would torture the dwarf until he made the weapon he wanted.

No, I vowed. He wouldn't.

I rubbed Zoltan's charm to activate it—I hadn't tested it and could only pray that it worked—and flung out four of the glass spheres. They shattered as they hit the far wall.

I'm going to need your help as soon as possible, Sindari, I thought, grabbing the last two spheres and my grenades and rolling out from under the orb and away from everyone left in the chamber. I stuffed the spheres in my pocket for later.

The two shifters plastered to the orb didn't move, but the lion shifter must have seen where the spheres had originated. He lunged under the orb and raked his claws through the spot where I'd been. His eyes widened, locking right on to me—he was close enough to see through my charm's magic.

As I scrambled back to the wall, greenish gas wafted from the broken spheres. The lion shifter crouched to spring for me, but he broke out in coughs, his eyes tearing as if a baseball bat had slammed into his nose. His three buddies, including the two fastened to the orb, also started coughing.

"What *is* that stuff?"

"She's in here," the lion spat between coughs. He'd lost sight of me when I backed away, and his watering eyes scanned the chamber for me. "Get her!"

They swatted at the air with their claws, snot streaming from their noses and tears streaking down their cheeks.

So far, the gas didn't bother me. With my grenades in hand, I rushed to the control box.

I couldn't tell what Dob had done, and I didn't care. I stuffed two grenades inside, pulled the pins, then whirled and ran around the orb, dropping the other two grenades under it. Whatever the artifact truly did, if the dark elves had made it, I was sure it was pure evil.

As I sprinted for the tunnel, I almost crashed into Kurt running back into the chamber. I was fast enough to dodge and flatten myself to the wall, but he was close enough to see through my charm. He whirled and grabbed my arm.

I slammed a palm into his nose. The blow would have flattened a normal human, but he didn't let go as his head whipped back. He recovered with an angry snarl and raked a clawed hand at my face.

In the tight quarters, it was hard to bring my sword to bear, but I ducked his swipe and rammed my shoulder into his gut with all my strength. He slammed into the wall behind him, and his grip loosened. I twisted my wrist and tore it free, then sliced Chopper at him when he lunged at me. The blade flared blue and cut into the side of his neck, sinking in deeply.

As he screamed, the first two grenades went off.

The lavender light dimmed and went out, but before I could feel any triumph, it flared back up. Kurt, blood gushing from the side of his neck, was startled by the explosion. It gave me the opportunity to sink Chopper deep into his gut.

He roared, still not dead, and threw himself at me, but Sindari flew in from the side and crashed into him. His momentum knocked Kurt into the chamber as the third and fourth grenades blew. I had no doubt Sindari would finish off what I'd started. And I wouldn't tell him to stop.

There would be repercussions later, but if I wanted to get out of here, I couldn't worry about killing these guys.

The lavender light went out again, this time for longer. Maybe the grenades I'd tossed right under the orb had taken it out.

I rushed down the tunnel toward the chamber with the dwarf, the faint light of Chopper guiding me as the thunderous sounds of stone cracking and snapping erupted back in the orb room. Rocks tumbled down in the tunnel behind me, and a sound like shattering glass rose over the cacophony. I hoped it was the orb being destroyed.

A snap came from right under me, and the tunnel floor shuddered. Only the dragon's aura kept me from rushing straight out into the dwarf's chamber. Dob was standing in there, right in front of the prisoner.

When I stepped warily out, he faced me, as if he knew exactly where I was. He probably did.

Behind me, Sindari roared, but it sounded like he was still back in the chamber. Maybe finishing off the shifters so they couldn't get at my back while I faced Dob.

But Dob wasn't alone. The bare-chested Otto and another shifter in tiger form stood near the door, blocking the exit. Hell.

The vault door was open, and the sounds of weapons fire came from the house above, but I couldn't get out without going through the two shifters. Nor could I leave the dwarf. Dob held a palm face-down toward the bearded prisoner, who was alert now, the chain at his ankle snapped, but he was writhing in pain from whatever Dob was doing to him.

I wanted to help him, but the shifters had heard my footsteps. The tiger sprang into the air toward my face.

I dove under him, turning mid-roll to twist and jam Chopper upward. I caught the tiger in the belly. He screeched and raked me with his back legs before I could jump up and get out of the way. Pain blasted my side where the claws caught me.

Otto, hearing my gasp, charged straight toward me. I yanked out Fezzik and rained fire at him. The tiger, though bleeding from a gut wound, spun and also charged at me.

Nin's magical bullets bit into the shifters' inhumanly tough skin. The tiger yelped, turned, and raced down the dusty tunnel, but Otto wasn't ready to flee. He shifted into panther form, and hundreds of pounds of muscle and fang leaped at me.

Still firing, I sprang to the side, just missing another raking from savagely fast claws. My aim was true, and rounds pummeled his chest, blood spattering the earthen floor, but Otto's rage carried him after me. I backed up until I reached a wall, then switched to Chopper to keep him at bay and strike whenever I had the opportunity. The blade was a blue blur in the air between us, metal clanging against claw and fang. Blood gushed onto the gray stone floor.

Screams of pain came from the direction of the orb chamber, followed by Sindari's chilling roar. He still sounded busy.

One of Otto's paws slipped through, claws extending as they swept toward my throat. I whipped my head back, but he caught my leather thong. It snapped and my charms tumbled to the floor. I lunged but only caught one. The lock-pick charm.

Otto slashed at me, taking advantage of my break in the fight. I stuffed the charm in my pocket and whipped my sword in to deflect him.

As I pressed Otto back with a combination of feints and lunges, I was aware of Dob turning slowly away from his torture session to regard us. No, to regard *me*.

His silver-blue eyes narrowed, and out of the edge of my vision, I saw the lightbulb click on for him as he saw me for the first time, my cloaking charm now on the floor and useless. He'd just realized I wasn't some random intruder. I had to finish off Otto fast and figure out how to deal with Dob.

Sindari roared again, but it was distant, back in the orb room. He couldn't help me. Otto backed me up again, and I struggled to keep those fangs and claws from reaching me. He had three weapons—fangs and two sets of claws—and all I had was Chopper. Fezzik had riddled him with bullets, but it wasn't enough. Chopper could take off his head. I just needed an opening.

But he was incredibly fast, amped up on rage and bloodlust. Whereas my body ached, and my lungs burned from the exertion. I slashed for his head, but he ducked, and I barely clipped his ear, taking off the tip. He didn't appear to notice. He came in low, slashing for my shin. I tried to back further, but I was against the wall again. I slid the blade toward his feline face, not expecting to hit but hoping to distract, then leaped into the air, somersaulting over him. As I landed behind him, I spun and lashed out.

One of the glass spheres I'd stuffed in my pocket tumbled out when I was upside down. It shattered on the ground as Otto whirled toward me, already lunging in.

With my charm on the floor somewhere, I caught a whiff immediately. Damn it. I held my breath, backed away, and hoped that Otto, who was closer to it, would be more affected.

The gas filled the air, and he jerked back in the opposite direction. That was my chance. He sneezed, and in that split second, I swept Chopper in for a logger's chop. Even with my bodyweight behind it, and the magic of the blade, it didn't fully take his head off, but it cut halfway through. That was enough to sever his spine.

As the fight finally faded from the ferocious panther, I tore the blade free, and spun toward Dob. Too late.

Bolts of electricity streaked across the room and slammed into my body at a dozen points. Agony blasted me from each spot, and a scream escaped my mouth before I could clamp it shut.

I pitched onto my side, my legs refusing to hold me upright. They twitched as if volts of electricity were coursing through them. Maybe they were.

My fingers wanted to spasm open and drop Chopper, but through the pain, I clenched down, as if the sword was my lifeline. The acrid gas in the air stung my eyes and throat, but that was the least of my problems.

Dob strolled toward me, his hands folded calmly on his flat stomach. He was the elf again, his face handsome and pleasant. With all that lightning coursing across the chamber and into me, he should have been the ugly zit of an emperor from *Return of the Jedi*. All he was lacking was the maniacal cackle and the dramatic finger movements.

He stopped a few feet away, and the lightning paused, the chamber sinking into dimness. For a moment, the agony eased from extreme unrelenting pain to sharp throbbing pain. I was on my hands and knees, every muscle in my body quaking. Chopper was beneath me, but I couldn't grip it, couldn't rise, couldn't do more than twitch my head to the side to glare up at Dob through spastically blinking eyelids.

Dob's nose wrinkled. He flicked his fingers, and the gas disappeared from the air.

It was little relief. Dob was glaring at me, and I couldn't move.

"You cut off my toe," he said. "I'd kill you for that alone, you presumptuous mongrel excrement, but it will be even better, knowing your death will hurt that pompous scale-rotted dog."

Was that Zav?

"This is the point," I muttered, groping for something I could do to get out of this, "where it would be nice if my father showed up and threw you into a bottomless pit."

He didn't get the reference. Not surprising. I regained just enough control of my fingers to wrap them around Chopper's hilt. Still on my hands and knees, I used my body to hide the movement.

On the far side of the chamber, the dwarf rose to a sitting position. I wished I could count on him to help, but he didn't look strong enough to even stand up.

Coming, Sindari whispered into my mind as Dob turned his head toward the tunnel.

Careful. He's ready for you.

Streaks of lightning shot down the tunnel. Dob's focus was in that direction, his face turned away from me.

I leaped to my feet, wobbled, and gained my balance. I swung Chopper at Dob's neck, hoping he was distracted enough.

But my blade halted, as if it had hit an iron wall, inches from his neck. His head turned slowly back toward me. He lifted a hand toward me. I tried to sprint for the door, telling myself I could come back for the dwarf if I could figure out a way to escape Dob. But power wrapped all around me, pinning me in place, one of my legs raised ridiculously in the air.

Dob smiled, a predatory smile that wasn't appropriate on an elven face, and stepped close. I saw my death in his cold eyes.

Then he paused, looking toward the cement ceiling.

"He's coming," Dob murmured.

Zav? I started to feel a shred of hope, but Dob probably sensed him from ten miles away. I couldn't feel him yet. Wherever he was, it would take him time to fly here, and Dob could kill me in a second.

Once again, I tried to move my muscles. It didn't work. All I felt was the pain ricocheting through my body.

Wait, could the lock-pick charm work? It wasn't exactly an enchantment that held me, but maybe...

"Unfortunately for him, he'll find only your body when he arrives." Dob's gaze settled on me again.

I mentally willed the lock-pick charm to unlock this magical cage around me. It didn't work. But it also hadn't worked the first time I'd tried it on the dark-elf bonds.

Dob lifted a single finger, morphing his nail into a glistening sharp talon and leaning close to cut my throat. I threw all of my energy into that charm. With the mental roar of a tiger, I commanded it to open the cage.

Something snapped, echoing in my brain, and I had control of my limbs. Dob was only inches away. I whipped Chopper straight at his face.

He stumbled back, the blade sinking into his cheek. But he recovered and flung a wave of power at me before Chopper could take off his head. Once again, I was thrown back against the wall, my head cracking hard. What did it take to kill this bastard?

I waved Chopper defensively as Dob, bloody and furious, strode toward me. Blackness edged my vision.

A bang sounded from above, and the ceiling crashed down all around us. Huge blocks of cement fell, and I flung my arms up to protect my head. A slab of rock struck my shoulder, knocking me to my knees again.

Sindari surged into view as more and more debris rained down from above. A refrigerator slammed into the floor right next to Dob, and I gaped in bewilderment.

Sindari stood over me, protecting me as more cement, earth, chunks of flooring, and even furniture came down from above. Then, the black scales of a massive dragon came into view. Zav plucked the elven version of Dob out of the debris and rose up, great wings stirring the dust, whipping my braid around with their wind.

I scrambled out from under Sindari to peer up at the hole above us, not just in the floor of the house but in the roof. Dob turned into the silver dragon even as Zav gripped him in his talons. Nothing but the cloudy night sky was above them. They flew apart, raking and slashing at each other, and then disappeared from view.

A cutting board slid off a counter and tumbled through the hole, landing near the vault door. Zav had slammed right through the roof of the house, through the kitchen floor, and through the cement ceiling of this chamber.

One of the Pardus brothers' shifter buddies came into view, staring into the hole at us. I reached for Fezzik. The shifter was bare-chested but gripped a gun in both hands, as if he'd been in the middle of a war.

Somewhere behind him, shots rang out, and tires squealed in the street. The shifter rushed out of view.

I believe the orb is destroyed, Sindari told me, shaking dust from his silver fur. *The shifters that were back there are dead. I had to ensure they would not come out to gang up on you.*

I understand. Thank you.

I hadn't wanted to kill the shifters, just stop the threat to Nin. But I couldn't be surprised things had gone this way. The one being I did wish dead was up there fighting with Zav. I hoped there had been time for Zav to properly heal and that he could once again best Dob.

But what if he'd only come back to Earth because he knew I was in danger? What if there *hadn't* been time for him to heal fully, and what if Dob could take advantage of that?

CHAPTER 29

A rough voice spoke from the side, and I jumped. The dwarf. He was half covered in blocks of cement and faux wood boards from the kitchen floor.

"What'd he say? Sindari, can you find my charms? Otto tore them off. I'm going to try to help this guy."

I can easily find mine. I am attuned to it.

Good, if you could be attuned to the other ones, too, I'd appreciate it.

I climbed over rubble and pulled broken chunks of cement off the dwarf, rock dust turning him an ashen gray. Normally, I would have expected a dwarf to be nearly indestructible and eat boulders for breakfast, but this guy had been half-dead even before the dragon started tormenting him.

A screech sounded above, and I jumped again, pointing Fezzik at the hole.

Dob flew past with Zav right on his tail. Zav snapped down, his large fangs flashing before they sank into that tail. Dob roared and twisted in the air, slashing at Zav.

Half fighting, half flying, they somehow stayed aloft. Drops of water spattered down from above. No, I realized, as I spotted fresh red splashes on the debris. Drops of blood. The writhing dragons tumbled out of view, and a second later, a thump reverberated through the earth. Had they struck down?

Gunfire punctuated the roars and screeches, reminding me that the battle wasn't over. As soon as I freed the dwarf, I had to get up there and help Dimitri and the werewolves. And Zav, if I could. I couldn't assume he would be able to best the tricky Dob a second time. And there were still shifters up there to worry about.

A callused hand gripped mine. The dwarf met my gaze, then spoke in a string of words I didn't understand.

"Sindari?" I asked hopefully.

Here. Sindari trotted over with my broken leather cord in his mouth and two charms, his cat figurine and the translation trinket. He laid both down. *I will gather the others. I brought the most important ones.*

"I see. Thank you." I grabbed both, rubbed the translation charm, and patted the dwarf's hand. He was still gripping my wrist. "Go ahead."

He frowned, no understanding in his eyes. Unfortunately, the charm did not work both ways.

I pointed to my chest. "Val."

More gunfire sounded, bullets whizzing right above the hole. It was a ludicrous time to try to communicate with someone. I went back to shoveling the debris off him. We could play Charades later.

"I'm sorry I do not speak your language," the dwarf said. "I am Belohk. You have saved my life and slain my captors. You are a mighty warrior."

"I'm glad you think so." It was legions above the dragons calling me a mongrel and a criminal.

I know a few words in his language, Sindari said, bringing more charms over. The thong was broken so I could only stick them in my pocket for now and hope I didn't lose any. *I'll attempt to share what you're saying.*

Good. Thank you.

"I should have realized as soon as I saw your sword. The blade of Dondethor, a true master craftsman."

I was in the middle of heaving a slab of rock off him, my battered body protesting the effort, and almost dropped it on my foot. "You know who made my sword?"

He—Belohk—looked at Sindari, waiting for a translation. Then he nodded. "The work of the legendary craftsman Dondethor is recognizable by all good dwarves. One of his works hangs in the museum in the Granite Castle deep in the First Mine."

"Is he still alive? Is there an instruction manual for the sword that I can buy?"

His forehead creased. I probably shouldn't have asked that. His estimation of how great a warrior I was had likely plummeted. What kind of warrior didn't know the history of her weapons?

But I might never get another chance to talk to a dwarf. I had to put dignity aside and learn what I could.

"Dondethor passed to the realm of the blessed ancestors more than ten thousand years ago."

Hell.

"The secrets of the blades are passed from father to son, mother to daughter. They are not written down. Did your father or mother not share them with you?"

"No, I got the sword from a zombie lord. I didn't ask him if his parents had shared the operational instructions with him."

As Belohk digested that—or maybe indigested it, as his pained frown suggested—he rolled onto his hands and knees and pushed himself to his feet. He wobbled, and I grabbed him to give him support.

"Then the sword was stolen from the original owner. It should be given back."

Give back Chopper? I didn't shake my head with vehement rejection, even if that was my first reaction, but made myself ask, "Do you know who it belongs to and where the family would be found?"

If I seemed cooperative, maybe he would be more likely to help me. And I *was* cooperative, however reluctantly. I'd had the sword for ten years, so I wanted very much to state it was mine, but Zav had also implied it was stolen. If I ever did find the legitimate owner, I would feel compelled to give it back.

"I do not know," Belohk said. "Sometimes, great weapons were given as gifts to kings and queens and emperors and empresses from other lands. A few were even sacrificed to dragons for appeasement. I could take you to my homeland to do the necessary research, but I am a prisoner here."

"How did you end up in this situation?"

Maybe I'd better get his mind on that and give up on getting more information about Chopper. If I kept asking about it, he might feel compelled to try to take it from me so that he could deliver it to its rightful owner. If that owner showed up with provenance, I would return Chopper, but I wouldn't go looking for him or her.

"I was kidnapped and sold and dragged into this… forsaken realm. Which has no portals, no way back. No way home." He turned haunted eyes on me. "I have a wife and children and grandchildren. And it is a volatile time back home. I worry about them."

"If I could get you back home, I would. Trust me."

Clumps of dirt and flooring tumbled down, and I whirled, again pointing Fezzik upward.

Dimitri was leaning over the edge. He jerked back out of sight. I lowered the weapon, and he poked his head over the side again.

"We've got a problem." He looked toward a portion of the sky that wasn't visible to me from down in the hole.

"Just one?"

"It's a big one. I think our dragon is losing."

I swore. "I'm coming up."

"Zav seemed to be kind of injured from the beginning, and the other one is taking advantage."

I'd been afraid of that.

Dimitri offered me a hand, but I pulled myself up into the wreckage of the kitchen on my own. Not because I was too proud to accept help but because I didn't want him to get hurt because he was focused on me.

The gunfire had dwindled, but the dragons were still fighting nearby, snarls and roars alternating with loud thuds. I saw only Dimitri's van out in front of the house—the kitchen and living room walls had been flattened, interior and exterior, leaving the view to the street open. Maybe when the dragon fight had broken out, the werewolves had decided their job was done. I didn't blame them.

Flames turned the gray night sky orange, and I looked up in time to see Dob spewing fire from his maw, the size and roiling heat of that gout a hundred times what any flamethrower could produce. Zav, swooping low as he tried to evade the attack, took the brunt of it. He disappeared entirely inside of the fire even as it spewed past, engulfing one of the neighboring houses and a tree.

Fear for him had me running through the wrecked living room to a spot where I could see better, where I could *help* better. Would that fire kill him, or could his defenses handle it?

Zav flew out of the flames but couldn't turn quickly enough to avoid hitting the house. He crashed through an exterior wall, clipping a chimney hard enough to knock it down, the bricks tumbling all around him.

Dob roared and swooped out of the sky toward Zav, talons as long as swords outstretched for the kill. Zav lay crumpled among the wreckage, the bricks half burying him.

I took cover behind a corner of the Pardus house that was still standing and leveled Fezzik in Dob's direction. The bullets wouldn't hurt him, and I knew it, but if I could distract him for a moment...

As he dove, I opened up with automatic fire and emptied the entire magazine.

The rounds didn't bounce off his silver scaled hide, but they also didn't do any damage. They *did* make Dob spread his wings to slow his descent and glare in my direction. His eyes flared with silver light, and I flattened myself to the ground, anticipating an attack.

Raw power slammed into the corner of the house, obliterating it. Chopper must have given me some protection, or maybe Dob had aimed too high, for the brunt of it went over me.

Behind me, Dimitri swore as drywall and wood blew all the way out to the river. He'd also flattened himself to the ground.

"Stay down!" I yelled back at him. "Go down in the basement!" At least no stray debris would slam into him down there.

As the wave of power waned, I knelt up, loading another magazine.

Dob's diving attack had turned into a landing. Now, he crouched in the grass a dozen feet from the unmoving Zav. His focus shifted back to his dragon nemesis, but I fired again, aiming for his glowing eyes, hoping in vain to find a vulnerable spot.

Just as it occurred to me that he was on the ground, so I might be able to reach him with Chopper, Zav burst out of the bricks.

Dob was so close to him that he didn't have time to spring away. Zav hit him with the speed of a maglev train.

They tumbled across the grass, mowing down another house. Wood splintered as the roof collapsed atop them. Shingles flew as the dragons bit and clawed and flung power. A woman in a bathrobe shrieked, ran out the back door, and sprinted down the street barefoot without looking back.

Fire shot out of the end of the structure where the dragons were fighting and hit the house next door. It burst into flames as if it had been doused with gasoline.

Another wall crashed down, and the wild dragon battle rolled into the back yard.

I ran for a tree, not wanting to risk giving up all cover, but I had to see what was going on. Out of ammo, I holstered Fezzik and pulled out Chopper. If Dob rolled close to me, I was going to pulverize him like a meat grinder.

I darted for a closer tree, the flames burning the top branches not deterring me. To my left, the river flowed past, reflecting the fires of the neighborhood. From my new spot, I could see the dragons wrestling and biting in the back yard.

Before I could lunge in to stab at Dob's silver hide, Zav launched him into the air with an attack that looked almost as much physical as mental. Dob somersaulted as he sailed over my burning tree, knocking the top off on his way past.

Burning branches fell toward me, and I leaped out of the way. Dob splashed down into the river, water spraying me from twenty feet away.

I expected Zav to press his advantage, to rush after Dob and finish him, but he slumped down, one of his wings appearing broken. Blood ran from dozens of deep gashes in his black scales, gashes that left the pink of the muscle visible.

In the river, Dob lay on his back, his belly exposed. This was the time to attack.

His head lolled to the side, his furious gaze pinning me. And then his mind was in my mind, commanding me to take Chopper and rush toward Zav, to drive it into his chest. Into his *heart*.

The image of it making a killing blow filled my thoughts with such vividness that for a second, I believed it had already happened. I'd killed Zav, and now I would revel in his death, feel the power of being the greatest warrior in the world, the only one to kill a dragon.

Horror flooded me as my legs started to carry me toward the wounded Zav.

"No," I snarled, my hands shaking on Chopper's hilt. "*No!*"

I was so tired of being used by that dragon—by *all* dragons. Fury boiled over in me, and I channeled all of my mental strength into my legs and into Chopper.

Jerking around so hard it gave me whiplash, I sprinted toward Dob. He had to be gravely injured, because he still lay there in the water on his back, his head barely turned to stare at me, to try to manipulate me.

"Not this time!" I roared and sprinted to the edge of the bank and leaped out onto him.

I sensed his surprise—he couldn't believe his mind control hadn't worked—and he tried to raise his magical defenses, but I landed on his chest with Chopper leading. The blade plunged down into scale and flesh, snapping a rib and driving deeper.

The dragon stiffened under me. Magical mental claws tore at my mind. A fiery jolt raced up my arm, and the sword flared such a brilliant blue that it brought tears to my eyes. Pain hammered every nerve of my body, but I didn't let go—*refused* to let go. I plunged Chopper all the way to the hilt.

Dob convulsed, water splashing all around him. I thought he would rise and attack me again. But then he grew still. Completely still. Slowly, his aura faded, and the magical power he'd always radiated disappeared.

I crouched there for a long moment, my muscles shaking, my hands still wrapped around Chopper's hilt. Finally, I summoned the strength to stand and pull out the long blade. Dob was dead.

As I crawled out of the river and dragged myself up onto the bank, my entire body throbbed with pain. I had to pause to throw up. It felt like all of my energy had gone into that killing blow. It had been worth it.

The Pardus house was flattened and five of the neighboring homes had suffered similar fates. Four others were on fire. Countless trees burned.

Dimitri rushed out of the rubble and headed for me, but he paused and looked back. Zav, still in his black dragon form, limped across the wreckage of the house toward me.

What did you do? his telepathic voice rang in my mind, full of disbelief and rage.

"Uh?" I glanced at the dead silver dragon and then back to him as he halted in front of me.

Even injured, his huge muscled form radiated power. Blood ran from deep gouges in his scales, but the wounds did nothing to diminish his gravitas. His eyes flared violet as they bored into me.

I shifted uneasily, Chopper held loosely in my grip. "Maybe you didn't see it, but I defended myself and took care of the guy harassing you."

Took care of him! Zav shifted into human form, his eyes still glowing, as if fueled by anger. "You killed a dragon. I only sought to defeat him. It was my duty to take him back for punishment and rehabilitation." His voice rang with just as much power when he was in human form. Maybe more, since everybody heard it now.

Dimitri had been on the way over, but he hung back. The dwarf had climbed out of the hole and was watching.

The heat of embarrassment scorched my cheeks. It was bad enough Zav was yelling at me when I'd *helped* him, but he didn't need to do it in front of other people.

"You said yourself that his family would get him out of that if you brought him in," I said.

"That's not a reason to circumvent the law and *murder* a dragon." Zav stalked past me and toward the river where the lifeless Dob lay, too large to be fully submerged in the water.

I would have to call someone at Willard's office to come out and get the body, especially if dead dragons were no longer hidden from those without magical power. I imagined that couple with the stroller, walking the path on the opposite side of the river in the morning and coming around the bend to see Dob belly-up in the water.

"As we've discussed before," I called, refusing to trail after him like a whipped hound, "your laws are not the laws here on Earth. That bastard killed all the workers in that water plant. The government paid me to kill him."

"How wonderful that you'll be *paid* for your assassination job," Zav shot over his shoulder before leaping out onto Dob's belly.

I clenched my hand so tightly around Chopper that my knuckles ached.

Zav reached the spot where I'd driven the blade into Dob's heart. I had no delusions that I'd ever be able to kill another dragon. Only Dob's grievous injuries and being depleted from his battle with Zav had allowed me to get past his magical defenses and strike a fatal blow.

Zav laid a hand on the wound.

"You're not going to bring him back to life, are you?" I blurted.

Was that possible? I didn't know, but the last thing I wanted was that asshole and his vendetta against me to be alive so he could retaliate.

"Even a dragon cannot bring others back to life," Zav said scornfully without looking at me.

"Then what—" I stopped when Sindari bumped my hip.

He'd come to stand next to me. *Let it go, Val. He is angry and might lash out if you continue to pester him.*

I'm not pestering him. I'm verbally defending myself.

Yes, but it offends people when you do that.

Well, screw those people. "And screw *him*." I thrust my sword in Zav's direction.

He was twenty feet away, but he leveled a warning glare in my direction. I stubbornly kept my sword up until he looked back down at what he was doing. Whatever that was. Then I wiped Chopper's blade and sheathed it.

I didn't sense any shifters still around—Zav and Belohk were the only full-blooded magical beings within my range—and I didn't truly want to pick a fight with Zav. Even if he *was* being an ass. Sindari was right. I shouldn't assume that Zav wouldn't lash out at me if he was angry... and a dragon having a tantrum could kill someone by accident.

"What's he doing?" I could sense Zav using his magic, applying it to Dob's corpse.

Maybe he will create a portal to take the dragon's body back to his realm, Sindari suggested.

I'd seen Zav make a portal before, and it hadn't looked like this. The wound on Dob's chest closed up.

"Uh, is it possible to heal a dead body?" I glanced at Sindari. "And why would you want to?"

It will not make the dragon less dead, but since he's so recently deceased, perhaps it is possible. Or maybe he is filling in the hole by some superficial means.

"Are you all right, Val?" Dimitri came up beside us.

"Yes. Thank you for your help tonight."

At least *somebody* here could be courteous and grateful for assistance.

"Did you see the exploding barrel I made? It took out the front door and that window." Dimitri pointed toward the utterly smashed house. "Which was more impressive before Zav showed up and just flattened everything."

"You did well. I'm glad you were distracting the shifters in the house, because Sindari and I had our hands full with the ones under the house."

Reluctantly, I admitted that I'd be dead now if Zav hadn't shown up.

Of course, if Zav had never come to this world, then Dob never would have, either, and I wouldn't have been threatened by *any* dragons.

I nodded, convinced this meant that I did not owe Zav an expression of gratitude, and I certainly wasn't going to apologize for killing the dragon who'd been trying to use me *again*. After trying to kill me.

For whatever reason, Zav didn't fix any of dead Dob's other wounds. There were talon marks all over. Once my sword puncture had been repaired, Zav hopped back to the bank, leaping twenty feet as if he were a cat instead of a human.

He stopped in front of me, not acknowledging Dimitri at all. Judging by the uneasy way Dimitri shifted away from him, he was probably fine with that.

"If the Dragon Justice Court learns that you killed a dragon, they will send someone to collect you for punishment and rehabilitation."

"Rehabilitation? Rehabilitation for *what*? All I did was defend myself. I don't know if you noticed, but he was trying to put me in your way again. No, he was trying to get me to *kill* you."

"I noticed." Zav looked toward the stars and clouds above. "I must consider how I will answer questions on this matter. I will not implicate you." He walked away and waved an arm to form a shimmering silver portal in the air.

That was it? He was leaving? Would he be back?

"I would prefer not to be the one sent to collect you and turn you over to the court," he added.

A chill went through me at the idea of being dragged before this court of dragons. What kind of punishment and rehabilitation went on there, anyway? From what I'd heard, most of the magical beings who'd fled to Earth had considered it better to risk death here than to be brought in for that.

"Wait," I called as he turned into his dragon form and started toward the portal. "Will you take Belohk?" I pointed to where the white-haired dwarf had been quietly watching, a gnarled hand pressed to his injured side. "He was kidnapped and brought here against his wishes. Will you take him back to his home?"

Zav looked at me, then at the dwarf, and several long moments passed as they seemed to communicate telepathically. The dwarf walked toward him and the portal, but paused to come to me first. He gripped my hand, and I quickly activated my translation charm.

"Thank you for helping me. If ever you come to my world, I shall assist you in researching your sword."

I didn't see how that would ever happen—it wasn't as if Zav was inviting *me* through his portal—but I thanked him and patted him on the shoulder before he walked away. Zav leaped through the portal, and Belohk followed. A second later, the shimmering gateway disappeared, leaving me alone with Dimitri and Sindari and a huge mess.

You have put him in a difficult situation, Sindari observed.

Who? Zav?

They will ask him how Dob died. The death of a dragon is not a thing that can go unreported. He will either have to take the blame—and the punishment inherent in that—or tell the truth and risk being sent back to collect you for punishment. If not him, then it would be another. For a human—or even an elf—to kill a dragon is not a small thing, and it would not be forgiven by other dragons.

What would you have had me do, Sindari? Let Dob take control of me again? He was going to kill me if I didn't kill him first.

I acknowledge that, and I do not know if there was a better solution.

Besides, he was trying to kill Zav. Don't tell me he wasn't. If he'd succeeded, wouldn't he have been brought before their justice court?

Likely, but with a story rehearsed to tell. Since he loathed you, he might have put the blame on you.

Great.

I do not believe Zavryd is someone who likes to besmirch his honor by lying.

Which he was now going to have to do to protect me. Fantastic. Why'd I have to cross paths with an *honorable* dragon?

"Is anybody else completely tired of dragons and shifters and ready to get out of here?" I asked.

Dimitri raised his hand. "I thought you'd never ask."

Police sirens wailed in the distance. If Zav had been casting some magic to keep anyone outside of the area from noticing the carnage going on… it was gone now. It was cowardly, but I didn't want to deal with explaining any of this.

I'd leave a message at Willard's office and explain everything. That would have to be enough. I was done. So very done.

EPILOGUE

I was cleaning my apartment when someone knocked on the door. Technically, I was lying on the floor, staring desolately at the ceiling and *thinking* about cleaning the apartment. Earlier, I'd picked up the books and clothes strewn around the living room, but I'd lost motivation.

Even though the last thing I wanted was to give Zav free rent in my mind, I kept playing the night before over in my mind and wondering if I had done the wrong thing or if he was an uptight over-reacting huge pain in the ass.

"It's Willard," came the muffled call when I didn't get up to open the door.

Thus ended my afternoon of deep reflection, also known as brooding.

"Come in."

Willard walked in and peered around before spotting me on the floor. "Are you injured? You didn't mention being hurt last night when you were asking for a corpse removal team to come out to Bothell with a very large stretcher." Judging from the twitch of her eyebrows, that hadn't been the proper way to inform the office that they had to figure out how to bag and tag the massive dragon clogging up the Sammamish River.

"My injuries are minor. They're healing."

Maybe not minor, but they *were* healing. In a couple of days, I shouldn't have even a bruise. Someday, I would figure out why my half-elven blood

263

could tackle broken bones, bullet wounds, and claw slashes, but not elevated inflammatory markers. Something didn't seem right there.

"So," Willard said, "you're just lying on the floor because it's comfortable?"

"This happened to be where I was when I got tired of cleaning and was overcome with weariness and ennui. The couch was too far away." I waved at the three-seater all the way on the other side of the coffee table.

"Ennui? Shit, did you call your therapist?"

"I will on Monday. She may give up on me. I almost got her favorite yoga studio blown up."

"The *almost* in that sentence gives it a significantly different meaning than if the word hadn't been there."

"And yet she sent me a link to some online yoga videos and suggested that might be better for me. Or those around me."

Willard closed the door and sat on the couch. She was in her army uniform, her hat in hand, her wiry gray-shot hair recently cut. She had gained a couple of pounds since leaving the hospital but didn't yet look like her usual tough-as-nails self.

"Some people stand up and salute me when I walk into a room," she pointed out, waving an envelope.

"Yes, Colonel. Right away, Colonel." I waved two fingers at my temple.

"Every time we work together, I'm amazed you made it ten years in the army."

"It was nine, and I got assigned extra duties a lot."

"I'm shocked."

The roar of rush-hour traffic and honking of horns penetrated my windows, meaning I'd spent more time on the floor with my ennui than I'd realized. "You on the way home for the day?"

"Yup. I've got a long drive back to Fort Lewis, and I thought I'd wait for the traffic to die down. And come pay you. I think that's the quickest you've closed an impossible assignment."

I couldn't manage a smile. I hadn't even been trying to kill Dob, just help Nin.

It occurred to me that I should be a decent hostess and get up and offer Willard something from the fridge. My dark-elf intruder hadn't molested the bottles of hard cider or cans of La Croix.

Instead of moving, I announced, "I hate dragons."

"All of them? You've only met two."

"*All* of them."

"Even the one that makes you tingle?"

I shot her a dirty look. "Yes."

The memory of the heated kiss-and-rub session in the water-treatment plant crashed into my mind, and my cheeks flushed red. That hadn't been Zav's fault, but...

"I hate anyone with that much power over me."

"Most people," Willard said, "who don't have magical swords and magical elven blood have to deal every day with people having power over them. That's life. The problem is when that power is misused."

"Yeah, yeah. But it's always misused. Even if it's not, there's your perception and knowledge that it could be at any time. That's why it's better to work for yourself and learn how to effectively knee people in the balls. Or boobs, should your tormentor be female."

"Of course. We should all solve the problems that arise from the inequalities between people by adopting isolationist tendencies interspersed with brute force."

"Did I invite you here to be reasonable and wise?"

"You didn't invite me at all."

"I knew it. I shouldn't have let you in."

"I came to pay you."

"Never mind. Help yourself to anything in the fridge. Just watch out for the stuff on the floor. I haven't cleaned in there yet."

Willard tossed the envelope onto the rug next to me and picked her way into the kitchen. "You didn't mention that your apartment had been ransacked again."

"Didn't I? I think it was a dark elf looking for a notebook I took when I was in their complex."

"Dark elves?" Willard took two berry-flavored cans of sparkling water out of the fridge and frowned at me. "Are you sure?"

"No. The note he or she left was in English. But the bone daggers looked like something dark elves would have. And I don't know who else would have stabbed a blade through Zav's face."

"Pardon?"

"His face in that poster." I waved to where it remained on the desk.

Willard dropped off one of the drinks next to me and went to look. "Should I find it odd that you have a poster of a shape-shifted dragon in your apartment, or is it simply another sign of the inevitable marriage?"

"Trust me, he's more likely to kill me—or tote me off for punishment and rehabilitation—after last night. He was *not* cool with me finishing off his enemy. Apparently, dragons don't kill dragons. It's a thing."

"Like homicide?"

"I guess. The note is on my bathroom counter in case you want to take it to your office for forensics stuff. Can you get fingerprints on dark elves?"

"Only if they're in the government database."

"I think the ink is someone's blood."

"That would let us know who they killed, not who they are."

"Look, Willard. I can only hand you so many clues. You're going to have to do some legwork on your own."

"Says the woman napping on the floor."

She disappeared into the bathroom, came out without commenting on the freshly stabbed black bra left on the counter, and waved the note. "I'll give it to the forensics tech on Monday."

"Good."

Willard came around the couch to frown down at me. "This ennui isn't like you. What's up?"

"Nothing." I didn't know how to explain my frustration with the Zav situation and would prefer not to try.

"It's clear that you need something to do in order to distract your mind from your woes."

"Are you going to ask me to hang out with you this weekend, Colonel? Is that allowed? Fraternizing with the lowly civilian contractor who doesn't properly salute you?"

"Oh, that's highly discouraged. But I signed the lease for a new less incendiary apartment in the city, and some of the guys from the office are coming to help me move tomorrow. I thought you might like to help."

"What can you possibly have to move? Didn't all your stuff burn?"

There went her judgmental eyebrows twitching again. Though maybe I shouldn't have made the joke. She'd probably lost a lot of her treasured belongings in the fire.

"Most of it, but I had a three-bedroom house on base at my last assignment, so I still have furniture in storage. And I bought some new exercise equipment to celebrate being alive." Her eyes narrowed. "I have some nice fifty-pound dumbbells you can carry into the apartment."

"You bought celebratory fifty-pound dumbbells? You're a weird woman."

"Says the pot to the kettle."

"Most women get the purple, pink, and teal dumbbell set that maxes out at twelve pounds." Admittedly, I would laugh my butt off if I saw Willard wielding a pink six-pound dumbbell.

"I used to have a squat rack in my bedroom."

"I bet that excites men and gets you a lot of dates."

She rolled her eyes. "Enjoy your money. I'll text you the address of the new place and see you tomorrow."

"I didn't say yes."

"You'll get tired of your ennui and want to come."

I waited until she left before opening the envelope. She'd arranged for the double combat bonus, as promised.

After taxes, there might be enough left to pay off the auto loan on the destroyed Jeep. That was a good thing, but I wasn't sure how I felt about being rewarded for this, since killing Dob had pissed off Zav and broken some Dragon Justice Court law.

I reminded myself of the dead goblins and workers in the water-treatment facility and decided I'd done the right thing. Zav was wrong—or naive about his silly judicial system—not me.

I carried the fifty-pound dumbbells out of Willard's Honda CRV, wondering what she did with them. Squats? Shoulder shrugs? Chest presses? The colonel was definitely a beast. I carried them easily enough, but that was more thanks to my father's blood than my exercise routine. When I went to the gym, I spent more time doing sprints, practicing sword-work, and pummeling the bags than hurling weights around.

Willard's "new" apartment was in another fifty-year-old building with external staircases and doors. Maybe she worried about being trapped in another fire—or an attack—and wanted to be able to flee straight outside. Given how her last apartment building had burned down, I couldn't blame her.

When I reached the second floor, Corporal Clarke, who'd been pressed into this duty along with two other soldiers from Willard's office, waited on the landing.

"I'd offer to help, but the colonel said you personally requested to unload her dumbbell set." He smirked, his dark brown eyes twinkling.

"She said to make the forty-something woman carry the heavy weights while you strapping youngsters carry shoeboxes?"

"You're forty-something, Thorvald? That can't be right."

"I've got a young face." The dumbbells were putting a strain on even my half-elven forearm muscles, so I passed him and headed into the apartment. It had a higher ceiling than the last one, with an overhead fan stirring the warm summer air. Here in Seattle, that counted as the air conditioning.

As I set the weights down on the rack in the living room, Clarke walked in, his fitted brown T-shirt showing off his bulging biceps as he carried in a flat-screen television. He winked again and hefted it up and down—either demonstrating how heavy the burden was or demonstrating the curve of his biceps—before settling it on the stand. After Clarke removed the blanket protecting the TV, he sidled over to me.

"Val, I've been meaning to ask…" He wriggled his eyebrows flirtatiously. "Can I see your tiger?"

"I thought you were going to make a pass at me."

"Nah, you're not my type."

I was fairly certain it wasn't because of my age.

"I've heard your tiger is amazing," Clarke added, "but I've never gotten to see him."

"Willard doesn't like me to take him out in her apartment. She has a cat."

A yowl came from the bedroom, as if Maggie was listening and had an opinion on this subject. That was possible, though she'd been yowling all morning. Probably protesting that the door to freedom was open, but she was locked behind bars in her cat carrier. From what I'd heard, she had already escaped twice from the apartment and down to an active bird feeder in a picnic area for the tenants. She'd been wooed back with canned tuna fish.

"We could do it on the landing out there. I've never seen a tiger up close. We don't have them in Jamaica. No lions or panthers either."

"You sound disappointed, but after the week I've had, I assure you that's a selling point." Maybe if I saved up like Nin, I could buy a house there and retire.

Clarke looked confused, but only for a second, before enlightenment dawned. "Ah, yes. I heard about the neighborhood you demolished in Bothell."

"I had help." I waved for him to follow me onto the landing, then touched my charm and summoned Sindari.

Another battle so soon? Sindari looked up and down the walkway and then out to the parking lot.

"No. One of Willard's soldiers wants to see you."

To see me? Sindari turned to face me, his green eyes judging. *You interrupted my stalking of the delicious* yerboka *so some tourist can gawk at me?*

"Oh, he's completely dope," Clarke said.

Completely what? Sindari asked.

Don't ask. Out loud, I said, "Dope? Does that rate higher or lower than dank?"

That had been Dimitri's adjective for Sindari.

"Dank? Who said that? He's not a dub bag of weed."

I do not understand the language this man is speaking, Sindari told me.

I know. Me either. Just look regal for him for a minute, and then you can go back to hunting.

He may not touch me.

Feeling persnickety today?

A yowl of complaint came from the bedroom.

"What is your tiger doing here?" Willard asked, coming up the stairs on the way back from the recycling bin. "You know Maggie doesn't like him."

"I know. That's why we're outside. Clarke wanted to see him." Maggie yowled.

"Maggie knows he's here." Willard frowned.

"Maggie was complaining even before he showed up," I said. "Does she like the new place? Should I have brought a housewarming gift for your cat?"

"You didn't bring one for me."

"Because I'm here doing manual labor for you. That's a gift that few receive."

"Uh huh." Willard pointed to the moving truck. "Lots more waiting in there for you, Corporal."

"Yes, ma'am." Clarke smiled, told me thanks, then slid a hand along Sindari's back as he descended the stairs.

The presumptuousness! Fortunately, Sindari glared at me instead of biting off Clarke's hand.

A neighbor came out of one of the apartments above, and I shooed Sindari inside. "You better stay out of sight, so Willard's neighbors don't think she has weird visitors. I'll be right back." As I jogged down the stairs, I silently added, *And don't scent-mark any of the furniture, or I'll ask Corporal Presumptuous to come back up here and rub his hands all over you.*

You are the oddest handler I've ever had.

You're welcome for making your life interesting.

Hm.

As I was toting the forty-five-pound dumbbells out of the SUV and to the stairs, a familiar orange camper van with galaxy curtains pulled into the parking lot. Dimitri waved out the open window. Nin sat in the passenger seat.

I nodded to let them know I'd be back in a minute. When I went inside to set down the dumbbells, Sindari was still by the door, rubbing his cheek on the back of a stationary exercise bike.

"Are you leaving your scent on that?"

Merely scratching an itch.

Maggie meowed plaintively, as if she knew exactly what was going on out in her living room. I squinted suspiciously at Sindari and vowed to look up all the ways felines left their scents on things.

"Dumbbells go in the bedroom, not the living room," Willard said, walking out as I was trying to leave.

"Is that official home-gym etiquette, or do you just like seeing me carry heavy weights around?"

"Yes." She pointed at Sindari. "What is your tiger doing?"

"Scratching an itch, he promises me."

"If Maggie is terrified to go near that exercise bike later, I'm going to dock your combat pay on the next assignment."

"Why would a cat *want* to go near an exercise bike?"

"Maggie likes to spin the pedals with her paws." Willard strode up to Sindari and made shooing motions with her hands. "Outside, large feline. Out."

Sindari gave her an indifferent look, then turned his gaze on me. *Not only did you not bring me forth to do battle, but I must endure the disrespect of humans who do not acknowledge my supreme eminence.*

"She's my boss. If you would be so kind as to go outside?" I waved at the door. "Dimitri is out there. I know you find his hands acceptable."

Sindari made a noise that sounded like the tiger equivalent of *hmmph.* He padded toward the door but brushed his side along the front of Willard's dark pants and shirt on the way out. She scowled and brushed at the impressive amount of silver fur that came off on her clothing.

"You need to groom that tiger. Maggie's going to have a fit."

Sindari sashayed out the door, his tail swaying jauntily. Since there were a handful of people around, I dismissed him back to his realm. Hopefully, he could finish that hunt.

Though I was eager to know what Zoltan had found, Nin intercepted me before I reached Dimitri.

"Thank you for your assistance with the Pardus brothers," she said formally and solemnly. "I know you did not wish to kill anyone, and that was never my wish either. I apologize for not foreseeing that my request would turn to such violence."

"It's all right. They were asses, and I probably would have ended up hunting them down for crimes sooner or later anyway." I remembered the shifter on the lawn who'd been eyeing the couple with the stroller.

"I am still sorry. Were you badly injured? Dimitri said the dragons were there."

"I'm all right. Thanks for asking."

"I am working on your armor already. I will attempt to make it so good that it protects you even from dragons."

"That's good, because I have a feeling I'm not done with dragons yet."

Unfortunately.

Dimitri looked over at me from his van. He stood beside it, talking to Clarke, who was telling an animated story, judging by the hand gestures. I couldn't tell if Dimitri was entertained or wanted a way to escape the garrulous corporal.

271

"Clarke," I said, walking up. "Willard wants you to personally carry the rest of the dumbbells up to the apartment."

"She said that? Does she want to admire my biceps?"

"Oh, I'm positive."

"I'm the delight of many older women," Clarke told Dimitri with a flirty wink identical to the one he'd given me. He strutted to the Honda, his arms held just so to display his ropy muscles.

"I've crossed paths with him numerous times in the last year," I said, "and I haven't the foggiest idea which way his tastes run."

"All ways, I think."

"I don't know exactly what that means, and I don't want to know." I pointed at the notebook and piece of paper. "Are those for me?"

"This is most definitely for you." Dimitri handed me the sheet of paper. "I'm on my way out of town. My landscaping employer has gotten a bunch of gigs and has work for me, so I'm going back to Bend. Zoltan asked me to deliver the notebook to you on my way out *if* you agree to pay him."

"Of course I'll pay him." I read the sheet of paper, expecting a translation of the notebook, but… "This is an invoice. For six-thousand-and-seven-hundred dollars." I thought about fainting. I'd never fainted in my life, but this seemed like an appropriate time to start.

"Yes. I understand it's itemized—charm, gas grenades, and translation services—for your bookkeeping convenience."

"He charged me more for the translation than for anything else."

"Because the translation took the longest. He said he settled on an official hourly rate for his services and billed you accordingly. He didn't charge you for materials."

"What a deal. Dimitri, professional hookers in Hollywood don't make this much per hour. *Lawyers* don't make this much per hour." I pointed a thumb at my chest. "*I* don't make this much per hour, and I risk my life every time I take a job."

Dimitri lifted his hands. "If you don't like his rate, you'll have to take it up with him. I'm just the delivery boy."

"I always assumed that if I was gouged by a vampire, blood would be involved." So much for getting out of debt on that car loan.

"Here. This is the part you want." Dimitri handed me the notebook.

I opened it and found a stack of folded papers inside, Zoltan's old-fashioned calligraphic handwriting detailing what he'd translated. The word *orbs* leaped out at me, and I shivered. Willard came down as I was scanning the pages, and I waved for her to come read over my shoulder.

"They're recipes and shopping lists with instructions for making what Zoltan translated as *poisonous pleasure orbs* along with several other devices," I said. "They're all called pleasure something-or-other."

"Was the one you saw poisonous?" Willard must have already read the report I'd turned in that morning.

"The shifters were pressing themselves right up against it, and it seemed like they'd been using it for a while, so it would have to be something long-term."

"That's possible," she said. "Dark elves are long-lived, so they wouldn't be in a hurry to get immediate results. Did any of the shifters who were using it live? If we could question one…"

"Maybe some of the ones who didn't come down into the basement. Nobody down there survived. Once Dob showed up, Sindari and I were in purely defensive mode. No time for sparing lives or questioning anyone."

"I'll talk to my informants in the north and see what I can learn in the next couple of weeks."

"You can start with this." I thrust the notebook and translation at Willard. "You better make a whole bunch of copies of this stuff and then throw the notebook in the Sound. The dark elves want it back, but I don't think we want them to have it back."

"No." Willard took it. "I wonder how many of these devices they've already made and how they intend to use them."

"I don't know, but if the shifters were an indication, they'll lure in a lot of people. They must plan to use honey instead of vinegar to get what they want."

"And what do they want?"

"I was hoping you knew that. You're the intelligence gatherer. I'm just the muscle."

Clarke walked past, carrying a set of dumbbells in each hand.

"My muscle isn't as prominent as some people's," I said, "but it's effective."

"I have no doubt of that. You took out six shifters and a dragon in one night."

"I had help. A lot of help. Sindari, of course, and if not for Zav, Dob would have killed me like an elephant smashing a beetle underfoot." Now that some time had passed, and I'd had a chance to consider how much trouble he might get in because of my actions, I felt more inclined to apologize to him, or at least thank him. But who knew if I would ever see him again?

Willard pulled out her phone and read a text. "Hm."

"Is that your landlord letting you know that your exercise equipment exceeds the weight allowance for the second floor?" I asked.

"No." She lowered the phone, her face grim. "The dragon's body disappeared out of the big storage unit we put it in until we could get a proper team to examine it."

"It *disappeared?*" Dimitri asked. "How does that happen?"

"Magic," I murmured.

I had a bad feeling the Dragon Justice Court had collected it and that I would soon find out if Zav's attempt to hide my role in killing Dob would work.

THE END

~

The adventure continues in Book 3, *Tangled Truths*.

CONNECT WITH THE AUTHOR

Have a comment? Question? Just want to say hi? Find me online at:
http://www.lindsayburoker.com
http://www.facebook.com/LindsayBuroker
http://twitter.com/GoblinWriter
Thanks for reading!

Printed in Great Britain
by Amazon